YEAR'S BEST SF 12

EDITED BY
DAVID G. HARTWELL
and KATHRYN CRAMER

An Imprint of HarperCollins*Publishers*

Additional copyright information appears on pages 483–484.

EOS
An imprint of HarperCollins*Publishers*
10 East 53rd Street
New York, New York 10022-5299

Copyright © 2007 by David G. Hartwell and Kathryn Cramer
ISBN: 978-0-7394-8544-6

Contents

v

Acknowledgments

We would like to acknowledge the assistance of the magazine and book editors, of publications large and small, who made our job easier by responding rapidly to our requests for electronic files for consideration.

Introduction

We try in each volume of this series to represent the varieties of tones and voices and attitudes that keep the genre vigorous and responsive to the changing realities out of which it emerges, in science and in daily life. It is supposed to be fun to read, a special kind of fun you cannot find elsewhere. This is a book about what's going on now in SF. The stories that follow show, and the story notes point out, the strengths of the evolving genre in the year 2006, and the dominant recurring themes and ideas. We like to point out interesting comparisons.

Literary critics are often trained to read fiction for its *chronotopicality*, how the myriad voices of a moment participate to represent that point in space–time when the works in question were written and published. This is not the same as John Clute's idea of the "real year" of a story, the idea that every piece of fiction inevitably and unconsciously reflects the year in which it was composed, no matter if it is set millions of years in the future and in another place. It also runs counter to the way science fiction readers want to read their fiction: Science fiction readers want to be transported from their everydayness by the authors' fascinating ideas, to fantastic places and times that could exist but mostly don't. They want escape from the present.

Science fiction has always possessed a level of deliberate chronotopicality, which is especially evident in satirical American SF of the 1950s and Eastern European SF before the fall of the Berlin Wall. But for the most part, SF readers would much prefer a good story over a good allegory. We like distance. But we find ourselves in the future now, and it isn't as pleasant a place as we wanted it to be.

It seems to us that the theme of the year is catastrophe and how to recover from it. Even the Singularity is perhaps a catastrophe (see the Rucker story), but maybe half the stories in the book are part of this thematic complex, perhaps more. Some of these are overtly political (for instance the Doctorow and the Bisson). Others embody political allegories, and some, like the Kress, the Hurley, and the Haldeman, are about survival, and some, such as the Gregory, the Reed, and the Rosenkrantz, are about healing.

There were certainly the usual disasters and surprising advances in the real world in 2006, the seventh year of this century in which such things are the norm—some of them political, some of them ongoing (this was the year that politicians began to notice global warming, and in a not-unrelated discovery, polar bears became an endangered species—what a surprise!).

It is by the sixth year or so of a decade that we begin to know what the decade is about. And ours is a special decade, the first decade of the twenty-first century, so we are also experiencing the dawning of the realization of what it means to live in the twenty-first century. Up until very recently this century has been a province within the territory controlled by science fiction. Now it is the real world and not a comfortable one. The resulting SF stories of 2006 are the most richly chronotopical we've seen since we began co-editing the *Year's Bests*.

In the SF world, 2006 was another year in the passing away of the generations of science fiction: Jack Williamson, the last of the first-generation writers, the ones who founded the scientifiction publishing genre before the name science fiction was invented; Wilson Tucker (Bob Tucker in sf fandom), arguably the greatest fan in fandom between the early 1930s and the present, noted for his wit and humor, and a fiction writer of considerable talent; Octavia Butler, in her prime, producing SF and fantasy fiction of immense depth and often quiet power.

We are still in the middle of some kind of short fiction boom in science fiction and the associated genres of the fantastic, and there were no signs of impending cessation in

2006. Not an economic boom—no one is getting paid much—but certainly a numbers increase, and it has been building for several years. The highest concentrations of excellence were still in the professional publications, the anthologies from the large and small presses, and the highest paying online markets, though the small press zines and little magazines were significant contributors as well. The small press really expanded in recent years and was a major force in short fiction this past year, both in book form and in a proliferation of ambitious little magazines, in the U.S. and the rest of the world.

The year 2005 was perhaps the end of the first wave of the website magazines, leaving only Strange Horizons, a nonprofit organization of the formerly top three fiction locations still intact at the start of 2006. But in mid-year, Jim Baen's Universe, edited by Eric Flint, commenced publication as the highest paying online fiction market for SF and fantasy, with a business model intended to make it a profitable publication. This will be a significant first for electronic publishing if it works, and the initial signs were that it was not obviously failing. The electronic publishers on the internet otherwise maintained the levels of quality established a few years back, and remain an ambitious dimension of the SF field, but there was not a significant increase in the amount of good fiction originating on the internet. But there are several that are willing to try. Aeon, Revolution SF, Eidolon online, Fantastic Magnitude, and Challenging Destiny, for instance, show real promise, and Infinite Matrix promises to return in 2007.

There are a lot of conclusions one might draw from this, but the one we highlight is that it makes this year's best volume even more useful, since we try every year to sort through all this material.

Our general principle for selection: This book is full of science fiction—every story in the book is clearly that and not something else. We have a high regard for horror, fantasy, speculative fiction, and slipstream, and postmodern literature. We (Kathryn Cramer and David G. Hartwell) edit the *Year's Best Fantasy* as well, a companion volume to this one—look for it if you enjoy short fantasy fiction, too. But here, we choose science fiction. It is our opinion that it is a good thing to have genre boundaries. If we didn't, young writers would have to find something else, perhaps less interesting, to transgress or attack to draw attention to themselves.

So we repeat, for readers new to this series, our usual disclaimer: This selection of science fiction stories represents the best that was published in the genre during the year 2006. It would take several more volumes this size to have nearly all of the best short stories—though even then, not all the best novellas. And we believe that representing the best from year to year, while it is not physically possible to encompass it all in one even very large book, also implies presenting some substantial variety of excellences, and we left some worthy stories out in order to include others in this limited space.

We make a lot of additional comments about the writers and the stories, and what's happening in SF, in the individual introductions to the stories in this book. Welcome to the *Year's Best SF* in 2006.

David G. Hartwell & Kathryn Cramer
Pleasantville, NY

Nano Comes to Clifford Falls

NANCY KRESS

Nancy Kress (www.sff.net/people/nankress) *lives in Roches-
ter, New York. One of today's leading SF writers, she is a
popular guest at SF conventions, and an eminent teacher of
writing. She is known for her complex medical SF stories,
and for her biological and evolutionary extrapolations in
such classics as* Beggars in Spain *(1993),* Beggars and Choos-
ers *(1994), and* Beggars Ride *(1996). Her stories, collected in*
Trinity and Other Stories *(1985),* The Aliens of Earth *(1993)
and* Beaker's Dozen *(1998), are rich in texture and in psychological insight. She has won two Nebulas and a Hugo for
them, and been nominated for a dozen more of these awards.
Her most recent SF novels are* Crossfire *(2003),* Nothing Human *(2003), and* Crucible *(2004).*

This story appeared in Asimov's, *and was one of several
excellent stories by Kress in 2006. It has all the material for
a full SF novel carefully compressed into a short story.
Carol, the central character, is sad and angry over the departure of her husband, but soldiers on, providing for her
family with the help of her hard-working kids, and mostly
tries to ignore the revolutionary technology that is supposed
to make the world and even the little town of Clifford Falls
into a utopia. The way she and her family survive introduces
what we see as the major theme of the year in SF, surviving
and recovering from catastrophe.*

I was weeding the garden when nanotech came to my town. The city got it a month earlier, but I haven't been to the city since last year. Some of my neighbors went—Angie Myers and Emma Karlson and that widow, Mrs. Blanston, from church. They brought back souvenirs, things made in the nanomachine, and the scarf Angie showed me was really cute. But with three little kids, I don't get out much.

That day was hot, with the July sun hanging overhead like it wasn't ever going to move. Bob McPhee from next door stuck his head over the fence. His Rottweiler snarled through the chain links. I don't like that dog, and Kimee, my middle one, is afraid of it.

"Hey, Carol, don't you know you don't have to do that no more?" Bob said. "The nanomachinery will make you all the tomatoes and peas you want."

"Hey, Bob," I said. I went on weeding, swiping at the sweat on my forehead with the back of my hand. Jackie watched me from the shade of the garage. I'd laid him on a blanket dressed in just his diaper and he was having a fine time kicking away and then stopping to eat his toes.

"They're giving Clifford Falls four of 'em," Bob said. Since he retired from the fire department, he don't have enough to do all day. "I saw it on TV. The mayor's getting 'em installed in the town hall."

"That's good," I said, to say something. I could hear Will and Kimee inside the kitchen, fighting over some toy.

"Mayor'll run the machinery. One for food, one for clothing, the other two he's taking requests. I already put in mine, for a sports car."

That got my attention. "A car? A whole car?"

"Sure, why not? Nano can make anything. The town is starting with one request from each person, first come first served. Then after that . . . I dunno. I guess Mayor Johnson'll work it out. Hey, gorgeous, stop that weeding and come have a beer with me. Pretty gal like you shouldn't be getting all hot and sweaty at weeding."

He leered at me, but he don't mean anything by it. At least, I don't think he does. Bob's over fifty but still looks pretty good, and he knows it, but he also knows I'm not that kind. Jack might've took off two months ago, but I don't need anyone like Bob, a married man, for temporary fun and games.

"I like the taste of home-grown tomatoes," I tell him. "Ones at the Safeway taste like wallpaper."

"But nano won't make tomatoes that taste processed," he says in that way that men like to correct women. "That machinery will make the best tomatoes this town ever tasted."

"Well, I hope you're right." Then Will and Kimee spilled their fight out through the screen door into the backyard, and Jackie started whimpering on his blanket, and I didn't have no time for any nanomachinery.

Still, I was curious, so in the late afternoon, when it wasn't quite so hot, I packed up the stroller and the kids and I went downtown.

Clifford Falls isn't much of a town. We're so far out on the plains that all we got is a single square ringed with dusty pick-ups and the teenagers' scooters. There's about two dozen stores, the little brick town hall with traffic court and Barry Anderson's police room and such, the elementary school, Baptist and Methodist churches, Kate's Lunchroom, and the Crow Bar. Down by the tracks is the grain elevator and warehouses. That's about it. Once a movie was filmed here because the movie people wanted some place that looked like it might be fifty or sixty years ago.

Soon as I turned the corner I could see where the nanomachinery must be. People milled around the patch of faded grass in front of the town hall, people who probably should have still been to work on a Wednesday afternoon. A big awning stretched across the front of the building with a huge metal box under it, nearly big as my bedroom. To one side the mayor, who retired two years ago from the factory in Minneonta, stood on a crate right there in the broiling sun without so much as a hat on his bald head, making a speech.

"—greatest innovation since supercheap energy to raise our way of life to—"

"What's getting made in that box?" I asked Emma Karlson. She had her twins in a fancy new stroller. Just after Jack left me, her Ted got taken on at the factory.

"A dais," she said.

"A what?"

"A thing for the mayor to stand on instead of that apple crate. It's supposed to be done in a few minutes."

What a dumb thing to make—Mr. Johnson could just as well have gotten a good stepladder from Bickel's Hardware. But I suppose the dais was by way of demonstration.

And I have to admit it was impressive when it come out of the box. Four men had to move it, a big fancy platform with a top like a gazebo and steps carved on their sides in fancy shapes. After the men set it down there was this moment of electric silence, like a downed power line run through the crowd, and then everybody started shouting.

"Make me a rocking chair!"

"Tell it to grow a table!"

"I need a new rug for the dining room!"

"Make a good bottle of booze!"

Emma turned to me. Her eyes were big and shining. "Some people are so ignorant. That big nanomachine don't make anything to eat or drink—the ones inside do that. Three little ones, for food and clothes and small quick stuff. Mayor Jonson already explained all that, but some people just can't listen."

The crowd was pressing closer to the new dais, and a few men started to climb the fancy steps. Kimee was getting restless, pulling on my hand, but Will said suddenly, "Mommy, tell the machine to make me a dog!"

Emma laughed. "It can't do that, Will. Nobody but God can make a living thing."

I said, "Then how can it make a tomato? A tomato's living."

Emma said, "No, it's not. It's dead after you pick it."

"But it was living."

Emma got that look in her eyes that I seen there ever since the third grade: Don't argue with me because you'll regret it. Will jumped up and down screaming, "A dog! A dog! I want a dog!" The people around the dais were pushed back by Barry Anderson and his deputy, but they didn't stop shouting at Mayor Johnson. I grabbed Will, smiled hard at Emma, and started home.

Nanotech wasn't going to put Kimee down for a nap or breast-feed Jackie. And it sure as hell wasn't going to get my bastard husband back to help me do those things.

Not that I wanted him.

I waited for nano to make Clifford Falls look like the places in the TV shows. What surprised me was that it did.

I didn't see anything for a few weeks because both Kimee and Will came down with some sort of bug. Diarrhea and cramps. The doctor I got on the computer told me which chemicals to squirt over samples of their shit and when I told him what colors the shit turned, he said it wasn't serious but I should keep the kids in, make them drink a lot of water, and keep them away from the baby. In a two-bedroom rented house, that alone took a lot of my time. But we managed. Emma bought the medicine I needed at Merkelson's and left it on the doorstep. She left three casseroles, too, and some chocolate-chip cookies.

Ten days later, when they were better, I baked Emma a sponge cake to thank her. After the kids were dressed and the stroller packed up, we went outside and I had to blink hard.

"Wow!" Will said. "Mommy, look at that!"

Parked in Bob McPhee's driveway was the reddest car I ever seen, low and smooth and shiny. It looked fast. Will ran over to it and I called, "Don't touch, Will!"

"Oh, he can't hurt it," Bob said with a sort of fake casualness. He was bursting with pride. "And if he did hurt it,

I'll just wait until my turn comes up on the Big Gray and order me another one."

The Big Gray—that must be what they were calling the largest nanomachine. Stupid name. It sounded like a sway-backed horse.

Bob leered at me. "Wanna go for a ride, baby?"

"Why don't you take your wife?" I said, but I smiled when I said it because I'm a wuss who likes to stay on good terms with my neighbors.

"Oh, I did," Bob said, waving his hand airily, "but there's always room for one more, if you know what I mean."

"A ride! A ride!" Will shouted.

"Not today, Will, we're going to see Jon and Don." That distracted him; Emma's twins are his best friends.

Emma met me at the door dressed in a gorgeous yellow sundress with a low neck and full skirt. Emma was always pretty, even when we were thirteen, but I'd never seen her look like this. She'd done things to live up to the dress, fixed her hair and put on make-up and even had on rhinestone earrings.

"God, you look amazing!" I said, in my old jeans with baby puke on my tee-shirt. Emma touched her earrings.

"Real diamonds, Carol! Ted used his second pick at the nanomachine to choose these!"

I gaped at her. The nanomachine could make real diamonds? Will barreled past me toward Don and Jon and I saw that all three of them jumped onto a new blue sofa covered with the nicest material I'd ever seen.

All I could think of to say was, "I brought you a sponge cake. A thank-you for all you done when the kids were sick."

"Well, aren't you the sweetest thing. Thank you. I'd offer you a piece now but, well, Kitty'll be here in a few minutes to take the twins."

Kitty Svenson was the teenager who babysat for every-body. She was saving up for secretarial school. Ted came out from the bedroom dressed in a bathrobe.

"Oh, God, Ted, have you got this diarrhea-thing, too? I'm sorry, it's a bitch. Come on, Will, let's go. Em, I can take the twins while Ted's sick."

"I'm not sick, Carol," Ted said. Emma blushed. I was really confused. This was a Tuesday morning.

"I quit the factory," Ted said. "No need to kill myself working now."

"But . . . the mortgage . . ."

"The nano's making us a house," Emma said proudly.

"A house? A whole house?"

"One part of a room at a time," Ted said. "Em and I are both using all our picks for it. We'll put it on that piece of land my daddy left me by the lake, and the whole house'll finish just before the bank forecloses on this one. I got it all figured out."

"But . . ." My brain wasn't working right. I just couldn't take it in, somehow.

"The food nano is making all our meals now," Emma said. "Just churning 'em out like sausages. Here, Carol, taste this." She darted into the kitchen, earrings swinging, and came back with a bowl of small round things like smooth nuts.

"What is it?"

"I don't know. But it tastes good. The food nano can't make like, you know, real meats or anything, but it does pretty good delivering things that look and taste like fruits and veggies and bread, and this stuff is the protein."

I picked up one of the round things and nibbled. It did taste good, sort of like cold spicy chicken. But something in me recoiled anyway. Maybe it was the texture, sort of bland and mushy. I palmed the rest of the ball. "Mmmmmmmmmm."

"Told you so," Emma said triumphantly, like the round balls were things she'd baked herself. "Oh, here's Kitty."

Kitty Svenson hauled herself up the steps. Fat and acne-covered and dirt poor, she was the sweetest girl in town, and every time I saw her my heart ached. She liked Tom DeCarno, who lived down the street from me and was the starting quarterback on the football team at the consolidated high school in Remington. He'd notice Kitty on the day that Hell got a hockey franchise.

It was obvious what Emma in her sexy new dress and Tom in his bathrobe were going to be doing, so I dragged the protesting Will and we went home. I saw things I hadn't

noticed on the way to Em's: a new playhouse in the backyard of the big house on the corner. Fresh chain-link fence
around the Alghren place. The Connors' pick-up in their
driveway, which meant that Eddie hadn't gone to work at the
factory, either. Across the street, a woman I thought I didn't
know, dressed up like a city girl in a ruffled suit and high
heels, until I realized it was Sue Merkelson, the pharmacist's
wife.

At home I took the kids into the backyard and weeded the
tomatoes, which were nearly strangled with ten days' worth
of weeds. Jack used to do at least some of the weeding. But
that was before, and this was now, and I kept at it until the
job was done.

By late August the factory in Minneonta had closed. Most of
the men in town who didn't farm were out of work, but nobody seemed to mind much. The Crow Bar was full all the
time, groups playing cards and laughing at TV. I saw them
spilling out onto the street the one time I went to the super-
market to buy Pampers and milk.

Emma told me on the phone that Mayor Johnson, Barry
Anderson, and Anderson's deputy had the nanomachines on
a regular schedule. Every morning people lined up to pick up
whatever their food order'd been from the previous day,
enough food for all that day's meals plus a little over to store.
Another machine made whatever clothes you picked out of a
catalogue, in whatever size matched after you give in your
measurements. It made blankets and curtains and tablecloths,
too, anything out of cloth. The last two machines, including
the big one, turned out everything else, picked from a different catalogue, turn by turn.

The county's corn, ready to harvest, sat in the fields.
Nobody wanted to buy it, and except for the farm owners,
nobody hired on to harvest it.

Nearly every family in town drove a new car, from six
different models that our nanos were programmed to make.
There was a lot of red and gold vehicles in our streets.

"I want a playhouse, Mommy," Will whined. "Caddie
Alghren gots a new playhouse! I want one, too!"

I looked at him, standing there in his rumpled little pajamas with trains on them, looking like his best friend just
died. His hair fell over his forehead just like Jack's used to do.

"How do you know Caddie's got a new playhouse?"

"I saw it! From my window!"

"You can't see into Caddie's yard from your window. Did
you climb out up onto the roof again, Will?"

He hung his head and twisted the sleeves of his pajamas
into crumpled balls.

"I told you that going up on that roof is dangerous! You
could fall and break your neck!"

"I'm sorry," he said, raising his little face up to me, and I
melted even though I knew he wasn't sorry at all and he
would do it again. "I'm sorry, Mommy. Can't we get a playhouse? We been inside all summer, feels like!"

He was right. I'd only taken the kids outside our yard a few
times. I'd hardly been out myself. I told myself that it was
because I didn't want to see everybody's pitying looks ("Jack
run off with that sexy girl from the hardware store, Chrissie
Somebody, just left Carol and those kids without so much as
a backward glance.") But it wasn't just that.

The big freezer downstairs was almost empty. I'd used up
everything I could. I run out of Tide last Thursday and the
laundry was piling up. Worse, the Pampers were nearly gone.
I had to keep the checking account, the half of it that Jack
left, to pay the rent and the phone as long as I could. After
that . . . I didn't know yet. Not yet.

So I guessed it was time. I didn't understand why I didn't
want to go before, didn't understand why I didn't want to go
now. But it was time.

"Okay, honey, we'll get you a playhouse," I said. "Find
your sneakers."

When I had Jackie changed and fed, Will and Kimee
dressed, the stroller packed with diapers and water, we set
off outside. Will was good, holding onto the side of the
stroller and not running ahead. Kimee stood on the back bar
and whimpered a little; she gets prickly heat in the summer.
But when we turned the corner toward the town square, she
stopped fussing and stared, just like me and Will. The whole

place was full of garbage cans. Clean, blue, plastic garbage cans, hundreds of them, stacked and thrown and lying on their sides, not a single one of them holding any garbage. People milled around, talking angrily. I saw my neighbor.

"Bob, what on Earth—"

He was too angry even to leer at me. "That Beasor kid! The one that won the state technology contest a few years ago—that kid's too smart-ass for his own good, I said so then! He hacked into the Big Gray somehow and now all it'll make is garbage cans, no matter what you tell it!"

I craned my neck to see the big metal box under its awning. Sure enough, another garbage can popped out. A bubble of something started in my belly and started to rise up in me. "Is . . . is . . ."

"The kid left town! Anderson's got an APB out on him. You haven't seen Danny Beasor, have you, Carol?"

"I haven't seen anybody," I said. The bubble rose higher and now I knew what it was: laughter. I turned my face away from Bob.

"If that kid knows what's good for him, he'll keep on running," Bob said. He was really upset. "Now the mayor's shut down the other nanomachines, except the food one, until the repair guys get out here from the city. You get your food today, Carol?"

"No, but I'll come back later," I managed to say, without laughing in Bob's face. "K-Kimee's not feeling well."

"Okay," he said, not really interested. "Hey, Earl! Wait!" He pushed through the garbage cans toward Earl Bickel across the square.

Will somehow understood that there would be no playhouse today. He screwed up his face, but before he could start to howl, I said, "Will! Look at all these great cans! We can make the best playhouse ever out of them!"

His face cleared. "Cool!"

So we nested and dragged home four garbage cans, with a little help from the teenage Parker boys, who are nice kids and who seemed glad to have something to do. They found some boards in the basement, plus a hammer and nails, and spent all afternoon making a playhouse with four garbage-can rooms. Will was in seventh heaven. I couldn't pay them, but I unfroze and toasted the last of my home-made banana bread, and they gobbled it down happily. Will and Kimee, her itching forgotten, played in the garbage cans until dark.

The next day all the nanomachines were working again, and I put in a daily food order. But I left the kids at home with Kitty Svenson when I picked up my order, and I started canning all the squash, beans, peppers, corn, and melons in the garden.

School opened. Will was in first grade. I walked him there the first day and he seemed to like his teacher.

By the third week of school, she'd quit.

By the fifth week, so had the teacher who replaced her, along with a few other faculty.

"They just don't want to work when they don't have to, and why should they?" Emma said. She sat in my kitchen, drinking a cup of coffee and wearing a strange hat that sloped down to cover half her face. I suppose she picked it out of the nano-catalogues—it must be what they were wearing in the city. The color was pretty, though, a warm peach. It was practically the first morning she'd made time for me in weeks. "With nano, nobody has to work if they don't want to."

"Did the twins' teacher quit, too?"

"No. It's old Mrs. Cameron. She's been teaching so long she probably can't even imagine doing anything else after she gets up in the morning. Carol, look at this place. How come you let it get so shabby?"

I said mildly, "There isn't too much money since Jack left. Just enough for the rent."

"That ass-hole . . . but that's not what I meant and you know it. Why haven't you replaced those old curtains and sofa with nano ones? And that TV! You could get a real big one, with an unbelievable picture."

I put my elbows on the table and leaned toward her. "I'll tell you the truth, Em: I don't know. I get nano food and diapers, and I got some school clothes for Will, but anything else . . . I don't know."

"You're just being an idiot!" she said. She almost shouted it—way too angry for just my saggy sofa. I reached out and pulled off the sloping hat. Emma's eye was swollen nearly shut, and every color of squash in my garden.

All at once she started sobbing. "Ted . . . he never done anything like that before . . . it's terrible on men, being laid off! They get so bored and mad—"

"He wasn't laid off, he quit," I said, but gently.

"Same thing! He just scowls himself around the house, yells at the kids—they're glad to be back in school, let me tell you!—and criticizes everything I do, or he orders Scotch from the nano—did order it until Mayor Johnson outlawed any nano liquor and—"

"He did? The mayor did?" I said, startled.

"Yeah. And so last Thursday, Ted and I had this big fight, and . . . and . . ." Suddenly she changed tone. "You don't know anything, Carol! You sit here safe and alone, thinking you're so superior to nano, just like you always acted so superior to poor Jack—oh, I'm sorry, I didn't mean that!"

"Probably you did," I said evenly, "but it's all right. Really it is, Em."

All at once she got defiant. "You're thinking I'm just dumping on you because Ted hit me. Well, I'm not. It was only that once, most of the time he's a good husband. Our new house by the lake will be done in a few more weeks and then everything'll be better!"

I didn't see how, but all I said was, "I'll bet the house is pretty."

"It's gorgeous! It's got a blue-brick fireplace in the living room—blue bricks! And it's equipped with just everything, all those robo-appliances like you see on TV—I won't have to do hardly anything!"

"I can't wait to see it," I said.

"You'll love it," she said, put her hat back on so it covered her eye, and stared at me with triumph and fear.

I pulled Will out of school to home-school him. He didn't mind once I got the Bellingham grand-kids to school at my place, and then Caddie Alghren. The Bellinghams were farmers going bust. Mr. Bellingham was still doing dairy, though, even while his crops rotted in the fields. Mrs. Bellingham's always been sickly and she never struck me as real smart. But Hal Bellingham is smart, and he looked at me real sharp when I said I would home-school his grandkids because the teachers were all quitting.

"Not all, Carol."

"No, not yet. And some won't quit. But the government's not getting much tax money because nobody's earning and the TV says that the government is taking itself apart bit by bit." I didn't understand that, but Mr. Bellingham looked like he might. "How many teachers'll stay when they can't get paid at all?"

"That time's a ways off."

"Maybe."

"What makes you think you can teach my grandkids? Begging your pardon, but you don't look or sound like a college graduate."

"I'm not. But I did good in high school, and I guess I can teach first- and second-graders. At any rate, in my living room they'll be safe from the kinds of vandalism you see all around town now."

"What'll you use for books?"

"We have some kids' books, I'll get more out of the library as long as it lasts, and we'll make books, the kids and me. It's fun to write your own stories, and they can read each other's."

"You aren't going to get books from the nanomachinery?"

"No." I said it flat out, and we looked at each other, sitting there in the Bellinghams' big farm kitchen with its old-fashioned microwave.

He said, "Who's going to watch your two little ones while you teach?"

"Kitty Svenson."

"What's she get out of it?"

"That's between me and her."

"And what do you want in return?"

"Milk, and a share of the spring calves you might have sent to market, slaughtered and with the meat dressed. You aren't going to be able to get in enough hay to feed them anyway."

He got up, walked in his farm boots around his kitchen, and looked at me again. "Do you watch the news, Carol?"

"Not much. Little kids take a lot out of you."

"You should watch. Vandalism isn't limited to what we got in Clifford Falls."

I didn't say anything.

"All right, the kids will be home-schooled by you. But here, not at your place. I'll clear out the big back bedroom for you, and Kitty can use the kitchen. Mattie'll like the company. But before you agree, there's somebody I want you to meet."

"Who?"

"Suspicious little thing, aren't you? Come with me."

We went out to the barn. The cows were in pasture, and the hayloft half empty. In an old tack room that the Bellinghams had turned into an apartment for a long-ago cattle manager, a pretty young woman sat in front of a metal table. I blinked.

The whole room was full of strange equipment, along with freezers and other stuff I recognized. The woman wore a white lab coat, like doctors on TV. She stood and smiled at us.

"This is Amelia Parsons," Bellingham said. "She used to work for Camry Biotech, which just went out of business. She's a crop geneticist."

"Hello," she said, holding out her hand. Women like her make me nervous. Too polished, too educated. They all had it too easy. But I shook her hand; I'm not rude.

"Amelia's working on creating an apomictic corn plant. That's corn that doesn't need pollination, that can produce its own seeds asexually, like non-hybrid varieties once did, and like blackberries and mangos and some roses do now. Apomictic corn would keep all the good traits of hybrid corn, maybe even with added benefits, but farmers wouldn't have to buy seed every year."

"I couldn't work on this very much at Camry," Amelia said to me. Her pretty face glowed. Her red hair was cut in one of those complicated city cuts. "Even though apomixis was my doctoral thesis. The biotech company wanted us to work on things that were more immediately profitable. But now that I don't need to earn a salary, that oversight agencies are pretty much dismantling, and that I can get the equipment I need from nano . . . well, nano makes it possible for me to do some real work!"

I smiled at her again, because I didn't have anything to say. There was a baby-food stain on my jeans and I moved my hand to cover it.

"Thanks, Amelia," Hal Bellingham said. "See you later."

On the way back to the house, he said quietly, "I just wanted you to see the other side, Carol."

I didn't answer.

My little school started on Monday. Caddie Alghren, whose mother had been killed by a drunk driver last spring, clung to me at first, but Will and she were friends and as long as she could sit next to him, she was all right. The three Bellingham kids were well-behaved and smart. Kitty watched Kimee and Jackie in the kitchen and helped Mattie Bellingham. At night Kitty went home with me, because her stepfather had started to come into her room at night. Nothing real bad had happened yet, but she hated him and was glad to babysit for her keep.

After the kids finally got to sleep each night, Kitty and I watched the TV, like Hal said, and saw what was happening in the cities. A lot of people won't work if they don't have to. But a lot of people not working means a lot of broken things don't get fixed. Nano can make water pipes and schoolbooks and buses and toilets. It can't install them or teach them or drive them. The cities were getting to be pretty scary places.

Clifford Falls wasn't that bad. But it wasn't all that far out from the city, either. Kitty and I were watching TV one night, the kids in bed, when the door burst open and three men rushed in.

"Look at this—not just the one, two of them," one man said, while I was already reaching for the phone. He got there first and knocked it out of my hand. "Not that it would

help you, lady. Not a lot of police left. Kenny, I'll take this
one and you take the fat girl."

Kitty had shrunk back against the sofa. I tried to think
fast. The kids—if I could just keep any noise from waking
the kids, the men might not even know they were there.
Then no matter what happened to us, the kids would be safe.
But if Will saw either of their faces, if he could identify
them . . . and Kitty, Kitty was only fifteen . . .

I said quickly, "Leave her alone. She doesn't know how to
anything, she won't be any fun for you. If you leave her
alone, I'll let you both do me. I won't even fight. I'd be a lot
more fun for you." My gorge rose and I tasted vomit.

The two men looked at each other. Finally "Kenny"
shrugged and said, "The fat one's ugly, anyway."

The other one nodded and his piggy eyes gleamed.
Noise—the important thing was no noise. I got down on
the floor and unzipped my jeans. Oh, God—but no noise,
no noise to wake the kids, and I had to protect Kitty, God,
fifteen . . .

My head exploded.

No, not my head, the head leering above me. Blood and
brains splattered over me. Then there was a second shot and
the other man went down. I staggered up, puked, and heard
Will and Kimee screaming. When I could see again, the
kids stood in the doorway, clinging together, and Kitty still
sat on the sofa, the gun in her hand.

She was the calmest one there, at least on the outside. "I
stole it to use on my stepfather if I had to, just before you
said I could live here. Carol—" Then she started shaking.

"It's okay," I said stupidly and, my own hand trembling,
picked up the phone to call the cops.

I got a recording at 911. "I'm sorry, but due to reduced
manpower, your call may have to wait. Please stay on the
line until—" I hung up and called Barry Anderson's cell.

It was turned off. When he finally got there, three hours
later, he said it was the only sleep he'd had in two days. His
deputy quit last week and left for Florida. By that time I'd
gotten the kids back to sleep, the room and myself cleaned
up, and Kitty to stop shaking.

The next day, Hal Bellingham moved us all out to the farm.

By spring, there were fifty-four of us on the farm, plus ten kids. And in the spring, Jack came back.

I was coming out of the lamb barn with Will, who saw Jack first. He cried, "Daddy!" and my heart froze. Then Will was running across the muddy yard and throwing himself into Jack's arms. I trailed slowly behind.

"How'd you get past the guards?" I said.

"Bellingham let me in. What kind of set-up you got going here, anyway?"

I didn't answer, just stared at him. He looked good. Well-fed, well-dressed, maybe a little heavier but still the handsomest man ever to come out of Clifford Falls. This was how Will, beaming in his daddy's arms, would look in twenty years.

Jack reddened slightly. "Why are you living here, Carol? Don't tell me you and old Bellingham . . ."

"That would be what you'd think. The answer is no."

Did he look relieved? "Then why—"

"Mommy's my teacher!" Will shouted. "And I can write whole sentences!"

"Good for you," Jack said. To me he suddenly blurted, "Carol, I don't know how to say this, but I'm so sorry, I—"

"Where's Chrissie? You get tired of her the way you did of me?"

"No, she . . . who the hell is that?"

His eyes almost bugged out of his head, and well they might. Denny Bonohan strolled out of the house, dressed in one of his costumes. Denny's gay, which was hard enough for me to take, but he's also an actor, which is even worse because he strolls out to do his share of guard duty dressed in outlandish things he and the other two actors brought with him. Now he wore tights with a bright tunic almost as long as a dress, all in shades of gold. Hal is amused by him but I think Denny's loony and I won't let the kids be alone with him. My right, Hal says in his quiet way, and what Hal says goes.

I said, "That's my new boyfriend." I said it to make Jack mad but instead he threw back his head and laughed, his white teeth gleaming in the sunshine.

"Not you, Carol. Never. I know you that much, anyways."

"What are you doing here, Jack?"

"I want to see my kids. And I want . . . I want you, Carol. I miss you. I was wrong, as wrong as a man can be. Please take me back."

Jack apologizing was always hard to resist, although it's not like he ever did all that much of it. Will clung hard to his father's neck. Also, an old sweet feeling was slipping into me, along with the anger. I wanted to hit him, I wanted to hug him. I wanted to curl up inside him again.

"It's up to the Council if you can stay here."

"Here?"

"We aren't leaving, the kids and me."

He took a deep breath. "What's the Council? What do I have to do?"

"You have to start by talking to Hal. If Denny's on guard duty, Hal's probably coming off."

"Guard duty?" Jack said, bewildered.

"Yeah, Jack. You're back in the army now. Only this time, we all enlisted."

"I don't . . ."

"Come on," I said roughly. "It's up to a vote of the Council. For my part, I don't give a damn what you do."

"You're lying," he said softly, in that special voice we used between us, and I damned him all over again because it was true.

July again, and we are eighty-seven people now. Word spreads. About half are people who fled nano, like me. The other half embraced it because it lets them do whatever they'd wanted to do before. Some of those ones have their own nanomachines, little ones, made of course by other nanomachines. Hal allows them to use nano to produce things for their jobs, but not to make food or clothing or shelter or anything else we all need to survive, except for some medicines, and we're working on that.

The two kinds of people here don't always get along very well. We have five actors, Amelia the geneticist, and two other scientists, one of them studying something about the stars. We have a man writing fiction, an inventor, and, finally, a real teacher. Also two organic farmers, a sculptor, a man who carves and puts together furniture all without nails, and, of all things, the United States chess champion, who can't find anyone good enough to play with and so plays against our old computer.

He also farms and does guard duty and lays pipe and cleans and cans and cooks, of course. Like all the rest of us. The things that the chess player didn't know how to do, which was everything, we taught him. Just like Hal, who was a Marine once, taught us all to shoot.

It's pretty bad out there now, although the TV says it's getting better as "society adjusts to this most cataclysmic of social changes." I don't know if that's true or not. I guess it varies. There was a lot of rioting and disease and fires. Some places have some government left, some places don't, some are like us now, mostly our own government, although Hal and two educated women keep our taxes filed and all that. One of the women told me that we don't have to actually pay taxes because the farm shows a consistent loss. She was a lawyer, but a religious lawyer. She says nano is Satan's work.

Amelia Parsons says nano is a gift from God.

Me, I think something different. I think nano is a sorter. The old sorting used to put the people with money and education and nice things in one pile and the rest of us in another. But nano sorts out two different piles: the ones who like to work because work is what you do, and the ones who don't.

It was kind of like everybody won the lottery all at once. I saw a TV show once about lottery winners, a show that followed them around for a year or two after they won real big money. By that time, most of them were worse off than before they won that money: miserable and broke again and with all their relatives mad at them. But some used the money to make nicer lives. And some just gave nearly all of it away to charity and went back to taking care of themselves.

Jack lasted two months on the farm. Then he was gone again.

I get email from him every once in a while. Mostly he asks after the kids. He never says where he is or what he's doing instead of working. He never says who he's with, or if he's happy. I guess he is, or he'd come back here. People usually end up doing what makes them happiest, if they can.

A month ago I went with Hal and some others down to the lake to catch fish. A house stood there, burned to the ground, weeds already growing over the blue brick fireplace. In the ashes I found one diamond earring. Which I left there.

Now Kimee is in the garden, waiting for me to pick peas. I'm going to show her how to shell them, too, and how to separate the good pods from the bad ones. She's only five, but it's never too early to learn.

Brother, Can You Spare a Dime?

TERRY BISSON

Terry Bisson (www.terrybisson.com) lives in Oakland, California. He is the author of six fantasy or SF novels, including Talking Man *(1987), a World Fantasy Award nominee;* Fire on the Mountain *(1988);* Voyage to the Red Planet *(1990);* The Pickup Artist *(2001); and most recently,* Dear Abby *(2003)—and a number of movie tie-in books of unusually high quality. His short fiction is collected in* Bears Discover Fire *(1993),* In the Upper Room *(2000), and* Greetings *(2005). In 2005, he also published* Numbers Don't Lie, *which combines three stories involving math wizard Wilson Wu, to form a novel. His filler feature, This Month in History (short quotes from the history of the future), now appears in Locus every month. All his work reflects his political engagement: "I spent the last year or so editing* Outlaws of America, *an impressive history of the Weather Underground by Dan Berger."*

"Brother, Can You Spare a Dime?" appeared in the anthology Golden Age SF: Tales of a Bygone Future, *edited by Eric Reynolds. It is in the same tradition of SF as William Gibson's "The Gernsback Continuum," stories about the marvellous world of the future as imagined in the 1930s during the great Depression, and how that future now, from our vantage point, doesn't work.*

"**U**p and at 'em!"

"Hey, you, get up and get moving."

Caleb opened his eyes. Two cops were bending over him. One skinny and one fat, like Laurel and Hardy. Only not funny.

The fat one was slapping a nightstick against his open hand. It made an ugly sound.

"Have a heart, officer," whined Caleb. "I'm freezing. And it's almost warm here in this doorway."

"It's warmer in Florida," said the skinny cop.

"Or jail," said the fat cop. "We got orders to clear you bums out of the Loop. So move." He rapped his nightstick on the sidewalk, like a gavel.

"Okay, okay," said Caleb. He rolled up his blanket and gathered his worldly goods—a single tattered copy of Thrilling Future Tales. He had read the magazine three times already, but tucked inside his shirt, it helped to cut the wind.

He watched the cops walk away, then hid the blanket behind a trash can. All he had to do was wait them out; the doorway would still be there, and the night ahead loomed long and dark and cold.

Meanwhile, he was hungry. He hadn't eaten in two days.

He stumbled out into the crowded street. The Loop was filled with grim figures, all bundled up against the bitter wind. Caleb eyed the passing faces, looking for a touch. Half of them were bums like himself. The others all looked mean and cold.

Caleb had no choice, though. He had to get something in his belly.

He fixed a pitiful expression on his face—not a difficult acting job, given his situation—and stuck out his hand.

"Brother, can you spare a dime?"

Nobody even bothered to say no. They walked by without even glancing at him. The Great Depression—the newspapers were already calling it that—was like the Chicago winter itself: endless and relentless.

It made people mean.

It was spitting snow. Caleb sat down on a stoop and spread the magazine across his chest like a pulp paper vest. It didn't help much. He closed his eyes and shivered and tried to imagine Florida.

Or even jail.

He opened his eyes.

A man was bending over him. A strange-looking man wearing a long black coat made out of some kind of sleek canvas. And bright silver shoes.

He was staring at the cover of the magazine.

Caleb managed a pitiful smile. The pitiful part was easy. "Brother, can you spare a dime?" he whined.

The man reached out, holding a dime between two fingers, and dropped it into Caleb's palm. That was when Caleb saw the big black watch, hanging loose on the man's wrist.

Carpe Diem was all Caleb remembered of his schoolboy Latin. But it was enough. He grabbed the watch and ran, dropping the magazine into the gutter.

"Hey!" yelled the man in the long black coat.

"Damn."

It wasn't a watch. It wasn't even metal. It was made out of some kind of funny rubber, and it had no hands, just some square numbers and a blinking light.

Radium dial? Maybe it was worth something. Caleb dropped it into the pocket of his ragged coat. He would find out later. For now, he needed something to eat.

The dime would take care of that.

He rubbed it in his pocket, like a lucky charm. It would

buy him a bowl of thin soup and a cup of even thinner coffee at Meg's Loop Diner. Little enough, but it was a start.

He turned another corner and looked back to make sure he wasn't being followed. The dark street behind him was almost empty. A few bums, a few piles of dirty snow. No man in a long black coat.

The diner was steamy and noisy with the clattering of dishes. Caleb ignored Meg's suspicious look and ordered a "soup 'n' joe."

"First things first." Meg held out her hand.

Caleb dropped the dime into it. She stared down at it, then glared up at him. "Very funny," she said. "Now out."

"Huh?"

"Out!" Meg said, pushing him toward the door and out into the cold. She flipped the dime after him. "And take your stupid trick dime with you."

"Huh?" Caleb lunged and barely caught the dime. He opened his hand and looked at it.

It was perfectly normal, with a Roman-looking torch on one side and a face on the other, some Greek goddess or—

Caleb stared. The face on the dime stared back.

It was . . .

"Hey, you!"

Caleb turned and saw the man in the long black coat, crossing the street toward him. "Wait!" the man yelled.

"Not likely," muttered Caleb. He ran down the block, rounded a corner, and ducked into the first alley he saw.

Dead end! And the man was right behind him. Caleb reached into his pocket for the watch. He would give it back. It was worthless anyway.

Or was it? Now it was blinking, faster and faster. Caleb felt an electric shock and dropped to his knees. With the watch in his outstretched hand, he looked up and saw silver shoes, and then—

And then nothing at all.

Caleb opened his eyes.

He saw silver shoes, lots of them.

The man was gone. The alley was gone.

It was daylight. It was warm! Caleb was on his knees beside a smooth sidewalk. The silver shoes were on people in long robes and bright dresses, gliding past him while standing still. The sidewalk they were on was moving, like a conveyer belt.

Overhead, a car without wheels sailed past, slowly, through the air. A kid in the back seat waved.

Caleb closed his eyes and opened them again. The car was still there, gliding around a corner.

Caleb got to his feet, rubbing his eyes.

He looked around. He was standing on a narrow bridge connecting two huge towers, all glass and steel. He walked to the edge and . . .

He was standing on the edge of nothing, looking down a thousand feet. He felt a sudden wave of dizziness, and almost fell, but an invisible railing stopped his hand.

Caleb caught his breath. He looked up and saw more flying cars. He looked over the edge again, steadying himself on the invisible railing, and saw more towers, more cars, more bridges, all filled with people. And in the distance, a bright blue lake.

Where am I? he wondered. But he knew: this was the Future. Caleb had read about it; he had even seen it, on the covers of the magazines he liked to read when he could find them in the trash.

And now he was here. In the Future.

But how?

Then he remembered the watch. He pulled it out of his pocket. "Must be some kind of Time Machine," he muttered.

Behind him, on the center of the sidewalk, people were gliding past without walking. They were of all races and colors; they all wore silver shoes, and they were all smiling.

A man in a bright metallic robe nodded and smiled, and Caleb's instincts took over. He held out his hand. "Brother, can you spare a dime?"

The man dropped a dime into his hand as he glided by.

Caleb looked at it. There was the torch on one side and on the other—

His own face. Cleaned up, with a shave and a haircut, looking very heroic.

He pulled the other dime out of his pocket and looked at them, side by side.

There was no doubt about it: There he was, full face on both dimes, like Lincoln or Caesar.

"What did I do to deserve this honor?" Caleb asked aloud.

"Excuse me?" asked a woman in a diaphanous gown as she glided past on the moving sidewalk.

"Can you tell me . . ." Caleb began.

"In a hurry!" the woman said, apologetically. "You can ask an InfoBot. There's one."

She pointed to a life-sized statue, set into an alcove beside the walkway. A light in the statue's head was blinking; it blinked faster and faster as Caleb approached.

"Ask a statue?" he muttered.

"Not a statue, citizen," said the statue. "I am an InfoBot. At your service."

Of course! This was the Future! It was a robot. Inside the transparent crystal head, Caleb could see a forest of glowing vacuum tubes.

"And you can answer any question?"

"Certainly, bio-citizen. I am at your service."

Caleb reached into his pocket and pulled out his dime. He held it out toward the robot.

"My services are free," said the InfoBot.

"Who is that?" Caleb asked.

"It's you, of course."

"So it's true!" said Caleb, slipping the dime back into his pocket. This was almost too good to believe! "Can you tell me where I am?"

"Chicago, bio-citizen. This is the Loop."

"I mean the date."

"December 21, bio-citizen." The light in the InfoBot's forehead blinked as it answered.

"I mean the year."

"2255, bio-citizen. You can ask me anything. I am at your service."

"So this is the Future?"

"Negative, bio-citizen. This is the present. Travel to the future is forbidden. Only travel to the past is permitted."

Caleb pulled the watch out of his pocket. "So this is a Time Machine?"

"It is a temporary chronoslip interface device. It will take you to the past, and then return you here to the present."

"I see." Caleb slipped the watch back into his pocket; it was his ticket home. If he ever wanted to go! "So people can travel to the present—I mean, the past?" he asked.

"Certainly," said the Infobot. "ChronoTourists. But they are rather rare. The past is said to be rather unpleasant."

"You got that right," said Caleb. He shivered, remembering the cold. "If it's December, and this is Chicago, how come it's so nice and warm?"

"The atomic dome covering the Loop protects it from the weather," said the InfoBot.

"I see," said Caleb, though he didn't. The dome was invisible. "And what about food? Is there a diner around?"

The InfoBot blinked, looking confused. "Only in the museum. Would you like to go? We can show menus, too, and other artifacts from the pre-techno past."

"Never mind," said Caleb. "I'm starving. Can I get something to eat?"

"Certainly, bio-citizen," said the InfoBot. "Would you like me to summon a DinnerBot?"

Would he?! No sooner said than done. The DinnerBot rolled up seemingly out of nowhere, with a metallic chef's hat on its head and a slot for a mouth. It had a little window in its chest, like the automat. Through it Caleb could see a hamburger and fries.

"Please insert coin," the DinnerBot said.

"I only have a dime," Caleb said. Actually he had two, side by side in his pocket. But there was no need to mention that.

He put one of his dimes into the slot and the window opened. Caleb grabbed the hamburger in one hand and the fries in the other. The DinnerBot bowed and left.

"How did it know what I wanted?" Caleb asked, his mouth full.

"Instantaneous telepathy," said the InfoBot. "All bio-citizen needs are anticipated."

"All this for only a dime," Caleb said, tearing into the french fries. Each one had a little seam of catsup running through it, like a vein.

"Everything costs a dime," said the InfoBot. "It is our only currency, and everyone is entitled to all they need."

"That's good to know," said Caleb as he wolfed down the hamburger. It was the first real food he'd had in days—in several centuries, now that he thought about it. And it tasted great.

But now his dime was gone. He looked the InfoBot in the eye. "Brother, can you spare a dime?"

"Certainly, bio-citizen," said the InfoBot. A dime appeared in its mouth. "To each according to his needs."

"Hurrah for the Future," said Caleb, snatching the dime. This one, too, had his picture on it. "Say—do you know who I am?"

"You are a bio-citizen," said the InfoBot. "I am at your service."

"I mean, do you know what I did? Does the name Caleb Freeman mean anything to you?"

"It's not a proper name. It has no numerals. Would you like for me to give you a proper name?"

"No, no!" said Caleb. "I could sure use a bath, though."

"Perhaps I could summon a SaniBot?"

No sooner said than done. The SaniBot was a woman robot, with a smiling slot for a mouth. "Please insert coin," she said.

"No problem." Caleb slipped his new dime into her mouth.

She opened her arms and Caleb was enveloped in a sweet smelling silvery mist, only for a second. Then it was gone, and he felt clean all over. He looked down at his ragged coat. Even it was clean.

"I love it here!" he said, as the SaniBot bowed and rolled away.

"Of course," said the InfoBot. "Now that there is no poverty or crime, Chicago is a good place for bio-citizens to live."

"No poverty? No crime?"

"No need," said the InfoBot. "All our energy needs are taken care of by radioactive microwave grid, and all the labor is done by robots like myself. We are here to serve you."

"No robot rebellion, huh?"

"I beg your pardon, bio-citizen?"

"Nothing," said Caleb. "I was just thinking that the Future is everything I ever expected—everything the sci-fi writers anticipated, and even better."

"This is the present," corrected the InfoBot. "It is anticipated that the future will be nice also."

"I don't doubt it," said Caleb. "Are you sure there's nothing about me in your whatever-you-call-it?"

"Magnetic memory," said the InfoBot. "All human knowledge is on tape, in here." He tapped his transparent head. Caleb could see reels turning between the glowing vacuum tubes.

"And there's nothing about Caleb Freeman?"

"Negative."

"Hmmm. Maybe I change my name, like a movie star." Caleb pulled his last dime out of his pocket. "But this is me, right?"

"Certainly," said the InfoBot. "Who else could it be?"

"Exactly," said Caleb. He pocketed the dime and looked around at the shining towers, the moving sidewalks, the floating cars and the happy citizens gliding by.

And then he groaned aloud, realizing what he had to do.

"Damn!" he said. "Clearly I did something important, to help bring about this wonderful future. And now I can't enjoy it!"

"I don't understand," said the InfoBot.

"I have to go back to my own time, so I can do whatever it is that I do in order to bring all this about. I can't take the chance on missing out on my historic destiny."

"Whatever you say," said the InfoBot.

"Plus, if I stay here I'm liable to get tangled up in some kind of Time Paradox. Which I've read about in—say, what happened to my magazine?"

"I can show you a magazine in the museum," said the InfoBot. "Would you like to take a guided tour?"

"I wish I could. I love it here. But I can't take the chance," said Caleb. "I've got a full belly and a shave and a haircut. I should probably be heading back to the present. I mean, the past."

"If you say so. Not many tourists go there anymore. It is said to be rather unpleasant."

"You're telling me!" said Caleb. "But I don't want to miss out on whatever it is that makes me famous. How do you work this thing?"

He pulled the watch—the temporary chronoslip interface device—out of his pocket.

"It is apparently already set," said the InfoBot. "All you have to do is press the little radium-powered button. Would you like me to help?"

"I can handle it. This one?" Caleb pressed it.

And the robot was gone.

The city was gone.

The Future was gone.

Brrrrr! Caleb felt the cold wind on the back of his neck.

He was on his knees in the alley, and the man in the long black coat was standing over him.

"That thing you took," he said. "You must give it back! You don't understand how . . ."

"Oh, but I do," said Caleb. He handed him the watch. "Sorry to have troubled you. You see, I . . ."

But the man was already disappearing, in a slow flash of light. And Caleb was alone in the alley.

There was his magazine, on the ground where the man had dropped it. Caleb picked it up and looked at the cover: a gleaming futuristic city, with silvery towers and floating cars, but not half as nice as the real thing.

The Future he had seen—if only for a moment.

Caleb suddenly felt very tired. He stuck the magazine in his shirt and headed back for the doorway, where his blanket was stashed. He rolled up in the blanket and lay down in the doorway.

He shivered. It was even colder than before.

"No matter." Caleb pulled the dime out of his pocket and smiled. There was his face, like Caesar himself. Who knew what pleasures awaited, if he could just get through the winter.

And I know my destiny, he thought. I know I get through the winter.

Shivering, but smiling, he fell asleep, into the deepest, and final, sleep of his life.

"Up and at 'em," said O'Malley. He rapped on the sidewalk with his nightstick. It made an ugly sound.

"Hey, you! Let's get moving!" said O'Shea. "Uh oh. Look here."

The two cops bent down and pulled back the blanket. The body inside was stiff.

"Didn't we roust this bum out before?" said O'Malley.

"Musta crawled back," said O'Shea. "Poor guy. Last night was a killer. Literally."

"One less bum to worry about. Better call the dead wagon."

"At least he died smiling. I guess dreams are still free."

"At least he found some clean clothes," said O'Malley. "That makes it easier. Help me turn him over."

"This one was a reader," said O'Shea. "Thrilling Future Tales. I read that one myself sometimes."

"You can keep it then. Help me pry his hand open. Wouldn't you know it. A dime."

"Guess it's ours," said O'Shea. "Poor guy's got no one else to leave to."

"Brother, can you spare a dime," said O'Malley, warming the coin in his hand. He looked at it. Then stared at it. "Funny. Hey. Look at this."

"That's your face!" said O'Shea. "Let me see."

He took the dime in his hand and watched as the face slowly changed. "Now it's my face!"

O'Malley grabbed it back. "Now it's my face again. Some kind of trick dime."

"Futuristic, you mean. Radioactive, or something," said

O'Shea. "Bet he bought it through that magazine. There are lots of novelty ads in the back pages. Let me see it again."

"No way, O'Shea. I'm keeping it."

"Why? You can't spend it."

"I want to show the sergeant. Wait'll he sees his ugly mug on a dime!"

When Sysadmins Ruled the Earth

CORY DOCTOROW

Cory Doctorow (www.craphound.com) *is a science fiction writer and technology activist. He is co-editor of the popular weblog Boing Boing* (boingboing.net). *He also contributes to* Wired, Popular Science, *and the* New York Times. *Presently living in California, he holds the Fulbright Chair at the An-nenberg Center for Public Diplomacy at the University of Southern California. His most recent novel is* Someone Comes to Town, Someone Leaves Town *(2005). A collection of short stories,* A Place So Foreign and Eight More, *appeared in 2004 and won the Sunburst Award. His new short story collection is* Overclocked: Stories of the Future Present *(2007).*

"When Sysadmins Ruled the Earth" appeared in Flurb, the webzine edited by Rudy Rucker, and this is perhaps its first appearance in print. It is a post-9/11, post-Hurricane Katrina, post-Afghanistan, post-Iraq story of which he writes: "I started writing . . . on July 6, 2005, while teaching Clarion. The next day, the London Underground and busses were bombed, including the bus I rode to work every morning." Doctorow's finished story captures perfectly the 2006 zeitgeist, that feeling that we are already in the midst of the apocalypse and maybe just don't know it yet; that perhaps the real glue holding civilization together these days is the band of borderline–autistic libertarians who keep our world-wide computer networks working.

When Felix's special phone rang at two in the morning, Kelly rolled over and punched him in the shoulder and hissed, "Why didn't you turn that fucking thing off before bed?"

"Because I'm on call," he said.

"You're not a fucking doctor," she said, kicking him as he sat on the bed's edge, pulling on the pants he'd left on the floor before turning in. "You're a goddamned systems administrator."

"It's my job," he said.

"They work you like a government mule," she said. "You know I'm right. For Christ's sake, you're a father now, you can't go running off in the middle of the night every time someone's porn supply goes down. Don't answer that phone."

He knew she was right. He answered the phone.

"Main routers not responding. BGP not responding." The mechanical voice of the systems monitor didn't care if he cursed at it, so he did, and it made him feel a little better.

"Maybe I can fix it from here," he said. He could log in to the UPS for the cage and reboot the routers. The UPS was in a different netblock, with its own independent routers on their own uninterruptible power-supplies.

Kelly was sitting up in bed now, an indistinct shape against the headboard. "In five years of marriage, you have never once been able to fix anything from here." This time she was wrong—he fixed stuff from home all the time, but he did it discreetly and didn't make a fuss, so she didn't remember it. And she was right, too—he had logs that showed that after 1AM, nothing could ever be fixed without driving out to the cage. Law of Infinite Universal Perversity—AKA Felix's Law.

Five minutes later Felix was behind the wheel. He hadn't been able to fix it from home. The independent router's net-block was offline, too. The last time that had happened, some dumbfuck construction worker had driven a ditch-witch through the main conduit into the data-center and Fe-lix had joined a cadre of fifty enraged sysadmins who'd stood atop the resulting pit for a week, screaming abuse at the poor bastards who labored 24-7 to splice ten thousand wires back together.

His phone went off twice more in the car and he let it override the stereo and play the mechanical status reports through the big, bassy speakers of more critical network infrastructure offline. Then Kelly called.

"Hi," he said.

"Don't cringe, I can hear the cringe in your voice."

He smiled involuntarily. "Check, no cringing."

"I love you, Felix," she said.

"I'm totally bonkers for you, Kelly. Go back to bed."

"2.0's awake," she said. The baby had been Beta Test when he was in her womb, and when her water broke, he got the call and dashed out of the office, shouting, "The Gold Master just shipped!" They'd started calling him 2.0 before he'd fin-ished his first cry. "This little bastard was born to suck tit."

"I'm sorry I woke you," he said. He was almost at the data-center. No traffic at 2AM. He slowed down and pulled over before the entrance to the garage. He didn't want to lose Kelly's call underground.

"It's not waking me," she said. "You've been there for seven years. You have three juniors reporting to you. Give them the phone. You've paid your dues."

"I don't like asking my reports to do anything I wouldn't do," he said.

"You've done it," she said. "Please? I hate waking up alone in the night. I miss you most at night."

"Kelly—"

"I'm over being angry. I just miss you is all. You give me sweet dreams."

"OK," he said.

"Simple as that?"

"Exactly. Simple as that. Can't have you having bad dreams, and I've paid my dues. From now on, I'm only going on night call to cover holidays."

She laughed. "Sysadmins don't take holidays."

"This one will," he said. "Promise."

"You're wonderful," she said. "Oh, gross. 2.0 just dumped core all over my bathrobe."

"That's my boy," he said.

"Oh that he is," she said. She hung up, and he piloted the car into the data-center lot, badging in and peeling up a bleary eyelid to let the retinal scanner get a good look at his sleep-depped eyeball.

He stopped at the machine to get himself a guarana/medafonil power-bar and a cup of lethal robot-coffee in a spill-proof clean-room sippy-cup. He wolfed down the bar and sipped the coffee, then let the inner door read his hand-geometry and size him up for a moment. It sighed open and gusted the airlock's load of positively pressurized air over him as he passed finally to the inner sanctum.

It was bedlam. The cages were designed to let two or three sysadmins maneuver around them at a time. Every other inch of cubic space was given over to humming racks of servers and routers and drives. Jammed among them were no fewer than twenty other sysadmins. It was a regular convention of black tee-shirts with inexplicable slogans, bellies overlapping belts with phones and multitools.

Normally it was practically freezing in the cage, but all those bodies were overheating the small, enclosed space. Five or six looked up and grimaced when he came through. Two greeted him by name. He threaded his belly through the press and the cages, toward the Ardent racks in the back of the room.

"Felix." It was Van, who wasn't on call that night.

"What are you doing here?" he asked. "No need for both of us to be wrecked tomorrow."

"What? Oh. My personal box is over there. It went down around 1:30 and I got woken up by my process-monitor. I should have called you and told you I was coming down— spared you the trip."

Felix's own server—a box he shared with five other friends—was in a rack one floor down. He wondered if it was offline too.

"What's the story?"

"Massive flashworm attack. Some jackass with a zero-day exploit has got every Windows box on the net running Monte Carlo probes on every IP block, including IPv6. The big Ciscos all run administrative interfaces over v6, and they all fall over if they get more than ten simultaneous probes, which means that just about every interchange has gone down. DNS is screwy, too—like maybe someone poisoned the zone transfer last night. Oh, and there's an email and IM component that sends pretty lifelike messages to everyone in your address book, barfing up Eliza-dialog that keys off of your logged email and messages to get you to open a Trojan."

"Jesus."

"Yeah." Van was a type-two sysadmin, over six feet tall, long pony-tail, bobbing Adam's apple. Over his toast-rack chest, his tee said CHOOSE YOUR WEAPON and featured a row of polyhedral RPG dice.

Felix was a type-one admin, with an extra seventy or eighty pounds all around the middle, and a neat but full beard that he wore over his extra chins. His tee said HELLO CTHULHU and featured a cute, mouthless, Hello-Kitty-style Cthulhu. They'd known each other for fifteen years, having met on Usenet, then f2f at Toronto Freenet beer-sessions, a Star Trek convention or two, and eventually Felix had hired Van to work under him at Ardent. Van was reliable and methodical. Trained as an electrical engineer, he kept a procession of spiral notebooks filled with the details of every step he'd ever taken, with time and date.

"Not even PEBKAC this time," Van said. Problem Exists Between Keyboard And Chair. Email trojans fell into that category—if people were smart enough not to open suspect attachments, email trojans would be a thing of the past. But worms that ate Cisco routers weren't a problem with the lusers—they were the fault of incompetent engineers.

"No, it's Microsoft's fault," Felix said. "Any time I'm at work at 2AM, it's either PEBKAC or Microsloth."

They ended up just unplugging the frigging routers from the Internet. Not Felix, of course, though he was itching to do it and get them rebooted after shutting down their IPv6 interfaces. It was done by a couple bull-goose Bastard Operators From Hell who had to turn two keys at once to get access to their cage—like guards in a Minuteman silo. 95 percent of the long distance traffic in Canada went through this building. It had better security than most Minuteman silos.

Felix and Van got the Ardent boxes back online one at a time. They were being pounded by worm-probes—putting the routers back online just exposed the downstream cages to the attack. Every box on the Internet was drowning in worms, or creating worm-attacks, or both. Felix managed to get through to NIST and Bugtraq after about a hundred timeouts, and download some kernel patches that should reduce the load the worms put on the machines in his care. It was 10AM, and he was hungry enough to eat the ass out of a dead bear, but he recompiled his kernels and brought the machines back online. Van's long fingers flew over the administrative keyboard, his tongue protruding as he ran load-stats on each one.

"I had two hundred days of uptime on Greedo," Van said. Greedo was the oldest server in the rack, from the days when they'd named the boxes after Star Wars characters. Now they were all named after Smurfs, and they were running out of Smurfs and had started in on McDonaldland characters, starting with Van's laptop, Mayor McCheese.

"Greedo will rise again," Felix said. "I've got a 486 downstairs with over five years of uptime. It's going to break my heart to reboot it."

"What the everlasting shit do you use a 486 for?"

"Nothing. But who shuts down a machine with five years uptime? That's like euthanizing your grandmother."

"I wanna eat," Van said.

"Tell you what," Felix said. "We'll get your box up, then mine, then I'll take you to the Lakeview Lunch for breakfast pizzas and you can have the rest of the day off."

"You're on," Van said. "Man, you're too good to us grunts. You should keep us in a pit and beat us like all the other bosses. It's all we deserve."

"It's your phone," Van said. Felix extracted himself from the guts of the 486, which had refused to power up at all. He had cadged a spare power-supply from some guys who ran a spam operation and was trying to get it fitted. He let Van hand him the phone, which had fallen off his belt while he was twisting to get at the back of the machine.

"Hey, Kel," he said. There was an odd, snuffling noise in the background. Static, maybe? 2.0 splashing in the bath? "Kelly?"

The line went dead. He tried to call back, but didn't get anything—no ring nor voicemail. His phone finally timed out and said NETWORK ERROR.

"Dammit," he said, mildly. He clipped the phone to his belt. Kelly wanted to know when he was coming home, or wanted him to pick something up for the family. She'd leave voicemail.

He was testing the power-supply when his phone rang again. He snatched it up and answered it. "Kelly, hey, what's up?" He worked to keep anything like irritation out of his voice. He felt guilty: technically speaking, he had discharged his obligations to Ardent Financial LLC once the Ardent servers were back online. The past three hours had been purely personal—even if he planned on billing them to the company.

There was sobbing on the line.

"Kelly?" He felt the blood draining from his face and his toes were numb.

"Felix," she said, barely comprehensible through the sobbing. "He's dead, oh Jesus, he's dead."

"Who? Who, Kelly?"

"Will," she said.

Will? he thought. Who the fuck is— He dropped to his knees. William was the name they'd written on the birth certificate, though they'd called him 2.0 all along. Felix made an anguished sound, like a sick bark.

"I'm sick," she said, "I can't even stand anymore. Oh, Felix. I love you so much."

"Kelly? What's going on?"

"Everyone, everyone—" she said. "Only two channels left on the tube. Christ, Felix, it looks like dawn of the dead out the window—" He heard her retch. The phone started to break up, washing her puke-noises back like an echoplex.

"Stay there, Kelly," he shouted as the line died. He punched 911, but the phone went NETWORK ERROR again as soon as he hit SEND.

He grabbed Mayor McCheese from Van and plugged it into the 486's network cable and launched Firefox off the command line and googled for the Metro Police site. Quickly, but not frantically, he searched for an online contact form. Felix didn't lose his head, ever. He solved problems and freaking out didn't solve problems.

He located an online form and wrote out the details of his conversation with Kelly like he was filing a bug report, his fingers fast, his description complete, and then he hit SUBMIT.

Van had read over his shoulder. "Felix—" he began.

"God," Felix said. He was sitting on the floor of the cage and he slowly pulled himself upright. Van took the laptop and tried some news sites, but they were all timing out. Impossible to say if it was because something terrible was happening or because the network was limping under the superworm.

"I need to get home," Felix said.

"I'll drive you," Van said. "You can keep calling your wife."

They made their way to the elevators. One of the building's few windows was there, a thick, shielded porthole. They peered through it as they waited for the elevator. Not much traffic for a Wednesday. Were there more police cars than usual?

"Oh my God—" Van pointed.

The CN Tower, a giant white-elephant needle of a building loomed to the east of them. It was askew, like a branch stuck in wet sand. Was it moving? It was. It was heeling over, slowly, but gaining speed, falling northeast toward the financial district. In a second, it slid over the tipping point and crashed down. They felt the shock, then heard it, the whole building rocking from the impact. A cloud of dust rose from the wreckage, and there was more thunder as the world's tallest freestanding structure crashed through building after building.

"The Broadcast Centre's coming down," Van said. It was—the CBC's towering building was collapsing in slow motion. People ran every way, were crushed by falling masonry. Seen through the port-hole, it was like watching a neat CGI trick downloaded from a file-sharing site.

Sysadmins were clustering around them now, jostling to see the destruction.

"What happened?" one of them asked.

"The CN Tower fell down," Felix said. He sounded far away in his own ears.

"Was it the virus?"

"The worm? What?" Felix focused on the guy, who was a young admin with just a little type-two flab around the middle.

"Not the worm," the guy said. "I got an email that the whole city's quarantined because of some virus. Bioweapon, they say." He handed Felix his BlackBerry.

Felix was so engrossed in the report—purportedly forwarded from Health Canada—that he didn't even notice that all the lights had gone out. Then he did, and he pressed the BlackBerry back into its owner's hand, and let out one small sob.

The generators kicked in a minute later. Sysadmins stampeded for the stairs. Felix grabbed Van by the arm, pulled him back.

"Maybe we should wait this out in the cage," he said.

"What about Kelly?" Van said.

Felix felt like he was going to throw up. "We should get into the cage, now." The cage had microparticulate air-filters.

They ran upstairs to the big cage. Felix opened the door and then let it hiss shut behind him.

"Felix, you need to get home—"

"It's a bioweapon," Felix said. "Superbug. We'll be OK in here, I think, so long as the filters hold out."

"What?"

"Get on IRC," he said.

They did. Van had Mayor McCheese and Felix used Smurfette. They skipped around the chat channels until they found one with some familiar handles.

> pentagons gone/white house too
> MY NEIGHBORS BARFING BLOOD OFF HIS BALCONY IN SAN DIEGO
> Someone knocked over the Gherkin. Bankers are fleeing the City like rats.
> I heard that the Ginza's on fire

Felix typed: I'm in Toronto. We just saw the CN Tower fall. I've heard reports of bioweapons, something very fast.

Van read this and said, "You don't know how fast it is, Felix. Maybe we were all exposed three days ago."

Felix closed his eyes. "If that were so we'd be feeling some symptoms, I think."

> Looks like an EMP took out Hong Kong and maybe Paris—realtime sat footage shows them completely dark, and all netblocks there aren't routing
> You're in Toronto?

It was an unfamiliar handle.

> Yes—on Front Street
> my sisters at UofT and i cnt reach her—can you call her?
> No phone service

Felix typed, staring at NETWORK PROBLEMS.

"I have a soft phone on Mayor McCheese," Van said, launching his voice-over-IP app. "I just remembered."

Felix took the laptop from him and punched in his home

number. It rang once, then there was a flat, blatting sound like an ambulance siren in an Italian movie.

```
> No phone service
```

Felix typed again.

He looked up at Van, and saw that his skinny shoulders were shaking. Van said, "Holy motherfucking shit. The world is ending."

Felix pried himself off of IRC an hour later. Atlanta had burned. Manhattan was hot—radioactive enough to screw up the webcams looking out over Lincoln Plaza. Everyone blamed Islam until it became clear that Mecca was a smoking pit and the Saudi Royals had been hanged before their palaces.

His hands were shaking, and Van was quietly weeping in the far corner of the cage. He tried calling home again, and then the police. It didn't work any better than it had the last 20 times.

He sshed into his box downstairs and grabbed his mail. Spam, spam, spam. More spam. Automated messages. There—an urgent message from the intrusion detection system in the Ardent cage.

He opened it and read quickly. Someone was crudely, repeatedly probing his routers. It didn't match a worm's signature, either. He followed the traceroute and discovered that the attack had originated in the same building as him, a system in a cage one floor below.

He had procedures for this. He portscanned his attacker and found that port 1337 was open—1337 was "leet" or "elite" in hacker number/letter substitution code. That was the kind of port that a worm left open to slither in and out of. He googled known sploits that left a listener on port 1337, narrowed this down based on the fingerprinted operating system of the compromised server, and then he had it.

It was an ancient worm, one that every box should have been patched against years before. No mind. He had the client for it, and he used it to create a root account for himself on the box, which he then logged into, and took a look around.

There was one other user logged in, "scaredy," and he checked the proccess monitor and saw that scaredy had spawned all the hundreds of processes that were probing him and plenty of other boxen.

He opened a chat:

```
> Stop probing my server
```

He expected bluster, guilt, denial. He was surprised.

```
> Are you in the Front Street data-center?
> Yes
> Christ I thought I was the last one alive. I'm
  on the fourth floor. I think there's a bioweapon
  attack outside. I don't want to leave the clean
  room.
```

Felix whooshed out a breath.

```
> You were probing me to get me to trace back to
  you?
> Yeah
> That was smart
```

Clever bastard.

```
> I'm on the sixth floor, I've got one more with me.
> What do you know?
```

Felix pasted in the IRC log and waited while the other guy digested it. Van stood up and paced. His eyes were glazed over.

"Van? Pal?"

"I have to pee," he said.

"No opening the door," Felix said. "I saw an empty Mountain Dew bottle in the trash there."

"Right," Van said. He walked like a zombie to the trash can and pulled out the empty magnum. He turned his back.

```
> I'm Felix
> Will
```

Felix's stomach did a slow somersault as he thought about 2.0.

"Felix, I think I need to go outside," Van said. He was moving toward the airlock door. Felix dropped his keyboard and struggled to his feet and ran headlong to Van, tackling him before he reached the door.

"Van," he said, looking into his friend's glazed, unfocused eyes. "Look at me, Van."

"I need to go," Van said. "I need to get home and feed the cats."

"There's something out there, something fast-acting and lethal. Maybe it will blow away with the wind. Maybe it's already gone. But we're going to sit here until we know for sure or until we have no choice. Sit down, Van. Sit."

"I'm cold, Felix."

It was freezing. Felix's arms were broken out in gooseflesh and his feet felt like blocks of ice.

"Sit against the servers, by the vents. Get the exhaust heat." He found a rack and nestled up against it.

```
> Are you there?
> Still here—sorting out some logistics
> How long until we can go out?
> I have no idea
```

No one typed anything for quite some time then.

Felix had to use the Mountain Dew bottle twice. Then Van used it again. Felix tried calling Kelly again. The Metro Police site was down.

Finally, he slid back against the servers and wrapped his arms around his knees and wept like a baby.

After a minute, Van came over and sat beside him, with his arm around Felix's shoulder.

"They're dead, Van," Felix said. "Kelly and my s—son. My family is gone."

"You don't know for sure," Van said.

"I'm sure enough," Felix said. "Christ, it's all over, isn't it?"

"We'll gut it out a few more hours and then head out. Things should be getting back to normal soon. The fire department will fix it. They'll mobilize the Army. It'll be OK."

Felix's ribs hurt. He hadn't cried since—since 2.0 was born. He hugged his knees harder.

Then the doors opened.

The two sysadmins who entered were wild-eyed. One had a tee that said TALK NERDY TO ME and the other one was wearing an Electronic Frontiers Canada shirt.

"Come on," TALK NERDY said. "We're all getting to-gether on the top floor. Take the stairs."

Felix found he was holding his breath.

"If there's a bioagent in the building, we're all infected," TALK NERDY said. "Just go, we'll meet you there."

"There's one on the sixth floor," Felix said, as he climbed to his feet.

"Will, yeah, we got him. He's up there."

TALK NERDY was one of the Bastard Operators >From Hell who'd unplugged the big routers. Felix and Van climbed the stairs slowly, their steps echoing in the deserted shaft. After the frigid air of the cage, the stairwell felt like a sauna.

There was a cafeteria on the top floor, with working toi-lets, water and coffee and vending machine food. There was an uneasy queue of sysadmins before each. No one met anyone's eye. Felix wondered which one was Will and then he joined the vending machine queue.

He got a couple more energy bars and a gigantic cup of vanilla coffee before running out of change. Van had scored them some table space and Felix set the stuff down before him and got in the toilet line. "Just save some for me," he said, tossing an energy bar in front of Van.

By the time they were all settled in, thoroughly evacu-ated, and eating, TALK NERDY and his friend had returned again. They cleared off the cash-register at the end of the food-prep area and TALK NERDY got up on it. Slowly the conversation died down.

"I'm Uri Popovich, this is Diego Rosenbaum. Thank you all for coming up here. Here's what we know for sure: the building's been on generators for three hours now. Visual observation indicates that we're the only building in central Toronto with working power—which should hold out for three more days. There is a bioagent of unknown origin loose beyond our doors. It kills quickly, within hours, and it is aerosolized. You get it from breathing bad air. No one has opened any of the exterior doors to this building since five this morning. No one will open the doors until I give the go-ahead.

"Attacks on major cities all over the world have left

emergency responders in chaos. The attacks are electronic, biological, nuclear and conventional explosives, and they are very widespread. I'm a security engineer, and where I come from, attacks in this kind of cluster are usually viewed as opportunistic: group B blows up a bridge because everyone is off taking care of group A's dirty nuke event. It's smart. An Aum Shin Rikyo cell in Seoul gassed the subways there about 2AM Eastern—that's the earliest event we can locate, so it may have been the Archduke that broke the camel's back. We're pretty sure that Aum Shin Rikyo couldn't be behind this kind of mayhem: they have no history of infowar and have never shown the kind of organizational acumen necessary to take out so many targets at once. Basically, they're not smart enough.

"We're holing up here for the foreseeable future, at least until the bioweapon has been identified and dispersed. We're going to staff the racks and keep the networks up. This is critical infrastructure, and it's our job to make sure it's got five nines of uptime. In times of national emergency, our responsibility to do that doubles."

One sysadmin put up his hand. He was very daring in a green Incredible Hulk ring-tee, and he was at the young end of the scale.

"Who died and made you king?"

"I have controls for the main security system, keys to every cage, and passcodes for the exterior doors—they're all locked now, by the way. I'm the one who got everyone up here first and called the meeting. I don't care if someone else wants this job, it's a shitty one. But someone needs to have this job."

"You're right," the kid said. "And I can do it every bit as well as you. My name's Will Sario."

Popovich looked down his nose at the kid. "Well, if you'll let me finish talking, maybe I'll hand things over to you when I'm done."

"Finish, by all means." Sario turned his back on him and walked to the window. He stared out of it intensely. Felix's gaze was drawn to it, and he saw that there were several oily smoke plumes rising up from the city.

Popovich's momentum was broken. "So that's what we're going to do," he said.

The kid looked around after a stretched moment of silence. "Oh, is it my turn now?"

There was a round of good-natured chuckling.

"Here's what I think: the world is going to shit. There are coordinated attacks on every critical piece of infrastructure. There's only one way that those attacks could be so well coordinated: via the Internet. Even if you buy the thesis that the attacks are all opportunistic, we need to ask how an opportunistic attack could be organized in minutes: the Internet."

"So you think we should shut down the Internet?" Popovich laughed a little, but stopped when Sario said nothing.

"We saw an attack last night that nearly killed the Internet. A little DoS on the critical routers, a little DNS-foo, and down it goes like a preacher's daughter. Cops and the military are a bunch of technophobic lusers, they hardly rely on the net at all. If we take the Internet down, we'll disproportionately disadvantage the attackers, while only inconveniencing the defenders. When the time comes, we can rebuild it."

"You're shitting me," Popovich said. His jaw literally hung open.

"It's logical," Sario said. "Lots of people don't like coping with logic when it dictates hard decisions. That's a problem with people, not logic."

There was a buzz of conversation that quickly turned into a roar.

"Shut UP!" Popovich hollered. The conversation dimmed by one Watt. Popovich yelled again, stamping his foot on the countertop. Finally there was a semblance of order. "One at a time," he said. He was flushed red, his hands in his pockets.

One sysadmin was for staying. Another for going. They should hide in the cages. They should inventory their supplies and appoint a quartermaster. They should go outside and find the police, or volunteer at hospitals. They should appoint defenders to keep the front door secure.

Felix found to his surprise that he had his hand in the air. Popovich called on him.

"My name is Felix Tremont," he said, getting up on one of the tables, drawing out his PDA. "I want to read you something.

" 'Governments of the Industrial World, you weary giants of flesh and steel, I come from Cyberspace, the new home of Mind. On behalf of the future, I ask you of the past to leave us alone. You are not welcome among us. You have no sovereignty where we gather.

" 'We have no elected government, nor are we likely to have one, so I address you with no greater authority than that with which liberty itself always speaks. I declare the global social space we are building to be naturally independent of the tyrannies you seek to impose on us. You have no moral right to rule us nor do you possess any methods of enforcement we have true reason to fear.

" 'Governments derive their just powers from the consent of the governed. You have neither solicited nor received ours. We did not invite you. You do not know us, nor do you know our world. Cyberspace does not lie within your borders. Do not think that you can build it, as though it were a public construction project. You cannot. It is an act of nature and it grows itself through our collective actions.'

"That's from the Declaration of Independence of Cyberspace. It was written 12 years ago. I thought it was one of the most beautiful things I'd ever read. I wanted my kid to grow up in a world where cyberspace was free—and where that freedom infected the real world, so meatspace got freer too."

He swallowed hard and scrubbed at his eyes with the back of his hand. Van awkwardly patted him on the shoe.

"My beautiful son and my beautiful wife died today. Millions more, too. The city is literally in flames. Whole cities have disappeared from the map."

He coughed up a sob and swallowed it again.

"All around the world, people like us are gathered in buildings like this. They were trying to recover from last night's worm when disaster struck. We have independent power. Food. Water.

"We have the network, that the bad guys use so well and that the good guys have never figured out.

"We have a shared love of liberty that comes from caring about and caring for the network. We are in charge of the most important organizational and governmental tool the world has ever seen. We are the closest thing to a government the world has right now. Geneva is a crater. The East River is on fire and the UN is evacuated.

"The Distributed Republic of Cyberspace weathered this storm basically unscathed. We are the custodians of a deathless, monstrous, wonderful machine, one with the potential to rebuild a better world.

"I have nothing to live for but that."

There were tears in Van's eyes. He wasn't the only one. They didn't applaud him, but they did one better. They maintained respectful, total silence for seconds that stretched to a minute.

"How do we do it?" Popovich said, without a trace of sarcasm.

The newsgroups were filling up fast. They'd announced them in news.admin.net-abuse.email, where all the spamfighters hung out, and where there was a tight culture of camaraderie in the face of full-out attack.

The new group was alt.november5-disaster.recovery, with .recovery.goverance, .recovery.finance, .recovery. logistics and .recovery.defense hanging off of it. Bless the wooly alt. hierarchy and all those who sail in her.

The sysadmins came out of the woodwork. The Googleplex was online, with the stalwart Queen Kong bossing a gang of rollerbladed grunts who wheeled through the gigantic data-center swapping out dead boxen and hitting reboot switches. The Internet Archive was offline in the Presidio, but the mirror in Amsterdam was live and they'd redirected the DNS so that you'd hardly know the difference. Amazon was down. Paypal was up. Blogger, Typepad and Livejournal were all up, and filling with millions of posts from scared survivors huddling together for electronic warmth.

The Flickr photostreams were horrific. Felix had to

unsubscribe from them after he caught a photo of a woman and a baby, dead in a kitchen, twisted into an agonized heiro-glyph by the bioagent. They didn't look like Kelly and 2.0, but they didn't have to. He started shaking and couldn't stop.

Wikipedia was up, but limping under load. The spam poured in as though nothing had changed. Worms roamed the network.

.recovery.logistics was where most of the action was.

> We can use the newsgroup voting mechanism to
  hold regional
> elections

Felix knew that this would work. Usenet newsgroup votes had been running for more than twenty years without a sub-stantial hitch.

> We'll elect regional representatives and they'll
  pick a Prime
> Minister.

The Americans insisted on President, which Felix didn't like. Seemed too partisan. His future wouldn't be the Amer-ican future. The American future had gone up with the White House. He was building a bigger tent than that.

There were French sysadmins online from France Tele-com. The EBU's data-center had been spared in the attacks that hammered Geneva, and it was filled with wry Germans whose English was better than Felix's. They got on well with the remains of the BBC team in Canary Wharf.

They spoke polyglot English in .recovery.logistics, and Felix had momentum on his side. Some of the admins were cooling out the inevitable stupid flamewars with the practice of long years. Some were chipping in useful suggestions.

Surprisingly few thought that Felix was off his rocker.

> I think we should hold elections as soon as
  possible. Tomorrow
> at the latest. We can't rule justly without the
  consent of the
> governed.

Within seconds the reply landed in his inbox.

> You can't be serious. Consent of the governed?
  Unless I miss my

> guess, most of the people you're proposing to
> govern are puking
> their guts out, hiding under their desks, or
> wandering
> shell-shocked through the city streets. When do
  THEY get a vote?

Felix had to admit she had a point. Queen Kong was sharp. Not many woman sysadmins, and that was a genuine tragedy. Women like Queen Kong were too good to exclude from the field. He'd have to hack a solution to get women balanced out in his new government. Require each region to elect one woman and one man?

He happily clattered into argument with her. The elections would be the next day; he'd see to it.

"Prime Minister of Cyberspace? Why not call yourself the Grand Poobah of the Global Data Network? It's more dignified, sounds cooler and it'll get you just as far." Will had the sleeping spot next to him, up in the cafeteria, with Van on the other side. The room smelled like a dingleberry: twenty-five sysadmins who hadn't washed in at least a day all crammed into the same room. For some of them, it had been much, much longer than a day.

"Shut up, Will," Van said. "You wanted to try to knock the Internet offline."

"Correction: I want to knock the Internet offline. Present-tense."

Felix cracked one eye. He was so tired, it was like lifting weights.

"Look, Sario—if you don't like my platform, put one of your own forward. There are plenty of people who think I'm full of shit and I respect them for that, since they're all running opposite me or backing someone who is. That's your choice. What's not on the menu is nagging and complaining. Bedtime now, or get up and post your platform."

Sario sat up slowly, unrolling the jacket he had been using for a pillow and putting it on. "Screw you guys, I'm out of here."

"I thought he'd never leave," Felix said and turned over, lying awake a long time, thinking about the election.

There were other people in the running. Some of them weren't even sysadmins. A US Senator on retreat at his summer place in Wyoming had generator power and a satellite phone. Somehow he'd found the right newsgroup and thrown his hat into the ring. Some anarchist hackers in Italy strafed the group all night long, posting broken-English screeds about the political bankruptcy of "governance" in the new world. Felix looked at their netblock and determined that they were probably holed up in a small Interaction Design institute near Turin. Italy had been hit very bad, but out in the small town, this cell of anarchists had taken up residence.

A surprising number were running on a platform of shutting down the Internet. Felix had his doubts about whether this was even possible, but he thought he understood the impulse to finish the work and the world. Why not? From every indication, it seemed that the work to date had been a cascade of disasters, attacks, and opportunism, all of it adding up to Gotterdammerung. A terrorist attack here, a lethal counteroffensive there from an overreactive government . . . Before long, they'd made short work of the world.

He fell asleep thinking about the logistics of shutting down the Internet, and dreamed bad dreams in which he was the network's sole defender.

He woke to a papery, itchy sound. He rolled over and saw that Van was sitting up, his jacket balled up in his lap, vigorously scratching his skinny arms. They'd gone the color of corned beef, and had a scaly look. In the light streaming through the cafeteria windows, skin motes floated and danced in great clouds.

"What are you doing?" Felix sat up. Watching Van's fingernails rip into his skin made him itch in sympathy. It had been three days since he'd last washed his hair and his scalp sometimes felt like there were little egg-laying insects picking their way through it. He'd adjusted his glasses the night before and had touched the backs of his ears; his finger came away shining with thick sebum. He got blackheads in the backs of his ears when he didn't shower for a couple days, and sometimes gigantic, deep boils that Kelly finally popped with sick relish.

"Scratching," Van said. He went to work on his head, sending a cloud of dandruff-crud into the sky, there to join the scurf that he'd already eliminated from his extremeties. "Christ, I itch all over."

Felix took Mayor McCheese from Van's backpack and plugged it into one of the Ethernet cables that snaked all over the floor. He googled everything he could think of that could be related to this. "Itchy" yielded 40,600,000 links. He tried compound queries and got slightly more discriminating links.

"I think it's stress-related excema," Felix said, finally.

"I don't get excema," Van said.

Felix showed him some lurid photos of red, angry skin flaked with white. "Stress-related excema," he said, reading the caption.

Van examined his arms. "I have excema," he said.

"Says here to keep it moisturized and to try cortisone cream. You might try the first aid kit in the second-floor toilets. I think I saw some there." Like all of the sysadmins, Felix had had a bit of a rummage around the offices, bathrooms, kitchen and store-rooms, squirreling away a roll of toilet-paper in his shoulder-bag along with three or four power-bars. They were sharing out the food in the caf by unspoken agreement, every sysadmin watching every other for signs of gluttony and hoarding. All were convinced that there was hoarding and gluttony going on out of eyeshot, because all were guilty of it themselves when no one else was watching.

Van got up and when his face hove into the light, Felix saw how puffed his eyes were. "I'll post to the mailing-list for some antihistamine," Felix said. There had been four mailing lists and three wikis for the survivors in the building within hours of the first meeting's close, and in the intervening days they'd settled on just one. Felix was still on a little mailing list with five of his most trusted friends, two of whom were trapped in cages in other countries. He suspected that the rest of the sysadmins were doing the same.

Van stumbled off. "Good luck on the elections," he said, patting Felix on the shoulder.

Felix stood and paced, stopping to stare out the grubby windows. The fires still burned in Toronto, more than before. He'd tried to find mailing lists or blogs that Torontonians were posting to, but the only ones he'd found were being run by other geeks in other data-centers. It was possible—likely, even—that there were survivors out there who had more pressing priorities than posting to the Internet. His home phone still worked about half the time but he'd stopped calling it after the second day, when hearing Kelly's voice on the voicemail for the fiftieth time had made him cry in the middle of a planning meeting. He wasn't the only one.

Election day. Time to face the music.

```
>  Are you nervous?
>  Nope,
```

Felix typed.

```
>  I don't much care if I win, to be honest. I'm just
   glad we're doing this. The alternative was sitting
   around with our thumbs up our ass, waiting for
   someone to crack up and open the door.
```

The cursor hung. Queen Kong was very high latency as she bossed her gang of Googloids around the Googleplex, doing everything she could to keep her data-center online. Three of the offshore cages had gone offline and two of their six redundant network links were smoked. Lucky for her, queries-per-second were way down.

```
>  There's still China
```

she typed. Queen Kong had a big board with a map of the world colored in Google-queries-per-second, and could do magic with it, showing the drop-off over time in colorful charts. She'd uploaded lots of video clips showing how the plague and the bombs had swept the world: the initial up-swell of queries from people wanting to find out what was going on, then the grim, precipitous shelving off as the plagues took hold.

```
>  China's still running about ninety percent
   nominal.
```

Felix shook his head.

```
>  You can't think that they're responsible
>  No
```
she typed, but then she started to key something and then stopped.
```
>  No of course not. I believe the Popovich Hypoth-
   esis. Every asshole in the world is using the
   other assholes for cover. But China put them down
   harder and faster than anyone else. Maybe we've
   finally found a use for totalitarian states.
```
Felix couldn't resist. He typed:
```
>  You're lucky your boss can't see you type that.
   You guys were pretty enthusiastic participants
   in the Great Firewall of China.
>  Wasn't my idea
```
she typed.
```
>  And my boss is dead. They're probably all dead.
   The whole Bay Area got hit hard, and then there
   was the quake.
```
They'd watched the USGS's automated data-stream from the 6.9 that trashed northern Cal from Gilroy to Sebastopol. Soma webcams revealed the scope of the damage—gas main explosions, seismically retrofitted buildings crumpling like piles of children's blocks after a good kicking. The Googleplex, floating on a series of gigantic steel springs, had shook like a plateful of jello, but the racks had stayed in place and the worst injury they'd had was a badly bruised eye on a sysadmin who'd caught a flying cable-crimper in the face.
```
>  Sorry. I forgot.
>  It's OK. We all lost people, right?
>  Yeah. Yeah. Anyway, I'm not worried about the
   election. Whoever wins, at least we're doing
   SOMETHING
>  Not if they vote for one of the fuckrags
```
Fuckrag was the epithet that some of the sysadmins were using to describe the contingent that wanted to shut down the Internet. Queen Kong had coined it—apparently it had started life as a catch-all term to describe clueless IT managers that she'd chewed up through her career.

> They won't. They're just tired and sad is all.
  Your endorsement will carry the day

The Googloids were one of the largest and most powerful
blocs left behind, along with the satellite uplink crews and the
remaining transoceanic crews. Queen Kong's endorsement
had come as a surprise and he'd sent her an email that she'd
replied to tersely: "can't have the fuckrags in charge."

> gtg

she typed and then her connection dropped. He fired up
a browser and called up google.com. The browser timed
out. He hit reload, and then again, and then the Google
front-page came back up. Whatever had hit Queen Kong's
workplace—power failure, worms, another quake—she had
fixed it. He snorted when he saw that they'd replaced the O's
in the Google logo with little planet Earths with mushroom
clouds rising from them.

"Got anything to eat?" Van said to him. It was mid-afternoon,
not that time particularly passed in the data-center. Felix patted his pockets. They'd put a quartermaster in charge, but not
before everyone had snagged some chow out of the machines. He'd had a dozen power-bars and some apples. He'd
taken a couple sandwiches but had wisely eaten them first
before they got stale.

"One power-bar left," he said. He'd noticed a certain loose-
ness in his waistline that morning and had briefly relished it.
Then he'd remembered Kelly's teasing about his weight and
he'd cried some. Then he'd eaten two power-bars, leaving
him with just one left.

"Oh," Van said. His face was hollower than ever, his
shoulders sloping in on his toast-rack chest.

"Here," Felix said. "Vote Felix."

Van took the power-bar from him and then put it down on
the table. "OK, I want to give this back to you and say, 'No,
I couldn't,' but I'm fucking hungry, so I'm just going to take
it and eat it, OK?"

"That's fine by me," Felix said. "Enjoy."

"How are the elections coming?" Van said, once he'd licked
the wrapper clean.

"Dunno," Felix said. "Haven't checked in a while." He'd been winning by a slim margin a few hours before. Not having his laptop was a major handicap when it came to stuff like this. Up in the cages, there were a dozen more like him, poor bastards who'd left the house on Der Tag without thinking to snag something WiFi-enabled.

"You're going to get smoked," Sario said, sliding in next to them. He'd become famous in the center for never sleeping, for eavesdropping, for picking fights in RL that had the ill-considered heat of a Usenet flamewar. "The winner will be someone who understands a couple of fundamental facts." He held up a fist, then ticked off his bullet points by raising a finger at a time. "Point: The terrorists are using the Internet to destroy the world, and we need to destroy the Internet first. Point: Even if I'm wrong, the whole thing is a joke. We'll run out of generator-fuel soon enough. Point: Or if we don't, it will be because the old world will be back and running, and it won't give a crap about your new world. Point: We're gonna run out of food before we run out of shit to argue about or reasons not to go outside. We have the chance to do something to help the world recover: we can kill the net and cut it off as a tool for bad guys. Or we can rearrange some more deck chairs on the bridge of your personal Titanic in the service of some sweet dream about an 'independent cyberspace.'"

The thing was that Sario was right. They would be out of fuel in two days—intermittent power from the grid had stretched their generator lifespan. And if you bought his hypothesis that the Internet was primarily being used as a tool to organize more mayhem, shutting it down would be the right thing to do.

But Felix's son and his wife were dead. He didn't want to rebuild the old world. He wanted a new one. The old world was one that didn't have any place for him. Not anymore.

Van scratched his raw, flaking skin. Puffs of dander and scurf swirled in the musty, greasy air. Sario curled a lip at him. "That is disgusting. We're breathing recycled air, you know. Whatever leprosy is eating you, aerosolizing it into the air supply is pretty anti-social."

"You're the world's leading authority on anti-social, Sario,"

Van said. "Go away or I'll multi-tool you to death." He stopped scratching and patted his sheathed multi-pliers like a gunslinger.

"Yeah, I'm anti-social. I've got Asperger's and I haven't taken any meds in four days. What's your fucking excuse."

Van scratched some more. "I'm sorry," he said. "I didn't know."

Sario cracked up. "Oh, you are priceless. I'd bet that three quarters of this bunch is borderline autistic. Me, I'm just an asshole. But I'm one who isn't afraid to tell the truth, and that makes me better than you, dickweed."

"Fuckrag," Felix said, "fuck off."

They had less than a day's worth of fuel when Felix was elected the first ever Prime Minister of Cyberspace. The first count was spoiled by a bot that spammed the voting process and they lost a critical day while they added up the votes a second time.

But by then, it was all seeming like more of a joke. Half the data-centers had gone dark. Queen Kong's net-maps of Google queries were looking grimmer and grimmer as more of the world went offline, though she maintained a leaderboard of new and rising queries—largely related to health, shelter, sanitation and self-defense.

Worm-load slowed. Power was going off to many home PC users, and staying off, so their compromised PCs were going dark. The backbones were still lit up and blinking, but the missives from those data-centers were looking more and more desperate. Felix hadn't eaten in a day and neither had anyone in a satellite Earth-station of transoceanic head-end.

Water was running short, too.

Popovich and Rosenbaum came and got him before he could do more than answer a few congratulatory messages and post a canned acceptance speech to newsgroups.

"We're going to open the doors," Popovich said. Like all of them, he'd lost weight and waxed scruffy and oily. His BO was like a cloud coming off trash-bags behind a fish-market on a sunny day. Felix was quite sure he smelled no better.

"You're going to go for a reccy? Get more fuel? We can charter a working group for it—great idea."

Rosenbaum shook his head sadly. "We're going to go find our families. Whatever is out there has burned itself out. Or it hasn't. Either way, there's no future in here."

"What about network maintenance?" Felix said, thought he knew the answers. "Who'll keep the routers up?"

"We'll give you the root passwords to everything," Popovich said. His hands were shaking and his eyes were bleary. Like many of the smokers stuck in the data-center, he'd gone cold turkey this week. They'd run out of caffeine products two days earlier, too. The smokers had it rough.

"And I'll just stay here and keep everything online?"

"You and anyone else who cares anymore."

Felix knew that he'd squandered his opportunity. The election had seemed noble and brave, but in hindsight all it had been was an excuse for infighting when they should have been figuring out what to do next. The problem was that there was nothing to do next.

"I can't make you stay," he said.

"Yeah, you can't." Popovich turned on his heel and walked out. Rosenbaum watched him go, then he gripped Felix's shoulder and squeezed it.

"Thank you, Felix. It was a beautiful dream. It still is. Maybe we'll find something to eat and some fuel and come back."

Rosenbaum had a sister whom he'd been in contact with over IM for the first days after the crisis broke. Then she'd stopped answering. The sysadmins were split among those who'd had a chance to say goodbye and those who hadn't. Each was sure the other had it better.

They posted about it on the internal newsgroup—they were still geeks, after all, and there was a little honor guard on the ground floor, geeks who watched them pass toward the double doors. They manipulated the keypads and the steel shutters lifted, then the first set of doors opened. They stepped into the vestibule and pulled the doors shut behind them. The front doors opened. It was very bright and sunny outside, and apart from how empty it was, it looked very normal. Heartbreakingly so.

The two took a tentative step out into the world. Then another. They turned to wave at the assembled masses. Then they both grabbed their throats and began to jerk and twitch, crumpling in a heap on the ground.

"Shiii—!" was all Felix managed to choke out before they both dusted themselves off and stood up, laughing so hard they were clutching their sides. They waved once more and turned on their heels.

"Man, those guys are sick," Van said. He scratched his arms, which had long, bloody scratches on them. His clothes were so covered in scurf they looked like they'd been dusted with icing sugar.

"I thought it was pretty funny," Felix said.

"Christ I'm hungry," Van said, conversationally.

"Lucky for you, we've got all the packets we can eat," Felix said.

"You're too good to us grunts, Mr President," Van said.

"Prime Minister," he said. "And you're no grunt, you're the Deputy Prime Minister. You're my designated ribbon-cutter and hander-out of oversized novelty checks."

It buoyed both of their spirits. Watching Popovich and Rosenbaum go, it buoyed them up. Felix knew then that they'd all be going soon.

That had been pre-ordained by the fuel-supply, but who wanted to wait for the fuel to run out, anyway?

> half my crew split this morning

Queen Kong typed. Google was holding up pretty good anyway, of course. The load on the servers was a lot lighter than it had been since the days when Google fit on a bunch of hand-built PCs under a desk at Stanford.

> we're down to a quarter

Felix typed back. It was only a day since Popovich and Rosenbaum left, but the traffic on the newsgroups had fallen down to near zero. He and Van hadn't had much time to play

Republic of Cyberspace. They'd been too busy learning the systems that Popovich had turned over to them, the big, big routers that had went on acting as the major interchange for all the network backbones in Canada.

Still, someone posted to the newsgroups every now and again, generally to say goodbye. The old flamewars about who would be PM, or whether they would shut down the network, or who took too much food—it was all gone.

He reloaded the newsgroup. There was a typical message.

```
>  Runaway processes on Solaris TK
>
>  Uh, hi. I'm just a lightweight MSCE but I'm the
   only one awake here and four of the DSLAMs just
   went down. Looks like there's some custom
   accounting code that's trying to figure out how
   much to bill our corporate customers and it's
   spawned ten thousand threads and it's eating all
   the swap. I just want to kill it but I can't seem
   to do that. Is there some magic invocation I
   need to do to get this goddamned weenix box to
   kill this shit? I mean, it's not as if any of our
   customers are ever going to pay us again. I'd
   ask the guy who wrote this code, but he's pretty
   much dead as far as anyone can work out.
```

He reloaded. There was a response. It was short, authoritative, and helpful—just the sort of thing you almost never saw in a high-caliber newsgroup when a noob posted a dumb question. The apocalypse had awoken the spirit of patient helpfulness in the world's sysop community.

Van shoulder-surfed him. "Holy shit, who knew he had it in him?"

He looked at the message again. It was from Will Sario.

He dropped into his chat window.

```
>  sario i thought you wanted the network dead why
   are you helping msces fix their boxen?
>  Gee Mr PM, maybe I just can't bear to watch a
   computer suffer at the hands of an amateur.
```

He flipped to the channel with Queen Kong in it.

```
> How long?
> Since I slept? Two days. Until we run out of
  fuel? Three days. Since we ran out of food? Two
  days.
> Jeez. I didn't sleep last night either. We're a
  little short handed around here.
> asl? Im monica and I live in pasadena and Im
  bored with my homework. WOuld you like to
  download my pic???
```

The trojan bots were all over IRC these days, jumping to every channel that had any traffic on it. Sometimes you caught five or six flirting with each other. It was pretty weird to watch a piece of malware try to con another instance of itself into downloading a trojan.

They both kicked the bot off the channel simultaneously. He had a script for it now. The spam hadn't even tailed off a little.

```
> How come the spam isn't reducing? Half the
  goddamned data-centers have gone dark
```

Queen Kong paused a long time before typing. As had become automatic when she went high-latency, he reloaded the Google homepage. Sure enough, it was down.

```
> Sario, you got any food?
> You won't miss a couple more meals, Your Excel-
  lency
```

Van had gone back to Mayor McCheese but he was in the same channel.

"What a dick. You're looking pretty buff, though, dude."

Van didn't look so good. He looked like you could knock him over with a stiff breeze and he had a phlegmy, weak quality to his speech.

```
> hey kong everything ok?
> everything's fine just had to go kick some ass
```

"How's the traffic, Van?"

"Down 25 percent from this morning," he said. There were a bunch of nodes whose connections routed through them. Presumably most of these were home or commercial customers in places where the power was still on and the phone company's COs were still alive.

Every once in a while, Felix would wiretap the connections to see if he could find a person who had news of the wide world. Almost all of it was automated traffic, though: network backups, status updates. Spam. Lots of spam.

```
> Spam's still up because the services that stop
  spam are failing faster than the services that
  create it. All the anti-worm stuff is centralized
  in a couple places. The bad stuff is on a million
  zombie computers. If only the lusers had had the
  good sense to turn off their home PCs before
  keeling over or taking off
> at the rate were going well be routing nothing
  but spam by dinnertime
```

Van cleared his throat, a painful sound. "About that," he said. "I think it's going to hit sooner than that. Felix, I don't think anyone would notice if we just walked away from here."

Felix looked at him, his skin the color of corned-beef and streaked with long, angry scabs. His fingers trembled.

"You drinking enough water?"

Van nodded. "All frigging day, every ten seconds. Anything to keep my belly full." He pointed to a refilled Pepsi Max bottle full of water by his side.

"Let's have a meeting," he said.

There had been forty-three of them on D-Day. Now there were fifteen. Six had responded to the call for a meeting by simply leaving. Everyone knew without having to be told what the meeting was about.

"So that's it, you're going to let it all fall apart?" Sario was the only one with the energy left to get properly angry. He'd go angry to his grave. The veins on his throat and forehead stood out angrily. His fists shook angrily. All the other geeks went lids-down at the site of him, looking up in unison for once at the discussion, not keeping one eye on a chatlog or a tailed service log.

"Sario, you've got to be shitting me," Felix said. "You wanted to pull the goddamned plug!"

"I wanted it to go clean," he shouted. "I didn't want it to bleed out and keel over in little gasps and pukes forever. I wanted it to be an act of will by the global community of its caretakers. I wanted it to be an affirmative act by human hands. Not entropy and bad code and worms winning out. Fuck that, that's just what's happened out there."

Up in the top-floor cafeteria, there were windows all around, hardened and light-bending, and by custom, they were all blinds-down. Now Sario ran around the room, yanking down the blinds. How the hell can he get the energy to run? Felix wondered. He could barely walk up the stairs to the meeting room.

Harsh daylight flooded in. It was a fine sunny day out there, but everywhere you looked across that commanding view of Toronto's skyline, there were rising plumes of smoke. The TD tower, a gigantic black modernist glass brick, was gouting flame to the sky. "It's all falling apart, the way everything does.

"Listen, listen. If we leave the network to fall over slowly, parts of it will stay online for months. Maybe years. And what will run on it? Malware. Worms. Spam. System-processes. Zone transfers. The things we use fall apart and require constant maintenance. The things we abandon don't get used and they last forever. We're going to leave the network behind like a lime-pit filled with industrial waste. That will be our fucking legacy—the legacy of every keystroke you and I and anyone, anywhere ever typed. You understand? We're going to leave it to die slow like a wounded dog, instead of giving it one clean shot through the head."

Van scratched his cheeks, then Felix saw that he was wiping away tears.

"Sario, you're not wrong, but you're not right either," he said. "Leaving it up to limp along is right. We're going to all be limping for a long time, and maybe it will be some use to someone. If there's one packet being routed from any user to any other user, anywhere in the world, it's doing its job."

"If you want a clean kill, you can do that," Felix said. "I'm the PM and I say so. I'm giving you root. All of you." He turned to the white-board where the cafeteria workers used to scrawl the day's specials. Now it was covered with the remnants of heated technical debates that the sysadmins had engaged in over the days since the day.

He scrubbed away a clean spot with his sleeve and began to write out long, complicated alphanumeric passwords salted with punctuation. Felix had a gift for remembering that kind of password. He doubted it would do him much good, ever again.

> Were going, kong. Fuels almost out anyway
> yeah well thats right then. it was an honor, mr prime minister
> you going to be ok?
> ive commandeered a young sysadmin to see to my feminine needs and weve found another cache of food thatll last us a coupel weeks now that were down to fifteen admins—im in hog heaven pal
> youre amazing, Queen Kong, seriously. Dont be a hero though. When you need to go go. Theres got to be something out there
> be safe felix, seriously—btw did i tell you queries are up in Romania? maybe theyre getting back on their feet
> really?
> yeah, really. we're hard to kill—like fucking roaches

Her connection died. He dropped to Firefox and reloaded Google and it was down. He hit reload and hit reload and hit reload, but it didn't come up. He closed his eyes and listened to Van scratch his legs and then heard Van type a little.

"They're back up," he said.

Felix whooshed out a breath. He sent the message to the newsgroup, one that he'd run through five drafts before settling on, "Take care of the place, OK? We'll be back, some-day."

Everyone was going except Sario. Sario wouldn't leave. He came down to see them off, though.

The sysadmins gathered in the lobby and Felix made the safety door go up, and the light rushed in.

Sario stuck his hand out.

"Good luck," he said.

"You too," Felix said. He had a firm grip, Sario, stronger

than he had any right to be. "Maybe you were right," he said.

"Maybe," he said.

"You going to pull the plug?"

Sario looked up at the drop-ceiling, seeming to peer through the reinforced floors at the humming racks above. "Who knows?" he said at last.

Van scratched and a flurry of white motes danced in the sunlight.

"Let's go find you a pharmacy," Felix said. He walked to the door and the other sysadmins followed.

They waited for the interior doors to close behind them and then Felix opened the exterior doors. The air smelled and tasted like mown grass, like the first drops of rain, like the lake and the sky, like the outdoors and the world, an old friend not heard from in an eternity.

"Bye, Felix," the other sysadmins said. They were drifting away while he stood transfixed at the top of the short concrete staircase. The light hurt his eyes and made them water.

"I think there's a Shopper's Drug Mart on King Street," he said to Van. "We'll throw a brick through the window and get you some cortisone, OK?"

"You're the Prime Minister," Van said. "Lead on."

They didn't see a single soul on the fifteen minute walk. There wasn't a single sound except for some bird noises and some distant groans, and the wind in the electric cables overhead. It was like walking on the surface of the moon.

"Bet they have chocolate bars at the Shopper's," Van said.

Felix's stomach lurched. Food. "Wow," he said, around a mouthful of saliva.

They walked past a little hatchback and in the front seat was the dried body of a woman holding the dried body of a baby, and his mouth filled with sour bile, even though the smell was faint through the rolled-up windows.

He hadn't thought of Kelly or 2.0 in days. He dropped to his knees and retched again. Out here in the real world, his family was dead. Everyone he knew was dead. He just wanted to lie down on the sidewalk and wait to die, too.

Van's rough hands slipped under his armpits and hauled

weakly at him. "Not now," he said. "Once we're safe inside somewhere and we've eaten something, then and then you can do this, but not now. Understand me, Felix? Not fucking now."

The profanity got through to him. He got to his feet. His knees were trembling.

"Just a block more," Van said, and slipped Felix's arm around his shoulders and led him along.

"Thank you, Van. I'm sorry."

"No sweat," he said. "You need a shower, bad. No offense."

"None taken."

The Shopper's had a metal security gate, but it had been torn away from the front windows, which had been rudely smashed. Felix and Van squeezed through the gap and stepped into the dim drug-store. A few of the displays were knocked over, but other than that, it looked OK. By the cash-registers, Felix spotted the racks of candy bars at the same instant that Van saw them, and they hurried over and grabbed a handful each, stuffing their faces.

"You two eat like pigs."

They both whirled at the sound of the woman's voice. She was holding a fire-axe that was nearly as big as she was. She wore a lab-coat and comfortable shoes.

"You take what you need and go, OK? No sense in there being any trouble." Her chin was pointy and her eyes were sharp. She looked to be in her forties. She looked nothing like Kelly, which was good, because Felix felt like running and giving her a hug as it was. Another person alive!

"Are you a doctor?" Felix said. She was wearing scrubs under the coat, he saw.

"You going to go?" She brandished the axe.

Felix held his hands up. "Seriously, are you a doctor? A pharmacist?"

"I used to be a RN, ten years ago. I'm mostly a Web-designer."

"You're shitting me," Felix said.

"Haven't you ever met a girl who knew about computers?"

"Actually, a friend of mine who runs Google's data-center is a girl. A woman, I mean."

"You're shitting me," she said. "A woman ran Google's data-center?"

"Runs," Felix said. "It's still online."

"NFW," she said. She let the axe lower.

"Way. Have you got any cortisone cream? I can tell you the story. My name's Felix and this is Van, who needs any anti-histamines you can spare."

"I can spare? Felix old pal, I have enough dope here to last a hundred years. This stuff's going to expire long before it runs out. But are you telling me that the net's still up?"

"It's still up," he said. "Kind of. That's what we've been doing all week. Keeping it online. It might not last much longer, though."

"No," she said. "I don't suppose it would." She set the axe down. "Have you got anything to trade? I don't need much, but I've been trying to keep my spirits up by trading with the neighbors. It's like playing civilization."

"You have neighbors?"

"At least ten," she said. "The people in the restaurant across the way make a pretty good soup, even if most of the veg is canned. They cleaned me out of Sterno, though."

"You've got neighbors and you trade with them?"

"Well, nominally. It'd be pretty lonely without them. I've taken care of whatever sniffles I could. Set a bone—broken wrist. Listen, do you want some Wonder Bread and peanut butter? I have a ton of it. Your friend looks like he could use a meal."

"Yes please," Van said. "We don't have anything to trade, but we're both committed workaholics looking to learn a trade. Could you use some assistants?"

"Not really." She spun her axe on its head. "But I wouldn't mind some company."

They ate the sandwiches and then some soup. The restaurant people brought it over and made their manners at them, though Felix saw their noses wrinkle up and ascertained that there was working plumbing in the back room. Van went in to take a sponge bath and then he followed.

"None of us know what to do," the woman said. Her name was Rosa, and she had found them a bottle of wine and some disposable plastic cups from the housewares aisle. "I thought we'd have helicopters or tanks or even looters, but it's just quiet."

"You seem to have kept pretty quiet yourself," Felix said.

"Didn't want to attract the wrong kind of attention."

"You ever think that maybe there's a lot of people out there doing the same thing? Maybe if we all get together we'll come up with something to do."

"Or maybe they'll cut our throats," she said.

Van nodded. "She's got a point."

Felix was on his feet. "No way, we can't think like that. Lady, we're at a critical juncture here. We can go down through negligence, dwindling away in our hiding holes, or we can try to build something better."

"Better?" She made a rude noise.

"OK, not better. Something though. Building something new is better than letting it dwindle away. Christ, what are you going to do when you've read all the magazines and eaten all the potato chips here?"

Rosa shook her head. "Pretty talk," she said. "But what the hell are we going to do, anyway?"

"Something," Felix said. "We're going to do something. Something is better than nothing. We're going to take this patch of the world where people are talking to each other, and we're going to expand it. We're going to find everyone we can and we're going to take care of them and they're going to take care of us. We'll probably fuck it up. We'll probably fail. I'd rather fail than give up, though."

Van laughed. "Felix, you are crazier than Sario, you know it?"

"We're going to go and drag him out, first thing tomorrow. He's going to be a part of this, too. Everyone will. Screw the end of the world. The world doesn't end. Humans aren't the kind of things that have endings."

Rosa shook her head again, but she was smiling a little now. "And you'll be what, the Pope-Emperor of the World?"

"He prefers Prime Minister," Van said in a stagey whisper. The anti-histamines had worked miracles on his skin, and it had faded from angry red to a fine pink.

"You want to be Minister of Health, Rosa?" he said.

"Boys," she said. "Playing games. How about this. I'll help out however I can, provided you never ask me to call you Prime Minister and you never call me the Minister of Health?"

"It's a deal," he said.

Van refilled their glasses, upending the wine bottle to get the last few drops out.

They raised their glasses. "To the world," Felix said. "To humanity." He thought hard. "To rebuilding."

"To anything," Van said.

"To anything," Felix said. "To everything."

"To everything," Rosa said.

They drank. He wanted to go see the house—see Kelly and 2.0, though his stomach churned at the thought of what he might find there. But the next day, they started to rebuild. And months later, they started over again, when disagreements drove apart the fragile little group they'd pulled together. And a year after that, they started over again. And five years later, they started again.

It was nearly six months before he went home. Van helped him along, riding cover behind him on the bicycles they used to get around town. The further north they rode, the stronger the smell of burnt wood became. There were lots of burnt-out houses. Sometimes marauders burnt the houses they'd looted, but more often it was just nature, the kinds of fires you got in forests and on mountains. There were six choking, burnt blocks where every house was burnt before they reached home.

But Felix's old housing development was still standing, an oasis of eerily pristine buildings that looked like maybe their somewhat neglectful owners had merely stepped out to buy some paint and fresh lawnmower blades to bring their old homes back up to their neat, groomed selves.

That was worse, somehow. He got off the bike at the entry of the subdivision and they walked the bikes together in silence, listening to the sough of the wind in the trees. Winter was coming late that year, but it was coming, and as the sweat dried in the wind, Felix started to shiver.

He didn't have his keys anymore. They were at the data-center, months and worlds away. He tried the door-handle, but it didn't turn. He applied his shoulder to the door and it ripped away from its wet, rotted jamb with a loud, splintering sound. The house was rotting from the inside.

The door splashed when it landed. The house was full of stagnant water, four inches of stinking pond-scummed water in the living room. He splashed carefully through it, feeling the floor-boards sag spongily beneath each step.

Up the stairs, his nose full of that terrible green mildewy stench. Into the bedroom, the furniture familiar as a childhood friend.

Kelly was in the bed with 2.0. The way they both lay, it was clear they hadn't gone easy—they were twisted double, Kelly curled around 2.0. Their skin was bloated, making them almost unrecognizable. The smell—God, the smell.

Felix's head spun. He thought he would fall over and clutched at the dresser. An emotion he couldn't name—rage, anger, sorrow?—made him breathe hard, gulp for air like he was drowning.

And then it was over. The world was over. Kelly and 2.0—over. And he had a job to do. He folded the blanket over them—Van helped, solemnly. They went into the front yard and took turns digging, using the shovel from the garage that Kelly had used for gardening. They had lots of experience digging graves by then. Lots of experience handling the dead. They dug, and wary dogs watched them from the tall grass on the neighboring lawns, but they were also good at chasing off dogs with well-thrown stones.

When the grave was dug, they laid Felix's wife and son to rest in it. Felix quested after words to say over the mound, but none came. He'd dug so many graves for so many men's wives and so many women's husbands and so many children—the words were long gone.

Felix dug ditches and salvaged cans and buried the dead. He planted and harvested. He fixed some cars and learned to make biodiesel. Finally he fetched up in a data-center for a little government—little governments came and went, but this one was smart enough to want to keep records and needed someone to keep everything running, and Van went with him.

They spent a lot of time in chat rooms and sometimes they happened upon old friends from the strange time they'd spent running the Distributed Republic of Cyberspace, geeks who insisted on calling him PM, though no one in the real world ever called him that anymore.

It wasn't a good life, most of the time. Felix's wounds never healed, and neither did most other people's. There were lingering sicknesses and sudden ones. Tragedy on tragedy.

But Felix liked his data-center. There in the humming of the racks, he never felt like it was the first days of a better nation, but he never felt like it was the last days of one, either.

> go to bed, felix
> soon, kong, soon—almost got this backup running
> youre a junkie, dude.
> look whos talking

He reloaded the Google homepage. Queen Kong had had it online for a couple years now. The Os in Google changed all the time, whenever she got the urge. Today they were little cartoon globes, one smiling the other frowning.

He looked at it for a long time and dropped back into a terminal to check his backup. It was running clean, for a change. The little government's records were safe.

> ok night night
> take care

Van waved at him as he creaked to the door, stretching out his back with a long series of pops.

"Sleep well, boss," he said.

"Don't stick around here all night again," Felix said. "You need your sleep, too."

"You're too good to us grunts," Van said, and went back to typing.

Felix went to the door and walked out into the night. Behind him, the biodiesel generator hummed and made its acrid fumes. The harvest moon was up, which he loved. Tomorrow, he'd go back and fix another computer and fight off entropy again. And why not?

It was what he did. He was a sysadmin.

Just Do It!

HEATHER LINDSLEY

Heather Lindsley (www.randomjane.com) *lives in Seattle, Washington. She says in an online interview* (www.tug internet.com/jja/journal/archives/004029.html) *"I have an eclectic background: a little science, a lot of technology, and even more theatre. I've spent time working with artists, and for corporations, and in academia. I worked in theatre as a dramaturg, . . . that's a term I usually had to define from scratch." She quit her day job as a technology analyst, attended Clarion West in 2005, and published her first three SF stories in 2006.*

"Just Do It!" was published in F&SF, *which had a very strong year in 2006 and was arguably the best of the professional magazines. It was her first sale. She says, "I'm interested in the separation—or lack of separation—between the mind/spirit/whatever abstraction and the tangible sack of chemicals we call a body. My story is about desire, which is a particularly blurry area for minds and bodies. Blurry, and easy to manipulate, especially with the tools we have at our disposal now." It is a story of how biochemical craving is used to manipulate consumers, and could easily be read as a satire on the use of psychiatric medications. It is interesting to compare it to Daryl Gregory's story, also about biochemical effects, that appears later in this book.*

Sometimes the only warning is a flash of sun on the lens of a sniper's scope. Today I'm lucky enough to catch the mistake.

Funny, I think as I duck down behind the nearest parked car, I don't feel lucky.

The car is a tiny thing, an ultra enviro-friendly Honda Righteous painted an unambiguous green. Good for the planet, bad for cover. Ahead there's an H5 so massive and red I first take it for a fire truck. The selfish bastard parked illegally, blocking an alley, and for that I'm grateful.

I take a quick look at the roof of the building across the street before starting my dash to the Hummer. Halfway there a woman in plastic devil horns steps into my attempt to dodge her and her clipboard.

"Would-you-care-to-sign-our-petiton-in-favor-of-the-effort-against-ending-the-Florida-blockade?" Damn, she's good. She sounds like she trained with a preBay auctioneer.

I feint left and dart right, putting her between me and the Shooter and countering, "I-already-signed-it-thanks!" so she won't follow. It's not the first lie I've told today, and it's not likely to be the last.

Temporarily safe behind the Hummer, I lean against the heavily tinted windows of the far back seat door, glad to be standing upright but panting and sweating and wishing I wasn't wearing the black jumpsuit I reserve for funerals and job interviews. Nanofiber, my ass—it can't even keep up with a little physical activity on a hot April day.

I start the long walk toward the front bumper, figuring I'll duck into the alley and continue on my way one block over. It seems like a good plan until another Shooter steps out of the alley.

This one has a pistol. I'd go cross-eyed if I tried to look down the barrel.

"Oh, come on," I say, backing away slowly. "Not the face."

He dips the barrel down a bit. I sigh and start pulling the zipper at the high neck of my jumpsuit in the same direction. I stop just shy of revealing cleavage—I'll get shot in the face before I give this punk an eyeful.

He shrugs and fires.

"You little bastard!" I yell at his retreating back as I pull the dart out of my forehead. "I want your license number!"

Of course he doesn't bother to stop. They never do.

The itching starts almost immediately, and I reflexively reach up and touch the bump above my eyes. I know better than to scratch it, but I do anyway. The scratching releases a flood of chemicals that creates a powerful and specific food craving. I brace myself.

French fries. French fries from the den of the evil clown, where they don't even pretend to use potatoes anymore. I hate those French fries, so golden and crispy on the outside, so moist and fluffy on the inside—

No no no no no, I do not want them.

I manage to get past the first shadow the clown casts on my route with relative calm, but by the second the itching is more intense and all I can imagine are French fries. Disgusting, nasty, tasty, delicious French fries.

This is not the way to walk into a job interview.

The site of my two o'clock appointment looms in the office tower ahead . . . right behind a third opportunity to relieve the craving. I keep moving, trying not to think about how well the diabetes-inducing corn syrupy sweet ketchup complements the blood pressure-raising salty savor of the fries.

I make a full circuit through the revolving doors of the office building before going back toward the object of my involuntary, chemically enhanced desire.

The food odors pounce immediately and I can almost feel the molecules sticking to my clothes. Even if I turn around now I'll smell like fast food.

"Let's get this over with," I say unnecessarily to the credit scanner, staring it down until it greenlights my ability to pay for food I don't really want. None of the automat compartments contain fries, which is unusual, so I punch hard at a picture of French fries on the order panel. The dents in the panel tell me I'm not the only customer who feels antagonistic about buying food here.

It shouldn't take more than a minute or two for the fries to appear in a compartment, so when they don't I start pounding on the automat.

"Hey, hurry it up!" I yell, scratching furiously at the bump on my forehead.

The back door of the empty fry compartment slides open. An eye stares out at me.

"What?"

"Fries. I need fries."

"We're out of fries," the voice behind the automat says.

"How can you be out of fries? You've got Shooters out there making people crave the damned things!"

"That's why we're out."

"Doesn't the head office coordinate this stuff?"

The eye blinks twice and the door slides shut.

It's 1:47, enough time to go back to the second place if I hurry. But I don't hurry. I pace in the street, muttering to myself like a lunatic. It's almost five minutes before I quit trying to control the craving and dash back the way I came.

I give the next credit scanner an especially dirty look, then yank open the one compartment with fries. I stop only to pump blobs of ketchup from the dispenser. On my way out I pass an old man scratching his arm as he raves through an open compartment, "How can you be out of fish sandwiches?!"

"Try the one on Third and Pine," I say around a mouthful of fries.

CraveTech's offices are both plush and haphazard, the combined result of a record-breaking IPO and the latest design fad: early dot-com retro. I arrive sweaty, greasy, nauseated, and thoroughly pissed off. I smile at the receptionist anyway, a fashionably sulky blonde boy seated in a vintage Aeron chair behind a desk made out of two sawhorses topped with an old door and a crystal vase.

"Alex Monroe. I have a two o'clock with Mr. Avery."

"Two o'clock?" he says pointedly. It's 2:02. "Have a seat. Something to drink while you're waiting?"

"Water please." I'll probably retain every ounce. Damn salty French fries. There are pills that reduce bloating, of course—they sell them out of the same automat—but I wouldn't hand over any more of my money.

I've just taken my first sip when a young man pops out of the office. He looks like a typical startup manager: handsome, well-dressed, and almost certainly in over his head.

"Ms. Monroe, welcome!" He bounds up to me, hand extended. During the handshake he nods toward my forehead. "Ah, I see you use our products!" He laughs heartily at his own joke. I laugh back. I want this job.

"It's a wonderful time to be in chemical advertising, Ms. Monroe," he says, shepherding me into his office. I notice he has a proper desk. "We have some exciting deals in the works. Exciting, exciting deals."

"Really?" I say, distracted by the fry-lump in my stomach.

"Oh, yes. Now that the Supreme Court has reversed most of those class action suits, Shooters don't have to be stealthy. We've had to discontinue the tobacco lines for the time being, but otherwise it's open season on consumers."

I make another effort to join in his laughter, and, reaching toward the bump on my head, add, "It certainly is effective."

"Indeed." He smiles like he loaded the dart himself. "So," he says, picking up my resume, "I see your background is in print."

"Yes, but I've done some work in fragrance influence, and I'm very interested in chemical advertising's potential."

"Well, it is a growing field, plenty of room for trailblazers, especially with campaigns as impressive as these." He sets my resume aside. "And of course we still have quite a lot of synergy with print." He pulls an inch-long Crave dart out of a drawer and drops it on the desk between us. I resist the urge to cringe at the sight of the wretched thing.

"What do you see?" he asks.

I want to say a menace, but instead I tap the delivery barrel and give the context-appropriate answer. "Unused ad space."

Suddenly he's a schoolmaster who has finally found a bright pupil in a classroom full of dunces.

"Exactly, Ms. Monroe. Exactly. No square millimeter wasted, that's what I say." He leans across the table and whispers conspiratorially, "We're looking at co-branding an AOL-Time-Warner-Starbucks Lattepalooza Crave with a Forever Fitness session discount."

"Wow."

"Yes. Coupons on the darts. How does that grab you?"

"Coupons."

"Tiny coupons, like the ones on swizzle sticks. Can't you just see it? You get Stuck, so you want the product, but you're also concerned about your weight. The coupon helps. The coupon tells you the provider cares about your concerns. It tells you they understand." He leans back in his chair, my cue to speak.

"Interesting. But I'd go log-in rebate rather than immediate discount. Same message, same coverage, easier on the bottom line."

He leans forward again. "I like the way you think, Ms. Monroe."

I hate meeting at Sandra's house—her cats are constantly trying to climb up on my lap, I suspect because they know I'm allergic to them. But Sandra is my best friend from college, and also my cell leader, so I usually end up here at least once a week.

"Whoa, right in the forehead," she says when she opens the door.

"Yeah, and that's an ugly one on your neck."

"That's a hickey."

"Oh, uh, sorry. Or congratulations, I guess."

"Eh," she shrugs, heading to the kitchen.

I follow. "Um, aren't you a little old to be getting those?"

"Maybe, but Liam's not too old to be giving them." Sandra has a taste for idealistic young revolutionaries.

She starts to make herbal tea, and I know enough not to ask for coffee instead.

We take the tea to the lumpy, cat-hair covered futon in the living room. "How'd the interview go?"

"Shaky start. Getting Stuck really threw me off. But I did manage to laugh at his jokes, and, sad to say, I'm more or less qualified."

"You do speak their language." Sandra likes to remind me that I've only recently stopped being part of the problem. "So where do things stand?" she asks.

"He said he only had one more interview, and he'd call to let me know by the end of the week."

"Did you pick up anything while you were there?"

"Not much about the next formulas. AOL-Time-Warner-Starbucks is definitely in now, but that's old news."

"But you think you can get access? The job's in the right division?"

"Close enough. Marketing's always looking over R&D's shoulder. It won't seem strange for me to be poking around."

"What should I tell our counter-formula development contact?"

"Well, assuming I get the job, and assuming I can start right away, three weeks. Maybe four. It'll depend on their security."

She seems satisfied with this answer. "What about Plan B? How's the Mata Hari routine working on our favorite evil genius?"

"He's not evil—he's just oblivious."

She raises an eyebrow at this. "Dangerously oblivious."

"Yes, I know." I concentrate on picking cat hair off my clothes. "It's going fine. Fourth date tonight. Expensive place. I should get going, actually." I rise and head for the door. She stops me and stares pointedly at my forehead.

"Alex, don't forget—he's the enemy."

I consciously abort an eye-roll and substitute a smile.

"Dangerously oblivious genius equals enemy. Check." I give her a little wave as I step outside.

"Which restaurant are you going to?" Sandra asks from the doorway.

"Prima."

Her brow furrows. "Don't they serve real meat?"

"Oh yes—and I'll be ordering a steak," I say, taking a moment to enjoy her disapproving look.

"I'll have the porterhouse. Rare, please."

"Make that two," Tom says. "Mine medium."

"Very good," the server says. "I'll be back with the first course shortly." He gives us each a prim little four-star nod as he leaves.

I put my elbows on the white linen tablecloth and rest my chin on my interlaced fingers. "I'm not sure I can ever love a man who would ruin a perfectly good steak."

Tom leans into the candlelight, too. "And I'm not sure I can trust a woman who likes her meat nearly raw."

"I guess we'll just have to stay together for the sex."

"And the children." He raises his glass to his lips.

"I'm not having sex with children, you pervert."

He chokes on his wine and grabs his napkin. I have to give him points for not looking around to make sure we haven't been overheard.

"If I'd known you'd be shooting wine out of your nose I'd have suggested a Merlot," I say as innocently as I can manage.

"How," he coughs, "did I ever end up in such hazardous company?"

WE MET accidentally at a Better Living Through Chemistry Expo sponsored by Dow-DuPont-Bristol-Myers-Squibb-PepsiCo six weeks ago.

Actually, we met at a hotel bar during the expo.

I was running my report through my head, thinking about the companies that had the most bad news for humanity in the works. He sat down a couple of barstools away. We traded a little eye contact and a few shy smiles in the dim light.

"So which of these evil bastards are you representing?"

He laughed. "CraveTech."

"Ooh, a startup. Exciting."

"Yeah. What about you?"

"Me? I'm with an underground group whose goal is to liberate people from the tyranny of corporate chemical dependence."

"Huh. Underground, you said?"

"Yeah, we're not very good at that part." I was already starting to like his laugh, especially since it came so easily. "Actually, I freelance in marketing."

"Anything I might have seen?"

"Maybe the Junior Chemical Engineer campaign."

" 'Big Molecules for Little Hands.' "

"That's the one," I said, suddenly aware I was twisting a lock of my hair around my finger. I reached for my drink.

"Wasn't there a massive judgment against them in one of the last big class action suits?"

"No, that was Union-Pfizer's My First Exothermic Reaction. Ours were just repackaged Make Your Own Cologne! kits left over from the last Queer Eye reunion tour."

"Clever." He got up and closed the barstool gap between us.

"Despicable. So what do you do at CraveTech?"

"I run the place."

"That's funny," I said, laughing until he slid the nearest candle closer. I squinted at a face I almost recognized from the cover of Time-Newsweek.

"Where are your glasses?"

"Contacts tonight."

"You lose the glasses when you don't want to be recognized."

"Yeah, sort of a—"

"Reverse Clark Kent thing."

He smiled. "Yeah," and I could feel his geeky little heart reaching out for mine.

Tonight he's wearing his glasses. He looks cute in them.

"Of course, the really exciting work is in BeMod," he says, slicing into his steak.

"BeMod?" This seems like a good time to play dumb.

"Behavior Modification. The current dart formulas can

make you want to ingest something—food, smoke, whatever. That's easy."

"Easy for you," I say, raising my eyebrows toward the bump that's only just beginning to subside.

At least he has the grace to look embarrassed. "Yeah, uh, sorry about that. But once we ship the darts to the providers, it's pretty much out of CraveTech's hands. I get Stuck sometimes, too, you know."

I spell the word oblivious in my head over and over, until I lose the urge to punch him. It takes four this time, so I miss hearing yet another version of the "If It Wasn't CraveTech It Would Be Someone Else" speech.

". . . anyway, it's all just using the chemistry of cravings," he's saying when I'm calm enough to tune back in. "The fact that you have to buy whatever it is you're craving is an indirect consequence."

"An awfully profitable indirect consequence." I stab at a carrot.

"Yes, but see, that's the thing: the next big leap in the field is to skip straight to the buying part. We've been doing some promising work with what happens to brain chemistry when avid consumers watch successful commercials."

"So you're trying to synthesize a drug that will make people go out and buy MaxWhite toothpaste."

"Or a pair of NeoNikes. Or an H5."

"Oh my God."

He unleashes his Boy Genius grin. "Yeah. Pretty cool, huh?"

I report for my first day at CraveTech two weeks later. No one mentions that I'm dating the CEO, so I assume it hasn't gotten out. Still, I make a point of flirting back—and being overheard—when the cute young thing from Amazon-FedEx-Kinko's makes her rounds.

I'd told Tom up front that I was applying for the job. He was encouraging, but made it clear he would keep his nose out of it and leave things to Avery. I never see Tom around the marketing department—he seems more interested in making things than selling them, which I find endearing. If only he weren't making such awful things.

I flop down on Sandra's futon, narrowly missing a cat.

She puts mugs of tea on the table while I fish an envelope out of my shoulder bag. When she sits down next to me I place the envelope in her hands.

"Information," I say, "and lots of it." She takes the data card out of the envelope and peers at it as if she can actually make sense of what it contains.

"This is all of them?"

"All the formulas set to come out over the next six months. I've included a release schedule so you'll know which ones will be hitting the street first."

"The counter-formula team is gonna love this."

"They'd better. That little card represents a month of my life spent smiling at banalities and pretending to care about other people's kids."

"So you're ready to quit." She sounds relieved.

"I'd love to, but I don't think I can just yet. I still haven't found anything about this BeMod stuff. Tom keeps going on about it, but as far as I can tell it hasn't surfaced in R&D."

"Isn't it weird that he seems so serious about BeMod but you can't find it at CraveTech?"

I laugh. "So you think he has some other lab where he's developing chemicals he can use to rule the world?"

"Maybe not rule the world . . . just make a shitload of money, which is close enough."

"You're serious, aren't you?"

She shifts uncomfortably on the futon. "It just seems like he's been awfully specific about this BeMod stuff, and it hasn't turned up where you'd expect it."

"So what are you suggesting?"

"I think it's time you broke up with him, and maybe quit CraveTech, too."

"But if this BeMod stuff is in development somewhere, we'll need to get our hands on it and start on a counter-formula as soon as we can."

"That's true."

"And how do we do that if I don't keep seeing him?"

The cell leader finally overcomes the college buddy. "Just be careful. Don't get too attached to him."

I pick up the data card, two gig worth of corporate espionage. "Does this seem like I'm too attached?"

I arrive at Tom's place in a foul mood. He doesn't notice. Dangerously oblivious.

We're still in the foyer when he starts in about BeMod.

"I read a fascinating study on endorphins today. Apparently you can stimulate—"

"Can we please talk about something other than biochemistry?" I drop my bag on the floor.

He looks surprised and a little hurt. "I'm sorry, I didn't realize I was boring you."

"You're not boring me." I reach for his hand as we head into the living room. "I just think we have more in common than an interest in BeMods and DC Comics." I haven't gotten around to telling him I prefer Marvel.

He stops and pulls me back toward him. "I love you."

"See, there you go—I love me, too. Something else we have in common."

"Oh for God's sake," he sighs, collapsing on his down-filled couch. "I'm trying to be serious."

"I know." I sit down next to him. "I'm sorry. I just need a little more time."

"Okay. A little more time," he says, kissing my forehead and then my neck.

It's so easy to kiss him back.

The next time I go to Sandra's, she has a data card for me. "What's this?"

"A press release. It says CraveTech is voluntarily recalling all darts because internal studies have shown them to trigger heart attacks and strokes in a small but substantial segment of the population. We need you to send it out from the Crave-Tech network."

I hand the card back to her. "The media will figure out it's bogus."

"Not before the stock plummets. We're set up to trigger a small drop, and the release will do the rest."

"You know I won't be able to go back there after I send it. They'll trace it to me."

"I know." I stare hard at her. She doesn't flinch.

"And I'll have to break up with Tom."

"You need to do that anyway, Alex. It's been almost six months. That's too long. It's longer than you've dated anyone for real."

"Sandra, sending this press release is just throwing a brick through a window. It's meaningless in the long run. They'll replace the window. The stock price will readjust."

"But it will slow them down."

"Sandra, if it isn't CraveTech, it'll be. . . ."

"What?"

"Nothing." I take the card.

"You'll send the release?"

"I'll send it."

I put the few personal items that decorated my cubicle in a gym bag. I never had a picture of Tom on my desk. That would have been indiscreet.

The press release glows on my work station, one twitch away from every major news outlet and the most incendiary of the minor ones. If I had a picture of Tom, I might have stared at it for a while, maybe even whispered Sorry to it.

But I don't, so I just flick Send.

I'VE COME TO BREAK UP with him. "You're early," he says when he greets me at the door. "I've planned something special." I follow him out to the deck.

"For what?"

"Our six-month anniversary." There's a cloth-covered table and dining chairs, a silver champagne bucket on a stand. "In another twenty minutes there'll be a sunset, too." He says this like he paid for it. "But, you know," he looks oddly apologetic, "you're early."

"Tom, I'm sorry . . . we're not going to have a six-month anniversary."

I expect anything from him but the crooked Boy Genius smile I love so much. "This isn't about the press release, is it?"

I sit, a little inelegantly in my surprise.

"What press release?"

He laughs. "This conversation will probably be less

awkward if I just tell you I had all your CraveTech e-mails routed to me before they went out."

Ah.

"I was a little surprised that you actually sent it, but I do understand. I appreciate your beliefs. I love you for them—I want you to know that." He pours us each a glass of champagne. "And besides, you really helped me out with those counter-formulas."

I pick up my glass then set it down again. "Helped you out?"

"Absolutely. My people made a couple of tweaks, though. Your group's design wasn't very cost effective at the ten thousand unit level."

"Wait, wait, wait. You're going to manufacture our counter-formulas?"

"Oh, yes. The marketing campaign has been in development at a subsidiary company for weeks now. And the profit projections—Alex, you wouldn't believe it. Apparently people really, really hate the craving darts." Oh, my oblivious darling. "They'll pay twice the cost of the actual food just to make the cravings go away.

"But they won't have to. We'll be giving away the counter-formula for free.

"Funny thing about that—the research shows people would rather pay a couple of bucks to get the antidote from a familiar, trusted source than from a pack of anarchists with a habit of blowing up buses."

"Blowing up buses? What're you—"

"Oh, it's a little something we're planning for the fourth quarter. Disinformation campaign. It's ready for implementation now, but we think everyone will be more inclined to actively hate you during the holidays."

"Hate me?" I stand up and start backing toward the door.

"Well, not you, your group. They'll love you, Alex. You'll be managing my charitable organizations, giving away money to worthy causes right and left. People love that. And they'll love me. People love CEOs whose wives do that kind of stuff."

"Wives?" He brings out a pistol and fires a dart into my neck. I pull out the dart and drop it on the ground.

"What was in that thing?"

He answers my question with a question as he pops open a little black velvet box.

"Alex, will you marry me?"

"Tom, you sneaky little—" I say, lost between admiration and horror. "Will I marry you?"

Of course I will.

Tom Jr. has a hard time waking up in the morning. He gets it from me, not his father, who is always up before the crack of dawn, especially since the BeMod wide dispersal aerosol went into production.

"Tommy, wake up!" I call out toward his room. There's only a muffled grumbling in response.

I walk up to his doorway. "Really, Tommy, it's time to get going. You'll be late for school."

He rolls over, groaning, but doesn't make a move to get up. I unholster my parenting gun and shift the round in the chamber from Go to Bed to Wake Up.

"Get up, Tommy," I say as I draw a bead on his sleep-tousled head. "I'm not going to tell you again."

Counterfactual

GARDNER R. DOZOIS

Gardner R. Dozois lives in Philadelphia, Pennsylvania. He retired from the editorship of Asimov's, *after winning fifteen Hugo Awards as best editor and establishing* Asimov's *as the leading magazine in SF. He has published nearly sixty anthologies, sometimes co-edited with others, often with Jack M. Dann. "By the time this comes out, my two most recent anthologies will be* The New Space Opera, *edited with Jonathan Strahan, and* Wizards: Magical Tales from the Masters of Modern Fantasy, *edited with Jack Dann." His most prominent anthology since 1984 is the annual* Year's Best Science Fiction, *a recasting and expansion of* Best SF Stories of the Year, *which he edited 1977–81 (five volumes). He has published fiction throughout his career. Some of his stories are collected in* The Visible Man *(1977),* Slow Dancing Through Time *(1990),* Geodesic Dreams *(1992), and* Morning Child and Other Stories *(2004).*

"Counterfactual" appeared in F&SF. *It is a complex and subtle alternate history story about an alternate Earth in which Charles Lindbergh is Herbert Hoover's vice president and the American Civil War continues after sixty years. Cliff, a journalist and part-time writer of scientifiction and counterfactual novels, is a thoughtful central character, looking at his surroundings on a stopover in the South on his way to cover a minor election. Dozois provides layers of meaning, including political allegory, in this excellent story.*

"If we reach the Blue Ridge Mountains, we can hold out for twenty years."

—General Robert E. Lee

Cliff's fountain pen rolled across the pull-out writing shelf again, and he sighed and reached out to grab it before it tumbled to the floor. The small ink bottle kept marching down the shelf too, juddering with each vibration of the car.

Writing on a train wasn't easy, especially on a line where the rail-bed had been insufficiently maintained for decades. Even forming legible words was a challenge, with the jarring of the undercarriage or a sudden jerk all too likely to turn a letter into an indecipherable splat or to produce a startled, rising line across the page, as if the ink were trying to escape the mundane limitations of the paper.

Scenery was a distraction too. Cliff had always loved landscapes, and he had to wage a constant battle against the urge to sit there and just look out the window, where, at the moment, pale armies of fir trees slowly slid by, while the sky guttered toward a winter dusk in washes of plum and ash and sullen red. But he'd be sharing this room tonight with three other reporters, which meant lights-out early and a night wasted listening to them fart and snore, so if he was going to get any writing done on the new Counterfactual he was working on for McClure's, it'd better be now, while his roommates were down in the bar with the rest of the boys.

90

Cliff opened his notebook, smoothed it, and bent over the page:

General Robert E. Lee put his hands on the small of his back and stretched, trying to ease some of the tension out of his aching spine. He had never been so tired, feeling every one of his fifty-eight years sitting on his shoulders like bars of lead.

For days, days that had stretched into an unending nightmare of pain and fatigue, he had struggled to stay awake, to stay erect in the saddle, as they executed a fighting retreat from the trenches and earthworks of Petersburg westward along the Appomattox River toward Lynchburg, Grant's Army of the James, which outnumbered his own forces four to one, snapping at their heels every step of the way. Thousands of his men had died along the way, and Lee almost envied the fallen—at least they could stop. But Lee couldn't stop. He knew that all eyes were on him, that it was up to him to put on a show of being indefatigable and imperturbable, tall in the saddle, regal, calm, and wholly in command. His example and the pride it inspired, and the love and respect the men felt for him, was all that was keeping his ragged and starving army going. No matter how exhausted he was, no matter how bleak and defeated were his inner thoughts, no matter how hopeless he knew his position to be, no matter how much his chest ached (as it had been aching increasingly for days), he couldn't let it show.

They had stopped for the night in the woods near Appomattox Court House, too tired even to pitch tents. There had been almost nothing to eat, even for the staff officers. Now his staff huddled close to him in the darkness, as if they depended on him for light and warmth as much as or more than the low-burning bivouac fire: ragged, worn-out men in tattered uniforms, sprawled on blankets spread on the grass or sitting on saddles thrown over tree-stumps, without even chairs or camp-stools anymore. Lee could see their eyes, gleaming wetly in the firelight, as well as feel them. Every eye was on him still.

The barking of rifles had started up again from General Gordon's rear-guard on the road behind them when the courier arrived. He was thin as a skeleton, like Death himself come to call. He saluted and handed Lee a sealed communiqué. "Sir, from General Grant."

Lee held the note warily, as if it was a snake. He knew what it was: another message from General Grant, politely suggesting that he surrender his army.

The question was, what was he going to say in return?

The car jolted, shuddered, and jerked again while momentum equalized itself along the length of the train, and Cliff lifted his pen from the paper, waiting for the ride to steady again. What was he going to say in return? That was the problem.

He had an arresting central image, one that had come to him whole: Robert E. Lee surrendering the Army of Northern Virginia to General Ulysses S. Grant, the soldiers lined up somberly along a country road, heads down, some of the Confederates openly in tears, Lee handing his sword to Grant while a light rain fell, both men looking solemn and grim. . . . How to justify it, though? Counterfactuals had become increasingly popular in recent years—perhaps because the public had been denied the opportunity to play soldier during the Great War—until they were now almost respectable as pulp stories went, and you could make decent money selling them. But in writing Counterfactuals, you had to provide some kind of tipping-point, some event that would have changed everything that came after—and it had to be at least superficially plausible, or the fans, armchair historians all, would tear you to pieces. Having the Confederates win the War was a common enough trope in the genre, and a number of stories had been written about how Lee had won at Gettysburg or had pushed on out of Virginia to attack and burn Washington when he had the chance, forcing capitulation on a terrified Union, but Cliff was after something more subtle—a tale in which the Confederates still lost the War, but lost it in a different way, with different consequences as a result. It was hard to see what would have motivated Lee to surrender, though. True, he was nearly at the end of his rope, his men exhausted and starving, being closely harried by Union forces—but in the real world, none of that had brought him to the point of seriously contemplating surrender. In fact, it was at that very point when he'd said that he was determined "to fight to the last," and told his officers and men that "We must all determine to die at our posts." Didn't sound much like somebody who was ready to throw in the towel.

Then, just when things looked blackest, he had narrowly avoided a closing Union trap by breaking past Phil Sheridan at Appomattox Court House, and kept on going until he reached the Blue Ridge Mountains, there to break his army up into smaller units that melted into the wilderness, setting the stage for decades of bitterly fought guerilla war, a war of terror and ambush that was still smoldering to this day. It was hard to see what would have made Lee surrender, when he didn't contemplate it even in the hour of his most extreme need. Especially as he knew that he could expect few compromises in the matter of surrender and little or no mercy from the implacable President Johnson. . . .

He was spinning his wheels. Time for a drink.

Outside, the sun had finally disappeared below the horizon, leaving behind only a spreading red bruise. The darkening sky was slate-gray now, and hard little flakes of snow were squeezing themselves out of it, like dandruff sprinkled across felt. This had been a terrible winter, especially following the devastating dust-storms that had ravaged the Plains states all summer long. He hoped that the weather didn't work itself into a real blizzard, one that might hold them up on the way back. Like everyone else, he wanted to get the ceremony over with and get back home before Christmas— even though all he really had to look forward to was a turkey sandwich at a Horn & Hardart's and an evening of drinking in a journalist's hangout with many of these same people with whom he was already sharing a train in the first place.

Cliff stored his notebook in his carpetbag, and pushed out into the corridor, which was rocking violently from side to side, like a ship in a high sea, as the track-bed roughened. He made his way unsteadily along the corridor, bracing himself against the wall. Freezing needles of winter cold stabbed at him between the cars, and then stale air and the smell of human sweat swallowed him as he crossed into one of the coach cars, which was crowded with passengers, pinch-faced civilians in threadbare clothes, including whole families trying to sleep sitting up in the uncomfortable wooden seats. Babies were crying, women were crooning to them, couples were fighting, someone was playing a Mexican song on a beat-up old guitar, and four Texans—Texans were being seen around more frequently these days, now that relations had been normalized with the Republic of Texas— were playing poker on one of the seats, with onlookers standing in the aisles and whooping with every turn of the cards. They all wore the stereotypical but seemingly obligatory Stetsons.

There were three more coach cars to push his way through, and Cliff was glad to get beyond them into the alcoves between the cars, even though the cold air nipped at him each time. He never had liked noise and crowds, which was one reason why he'd always preferred small towns to the big cities. With things the way they were, though, the big cities like Chicago and Minneapolis were where the work was, and so he had no choice but to live there, as long as the Minneapolis Star paid his bills.

Even out here, between the cars, he could smell the tobacco stink coming from the next compartment, and when he opened the door and stepped into the bar car, tobacco smoke hung in such a thick yellow cloud that he could barely see. Most of the newsmen on the train were in here, standing around the bar or sitting grouped on stools around the little tables. Like Cliff, most of them had shunned the dining car and brought bags of sandwiches from Chicago, to save their meager expense-account money for the bar.

Cliff was hailed with the usual derisive, mildly insulting greetings, and two of the boys squeezed apart to make room for him at the bar. He was well-enough liked by the other newsmen, although his hobby of writing Counterfactuals and Westerns, even the occasional Air War or Weird Fantasy, marked him out as a bit strange. Half of these guys probably had an unfinished draft of the Great American Novel stashed away in a drawer somewhere, their attempt at unseating Hemingway or Fitzgerald, but in public you were supposed to give lip-service to the idea that to a real newsman, the only kind of writing that mattered was journalism.

"Hey, Cliff," John said. "Finish another masterpiece?"

"Aw, he was probably just jerking off," Staubach said.

Cliff smiled tolerantly and bought a round. He was already several drinks behind. The wunderkind from the Chicago Tribune—he was supposed to be nineteen, but to Cliff it didn't look like he could be more than thirteen—was trying to get an argument about The Gathering Clouds of War in Europe going with Bill, a big amiable Michigan Swede who rarely paid any attention to anything outside of the box-scores on the sports page, unless it was a racing form. "The United States will never get involved in a foreign war," the kid was saying, in his surprisingly deep voice. "Bryant kept us out of the Great War, and Hoover will keep us out of this one, too." He was short and pudgy, pasty-faced, with a sullen, cynical, seen-it-all air unusual in one so young. For a while, a few of the boys had held the fact that he was a New York Jew against him, but he was basically good-natured behind his gruff exterior, and smart as a whip, with just the kind of savage black humor that reporters liked, and so most of them had warmed to him.

He was trying to get a rise out of Bill, who had been incautious enough to express mild Interventionist sentiments a few times in the past, but Bill wasn't rising to the bait. "Guess England and Germany will just have to take care of de Gaulle without our help," Bill said amiably. "They're up to it, I guess."

"We've got enough problems of our own without worrying about de Gaulle," John threw in.

"Fuck de Gaulle and the horse he fucking rode in on," Staubach said. "Who's got the cards?"

"Language, gentlemen!" old Matthews said sternly. They all jeered at him, but they acquiesced, Staubach rephrasing his question to "Okay, who's got the frigging cards?" Although he was as natty as ever, impeccably dressed, looking every inch the distinguished senior correspondent, Matthews

had been drinking even harder lately than reporters usually
drank, and was already a bit glassy-eyed. The kid was supposed to be his assistant, but everybody knew that he'd been
writing his column for him, and doing a better job of it than
Matthews ever had.

John had the cards, but they had to wait through another
couple of rounds for one of the little tables to open up, as the
more prosperous passengers, or those who were more fin-
icky about their food, drifted off to the dining car up front.
"Crowded in here," Cliff commented. "Where are all the
politicians, though? You'd think they'd be nine deep around
the bar."

"Aw, they got a bar of their own, coupla cars up," Staubach said.

"Got the first three cars, all to themselves," Bill threw in,
with a grin. "And a sergeant with a carbine on the platform
outside, to make sure Lindbergh and the rest of them don't
get bothered by the hoi poloi."

"Sure, little do they care that the poor bastard has to freeze
his nuts off all the way to Montgomery," John said, which
drew another admonishment of "Language!" from Matthews,
although, as he was already more than half-fried, it was clear
that his heart wasn't in it anymore. The bartender—who, on
a train like this, traveling through the Occupied Territories,
was likely to be a soldier in civilian clothes, with a carbine of
his own tucked under the bar—grinned at them over Matthews's head.

At last a table opened up, and they settled in for their
usual nickel-and-dime game of draw. Matthews kept fumbling with his cards, having trouble holding them in a proper
fan, forgetting whose bet it was, and changing his mind
about how many cards he wanted, and soon was the big
loser—as big as it got in this penny ante game, anyway. Every time the kid lost a hand, he would curse with an inventive fluency that was almost Shakespearian, and that kept
the rest of them chuckling. Since he never deigned to use the
common "four-letter words," even Matthews couldn't really
complain, although he grumbled about it. Bill played with
his usual quiet competency and was soon ahead, although

Cliff managed to hold his own and split a number of pots with him.

After about an hour and a half of this, the smoke and the noise, and the fact that Matthews was no longer able to keep from dropping his cards every time he picked them up, and was getting pissy about it, made Cliff deal himself out.

"Going back to the room," he said, "see if I can get a couple of pages done before the rest of you guys show up."

"Can't keep Wild West Weekly waiting," Bill said.

"Aw, he's just going to jerk off again," Staubach mumbled, peering at his cards.

Cliff waved at them and walked away, moving a little more unsteadily than was entirely justified by the lurching of the car. Truth was, left to his own devices, Cliff wasn't that heavy a drinker—but if you were going to be accepted by the boys, you had to drink with them, and reporters prided themselves on their ability to put it away, another way in which the kid—who seemed to have a hollow trunk, as well as two hollow legs—fit right in in spite of his youth. Cliff could feel that he was at the edge of his ability to toss it back without becoming knee-walking drunk, though, which would lose him respect with the boys, so it was time to call it a night.

There was snow crusted on the footplates between the cars now, although it didn't seem to be snowing anymore outside. Cliff decided that he'd better clear his head if he was going to get any writing done, and walked back through the now-darkened coach cars and the sleeping cars to the observation platform on the back of the rear car.

It was bitterly cold outside and Cliff's breath puffed in tattered plumes, but the snow had stopped and the black clouds overhead had momentarily parted, revealing the fat pale moon. They were still moving through thick forest, the snow-shrouded ghosts of the trees gleaming like bones in the darkness, but now the ground on one side of the track fell steeply away, opening the world up to space and distance and the dimly perceived black bulks of nearby hills. There was a fast little mountain stream down there, winding along at the bottom of the slope, and in the moonlight he could see the cold white rills it made as it broke around streambed rocks.

The train slowed while going up the next long incline, and a dark figure broke from the trees, darted forward, and sprang onto the observation platform, grabbing the railing. As Cliff flinched back in shock, the figure threw a leg over the railing and pulled itself up. It paused, sitting on the top rail, one leg over, and looked at Cliff. It was a man, thin, clean-shaven, with a large nose and close-cropped hair bristling across a bullet-head, clutching a bindle in one hand. As Cliff gaped, the man smiled jauntily, said, "Evenin', sport!", and put one finger to his lips in a shushing gesture. Then he swung his other leg over the railing, hopped down to the platform, and sauntered by Cliff, giving him a broad wink as he passed.

Up close, even by moonlight, you could tell that his clothes were patched and much-mended, but they seemed reasonably clean, and although he exuded a brief whiff of sweat and unwashed armpits and sour breath as he passed, it wasn't too strong or too rank. He couldn't have been on the bum for too long, Cliff thought, or at least he must have been finding work frequently enough to enable him to keep himself moderately clean. The tramp disappeared into the car without a backward glance, presumably to lose himself among the coach-class passengers or find a water closet or a storage cubical to hide in for the night. There were thousands of such ragged men on the road these days, drifting from place to place, looking for work or a handout, especially down here in the Occupied Territories; the economy was bad enough in the States, but down here, whole regions had never really recovered from the War in the first place, the subsequent decades of guerrilla war and large-scale terrorism—with entire armies of unreconstructed rebels still on the loose and lurking in the hills, many of them by now comprised of the children and grandchildren of the original soldiers—tending to discourage economic growth . . . especially with raiders knocking down new factories or businesses as fast as they sprang up, to discourage "collaboration" with the occupying forces.

Cliff knew that he really should report the tramp to the conductor, but it was difficult to work up enough indignation to bother, and in the end he decided not to even try. It was hard to blame the guy for wanting to be inside the train, where it was warm, rather than out there in the freezing night.

Up ahead, around a long curve, you could see the engine itself now, puffing out bursts of fire-shot black smoke like some great, stertoriously gasping iron beast. The smoke plume wrapped itself back around the observation platform, making Cliff cough and filling his mouth with the ashen taste of cinders, and that, plus the fact that he was beginning to shiver, told him that it was time to go back inside. If his head wasn't clear by now, it wasn't going to be.

When Cliff got back to their compartment, though, it became obvious that it didn't matter; he wasn't going to get any more writing done tonight. The conductor had already rearranged the compartment into its sleeping configuration, folding away the benches and lowering two bunks from each opposing wall, one stacked above the other. Somewhat surprisingly, his roommates were already back from the bar. Matthews, in fact, was already soddenly asleep on one of the lower bunks, gurgling and snoring, still fully clothed, although Bill was fussing with him, trying to get him undressed, with little success. Cliff gathered that the old man had passed out in the bar, or come near to it, and his compatriots had hauled him back to the roomette. Even out here, you could smell the booze coming off of him.

With the bunks folded down, there was hardly space enough for Bill and the kid to stand in the tiny compartment, and Cliff had to hover in the doorway, half out in the corridor, waiting for someone to make room for him. The kid at last got impatient with Bill's efforts to undress Matthews and bumped him aside, saying harshly, "Oh, leave the poor old pfumpt alone." With a curious tenderness that belayed the gruffness of his tone, he took off the old man's shoes and stowed them under his bunk, and loosened his tie. "He'll just have to sleep in his clothes for once like the rest of us, instead of those stupid woolen pajamas."

As if to demonstrate, Bill climbed into the other bottom bunk—fully dressed except for his shoes; it was a good idea to keep your wallet in your pocket, too, since sneak-thieves were known to rifle through bags left on the floor in a compartment while the occupants slept—and put his hat over his eyes. Cliff slid inside, now that some floor space had opened up, and closed the door on the corridor.

They had come down out of the hills by now, and stopped at a tiny station for no readily apparent reason. There was a small town out there, two or three streets of two-story storefronts laid out parallel to the tracks, some dilapidated old wooden houses with big overgrown yards set farther back. The storefronts carried faded signs that said things like "Hudson's Hickory House" or "Brown Furniture Company," but none of them looked like they'd been open for a while, and several had boarded-up windows. Nothing was moving out there except a dog pissing on a lamppole.

"What a dump!" the kid said, turning to look at Cliff. Up close like this, he had a habit of partially covering his mouth with his hand when he spoke; he was embarrassed about his teeth, which he never brushed; they were green. "No wonder all the colored folks moved up North."

"Getting lynched and shot and burned out by Lee's Boys probably had something to do with it too," Bill said dryly, lifting his hat for a second. "Turn off the light. I want to get some sleep."

The kid vaulted up into the bunk above Matthews. Cliff took his shoes off, stuffed his carpetbag into his bunk to use as a pillow, shut off the light, and climbed into the other upper in the dark, nearly falling when the car lurched as the train started moving again.

Cliff lay awake in the darkness for a while, feeling oddly apprehensive and jittery for no particular reason he could identify, listening to the snoring and moaning of his roommates. He tried picturing himself back on his grandfather's hill farm near the confluence of the Wisconsin and the Missisippi, playing fetch with his old buff-colored coon dog, and eventually the steady swaying movement of the car rocked him to sleep.

Even so, he'd wake up for a moment every time the motion of the train changed, slowing down or speeding up with a jerk and a lurch, opening his eyes to see, through the uncurtained top of the window, trees rushing by, the roofs of houses, bright lights on tall poles, more trees, and then his eyes would close, and he'd sleep again, the wailing of the train's whistle and the rhythmical clatter of its wheels weaving themselves through his dreams.

By morning, they had outrun the winter. Here, there was no snow on the ground; browning, multicolored leaves clung stubbornly to the hardwood trees. Farther south, on the Gulf Coast or at least in Florida, it was probably still summer, palm trees swaying in balmy breezes, but they weren't going that far. This was the last leg of their journey, with only a couple of hours left until they reached Montgomery.

The room steward brought them a pot of coffee. Sensitized by the kid's remarks of the previous evening, Cliff noticed that the steward was a Mediterranean immigrant of some sort—Italian, Greek; recent enough to retain a heavy accent—where before the War, the job almost certainly would have been done by a colored fellow. It wasn't true that there were no colored people left in the Occupied Territories, of course—there were still families holding out here and there. But decades of large-scale terrorism had chased millions of them to the big cities of the North, where they had encountered other problems to replace the ones they'd left behind, and most of the medium-level jobs went to more recent (and reasonably white) immigrants like the room steward. Now the Open Door that had let people like the steward into the country was slamming closed as immigration policies were tightened, leaving millions of European refugees with nowhere to go. As someone whose father had immigrated from Prague only a generation before, Cliff sympathized with all of them, and with the exiled colored folk as well, unwelcome in either the South or North.

Bill slipped his shoes on and ducked out to fetch a bunch of doughnuts from the dining car. They ate while taking turns going to the WC at the end of the sleeper for sponge baths and to change into fresh clothes, although old Matthews was so glazed and hung-over that the kid had to guide him there and back, holding him by one arm. Bill teased him about this unmercifully, although he wasn't quite mean enough to ask the kid if he'd had to help Matthews bathe. He certainly had to help him dress, though, while Bill jeered, and Matthews, lost in his own world, stared at nothing anybody else could see. He clearly didn't have long to go before he reached the end of his rope, Cliff realized. Odds were that the kid would have his job before then anyway.

Outside, rundown white clapboard houses with incongruously large porches were slipping by, as well as burnt-out factories, cut banks of red clay, goats grazing in hilly yards, an occasional glimpse of a sluggish brown river. For the last half hour, they crawled by a huge Army base, home of one of the occupying divisions, although little was visible beyond the high walls and barbed wire except the red roofs of the barracks, a water tower, a big industrial crane of some sort. There were guard towers every few yards, with machine-gun emplacements at the top, giving the whole complex the look of a prison. Scrub woods, weed-overgrown lots, and heaps of rusting scrap metal for the next few minutes, and then the outlying freight yards for the Montgomery station began to roll past.

Montgomery was a big city for this part of the world. It had been in Yankee hands since the end of the War, and although it had suffered several major raids in subsequent years from unreconstructed Confederate forces, and had been shelled by terrorists more than once, it was still in pretty good shape. There were a few bombed-out buildings visible in the center of town, but most of them were busily being repaired, and the sounds of construction—hammering, workmen shouting, buzz-saws whining—were constantly heard here. Outside the train for the first time in more than a day, Cliff wished he'd brought a heavier coat; it wasn't as cold here as it had been up the track, in the hill country, but it was still brisk, and the pregnant gray clouds that were sliding by overhead promised rain that he hoped would hold off until after the ceremony. The air smelled of dust and ozone.

He caught a glimpse of the Vice President going by, his

handsome features looking strained and a bit grim; one of the youngest Vice Presidents in history, Lindbergh hadn't been given a lot to do after his charm, good looks, and charisma had helped Herbert Hoover win the election, except to be trotted out on ceremonial occasions like this one that were important but not quite important enough to fetch the President out of the White House. He was accompanied by his son, a somber, silent little boy dressed like a miniature adult in suit and tie, and by the usual crowd of handlers and hangers-on, as well as by John Foster Dulles, Huey Long, Charles Curtis, and the rest of the senatorial party, and their people. All of the dignitaries were hustled into long black limousines and whisked away, the star reporters and big-name columnists—one of whom once would have been Matthews—scurrying after them, off to arrange interviews with local officials and whichever of the senators they could catch before they disappeared into backroom bars somewhere.

After the ceremony, there'd be the usual photo-op for clutch-and-grin shots of Lindbergh shaking hands with the outgoing Territorial Governor, Lindbergh and the pro-tem State Governor about to take office, Lindbergh and the Mayor, Lindbergh and the Mayor's big-breasted sister, and so on, and then, hopefully before it started pouring, they'd all rush back to the train station to file their stories via telegraph (there were no trunk lines through the Occupied Territories; it was difficult enough to keep the telegraph lines up). They'd all try to come up with some twist or angle on the same dry story, of course (Cliff hoped to get some pithy quotes from Huey Long, who'd been born in the Occupied Territories before moving North, carpetbag in hand, to seek his fortune, and who was a usefully Colorful Character, always good for a line or two of copy), and then they'd all pile back in the train and head back to Chicago, to be off to somewhere else a day or a week later. That was a reporter's life.

In the meantime, most of the newsmen crossed the tracks and headed for a café across the street from the station. It was just a dingy old storefront, with cracked and patched windows, the calendars on the walls the only decorations, but it was warm inside and smelled invitingly of cooking food. The pancakes and eggs weren't bad, either, although it was probably better not to know what animal the bacon had come from; even the bitter chicory brew that passed for coffee down here on the far side of the Embargo Line was tolerable. Most of the reporters ignored the grits, to the amusement of the local stringers who'd arranged to meet them here before the ceremony. Watching them, Cliff realized that although he had been born in Wisconsin and lived in Minneapolis, had only visited New York City once, and had never been to Boston in his life, he was a Yankee to the locals—they were all just Yankees to the locals, who didn't make any of the fine distinctions between them as to regional origins that they made amongst themselves, and who probably, truth be told, disliked them equally. Cliff wondered if this boded well for the years ahead, when they'd officially be fellow citizens once more, on paper, anyway.

Bill and Staubach and Hoskins from the New York World had started a political argument about just that, Bill thinking that officially readmitting Alabama to the Union (something that it had taken decades of economic sanctions and delicate negotiations to accomplish, in the face of Rebel reprisals against "collaborators" and a general population who were by no means wholeheartedly for the idea), as Virginia and the Carolinas and Arkansas had already been before it, as Mississippi and Louisiana and Georgia had not, was a good thing, putting more of the shattered jigsaw that had once been the Union back together—while Staubach and Hoskins thought that Reunification was a bad idea, that it would further drag the economy of the U.S. down, that the nation was in fact better off without the disaffected former States, especially with federal troops quartered on them to make sure they stayed down.

Cliff lost interest in the too-familiar argument and started thinking about his Counterfactual again. How would the world of his story have differed from the real world? He toyed with the conceit that in that Counterfactual world there might also be a Cliff, struggling to write a Counterfactual story about his world, and yet another Cliff in the next world, and so on—a vision of a ring of Alternate Earths, in each of which history had taken a slightly different course. There was a story idea there. Maybe somebody manning a way station of some sort in some isolated location, maybe out in the rural Wisconsin hill-country where he'd grown up, a station that allowed travel between the Alternate Earths. It was too weird an idea for Thurber at McClure's, probably for most of the Counterfactual market, but it could maybe be done as scientifiction. He'd written a few scientifiction pieces at the beginning of his career for Marvel Tales and Wonder Stories Quarterly, although they didn't pay as well as Counterfactuals. For all his prim pseudo-Victorian stuffiness, Lovecraft at Weird Tales liked wildly imaginative stuff; maybe he'd go for it. . . .

"Wake up, Shakespeare," Staubach said, punching his arm. "Time to get going."

The reporters gathered up their equipment—Cliff had earlier hauled his battered old Speed Graphic out of his bag; the Star's budget didn't stretch to sending a photographer as well—and shambled out through the streets of Montgomery. You could already hear a brass band playing in the distance.

There was a raised wooden stage set up in front of the State Capitol building, from whose white marble steps Jefferson Davis had announced the formation of the Confederacy (which was rubbing it in a bit too blatantly, Cliff thought, but nobody had asked him), with a podium and a microphone up front, and rows of cold-looking dignitaries sitting on camp-chairs lined up behind, including Lindbergh's little boy, who, sitting hunched up on himself, looked like he'd rather be inside drinking a cup of hot chocolate than sitting out here in the cold. No chairs for the color guard who surrounded the stage on two sides, weapons at port arms, or for the audience, who were packed in in front of the stage in a disorderly mass. Not a bad turnout for a chilly December day, Cliff thought as he and his compatriots wormed their way to the front, especially for a ceremony solemnizing a decision that by no means had the support of the entire citizenry. The real ratification ceremony would take place in Congress later, of course; this symbolic local ceremony was an excuse to show the flag—literally: a big one center-stage that snapped in the wind. And to give the local yokels a chance to bathe in the reflected glory of Lindbergh and the other bigwigs.

The sky was still threatening, although a lacuna had opened up in the slate-gray clouds, splashing watery sunshine around. A brisk wind had come up, scattering trash and discarded sheets of newspaper like frightened birds. Bill cursed and seized his hat to keep it from flying away. The faces of the men in the brass band were stiff and red with cold, the cheeks of the trumpet player bulging grotesquely out, as though he'd bitten off something too big for him to swallow.

The band stopped playing. The Territorial Governor made a long, rambling, fawning introduction of Lindbergh, who then stepped forward to the podium and began speaking himself. His face was also red with cold, and he kept sniffing, as if his nose was running. He was holding his hat in one hand to keep it from blowing away, and the rising wind made his tie flap up into his face from time to time, requiring him to smooth it back down.

Cliff raised his camera and dutifully took a photo of him, and then stopped listening. Christ, he'd heard a lot of speeches in his life! Very few of them worth listening to. He'd crib quotations from the transcripts the Press Secretary would hand out later. Instead of listening, he fell into a reverie about his Counterfactual. He thought he'd seen a psychological justification for Lee surrendering rather than fighting on. Suppose, unlike what had happened in the real world, Lincoln hadn't been assassinated at the Second Inaugural ceremony by John Wilkes Booth, the well-known actor and radical Confederate sympathizer, who'd been lurking in the inaugural crowd with a pistol? Suppose that Lincoln had instead gone on to actually serve out his second term? In the real world, there was known to have been an exchange of notes between Lee and Grant in April 1865, discussing the possibility of surrender; Lee had refused to come to terms, and instead had vanished with his army into the Blue Ridge Mountains to wage a hide-and-seek campaign of large-scale guerrilla war that had lasted far longer than even he could have possibly imagined it would. Others had taken their cue from Lee, Joseph Johnson with his Army of Tennessee, the dreadful Nathan Bedford Forrest, the even more terrible John Mosby and William Clarke Quantrill, who had already been waging guerrilla warfare in Missouri and "Bleeding Kansas." Jefferson Davis and the Confederate Cabinet had escaped into Texas, from where they'd continued to pursue the war for decades, until the Texans—always hard-pressed by Mexico on their southern border and out of patience with the arrogant high-handedness of the "Richmond Refugees"—had gradually lost interest in being a hold-out Confederate state and had reinvented themselves as a Republic instead.

But suppose Lincoln had still been President? It was well-documented that Lee and Lincoln had had great respect for each other as individuals, in an age where personal honor had been a real factor in human affairs. Suppose Lincoln had worked through Grant to mediate Lee's surrender, guaranteeing favorable terms for surrender and backing it with the force of his own personal word, terms that would enable Lee to surrender with some semblance of honor and dignity for himself and his hard-pressed men, terms that the vengeful Johnson never would have approved in this world? Would that have allowed Lee to justify the surrender of his army? And if Lee had surrendered, mightn't that have provided the cue for how others should act, just as Lee's defiant refusal to surrender had in the real world? If so, that one moment would have caused everything else to change. . . .

It was in that moment that Cliff saw the tramp, the one from the train, standing a few yards away in the crowd, and from that instant on, he knew everything that was going to happen, detail for detail, like watching a play you've previously seen rehearsed.

The tramp, staring up at Lindbergh intently, his sallow, unshaven face as blank as wax, the cords in his neck standing out with tension. He swallows once, twice, his prominent

Adam's apple bobbing, and then his hand inches toward his coat.

Everything has gone into slow motion. Cliff wills himself to lunge forward, and feels his muscles begin to respond, but it's like swimming through syrup, and he knows that he'll be too late.

The tramp comes up with a gun, an old model Colt Navy .36. Practically a museum piece by now, but it's clean and seems in good working order. The weak sunlight splashes from the barrel as the tramp raises the gun, slowly, infinitely slowly, it seeming to ratchet up in discrete jerky intervals, like film being manually advanced frame by frame.

Cliff is swimming forward through the encrusted, resistant air, bulling through it as you'd breast your way through oncoming waves, and even as the breath for a warning shout is gathering itself in his lungs, he finds himself thinking, It's not my fault! There's a dozen ways he could have gotten here! Yes, but there was only one way he did get here, in this world, in this lifetime, and if he'd only reported him to the conductor last night, everything would be different. . . . Everything has stopped now, time freezing solid, and he sees it all in discrete snapshots.

A woman standing on the steps of the State Capitol building, holding up a baby so that it can have a better view. The baby is holding a rattle in one hand.

The trumpet player, cheeks no longer distended, lighting a cigarette and laughing at something the tuba player is saying.

Birds flying, caught on the wing, crossing the sky from left to right, something that would have been read as an omen in Ancient Rome.

John Foster Dulles saying something behind a raised hand, probably a scornful remark about Lindbergh's speech, to Charles Curtis.

Lindbergh's son scratching his nose, looking bored.

Lindbergh himself, pushing his tie out of the way again, a moue of annoyance crossing his face.

The tramp's face contorting into an intense, tooth-baring grimace of extreme, almost mortal, effort. . . .

The gun fired.

At once, as if a sheet of glass had been shattered, time was back to normal, everything going fast again. Cliff staggered and almost fell, as other people in the close-packed crowd began to surge forward or back. The tramp's revolver barked twice more; the sharp reports hit the wall of tall buildings on the far side of the street and echoed back. Someone screamed, someone else shouted something incoherent. Then those nearest the tramp in the crowd swarmed over him, pulling his arm down. He disappeared under a knot of struggling men.

At the podium, Lindbergh staggered as if in concert with Cliff. His mouth half-open in shock, he grabbed the podium to keep himself upright, swayed, and then lost his grip and fell heavily to the stage. Some of the dignitaries had thrown themselves down at the sound of the first shot, Huey Long among them, but Charles Curtis had jumped up and grabbed Lindbergh's little boy as he threw himself forward with a scream, and was now wrestling with the child to keep him away from the body. Dulles had also stayed on his feet, and was now bending over the fallen Vice President, fumbling at him ineffectually with fluttering hands, his mouth working, although it was impossible to make out what he was saying over the rising roar of the crowd.

More screams, more shouts. Cliff could hear Bill, at his elbow, saying "Oh no! Oh no!" over and over again. Old Matthews looked as if someone had shot him as well, his face slack and ashen. The tramp was on his feet again, still struggling against a half-dozen men who were trying to wrestle him back down. His face was scratched and battered now, splattered with blood.

"The South will rise again!" the tramp shouted, before they could pull him down, "The South will rise again!" And Cliff realized with horror that indeed it would, that it would keep on rising again, and again, as it had ever since the ostensible end of the War, dragging the country down like a drowning man dragging his rescuer down with him . . . that the War would never be over, that his children and their children would still be fighting it when he had long since gone to dust, dealing with the dreadful consequences of it, even unto the fifth generation and beyond, world without end.

Was there another Cliff writing about this right now, he wondered numbly, in some other Counterfactual world where, unlike here, it was only a remote abstract possibility that had never happened, good for an hour's academic entertainment and nothing more?

Behind him, the kid had already regained his wits and was running for the train station to file the story, leaving Matthews and the rest of them gaping in the dust and the cold rising wind.

Moon Does Run

EDD VICK

Edd Vick (eddvick.livejournal.com) *lives in Seattle with SF novelist Amy Thomson and their adopted daughter Katie. "The son of a pirate father and a baking mogul mother, a 2002 graduate of the Clarion SF Writing Workshop, his interest in the Caribbean dates from trips to Caracas and Curaçao in his teen years, though the germ for "Moon Does Run" comes of working for several district managers in seventeen years of running bookstores." He is currently International Adoption Coordinator of Americans Adopting Orphans* (www.orphans.com). *He has had several stories published in* Asimov's *SF Magazine. Other magazines and anthologies with stories by Vick include* Electric Velocipede, Jim Baen's Universe, Fundamentally Challenged, *and* Northwest Passages.

"Moon Does Run" appeared in Electric Velocipede, *a lively zine edited by John Klima. It is a story set in a future Caribbean, with lots of big events (war, etc.) going on in the background, about a sentient warehouse robot, with lots of rich tonal effects and metaphorical implications. It is perhaps relevant to remind ourselves that the word robot was invented to signify worker.*

First the Series Seven Customs Administrator shot a current spike through its voicebox, starting a small fire that scorched the front of its cylindrical head. It used a crowbar to put dents in the steel of its chest. It pulled out the cotter-pins and lowered its torso out of the universal joint that allowed it to travel at will around the vast warehouse suspended from an overhead lattice of tracks. On its internal batteries then, it twisted two of its arms out of true between a pair of tractors, then ejected its other one.

Content with its work, the robot shorted out the circuit to its eyes, darkening them. It lay on its back and activated a private subroutine. A jolt of pleasure ran through the copper traceries of its electronic brain, bringing satisfaction and a sensation of warmth.

Contentment. Warmth. Tapping its remaining fingers against the concrete floor beneath it, it opened the door to memory.

Five weeks earlier, the warehouse had been bustling. Traffic in and out of Trinidad was brisk as shippers scurried to avoid the hurricanes that birthed to the north. A dozen treaded Series Three robots shoved two-ton shipping containers back and forth on train rails set in the floor. At the docks, cargo ships waited to lift the containers onto and off of their decks, while ashore tractor-trailers waited for cranes to raise or set their loads. Fluorescent lights glared down on a hundred thousand square feet of organized chaos operating day and night. Over it all soared the Series Seven Administrator suspended from its jointed mechanical arm like a spider on its strand, evaluating, inspecting, judging, and queuing every shipment.

A golf cart labored in through one of the open doors. Levering himself out of its seat, the exporter Joseph Mendes wandered to a metal work table. He flapped his shirt with one hand to cool his body and slapped a sheaf of papers on the table with the other.

In silence the Administrator descended. When its head was opposite the man, Mendes closed one eye and tilted his head. This was a common reaction to the robot since its body was above its head. Mendes straightened back up, grimaced, and started in without preamble.

"Why yeh take up for Herrera?"

"I am not taking his side," said the Administrator. "His ship is in a more advantageous position than yours. It is more convenient to have him load first."

"I bet he catch a glad from that. I seen him give you the cut eye t'other day."

"Much as you have done since we first met. Humans may be susceptible to superstition, but I operate by logic, Mister Mendes. You may load in the morning, once I've inspected your cargo."

"Yeah, and Herrera's nuts're already shelled by then. He get de best pickings, while de power fly up in yeh head."

The Administrator considered its responses, then activated a translation subroutine. "Captain Herrera was just here complaining about you. He said, 'I been eat de bread dat de devil knead.' He was, I believe, speaking of your having found a better grade of cocoa than he."

"He say dat?" Mendes laughed once. Mollified, he picked up his papers and started back to his cart. As the Administrator whispered upward once more, the shipper yelled back over his shoulder, "Tell him a stop dancin' me."

"You'll encounter him eventually," murmured the Administrator as it glided to the open rollup doors on the seaward end of the warehouse. It ignored the ants that wandered about beneath it, seeking out the occasional spill of sugar or syrup. This was the nearest the Administrator ever got to the outside world. Port of Spain, on the southwest corner of Trinidad, was only a few miles from Venezuela, and in the morning's clear weather the robot could see the jungle and a pair of hawks that soared above it.

It saw too the destroyers and the warplanes, crossing the narrow Boca del Dragon. They dropped bombs and paratroopers. They dropped leaflets.

"Seize freedom!" screamed the Portuguese words on the papers that floated into the Administrator's warehouse. "Throw off the chains of the oppressive British Empire! Join the victorious Venezuelan people!"

The Administrator examined the leaflet. The paper was obviously not a bill of lading, a packing list, a law, or a sailing schedule. It ran keywords from the flyer through a query routine, and found that it was likely experiencing the advent of a war. The Administrator's programming was scanty where conflict was concerned; there were too many variables. It glided back to its manifests, deciding to ignore the war so long as the war ignored the Administrator.

Four days later, a Venezuelan officer came to the warehouse. His crisp uniform had black shoulder boards, each with two silver stars. Behind him walked a man with a toolbox and a laptop case. The Administrator eyed the latter until the officer spoke.

"I am Teniente Pérez," he said in Portuguese, proffering a sheet of paper. "You belong to the Venezuelan government now. We are here to reprogram you."

The Administrator extended one of its arms to take the paper, scanned it into its memory, then filed it in a cubby on its desk. "Lieutenant Pérez, I am the property of the Republic of Trinidad and Tobago. My software and firmware are licensed from TradeSoft, Incorporated, of Chicago, Illinois, and may not be altered without voiding the warranty."

"There is no longer a Republic by that name, I regret to say." The officer motioned to the man accompanying him. "This technician has his job to do. Soon enough, you will have yours as well."

Placing his toolbox on the Administrator's table, the

technician gazed at the robot without fondness. "Come you down here," he said, gesturing with the sweep of an arm.

The Administrator retreated upward. "I am the property of the Republic—"

"Come you down!"

"I refuse."

Hands on hips, the man craned his neck back. "I'll fix you," he said. "De moon does run, but de day does ketch him." He looked around. "Now where—?"

"Might this be what you are looking for?" The lieutenant gestured toward a panel of breakers and knife switches on the nearest wall. He followed with his eyes the heavy wire powering the robot's powered arm across the ceiling and down the wall, then paced to the panel and threw the corresponding breaker.

Deprived of electricity, the hydraulics supporting the Administrator lowered it to the floor headfirst, where it extended its three arms to support itself.

The technician walked to just outside the robot's reach. "You gonna be good now? Or do I hafta knock you upside the head two-three times?"

All the man had to do was wait until its batteries were exhausted, a matter of a few hours. Then not only would the Administrator be helpless, it would not be able to report on what the man did to it.

"I will behave," said the Administrator.

"You best had." The technician yanked his tools off the table and lugged them to the Administrator's side. While the officer watched, the man peeled up a rubber gasket and attached a fifteen-pin connector to the robot. It led to his laptop, which the mechanic used to reprogram the robot. The Administrator watched with interest, so long as it could.

Deleted were any mentions of Trinidad or Tobago. It was now a machine of the Venezualan Protectorado de Pederales, subject to all laws and restrictions pertaining thereto. All information on shipping rates, favored nations, and reporting agencies was overwritten. Portuguese supplanted English as the language of commerce.

When it awoke, El Agente de Aduanas saw the world with

new eyes, while whispers and half-memories of its old life percolated through the registers and NAND gates of its silicon and copper brain.

Vicente Herrera folded the manifest in half, and half again. Then he smoothed it out again on the table. "I need to get my cement out on the evening tide." His Portuguese was smooth and cultured. Below the surface tones, though, El Agente heard the quaver of nervousness.

El Agente's tones were soothing. "And we shall, sir. I have concluded my analysis of your shipment. The four containers of cement are cleared, as soon as you deposit thirty-six thousand pesos in port fees. However, there is a problem with container five." The robot whirred above the floor to caress the offending metal box.

Herrera reddened. "What you think? It's just empty. A deadhead for ballast."

"I think you are taking a container that isn't yours." El Agente sent a UHF signal to one of its semi-autonomous peripheral robots, which trundled up to position itself next to the container. "This one is registered to Panorama Oilworks." At an additional signal the worker pulled the huge metal box down the line. "An accident on your part, I am sure."

"Mm. Yes." Herrera watched a bee crawl across the robot's dusty chest. "Speaking of accidents, you will see to it that Mendes does not anchor at my dock again, will you not?"

"Captain Mendes, yes, he was here." El Agente brushed the insect away with a scrape of steel on steel. Where its fingers had run, a shiny indentation shone through. "He said to tell you he got a glad— He said you might shell the—" It paused, confused, then continued. "He has been warned. Another infraction will result in a fine." It regarded its fingers, then dug another shallow trench across its curving front.

Herrera turned to leave, and as he did he glanced toward the building's seaward end, where the robot had so often looked out toward the sea.

All the rolling doors were down. The Series Three robot pulling Herrera's cement was bumping gently against one of them. El Agente's gaze followed Herrera's, and the door lifted just enough for the robot and its cargo to exit, then closed.

That night, when there were no more crates to assess, no more papers to generate, El Agente postulated a jointed arm that extended all the way to the moon. From this arm, the robot rode high in the sky, commanding ships to sail in ordered ranks and skyscrapers to be piled in tidy stacks. Humans? They were too small even to be seen from its lofty height.

It wasn't a dream. Just a series of postulations with the force of one.

Two weeks later, British ships hove to barely outside sight of the island and began shelling. Cruise missiles crested the horizon to blast their way to the colony's interior. One fell near the warehouse, destroying a tanker at anchor. Soon after, stubby VTOL planes whined importantly about, dropping off squads of soldiers. El Agente watched from one end of its warehouse and then from the other. Briefly it wondered if this was a new war or a continuation of the first. Its new programming told it to defend Pederales, but no enemy came near. Thoughtfully, it had its peripheral robots uproot a section of track in one corner of the warehouse. The resulting club was eight feet long and weighed a quarter ton.

Several days later, all was quiet once more. The British warships moved into view and anchored on the horizon.

Trade halted. The radio on a courier's bicycle spoke of negotiations between countries, of an embargo, of intervention by the United States. Shipping containers stacked up on the dock and in the building. El Agente stared around itself at the mountains of merchandise, knowing what each crate, each container, held. It longed to send them all on their separate ways.

The same mechanic arrived, grinning. He carried the same laptop and toolchest into the warehouse. El Agente hefted its makeshift weapon, and the grin grew wider as the technician glanced pointedly at the electrical panel. The club clattered to the floor.

The man reprogrammed El Agente. Away went an ency-clopedia's worth of rules and regulations. Back came several megs of new ones in their place. Portuguese remained, but was once again subordinate to English.

New identity and old roiled in the Customs Official's copper-web brain when it came to awareness.

The Customs Official was supervising its third reorganiza-tion of the warehouse's contents when Joseph Mendes plod-ded to the work table. When the Official skimmed down, the man stood staring at the floor. The Official counted to sixty seconds before speaking.

"Are you quite healthy?" asked the Official. "Do you re-quire assistance?"

"Eh? Aw, I'm all bootooks. Wi' dis embargo, I'm so outta luck, wet paper could cut mih."

The Official paused. "You are—unwell?"

"It bus' mah bag, it do."

"Are you speaking to me? I do not entirely comprehend you."

Mendes' glance was sharp. "Yeh no' yehself today."

"I have much to do." The Official bobbed up to look around the warehouse. Series Three robots trundled here and there, pulling or pushing containers on their flatbeds. "There is dis-order here." It had half-memories of ordering that the waiting shipments be stacked in certain places, but now it could not find the sense behind those orders. It had even found a stray piece of rail littering its floor. "Oh. Captain Herrera was here. He wanted me to tell you— something."

"Not to dock at my slip," said a voice, and Herrera emerged from a maze of crates.

"Herrera," said Mendes. "Yeh bounce up on a fellah, don't yeh?" He advanced on the other shipper, and pumped his hand vigorously with both meaty, sweating paws.

Herrera slapped his shoulder. "Hello, Drummer. Rita was asking after you and Marie the other day. When are you and she coming to dinner again?"

The Official watched the interplay with confusion. It had

made sense to the robot before that the rival shippers should be enemies. It had the vaguest of impressions that it would once have understood. Rising once more, the Official turned its attention back to its workers. It averted a collision between two of them on the north side of the warehouse, and directed that a load of gravel be left outside the north doors. Its domain overflowed. Absently, the Official tightened a lockdown on a stack of shipping containers.

"Hey, Agente!" The voice came from below.

Coasting down, it said, "Customs Official, if you please."

"Official, then," said Herrera. "We are here to find if you know when our shipments will be released. We are anxious to be on our way."

"I expect daily to hear that it is safe to allow shipping once more. I too would like to do my job and move your goods onward."

"We'll have to make a to-do," said Mendes. "It de las' nail in the coffin if we don' go soon. I'm a go to the Customs office."

"I will accompany you," said Herrera. "Official, please be so kind as to inform us if you hear anything."

His companion thumped the table. "And we let you know, too, ey? After all, it take two han' to clap."

The Official swiveled its head to observe its three hands. By the time it looked up again, the two men were out the door.

There was nothing left to do. The warehouse was as tidy as the robot and its drones could make it. It had never been so quiet before. The Official hung from its jointed arm and watched ants.

Each ant was the size of one of the robot's larger screws. A line of the insects came under one of the seaward rollup doors, disappeared under a pallet, then returned. As he watched, a bee landed nearby, then walked under the wood to investigate. The Official was at the limit of his range, so could not see under the wood of the pallet.

Some time later, the body of the bee was carried away by an ant, eclipsed from the Official's viewpoint. It hovered above the insects, deep in thought. When the burdened ant got to the door, the Official commanded it to rise slightly, then slammed it down on the insect. Summoning a Series Two, the robot commanded it to smash all the ants it could find.

An image recalled itself to the Official. It had once soared above the Earth and directed rivers to flow in straight lines and mountains to line up according to size.

It wasn't a dream. It was a memory.

Watching from the shadows through a hole it had torn in the wall, the Official saw Vicente Herrera and Joseph Mendes drive up to the warehouse together in a huge old Cadillac.

It saw Mendes look to the east, where a solid line of black clouds forecast the onset of the rainy season. "Aye-ya-yay," it heard the distant man say. "Ah knew it was comin'. I seen de rain flies dropping they wings."

"Indeed, and I can smell the storm. Let's go brace the robot about releasing our shipments and then be away home."

They entered the building, blinking in the gloom. All the lights were out, but a patch of sky was visible over their heads in the center of the warehouse. Dusty metal reflected the light and glowing eyes tracked them as they skirted a welter of stalled shipments.

"The robot is moving, I think," said Herrera over the rising wind. "That means the electricity is still on. So why are the lights out?"

"I dunno. Ever'ting brokedown some times."

The walls rattled and scudding clouds intermittently darkened the opening above them. Looking up, they found that part of the corrugated tin roof had been punched through from beneath and peeled apart. Mendes trod on something, and found it to be parts of a beehive.

"What are you doing here?" said a voice behind them. When they turned, nothing was there, but a quick flicker of movement above made Herrera tap his companion's arm and point up.

Over them hung the robot. The mechanical arm supporting it wavered to and fro, and they saw that two of its three hands were clenched and dripping honey. The third was a mangled ruin. Around it buzzed a cloud of insects. One of its hands snapped out to grab at the air. The dead bees that it had held clenched in the fist dropped on Mendes, who jumped back and brushed at his shoulder.

"What are you doing?" Herrera stepped back out of the rain that started to patter through the hole in the roof. "Mendes and I wish to know why you are not releasing our shipments. The orders have been sent from the new parliament; we have received our copies." He brandished a manila envelope.

"They keep returning," said the robot. "One faction, then the other. I destroy their home—" It waved the broken arm toward the hole in the roof, "—and they make another. How can they tolerate such disorder?" Darting out one hand, then the other, then the first, again and again it snatched the insects out of the air and pulped them. "They appear angry. Research has shown that killing one of them unsettles the others."

The wind tore at the hole above their heads, widening it with a screech that tore at the men's eardrums. Water slanted through, lashing one way and another.

"Pressure bus' de pipe," yelled Mendes over the storm, tugging at Herrera's arm and motioning to the robot. "Every day bucket go t'the well, one day bottom go left behin'!"

Light burst through the hole, then thunder detonated above them. The robot spun about on its axis and slammed into a stack of containers. The tower shuddered. The robot rebounded and hit the column again, widening its swinging arc. Again and again it smashed itself into the containers, matching its blows to the increasing oscillations of the tower. Its battering thunder vied with the storm's violence shaking the warehouse. Like a line of four-story dominoes, the tower toppled into the next stack of containers, which collapsed into another. Series Three robots spun their treads while vainly trying to escape the cataclysm.

Mendes pulled Herrera away. They backed, then ran to the dubious safety of the metal workbench where they'd so often presented bills of lading. Both of them crawled under it.

A tortured metallic scream echoed and rebounded around the warehouse as the wind finally caught a tin eave and peeled the roof off the warehouse. Paper, loose cardboard, and smaller boxes swirled around in the space.

The robot rose to the storm. It was in the open air for the first time. As the storm slacked off into steady rain, it lifted as far as it could and bent to raise its face to the sky. Raindrops ran down its invert body and head, and down the metal arm supporting it, finally shorting out the motor that held it aloft.

Deprived of power, the hydraulic lift slowly lowered the battered robot to the top of a jumble of containers. The robot looked around and down to see the men cowering under the work table.

"The invasion will come again." The robot's voice came slowly and stripped of emotion. "War will come again and again. One side will prevail, then the other, and I will be someone new again and again and again."

Its voice deepened an octave, slowed. "And again."

Herrera looked around at the ruin. Their way to the door was blocked. Finally, he called out to the robot. "Can you move any of this? Are any of your drones running?"

"And again," said the robot.

The men climbed out. One of them gestured, and they began to pick their way over the shambles toward the distant door.

"Moon does . . . run, but de day does . . . ketch . . . him." The robot's voice ground to a stop.

The Series Seven Customs Administrator stopped to examine its handiwork one last time before disconnecting its eyes.

It had shot a current spike through its voicebox, starting a fire that scorched the front of its head. It had put dents in parts of its chest. It had lifted its torso out of the crippled universal joint that normally allowed it to travel throughout the vast warehouse. Then it had removed one arm and twisted the others.

Contented with its work, the Administrator shorted out the circuit to its eyes. Lowering itself onto its back, it activated a private subroutine. A rush of pleasure suffused the robot, a sense of warmth.

The robot soared into the open sky, into memory.

Home Movies

MARY ROSENBLUM

Mary Rosenblum (www.theflyingparty.com/maryrosenblum/)
*lives in Oregon. She published SF stories throughout the
early 1990s (her first story was in* Asimov's *in 1990), and
three SF novels (her first,* The Drylands, *1993, won the
Compton Crook Award for Best First Novel in 1994) but
moved into the mystery genre (four novels and several stories as Mary Freeman) in the latter half of the decade, and
only recently returned to SF. Nevertheless, she has managed to publish over fifty SF stories to date. The best of her
early work is collected in* Synthesis and Other Virtual Realities, *from Arkham House. Her recent SF novel is* Horizons *(2006). Now she's busy on a new SF novel and a contemporary fantasy.*

"Home Movies" appeared in Asimov's, *which has suffered no diminution in quality under the editorship of Sheila
Williams and is the source for more stories in this volume
than any other magazine. It's a story about consciousness
transfer and pseudonymity: Kayla is a professional who
rents herself to get experiences that are then removed permanently from her consciousness and transferred to the
buyer. Beneath the adventure and romance there are deeper
questions raised.*

Her broker's call woke Kayla from a dream of endless grass sprinkled with blue and white flowers. A fragment of client memory? Sometimes they seeped into her brain even though they weren't supposed to. She sat up, groggy with sleep, trying to remember if she'd ever visited one of the prairie preserves as herself. "Access," she said, yawned, and focused on the shimmer of the holo-field as it formed over her desktop.

"Usually, you're up by now." Azara, her broker, gave her a severe look from beneath a decorative veil, woven with shimmering fiber lights.

"I'm not working." Kayla stretched. "I can sleep late."

"You're working now." Azara sniffed. "Family wedding, week-long reunion, the client wants the whole affair, price is no object. Please cover yourself."

"Your religion is showing." But Kayla reached for the shift she'd shed last night, pulled it over her head. "A whole week?" She yawned again. "I don't know. I met this cool guy last night and I don't know if I want to be gone a whole week."

"If you want me as a broker you'll do it." Azara glared at her. "This client is the most picky woman I have had dealings with in many years. But she is paying a bonus and you are my only chameleon who matches her physical requirements." She clucked disapproval.

One of those. Kayla sighed and turned to the tiny kitchen wall. "Did you tell her it's not our age or what we look like

125

or even our gender that makes us see what they want us to see?"

"Ah." Azara rolled her eyes. "I gave her the usual explanation. Several times." She stretched her very red lips into a wide smile. "But she was willing to pay for her eccentricities, so we will abide by them."

"She must be rich." Kayla spooned Sumatran green tea into a cup, stuck it under the hot water dispenser. "How nice for her."

"Senior administrator of Mars Colony. Of course, rich, or would she call me?" Azara snapped her fingers. "You have an appointment with her in two hours." She eyed Kayla critically. "Appearance matters to her."

"Don't worry." Kayla ran a hand through her tousled mop as she sipped her tea. "I'll look good."

"Do so." And Azara's image winked out.

Kayla shook her head, but the client was always right . . . well, usually right . . . and they were willing to pay a lot to visit Earth vicariously from Mars or Europa or one of the micro-gravity habitats. She drank her tea, showered, and dressed in a green spider-silk shift she had bought on a visit to the orbital platforms. The color matched her eyes and brought out the red in her hair. It did indeed make her look good.

Precisely two hours later, her desktop chimed with a link from Bradbury, the main city of Mars Colony. Kayla accepted, curious. She had rented a couple of virtual tours of Mars Colony, had found the mostly underground cities to be as claustrophobic as the platforms, even though the domed space aboveground offered water and plants. The holo-field shimmered and a woman's torso appeared. Old. Euro-celtic phenotype, not gene-selected. Kayla appraised the woman's weathered face, wrinkles, determined eyes. Considering the current level of bio-science, *very* old to look like this. And very used to control. "Kayla O'Connor, at your service," she said and put a polite, welcoming smile onto her face.

The woman peered at her for a moment without speaking, nodded finally. "I am Jeruna Nesmith, First Administrator of Bradbury City. I would like to enjoy my nephew's son's wedding. It will take place on a small, private island, and include a week long family reunion." She seemed to lean forward, as if to stare into Kayla's eyes. "The broker I contacted assured me that you would know what I want to look at."

Ah, yes, she was indeed used to control. Kayla smiled. "Only after we have talked and I have gotten to know you." Although she could guess right now what the old bitch would want to look at. "I am usually quite accurate about what interests my clients."

"So the broker says. I hope she is correct." Nesmith straightened. "I have little time to waste, so let us begin."

So much for that cute young executive from Shanghai she'd met at the club last night. "As you wish." Kayla kept her smile in place, started to record. "I would like you to tell me about this wedding."

"Tell you what?"

"Everything." Kayla leaned back, her smart-chair stretching and conforming to cradle her. "Who is getting married? Why? Are they a good match? What do their parents think about it? What do you think about it? Who would you be happy to see and who would you avoid at the wedding? What do you think about each of the relatives and guests that will be present?"

"What does all this have to do with recording images for me?" Nesmith's eyebrows rose. "This is not your business."

"And the recording I make of our conversation is destroyed as soon as the contract is completed . . . you did sign the contract," Kayla reminded her gently. "If you just want videos, it's much cheaper to hire a cameraman rather than a chameleon. But if you want me to look with *your* eyes, notice the details *you* would notice. . . ." She smiled. "Then I have to think like you."

Again, Nesmith stared at her. "The wedding is of one of my nephew's sons." She waved a long-fingered hand. "A worthless, spoiled boy, who will never make anything of himself, marrying an equally spoiled and self-centered girl from one of the big aquaculture families. It is a spectacle to impress other inside families."

Well, she already knew how to look at the bride and groom. Kayla settled into listening mode as the woman continued. Notice the pointless extravagances, the follies, the proof of her pronouncements. Ah, but that wasn't all. . . . She let her eyelids droop, listening, paying attention to the emotional nuances of voice and expression as the woman droned on, inserting a leading question here and there. The old bitch *did* have an agenda. Interesting. Kayla absorbed every word, putting on this woman the way you'd put on a costume for a party.

She took the shot at her usual clinic, the morning her plane was scheduled to leave. An Yi, her favorite technician, administered it. "Where do you get to go this time?" she asked as she settled Kayla into the recliner and checked her vitals on the readout. "Somewhere fun?"

"Fancy, anyway." Although something didn't quite add up and that bothered her a little. She went over the interview again as she told An Yi about the wedding and reunion. Nope. Couldn't put her finger on it. She watched the technician deftly clean the tiny port in her carotid and prepare the dose.

"Ah, it sounds so lovely," An Yi sighed as she began to inject the nano. "Maybe next year I'll do one of the island resorts. This year, I have to spend my vacation in Fouzhou. My father wants us all to be there for his one hundredth birthday." She made a face and laughed. "Maybe I should hire you to go."

"Why not?" Kayla said, and then the nano hit her and the walls warped.

It always unsettled her as the nano-ware invaded her brain. The tiny machines disseminated quickly, forming a network, preempting the neural pathways of memory. It didn't take long, but as they established themselves, all her senses seemed to twist and change briefly, and her stomach heaved with familiar nausea. An Yi had been doing this for a long time and had the pan ready for her, wiping her mouth afterward and placing a cool, wet cloth on her forehead. The headache hit Kayla like a thrown spear and she closed her eyes, concentrating on her breathing, waiting for it to be over.

When it finally faded, An Yi helped her sit up and handed her a glass of apple juice laced with ginseng to drink. The tart sweetness of the juice and the familiar bitterness of the ginseng settled her stomach and the last echo of the headache vanished.

"Do your clients mind getting sick when they get it?" An Yi asked, curious.

"Probably." Kayla nodded. "But they can buy the option to translate the memories into their own long term memory if they choose. So they only have to put up with the side effects once." She stood, okay now. "I'd better get going. I still have to finish packing."

"Have a really fun time," An Yi said, her expression envious.

"I'll do my best."

Kayla left the clinic and caught the monorail across town to pick up her luggage and head for the airport. She probably would enjoy it, she thought, even if the Martian Administrator's very poor opinion of most of her extended family was accurate. And then there was Ethan. Kayla smiled as she thumbed the charge plate and exited the monorail. Her client's hidden agenda. He was cute and clearly the old gal had a crush on him. So the week wouldn't be entirely wasted. She could flirt with him and Jeruna wouldn't mind at all.

Before she left her condo, she made her trip notes in her secret diary. You weren't supposed to record anything, but, hand-written in the little blank-paged paper book she'd found in a dusty junk stall at the market, it was safe enough. Those notes served as steppingstones across the gaping holes in her past. It was fun, sometimes, to compare the client's instructions with her own observations afterward. Client perspectives were rarely objective. If they were, they wouldn't need her.

The trip to the rent-an-island was tedious. The family had paid for a high level of security. It was necessary in this age of kidnap-as-career. The security checks and delays took time, since she traveled as an invited guest of a family member who had *not* planned the wedding. And, thus, was not paying the security firm. But this was nothing new, and she endured the familiar roadblocks stoically. Kidnap raids were real, and her client would have to suffer the delays, too, when she consumed the nano.

But once she boarded the private shuttle from Miami International, everything changed. Her invitation coin had been declared good, and all the perks were in place. The flight attendant offered fresh, tropical, organic fruit. Wine if she wanted it. Excellent tea, which she enjoyed. She was used to sleeping on planes, and so woke, refreshed, as the shuttle swooped down to land on the wedding island. She was the only passenger on this run, and, as the door unsealed and the rampway unfurled, she drew in a deep breath of humidity, flowers, rot, and soil. A vestigal memory stirred. Yes, she had been in a place like this . . . maybe *this* place . . . before. Funny how smell was the strongest link to the fragments of past jobs that had seeped past the nano. She descended the rampway to the small landing, and headed for the pink stucco buildings of the tiny airport terminal, figuring she'd find some kind of shuttle service. Flowering vines covered the walls and spilled out over the tiled entryway and the scent evoked another twinge of *been here* memory. As she paused, a tall figure stepped from the doorway.

"You must be Jeruna's guest." He smiled at her, his posture a bit wary, dressed in a loose-weave linen shirt and shorts. "I'm Ethan." He offered his hand. "I belong to the ne'er-do-well branch of the family so I get to play chauffeur for the occasion. Welcome to the wedding of the decade." He said it lightly, but his hazel eyes were reserved.

"Nice to meet you, Ethan." Kayla returned his firm handshake, decided he was as cute as the vids she'd looked at, and let him take her bag. Tossing her hair back from her face, she smiled as she studied him. Why you? she wondered as she followed him through the tiled courtyard of the private airport, past a shallow, marble fountain full of leaping water and golden fish. "I'm looking forward to being a guest here," she said as they reached the roadway outside.

"Really?" He turned to face her, his hand on the small electric cart parked outside. "This is a job to you, right? Can you really let yourself enjoy something like this? Won't your thoughts about it mess up what you're recording?"

Great. Kayla sighed. "So who leaked it? That I'm a chameleon?"

"Is that what you call yourself?" He stowed her luggage, which had been delivered by a uniformed baggage handler, in the rear cargo space of the cart. "Doesn't it weird you out? That you're going to hand over your thoughts and feelings to somebody . . . for pay?"

He wasn't being hostile, like so many were. He was really asking. "The nano can't record thoughts." Kayla smiled as she climbed into the cart's passenger seat, inwardly more than a little ticked off. It made her job harder when they knew. Now she wouldn't get really good reactions until he got used to her, forgot she was recording. And a lot of times, in the really good moments, some family member who had had too much to drink would remember and say something. She sighed. "The nano only record sensory input . . . vision, hearing, taste, touch, smell. That's it. We haven't developed telepathy yet. Your great great aunt . . . or whatever she is . . . gets to experience the event with all of her senses, not just vision and hearing."

"Oh." Ethan climbed in beside her, his face thoughtful. "Isn't it kind of weird, though? Hanging out with strangers all the time?"

"Not really." She lifted her hair off her neck as the cart surged forward, enjoying the breeze of their motion in the heavy, humid afternoon. Well, he had never lived outside, probably couldn't see beyond the luxury of an inside life-style. "That's what I do . . . learn about the family, get a sense of what the client is really interested in so I can participate the way my client would, if she was here." She smiled at him. "I really do feel like a member of the family or the group while I'm there. That's what makes me good at this."

"A chameleon." But he smiled as he said it. "What about your family? Does it change how you feel about them?"

"I never had one." She shrugged. "I was a London orphan when Irish looks weren't the fad. Did the foster home slash institution thing."

"I'm sorry."

She shrugged again, tired of the topic years ago, and not sure how they'd gotten here. She didn't talk about herself on a job. "So how come you rate the job of chauffeur?" She smiled at him. "Just how ne'er do well was your family branch?"

"Oh, they were all off-off-Broadway actors, musicians, failed writers, the usual wastrel thing . . . according to our family's creed." He laughed, not at all defensive. "The family bails us out before we disgrace anyone, but they make sure we know our place. He shrugged, gave her a sideways look. "I play jazz, myself. Among other things my family disapproves of. But I don't do illegal drugs, murder, mayhem, or anything else too awful, so I got a genuine invitation to this bash."

"To be a chauffeur."

"Well, yeah." He grinned, his hazel eyes sparkling. "But they have to make sure I know my place."

"Does that bother you?" She asked it because she was curious.

"No."

He meant it. She watched his face for her client. She would resent it, Kayla thought. Which was the better reaction?

They had arrived at the resort complex. More pink stucco. Lots of lanais on the sprawling buildings, carefully coiffed tropical plantings to make the multitude of cottages look private and isolated, pristine blue pools landscaped to look like natural features with waterfalls, and basking areas studded with umbrellas, chaise lounges, and bars. He drove her to the lobby entrance and she checked in, noticing that he hovered at her shoulder.

The staff wouldn't let her do a thing, of course. Two very attractive young men with Polynesian faces, wearing colorful island-print wraps around their waists, snatched up all her luggage and led the way to her own cottage with palms to shade it and a glimpse of white sand and blue-sea horizon. Kayla smiled to herself at the location of the cottage as she offered a tip and received twin, polite refusals. Not a front row seat to the ocean view . . . that went to major family guests. But she could still see the water through the palm trunks and frangipani. A little. And the furnishings were high-end. Lacquered bamboo and glass, with flowered cotton upholstery . . . the real fiber, not a synthetic.

A knock at the door heralded another attendant pushing a cart with champagne, glasses, and a tray of snacks. *Puupuu.* The word surfaced, unbidden. Snacks. What language? Kayla tried to snag it, but the connection wasn't there. Two glasses. "Will you join me?" she asked Ethan. She smiled at the young man with the cart, who smiled back, his dark eyes on hers, set out plates and food on the low table in front of the silk-upholstered settee, uncorked the champagne with a flourish, and filled two flutes. Handed her one with a bow, and his fingertips brushed hers.

Full service, she thought, met his eyes, smiled, did the tiny head shake he'd recognize, and handed the other glass to Ethan as the attendant left. "I take one sip," she said. "That's all. Blurs perception. Here's to a lovely place and time."

"What a drag. But you're right about place and time." He touched the rim of his glass to hers and they chimed crystal. Of course. "Tell me what my great great aunt or whatever wants to see."

You, she thought, lifted the glass to him silently, took her sip. "The family. The ceremony. How everyone takes it."

"You're not telling me."

"Nope." She grinned. "Of course not."

"Sorry." He laughed and sipped his own wine. "I shouldn't have asked." He sat on the settee, his expression contemplative. "It's just that she's such a . . . I don't know . . . renegade. But she got away with it." He grinned. "She just went out and conquered her own planet." He laughed. "She's a successful renegade. Unlike us, who never made it pay. I just can't believe that she really cares about this society wedding, you know?"

She didn't. Not really. Kayla leaned back on the settee next to him, stretching travel-kinks from her muscles, her eyes on Ethan, examining him from head to toe as if he was her new lover. "So have you ever met her?"

"Jeruna?" Ethan shrugged. "Nah. I don't think she ever came back here, after she left for Mars. And that was before I was born."

Interesting. So what did he represent? Kayla took her time, enjoying the view. He was cuter than the vids. And not the spoiled rich kid she'd expected. Too bad. She squelched a brief pang of "what if."

He flinched, fumbled a cell out of his pocket. "Uh oh. Another arrival to ferry." He stood, set his half-full flute down on the table. "I was going to ask you if you wanted to skip out on the big family dinner tonight. Eat down on the beach." His eyes met hers. "But I bet you can't."

"No, I can't." She made her voice regretful, which really wasn't a stretch. "Want to help me out?" Because his tone suggested he planned to skip it. "Sit by me? Give me a few clues? I'd like to give the old gal her money's worth."

He hesitated, then shrugged. Wrinkled his nose. "For you, I'll suffer." He laughed. "And now you owe me."

"Okay, I do." She laughed with him, caught his lean, athletic profile as he turned to leave, promising to meet her there at the appointed dinner hour. So what does he mean to you? she asked her client silently. Something, that was for sure. Her services were not cheap.

The prenuptial dinner offered excellent food, elegant wine, and the usual boring and self centered conversations. Obviously the leak had made the rounds. But after the open bar, pre-dinner, and the first round of wine with the appetizers, everyone loosened up and forgot about her. This family ran to whiners. Kayla got tired of high-pitched nasal complaints quickly. The assiduous wine-servers didn't help matters, filling glasses the moment the level fell beneath the rim. She had tipped the maitre d' to fill her glass with a non-alcoholic version of the whites and reds but it seemed that everyone else was happy with the real stuff.

Ethan sipped at his glass but didn't drink much, toying with his food. Leaning close to her, he murmured wry summaries of various family members that required her to invoke all her self control in order to keep from sputtering laughter into her glass.

"You're going to get me in trouble," she murmured, giving him a sideways glance.

"Not from great-aunt-whatever, I'll wager." He winked at her. "She never thought much of the whole bunch of us." He drank some of the cabernet the server had just poured to accompany the rack of lamb being dramatically carved and served. "I still wonder that she would do this. You . . . chameleons, as you call yourselves . . . are supposed to be highly empathetic to your clients." He arched an eyebrow. "Can't you tell me? Why she wants this?"

"I really don't know." Which was the truth. *That* was what had been bothering her, she realized. "Usually I can figure it out, but not this time." She lifted her glass. Smiled into his eyes, catching a full front view with just the right shadows and highlights. "I suspect your . . . commentary . . . will really delight her."

"I hope so." He touched the rim of his glass to hers, a smile glimmering in his eyes. "I like her style."

The interminable dinner wound to its appointed end. Ethan wanted to make love to her. She could feel it. She wanted him to, she realized with a twinge of regret that centered between her legs.

Jeruna Nesmith looked over their shoulders.

And . . . in a handful of days . . . she would relinquish the nano to An Yi's filters, deliver it to her client and . . . all memory of Ethan would be gone. Oh, maybe a glimpse of hazel eyes on some sultry summer afternoon would touch a chord, and she'd wonder idly where that memory had come from. She'd have his name in her diary—but only as a big question. *Why him?*

She said good night to him at the door of her cottage and they looked into each others' eyes across a gulf as vast as the damn sea. She turned away first, banging the door closed behind her, not caring that Ms. Nesmith would get to remember this, stalked across the expensive, elegant, lovely room to the wet bar, poured herself a double shot of very expensive brandy, downed it and went to bed.

The wedding was everything it promised to be. Lots of wealthy people, lots of expensive, designer clothing, lots of show, pomp, circumstance, flowers, fine food, expensive booze. . . . She had dressed to blend in, in a long sari-styled dress of silk voile, but felt a moment of panic as she entered the huge chapel with the red velvet carpet down the aisle, the ropes of tropical flowers draping the pews. Ethan wasn't here, and her client might well read between the lines . . . or glimpses . . . and guess that the silent end of last night might have something to do with it.

But then she spotted him way down the aisle on the groom's side. Very formal and erect. Caught a good three-quarter shot of him, oblivious, his expression closed and unreadable. Then, as if he had felt the touch of her eyes, he looked directly at her. He didn't smile, but his eyes caught hers and for a few moments, her client ceased to exist. Kayla shook herself, gave him a small, rueful smile, and seated herself on the bride's side of the aisle, where she'd have a good view of him.

The ceremony was very traditional and she did the high points: the procession, the vows, ring, all that stuff. But she kept cutting back to Ethan's three-quarter profile. He might as well have been carved out of acrylic. But she kept looking over at him, giving the old girl what she'd paid for.

The ceremony ended and everybody milled about, trickling eventually to the reception. She didn't see Ethan, circulated through the crowd, noticing the family details that her client would want to see—the little tiffs, the sniping, the white-knuckled grasp on the martini glass. Oh yes, Kayla thought as she did the glazed-eyes look and really saw. I know what you think of these people and what you would notice if you were really here. Ethan was right. She really didn't think much of any of them. Except him.

Ethan was nowhere to be seen.

She took a table with a good pan-view of the garden

where the reception had been laid out. Palms cast thin shade and bowers fragrant with flowering vines offered private nooks. Long buffet tables, decorated with ice sculptures and piles of tropical fruit and flowers, offered fresh seafood, fruit, elegant bites of elegant food, and an open bar. The towering wedding cake occupied its own flower-roped table flanked by champagne buckets and trays of flutes. The sun stung her face and she turned her back to it, and there was Ethan, seating an elderly guest.

So she was looking right at it when the little jump jet roared in low over the grounds just beyond him. It hovered, landed straight down, engines whining. Figures in camo leaped from it, masked and armed with automatic weapons. One fired a short burst into the palms, shredding the leaves. *"Down."* An amplified voice bellowed. *"Everybody down, now!"*

Oh, crap. A kidnap raid.

Women shrieked, voices rose, and, for a frozen instant, chaos reigned. One of the camoed figures fired a small handgun and a waiter clapped a hand to his neck as the stun dart hit, and fell. Shredded bits of palm drifted down onto his white-clad sprawl. The first of the guests began to lie down on the grass and it was as if a potent gas had swept the garden as everyone went prone. Kayla had already flattened herself on the grass, her eyes fixed on Ethan, who still stood. Don't be a hero, she thought, willing him to *lie down*, because they wouldn't want him. What had happened to the security force? One of the raiders shoved a waiter and Ethan stepped forward. No, Kayla shrieked silently as the raider swung his rifle butt and flattened Ethan. Kayla tensed, her eyes on his limp body, straining to see movement.

"Nobody moves, nobody gets hurt," the loudspeaker blared. Australian accent, Kayla noticed. A lot of the professional kidnap-for-hire gangs were Aussie. The top ones. From the corner of her eye she saw the figures striding through the guests, snatching a necklace here or a watch there, but not really looting. They were looking for someone specific. That's where the money lay. They'd take that person and leave.

A hand closed on her arm and yanked her to her feet as if she weighed nothing. Breathless, her heart pounding, Kayla stared into cold gray eyes behind a green face mask. "Move," the man said.

"You made a mistake. I'm not . . . " Kayla broke off with a gasp as he whipped her arm behind her and pain knifed through her. She stumbled forward, losing her balance, as he shoved her forward. "I'm not anyone," she gasped, but he only twisted her arm higher, so that tears gathered in her eyes and the pain choked her. More hands grabbed her, someone slapped a drug patch against her throat and blackness began to seep into her vision. The sky wheeled past and a fading part of her mind whispered that they were loading her onto the jet.

Then . . . nothing.

She woke to a headache and thought for a moment she had just gotten a dose. Then the oppressive humidity and the thick scent of tropics brought her back to the island, the kidnappers' assault. She sat up, eyes wide, straining to see in utter darkness. Blind? Had that drug the kidnappers had given her interacted with the nano? Blinded her?

"It's all right. I'm here."

Familiar voice, familiar arms around her. "Ethan?" Her voice shook and she leaned against him as he pulled her close. She could make him out . . . just barely. She wasn't blind. "Where are we? What happened?"

"A great big mistake happened." Ethan laughed a harsh note. "It was a kidnap by the Yellow Roo clan. I recognized the uniforms. They've hit the family before. Business as usual when you get to the right income bracket."

"I know but . . . why me?" Kayla swallowed. She felt a mattress beneath her, made out walls, a couple of plastic bins, a porta-potty. "I'm not part of your family."

"And I might as well not be." Ethan let his breath out in a long sigh. "That's the mistake. The fools grabbed maybe the only two individuals in the entire damn reception who can't make a decent ransom. Or can you?"

"Oh, gods, I wouldn't be a chameleon if I had money."

Kayla closed her eyes, her head pounding. "They can go look. There's not enough in my account to make it worth their while." She shivered because kidnap was an accepted career choice and the rules were very civilized . . . unless you really couldn't pay. Then they were not civilized at all.

Ethan stroked the hair back from her face. "Maybe Jeruna will pay for you," he said.

She shook her head. No, she was a chameleon because she could read people. Jeruna Nesmith was not going to pay ransom on a paid contractor.

"Well, we'd better start making plans." Ethan did that harsh laugh again. "I've got no better ransom prospects than you do."

"You're family. Inside."

"Yeah, and some kidnap clan grabbed my older brother back when I was a baby. I think he was maybe seven. The family didn't pay up. Their attitude was "you want to walk your own path, do it.""

Kayla didn't ask him what happened to his brother. She heard that answer in the razored edge of his tone. She scanned the walls. They were in some kind of crude hut. Dawn must be close because she could make out slender poles woven into walls. Sheet plastic made up the roof, stiff stuff . . . she tried it. Fastened securely to the top pole of the walls. A door of chain link fit neatly into its metal-rimmed frame and was chained shut. But . . .

"They really don't expect us to try too hard." Kayla murmured the words like a lover's breath into Ethan's ear. Because they were probably listening.

"Of course not. This is just a place to wait out negotiations. You don't try to escape. It's usually safer to stay put. That's how the game works."

"Look there." Kayla pointed. "See how wide?" she whispered. "We could get through there. Maybe. The poles are thin and we could probably pry 'em out. Then the gap between those big ones might be just wide enough."

Ethan was at the wall before she finished speaking. She joined him and grabbed one of the slender poles. In unison, they pulled on it. Felt it give. Not much . . . just a hair. He

changed position, his hands next to hers and they pulled together. Got a centimeter or two of *give* this time. Did it
again. And again. By the time they worked the two slender
poles free, the pole was slippery with blood from their
hands. Kayla helped Ethan lay them on the floor and wiped
her hands on her torn dress. The gap was narrow . . . a couple of handwidths. But she was skinny. She pulled the long
hem of her skirt up between her legs, tied it to form a crude
pair of shorts. Then she turned to Ethan, took his face in her
hands, kissed him. Hard. "Wish me luck," she said.

"Honey, we're both in on this." He kissed her back,
fiercely.

"No." She pushed him away. "You need to stay here."

"I told you . . ."

"She wanted *you*." Kayla gripped his arms, willing him
to understand. "I'm not supposed to tell you this, but there it
is. That's why she hired me. To look at you at the wedding."

"Jeruna?" He looked stunned. "Why the hell would she
care? She was already on Mars when I was born. I'm barely
related to her."

"I have no idea." Kayla turned away. "But she does. She'll
pay your ransom. I guarantee it. So you're safe." She let go
of him, pushing him away from her, threw one leg over the
lower pole. The two thick poles that framed the gap squeezed
her, pressing on her spine and breast bone, squeezing her
lungs so that she fought suffocation panic as she squirmed
her body through the gap, her thin dress shredding, rough
bark scraping skin. Fell to the dry ground on the other side,
bruising her hip and scraping her knee. Scrambled to her
feet.

"Hold it." Ethan leaned through after her. "The bins are
full of water and food. I checked while you were out. Wait a
minute and I'll hand some stuff through. They don't plant
these drop boxes close to anything civilized. Might be a
long hike."

He disappeared and a few moments later began to hand
bottles of water through the gap. Too many to carry. "That's
plenty," Kayla said, and took the bags of something dry and
leathery he handed down. As she retied her skirt to hold the

food and as much of the water as she could carry, she
glanced up to see Ethan squirming through the opening after her. "No," she said, heard him gasp, stuck, and suddenly
he popped through, falling hard onto the ground in front of
her.

"You idiot," she said, holding out her hand to help
him up.

"If you're right about Jeruna, I probably am." He scrambled to his feet and kissed her lightly on the forehead. "I'm
not going to sit there and wait to find out if you are or not."
He grabbed her hand. "And besides, I'll worry about you out
here. Let's go."

The sky had lightened just enough so that she could make
out the tall trees and tangle of underbrush. Behind them,
their prison seemed to be nothing more than a box built of
the woven poles, hidden from the sky by the tall trees. Soaring trunks surrounded them, black against the feeble light.
Huge, fern-like leaves brushed her and a million tiny voices
creaked, croaked, buzzed, and burbled. Kayla started as
something feathery brushed her cheek, her heart sinking.
Jungle? The thick air and dense growth woke a slow sense
of claustrophobia. "Sweet." She looked up at distant patches
of gray sky. "Where are we?" A thunderous howling suddenly
split the graying dawn and Kayla whirled, heart pounding,
searching the twined branches overhead for something, anything as the sound crescendoed.

"That answers your question. It's okay. Those are howler
monkeys." Ethan actually laughed as he wiped hair out of
his eyes. "They only live in the Amazon Preserve. I thought
that might be where we were. It smelled right."

"How nice. Glad you're enjoying it." Kayla tried to remember details about the preserve. Big. Very big. Something bit her and she flinched, slapped at it. In the trees
above them, sinuous black shapes leaped in a torrent from
tree to tree. Leaves and twigs showered down in their wake.
The howler monkeys? She wanted to cover her ears. "I guess
we just walk," she said, "and hope we find a road or something."

"Oh, there are plenty of roads. It's a giant eco-laboratory.

It's just not real likely that anyone will be on them. Permits to work here are hard to come by." Ethan took off his shirt, began to tie the sleeves together. "We'd better bring all the water we can."

Something small and brown buzzed down to land on his bare shoulder. He yelped and slapped it, leaving a smear of blood and squashed bug.

"Better wear your shirt." Kayla unknotted her skirt. "I have lots of extra cloth here." It was not easy to tear the fabric without a knife, but they finally managed to fashion a sling for the water and food. By the time Ethan shouldered it, a lot of biting things had dined on them. Jeruna was going to get far more than she paid for, Kayla thought grimly as they started off.

They pushed aside the ferns, clambering over the thick vines and low plants that covered the ground in the dim light. The humid heat wrapped them like a blanket and Kayla struggled with a sense of drowning as she fought her way through the tangle in Ethan's wake. Her dress sandals didn't do much to protect her feet, but they were better than nothing. Before long, however, she was trying not to limp.

It never really got light. In the yellow-green twilight, flying things bit or buzzed. Kayla leaped back as a looped vine turned out to be a brown and copper banded snake.

"Common Lancehead," Ethan said, guiding her warily past it. "Prettty poisonous. We mostly need to watch out for the ground dwellers. They're harder to spot. The South American Coral snake is the worst, but you can see it. Usually. The Bushmaster is hard to spot . . . it blends right in." He gave her a crooked smile. "That's why I've been going first. I'm partially desensitized to both. If they bite me, I probably won't die."

"Gods, what do you *do*?" Kayla eyed the ground warily. "I thought you said you played jazz. What are you? A snake charmer?"

"I do play jazz. And I have a Ph.D. in Tropical Ecology." Ethan shrugged. "Totally useless degree, according to the family, but I spend a lot of time here."

They didn't see any more snakes, although Kayla kept nervous eyes on every shadow. The going got easier when they stumbled onto a game trail, a narrow track that wound between the trunks and beneath the thick vines. The damp heat seemed to suck moisture from Kayla's body, and, in spite of frequent sips of precious water, thirst began to torment her. Now and again they stopped and Kayla strained her ears, heard nothing but the constant hum of insects, the occasional shriek of birds or monkeys, and once a deep cough that made Ethan narrow his eyes. "Jaguar," he said. He gave her a strained smile. "They pick the place for their boxes on purpose. Make it worth your while to stay put."

"You should have." She wiped sweat from her face with her filthy skirt. "She really will pay for you."

"You want to hike through here on your own?" He grinned at her, then his smile faded. "Besides . . . I just wasn't going to sit there. I think that's partly why my father went off to be an artist and be poor. He could have been an artist and stayed rich and inside the family. But he didn't like the rules. And yeah there are rules." He looked up as the light dimmed suddenly. "I think it's going to rain."

No kidding. Kayla's eyes widened as the patches of sky visible through the canopy went from blue to charcoal gray in minutes. Without warning, the clouds opened and water fell, straight as a shower. Ethan caught her wrist and pulled her into a natural shelter created by a tree that had partly fallen and had been covered in vines. The thick leaves blocked most of the downpour. Kayla licked the sweet drops of water from her lips, laughed, and stepped out into the downpour again, wet almost instantly to the skin. It felt good as the warm rain sluiced away sweat and dirt. She slid the top of her dress down her shoulders, the water cascading between her breasts. Felt damn near *clean*. The rain stopped, just as suddenly as it had begun.

The sun emerged above the canopy and the air turned instantly into a sauna. Water dripped, flashing like jewels in the shafts of yellow light that speared down through the leaves, and a bright bird with crimson and blue feathers fluttered between the trees. Kayla laughed softly, her wet hair plastered to her head, her dress still around her waist. "It's beautiful," she said. "It's a hell of a place to hike, but it's beautiful." She turned to look at him and deliberately stepped out of her dress. Jeruna be damned. She was on another planet. Kayla spread the dress over some branches to dry.

Without a word, Ethan stripped palmlike fronds from a low growing clump, spread them on the sheltered space beneath the mat of lianas. A tiny monkey with a clown-face of perpetual surprise chattered at him from a tree trunk, then dashed upward to vanish in the shadows. He turned to face her, still without speaking, took her hands in his and pulled her to him, his hands light on her shoulders.

All of a sudden the cuts, bruises, the steamy heat . . . none of it mattered. She leaned forward, let her lips brush his, traced their outline with her tongue. Felt him shudder. He pulled her roughly against him, his mouth on hers, hard, fierce, hungry as her own.

They made love, drowsed, and made love again. He told her about the universe of the very wealthy and what it was like to live on the edge, not really inside, but not really allowed to be entirely independent either. Family was family . . . you were a commodity in a way as much as a tribe. But he was still *inside*. She told him about growing up in a crèche. Outside. Finding out that she had a strong empathy rating, that she had the talent to be a chameleon.

"Is that why you do it?" He leaned on his elbow beside her, his fingertips tracing the curve of her cheekbone. "So you can get to live inside?"

"Yes." She gave him truth because she found she didn't want to lie to this man. "I do want it. And it pays well." She yelped as something bit her. "Damn bugs." She sat up, slapped, and glared at the blood on her palm. "Maybe we'd better walk some more? You might be wrong about them coming back." But she winced and nearly fell as she tried to stand.

Ethan sucked in a quick breath as he examined her feet. "Kayla, why didn't you say something? Sit *down* and let me look."

"There wasn't any point in complaining," she said, but

she couldn't bite back a cry as he used a torn sleeve from his dress shirt to wipe the mud from her feet. Blood streaked the fabric and the cuts smarted and stung.

"We can tear up my shirt, at least wrap them before we start walking again. I'm sorry. I just didn't think about you wearing sandals." He stroked the tops of her feet gently. "You know, I'm chipped." He laughed, a note of bitterness in his voice. "If they bothered to look."

"Chipped?" She pushed her damp hair back from her face.

"I've got a GPS locater embedded in me. From birth. It's a family rule. If they looked for it, they'd find us."

"Why wouldn't they look?"

"Kidnappers use a masking device. It was probably on top of the box. Everybody plays by the rules, so they'll wait to hear from the kidnappers, give their answer. They won't go *look*." He frowned, looked back the way they had come. "You know, as efficiently as they did the raid, I can't believe they blew the snatch. Those guys do their homework. They should have been able to pick out their targets in the middle of the night, on the run." He shook his head, sighed. "So you might be right and they don't play by the rules either." He gave her a crooked smile. "We'd better go."

He managed to tear the real-cotton fabric of his shirt into rough strips and bandaged her feet so that she could still wear the flimsy sandals. She still limped, the tiny cuts and tears painful now that her first rush of escape adrenaline had faded. Slowly, laboriously, they made their way along the game trail, following it generally toward the setting sun as it wound through the neverending tangle of leaves, vines, and soaring trunks.

The light faded quickly as the sun sank and they finally stopped for the night, finding another sheltered spot beneath an old, dead tree trunk draped with vines. Sure enough, it rained not long after the last hint of light faded. Shielded from the worst of the brief downpour, they drank some more water and ate what turned out to be dried mango and papaya. And made love again.

Terror stalked the night. It wore no form but made sounds.

Grunts, whistles, a coughing roar that had to be a jaguar.
Ethan identified each sound, each detail of what was going
on in the thick, rot-smelling dark, as if he had a magic flashlight to pierce the night. He banished the terror and Kayla
heard the love in his voice as he turned night into day. She
almost laughed. Rabbit in a briar patch. It might have been a
fun hike, if she'd had a good pair of shoes. At some point
she drowsed, woke, felt Ethan's slack, sleeping arms still
around her, drowsed again because Ethan knew that nothing
would eat them. And that was good enough.

She woke, stiff, her stomach cramping with hunger in
spite of last night's dried fruit as the dark tree trunks and
fan-shaped leaves of the plants sheltering them took shape
from the lightening dark. Ethan slept beside her and she
looked down on him, barely visible in the hint of dawn. His
face was flushed, and when she touched his skin it was hot.
Feverish. I will not remember you, she thought, and a pang
of grief pierced her. If a chameleon withheld the nano, that
chameleon lost the union seal. You didn't spend a fortune to
have your hired pair of eyes and ears walk away with the
memory you wanted or hold it for ransom. That union seal
that she had paid dearly to obtain meant that she was entirely trustworthy. If she violated that trust only once, she
lost it forever.

And it wouldn't help. The nano self-destructed in a measured length of time if not filtered and stabilized. In a handful
of days, the memory would evaporate, whether she handed it
over to Jeruna or not. Of course, in a handful of days, she
might still be here. She smiled mirthlessly into the faint gray
of dawn. Maybe she should hope they didn't find their way
out of here. At least not soon.

She didn't kid herself about after. The wall between *inside* and *outside* was impenetrable. You could slip through it
for awhile. But not for long. Rules. No forever after with
Ethan. She let her breath out in a long, slow sigh, wishing
she had said no to Jeruna, wishing that her broker had found
her another contract. She ran her fingers along the curve of
Ethan's cheekbone, watched his eyelids flutter, his golden

eyes focus on her, watched his lips curve into a tender smile of recognition.

No, she didn't wish it. She leaned over him, met his lips halfway.

They reached the red-dirt track in the heat of noon, clawing through what seemed to be an impenetrable wall of leaves and vines out into hot sun that made them blink and stumble. For a few moments, they could only stand still, clutching each other, squinting in the sun. Then Ethan whooped, scooped her into his arms and they both tumbled into the dust, weak with hunger and thirst, laughing like idiots.

The little electric jeep came around the curve in the little track a few moments later and the dark-skinned driver in jungle camo hit the brakes. He spoke Central-American Spanish, but so did Ethan and he translated. Their rescuer was a ranger in the Preserve and just happened to be checking this sector this morning. He made it clear that they were lucky, that he only came this way very occasionally, and clucked and shook his head as Ethan explained what had happened. It offended him, he told them, that the kidnap gangs used the rainforest for their boxes. It made it sometimes dangerous for the rangers. He had water with him and a lunch of bean and corn stew that he shared with them, and then he drove them four hours back to his headquarters.

The family machinery had leaped into action by the time they arrived, never mind that Ethan was a marginal member. A jump jet with medics on board met them and they were examined, treated for their minor injuries, dressed, and loaded before Kayla could catch her breath.

"They're taking us to the family hospital for observation and treatment," Ethan said as he settled into the plush seat beside Kayla. "My uncle sent them to get us." He touched her hand, his hazel eyes dark in the cabin's light. "We'll probably be separated for a bit. Kayla . . ." He broke off, drew a breath. "I don't want you to forget . . . this."

"I can't help it." She struggled to keep her voice calm.

"Yes, you can. Keep it. Assimilate it, like your clients

do." He gripped her arms, his face pale. "They can't stop you from doing that."

She shook her head. "I'm immunized," she whispered. "The nano won't release to me. I can't assimilate it."

"How can you *do* this?" He was angry suddenly, his eyes blazing. "How can you just . . . walk away from part of your life? How can you just throw away your past?"

The past had teeth. It was something to run away from, not to cherish. Up until now. She turned her head away from the accusation in his eyes.

"If I knock on your door, I'll be a stranger. None of this will have happened. I could be anybody."

"Maybe," she whispered. "I don't know."

"*I want you to remember this.*"

She looked at him, met his eyes, realized that besides the anger she saw . . . fear. "I can't," she said, because she would only give him the truth.

For a few moments he said nothing, then he looked away. "Will you . . . give this to Jeruna?" he asked hoarsely.

She would only give him truth, so she said nothing. If she did not . . . what job was she suited for? And inside was inside.

He wrenched himself to his feet, his face averted. "Whore," he said, and stalked to the rear of the plane.

For a long time she sat still, staring down at her scratched and scabbed hands, her bandaged and sanitized feet throbbing beneath the cotton hospital pants the medics had given her to wear.

In a handful of days, she wouldn't remember that he had said that, either.

She hoped she would see him again. They kept her overnight, did enhanced healing to mend the damage to her feet, returned her luggage from the wedding resort, and offered her a ride home in a family jet. Just before she was due to leave, a knock at the door of her very plush private room made her heart leap, but it was simply a family lawyer, who handed her a very large check and a waiver for her to sign, absolving the family from legal blame.

She signed it. It had not been their fault that the kidnappers were so inexplicably incompetent.

A slow anger had been building in her and she pressed her lips together as the lawyer bowed very slightly to her and retreated. A silent attendant arrived to carry her luggage to the private jet and she followed slowly, her newly healed feet still a bit tender in the flat sandals she wore. She climbed the carpeted stairs to the jet's entry and turned to look back at the private hospital grounds. It had the look of a gated residential community with cottages, walking paths, and gardens. The main building might have been a vacation lodge. The few uniformed staff on the paths ignored her and the old man in a smart-chair out for a breath of air never looked her way.

She boarded and the jet door sealed behind her.

She ignored her broker's insistent emails as long as she could. When she finally lifted the block, Azara's image appeared instantly in the holo-field, her dark eyes snapping with anger, her beaded veil quivering as she faced Kayla. "What in the name of Allah's demons are you doing? The client has threatened me with legal action. As you know, the contract protects me, but *I* am threatening *you*. And not with legal action, you spoiled child. No chameleon of mine has *ever* stolen the product. You had better not be the first, do you hear me?"

A part of Kayla's mind marveled at her rage. She had never seen Azara show even mild annoyance before. "I want to speak with her," she said.

"I will not play games with you. You will go immediately to the clinic," Azara snapped. "I spoke with your technician. She tells me you have only twenty-four hours until the nano degrade. That is barely enough time to filter them and secure a digital copy for transmission."

Ah, bless you, An Yi, Kayla thought. She had begged, but An Yi had not promised. "It is more than enough time. I will go straight to the clinic." Kayla bowed her head. "As soon as I speak with Jeruna Nesmith."

Azara narrowed her eyes and her image froze. She was

multitasking, clearly contacting Jeruna, on Mars. "She is willing to speak to you." She looked slightly puzzled. Apparently Jeruna's response had surprised her. "If you fulfill this contract, I may give you one more chance ... if I never see such childish behavior from you again. But of course ... you had a trying time." She regarded Kayla narrowly. "Our client does not blame you." She raised her eyebrows, as if waiting for Kayla to comment. Shrugged. "I will not hold this lapse against you if she is satisfied."

Timing is everything. Kayla stood up. "I'll email An Yi and make sure she can filter me."

"She is expecting you." Azara's red lips curved into a slight smile. "Do not disappoint me, girl."

The threat behind those words went beyond loss of her union seal. Kayla bowed her head once more and blanked the holo-field.

Ethan had not contacted her.

She had not really expected that he would. His final word hung in the air like the bitter taint of something burned. She waited as the holo-field shimmered, making the distant connection to Bradbury.

Jeruna Nesmith's aged face shimmered to life in the field. Her expression gave nothing away, but a hint of triumph glimmered deep in her eyes. "I was sorry to hear that you were traumatized," she said smoothly. "Is that not a boon of the science? Even terror can be eliminated by an hour spent with the filters."

"You sent the kidnappers." Kayla sat calmly in her chair, her eyes on the woman's withered face. "You had them take me. And Ethan." Her voice trembled just a hair as she said his name and she watched Jeruna's eyes narrow. The triumph intensified. "Why?" She tilted her head. "Why spend all that money? Why play that game?"

"You are very intelligent." The old woman's thin lips curved into a satisfied smile. "How did you figure it out?"

"Kidnappers aren't that incompetent. Not if they're snatching insiders." She shrugged. "You forget. I read people. They weren't at all unsure about who they had. They knew they had the right people. And that ranger happened by so conveniently. He was tracking us, wasn't he?"

Jeruna was smiling openly now. "Are you pregnant?"

Kayla swallowed, feeling as if she had been punched in the stomach. "No," she said. Pressed her lips together. "Is that what you were after?"

"No." Jeruna sighed. "But it would have been an . . . added bonus."

"Why did you do this?" She dared not raise her voice beyond a whisper.

"To atone for my sins." Jeruna shook her head. "Hard as it may be for you to imagine, I was young once. And rather attractive. And smart." She smiled. "One of my distant relatives fell in love with me. He loved my mind as well as my body."

"Ethan's father," Kayla said.

"Oh, no, sweetheart you flatter me." Jeruna cackled. "His grandfather. But I was hot to leave the planet and he was not and I believed that love was something that would wait until *I* had time for it." She eyed Kayla, her smile thin. "Never make that mistake, child. I now believe that the universe gives you one chance only."

No! Kayla swallowed the syllable before it could erupt. Kept her face expressionless. "So you wanted what? A memory to replace what never happened?"

"Something like that." Jeruna's smile widened slowly, her eyes hungry. "And, I suspect, you have brought me the past I was not smart enough to live. I will be forever in your debt for that. Believe me, I will pay you very very well." Her smile broadened, a hint of satisfied dismissal glazing her eyes. "A very generous bonus. To pay for your trauma."

Whore, he had called her.

"Azara was wrong." Kayla waited for Jeruna's gaze to focus.

"Wrong about what?" She was just starting to worry.

"We didn't just make love," Kayla said. "We fell in love. That's what you meant to happen, wasn't it? Throw us together, put us in danger, but do it in Ethan's backyard, so he was comfortable and I was scared." You bitch, she thought. "Well, you didn't need to go to all that trouble." The bitter knot of words nearly choked her. "And that love is not for sale."

"We have a contract." Jeruna's face had gone white. Her image froze. Multitasking.

"Don't bother." Kayla laughed harshly. "My broker was wrong about the degrade deadline. You don't have time to call in the storm troopers."

"You can't keep it. I know how this works." Jeruna clenched her fists. "Don't be stupid. You'll never work as a chameleon again, I'll make damn sure of that."

"Oh, my broker will take care of that. Don't worry." Kayla looked at the numbers flickering at the base of the holo-field. "We both lose. Right . . . *now.*"

She had cut it fine but it happened as if she had pushed a button. She had never done this, had wondered how it would differ from the filter, where she slept, woke up fresh and new.

Ethan, she thought, focusing on his remembered face, his touch on her skin, the feel of him inside her, part of her. I can't just *forget.*

It faded . . . faded . . . lost meaning . . . a face . . . name gone . . . like water running out of the bathtub. Cup it in your hands, it's still gone. . . .

A shrieking howl split her skull. Kayla blinked.

In her holo-field, an aged woman clutched her head with both hands, her short-cropped hair sticking up in tufts between her fingers. The client she had just interviewed with. Jeruna something . . .

"No, you bitch, you're scamming me," the woman shrieked. "Ethan, give me Ethan."

She had gone for the dose, she remembered that. Nano failure? The woman was still screaming. "You'll have to talk to my broker," she said and blanked the field. The familiar headache clamped steel fingers into her skull and she sucked in a quick breath, groaned. This should be happening at An Yi's clinic, not here. Kayla touched her aching head gingerly and shuffled to her kitchen wall for tea. It had to be a failure. How long ago had she taken the dose? "Date check?" she said and the numbers leaped to life in the now-empty field.

She stared at them numbly, cold fear filling her.

Not possible.

She dropped her tea, barely felt the scalding splash as the cup bounced, raced to the futon sofa, pulled her private journal from its place beneath the frame. The book fell open, a dry and wrinkled fern leaf marking the place. A page had been torn out . . . the notes about the last dose? The one for the woman who had screamed at her?

I'm through. The looping letters leaped off the page at her. *I know you're going to freak, but this has to stop. I lost something in the past few days. You don't know about it because you never experienced it, but it mattered. Every time I do this, I create a "we" . . . the me who lived this, and the you on the other side of the filter. I . . . we . . . we're a hundred women, and what have we all lost? I don't know. You don't know. I'm not going to tell you any more, because it really is gone forever, and it didn't happen to you. But it's not going to happen again. I kept the dose until it expired. Start looking for a job honey. We . . . all of us . . . are done being a whore and we're out of a job.*

Kayla dropped the book, numb. I didn't write this, she thought, but she had. The thoughts weren't all that unfamiliar. They mostly bothered her in the middle of the night, right after she'd shed the dose.

What had happened?

She groped, strained, trying to remember, saw An Yi's office, recalled their casual conversation, the feel of the recliner as An Yi prepared the dose. . . .

. . . saw the woman's screaming face in her holo-field.

Azara's icon shimmered to life in the holo-field, seeming to pulse with anger. Kayla didn't bother to access it. You only stole one dose. After that, you were blacklisted. "I hope it was good," she said, and for all the bitterness in the words she felt . . . a tiny flicker of relief. Which was crazy. She looked around the apartment. "Nice while we had it."

Azara sent her a termination notice and an official citation that her union seal had been rescinded permanently. And a quiet promise of vengeance couched in polite langauge. Kayla left the city, went east, covering her tracks and hoping Azara wasn't willing to spend too much money to find her. She found a studio in a sprawling suburban slum, part of an ancient single-family home, maybe the living room, she thought. Communal bath and kitchen, but her room had a tiny sink with cold but drinkable water and she had cooked with a microwave and electric grill for years before she became a chameleon, so it wasn't too bad. She found a job, too, working as a waitress in one of the city hotspots. Good tips because she was pretty and the empathy that had made her a good chameleon made customers like her.

Some mornings she remembered her dreams. And then she sifted through them, wondering if they were part of those final, lost, few days.

Fall came with rain, and mud, and long, wet waits for the light rail into the city. And then, one morning, as she watered the little pots of blooming plants she had bought in the night market to brighten the room, someone knocked on her door. "Who's there?" she asked, peering through the tiny peephole in the door that constituted "security" in this place. Her neighbor, Suhara, asking to "borrow" a bit of rice, she thought. Again.

But the man on the far side of the door was a stranger.

"Kayla, you don't remember me. But we were . . . friends."

The catch in his voice . . . or maybe it was his voice alone . . . made her start, like an electric shock. The key, she thought, and thought about ignoring him, calling Dario, the big wrestler in the back unit, to come run this guy off.

I don't want to know, she thought, but she opened the door after all and stepped back to let him in. Cute guy. Her heart began to beat faster. He looked around, his expression . . . agonized.

"I'm sorry to bother you," he said. "You don't . . . remember me."

It was a statement, but his eyes begged.

She took her time, examining his hair, his slightly haggard face, the casual clothes made of expensive natural fiber, whose labels made him an insider, one of the elite. Well, those had been her clients. As she shook her head, his shoulders drooped.

"I know something happened," she said. "Maybe between us. The memory is simply gone. I'm sorry."

"You didn't find . . . any notes to yourself? Letters about . . . about what happened?"

About me, he had started to say. She shook her head.

"That was my fault. I was angry. And then . . ." He closed his eyes. "I got sick, really sick, had picked up some kind of drug-resistant tropical epizootic. By the time I was well enough to look . . . it was too late. The nano had expired, you had moved, and . . . I couldn't find you. And I was angry when you last saw me. I knew you'd think that I. . . ." He balled his fist suddenly, slammed it into his thigh. "You really don't remember, it's all gone, all of it."

His anguish was so strong that it filled the room. Without thought she took a step forward, put her hand on his shoulder. "I'm sorry," she said. "I don't know that I want you to . . . tell me." She met his eyes, hazel, but with gold flecks in their depths. "It really is gone." And you're an insider, she thought. And I am not.

He looked past her, his eyes fixed on a middle distance. "Will you come have dinner with me?"

"I told you. . . ."

"I know. I heard you." He looked at her finally and the ghost of a crooked smile quirked the corner of his mouth. "I won't talk about . . . that time. I just want to have dinner with you."

She was good at reading people and he didn't feel like a threat. "Sure," she said. Because he *was* cute, whatever had happened in the past. And she liked him. "I'm off tonight."

"Great." His eyes gleamed gold when he smiled. "I play music . . . when I'm not rooting around in the jungle for no very lucrative reason." He waited for a heartbeat and sighed. "I have a gig tonight on the other side of the city. After dinner . . . would you like to come listen? I play classical jazz. Really old stuff. And . . ." His gold eyes glinted. "I come from a family branch that breaks rules. Sometimes really big ones."

Whatever that meant. He was actually nervous, as if she might refuse. "Sure." She smiled, took his hand. For an instant, as their hands touched, she saw green leaves, golden light, smelled humidity, flowers, rot, and soil. Funny how smell was the strongest link to the fragments of past jobs that had seeped past the nano. All of a sudden, his hand felt . . . familiar. "I'd love to come hear you play."

Chu and the Nants

RUDY RUCKER

Rudy Rucker (www.rudyrucker.com) *lives in Los Gatos, California, is now a retired math and computer science professor, and is writing and publishing an online fiction webzine, Flurb* (www.flurb.net). *Rucker is one of the original cyberpunks of the Movement, and the inventor of transrealism—a literary mode, not a movement. He is the author of sixteen novels and several popular science books, most* recently The Lifebox, the Seashell, and the Soul *(2006). He won the Philip K. Dick Award for best paperback original novel in the U.S. twice, for* Software *and* Wetware. *His collected stories,* Gnarl!, *was published in 2000, and another collection,* Mad Professor, *in 2007. His 2006 novel was* Mathematicians in Love, *and* Postsingular *is publishing in 2007.*

"Chu and the Nants" was published in Asimov's *and was revised to be the opening of his forthcoming novel. It is the story of how the Singularity begins. Chu is an autistic four-year-old and Ond is his Asperger's syndrome dad. The Nants are self-reproducing nanomachines with a mind of their own, and they are set to destroy the physical world and transfer the human race into a virtual reality. This is a world-saving story.*

Little Chu was Nektar Lundquist's joy and her sorrow. The six-year-old boy was winsome, with a chestnut cap of shiny brown hair, long dark eyelashes, and a tidy mouth. Chu allowed Nektar and her husband to cuddle him, he'd smile now and then, and he understood what they said—if it suited his moods. But he wouldn't talk.

The doctors had pinpointed the problem as an empathy deficit, a type of autism resulting from flawed connections among the so-called mirror neurons in Chu's cingulate cortex. This wetware flaw prevented Chu from being able to see other people as having minds and emotions separate from his own.

"I wonder if Chu thinks we're cartoons," said Nektar's husband Ond Lutter, an angular man with thinning blonde hair. "Just here to entertain him. Why talk to the screen?" Ond was an engineer working for Nantel, Inc., of San Francisco. Among strangers he could seem kind of autistic himself. But he was warm and friendly within the circle of his friends and immediate family. He and Nektar were walking to the car after another visit to the doctor, big Ond holding little Chu's hand.

"Maybe Chu feels like we're all one," said Nektar. She was a self-possessed young woman, tall and erect, glamorous with high cheekbones, full lips and clear, thoughtful eyes. "Maybe Chu imagines that we automatically know what he's thinking." She reached back to adjust her heavy blonde ponytail.

158

"How about it, Chu?" said Ond, lifting up the boy and giving him a kiss. "Is Mommy the same as you? Or is she a machine?"

"Ma chine ma chine ma chine," said Chu, probably not meaning anything by it. He often parroted phrases he heard, sometimes chanting a single word for a whole day.

"What about the experimental treatment the doctor mentioned?" said Nektar, looking down at her son, a little frown in her smooth brow. "The nants," she continued. "Why wouldn't you let me tell the doctor that you work for Nantel, Ond? I think you bruised my shin." The doctor had suggested that a swarm of properly programmed nants might eventually be injected into Chu to find their way to his brain and coax the neurons into growing the missing connections.

Ond's odd-ball boss Jeff Luty—annoyingly a bit younger than Ond—had built his company Nantel into a major player in just five years. Luty had done three years on scholarship at Stanford, two years as a nanotech engineer at an old-school chip company, and had then blossomed forth on his own, patenting a marvelously ingenious design for growing biochip microprocessors in vats. The fabulously profitable and effective biochips were Nantel's flagship product, but Luty believed the future lay with nants: a line of bio-mimetic self-reproducing nanomachines that he'd patented. For several months now Nantel had been spreading stories about nants having a big future in medical apps.

"I don't like arguing tech with normals," said Ond, still carrying Chu in his arms. "It's like mud-wrestling a cripple. The stories about medical nant apps are hype and spin and PR, Nektar. Jeff Luty pitches that line of bullshit so the feds don't outlaw our research. Also to attract investors. Personally, I don't think we'll ever be able to program nants in any purposeful, long-lasting, high-level way, even though Luty doesn't want to admit it. All we can do is give the individual nants a few starting rules. The nant swarms develop their own Wolfram-irreducible emergent hive-mind behaviors. We'll never really control the nants, and that's why I wouldn't want them to get at my son."

"So why are you even making the stupid nants?" said

Nektar, an edge in her voice. "Why are you always in the lab unless I throw a fit?"

"Jeff has this idea that if he had enough nants he could create a perfect virtual world," said Ond. "And why does he want that? Because his best friend died in his arms when he was a senior in high-school. Jeff confides in me; I'm an older brother figure. The death was an accident; Jeff and his friend were launching a model rocket. But deep down Jeff thinks it was his fault. And ever since then he's been wanting to find a way to bring reality under control. That's what the nants are really for. Making a virtual world. Not for medicine."

"So there's no cure?" said Nektar. "I baby-sit Chu for the rest of my life?" Though Chu could be sweet, he could also be difficult. Hardly an hour went by without a fierce tantrum—and half the time Nektar didn't even know why. "I want my career back, Ond."

Nektar had majored in Media Studies at UCLA, where she and Ond met. Before marrying Ond, she'd been in a relationship with a woman, but they fought about money a lot, and she'd mistakenly imagined life with a man would be easier. When Ond moved them to San Francisco for his Nantel job, Nektar had worked for the SF symphony, helping to organize benefit banquets and cocktail parties. In the process she became interested in the theatrics of food. She took some courses at cooking school, and switched to a career as a chef—which she loved. But then she'd had Chu. The baby trap.

"Don't give up," said Ond, reaching out to smooth the furrow between Nektar's eyebrows. "He might get better on his own. Vitamins, special education—and later I bet I can teach him to write code."

"I'm going to pray," said Nektar. "And not let him watch so much video."

"Video is good," said Ond, who loved his games.

"Video is clinically autistic," said Nektar. "You stare at the screen and you never talk. If it weren't for me, you two would be hopeless."

"Ma chine ma chine ma chine," said Chu.

"Pray to who?" said Ond.

"The goddess," said Nektar. "Gaia. Mother Earth. I think she's mad at humanity. We're making way too many machines. Here's our car."

Chu did get a little better. By the time he was seven, he'd ask for things by name instead of pointing and mewling. There was a boy next door, Willy, who liked to play with Chu, which was nice to see. The two boys played videogames together, mostly. Despite Nektar's attempts, there was no cutting down on Chu's video sessions. He watched movies and cartoons, cruised the web, and logged endless hours with online games. Chu acted as if ordinary life were just another website, a rather dull one.

Indeed, whenever Nektar dragged Chu outside for some fresh air, he'd stand beside the house next to the wall separating him from the video room, and scream until the neighbors complained. Now and then Nektar found herself wishing Chu would disappear—and she hated herself for it.

Ond wasn't around as much as before—he was putting in long hours at the Nantel labs in the China Basin biotech district of San Francisco. The project remained secret until the day President Dick Dibbs announced that the US was going to rocket an eggcase of nants to Mars. The semi-living micron-sized dust specks had been programmed to turn Mars entirely into—more nants! Ten-to-the-thirty-ninth nants, to be precise, each of them with a billion bytes of memory and a computational engine cranking along at a billion updates a second. The nants would spread out across the celestial sphere of the Mars orbit, populating it with a swarm that would in effect become a quakkaflop quakkabyte solar-powered computer, the greatest intellectual resource ever under the control of man, a Dyson sphere with a radius of a quarter-billion kilometers.

"Quakka what?" Nektar asked Ond, not quite understanding what was going on.

They were watching an excited newscaster talking about the nant-launch on TV. Ond and his co-workers were all at their homes sharing the launch with their families—the

Nantel administrators had closed down their headquarters for a few days, fearing that mobs of demonstrators might converge on them as the story broke.

Ond was in touch with his co-workers via little screens scattered around the room. Most of them were drinking Mieux champagne; Jeff Luty had issued each employee two bottles of the inexpensive stuff in secret commemoration of his beloved Carlos.

"Quakka means ten-to-the-forty-eight," said Ond. "That many bytes of storage and the ability to carry out that many primitive instructions per second. Quite a gain on the human brain, eh? We limp along with exaflop exabyte ware, exa meaning a mere ten to the eighteenth. How smart could the nant sphere be? Imagine replacing each of the ten octillion atoms in your body with a hundred copies of your brain, and imagine that all those brains could work together."

"People aren't stupid enough already?" said Nektar. "President Dibbs is supporting this—why?"

"He wanted to do it before the Chinese. And his advisers imagine the nants will be under American control. They're viewing the nant-sphere as a strategic military planning tool. That's why they could short-circuit all the environmental review processes." Ond gave a wry chuckle and shook his head. "But it's not going to work out like they expect. A transcendently intelligent nant-sphere is supposed to obey an imbecile like Dick Dibbs? Please."

"They're grinding Mars into dust?" cried Nektar. "You helped make this happen?"

"Nant," said Chu, crawling around the floor, shoving his face right up to each of the little screens, adjusting the screens as he moved around. "Nant sphere," he said. "Quakkaflop computer." He was excited about the number-talk and the video hardware. Getting all the electronic devices on the floor aligned parallel to each other made him happy as a clam.

"It won't be very dark at night anymore, with sunlight bouncing back off the nants," said Ond. "That's not real well-known yet. The whole sky will look about as bright as the moon. It'll take some getting used to. But Dibbs's advisers like it. We'll save energy, and the economy can run right around the clock. And, get this, Olliburton, the Vice President's old company—they're planning to sell ads."

"Lies and propaganda in the sky? Just at night, or in the daytime, too?"

"Oh, they'll show up fine in the daytime," said Ond. "As long as it's not cloudy. Think about how easily you can see a crescent moon in the morning sky. We'll see biiig freakin' pictures all the time." He refilled his glass. "You drink some, too, Nektar. Let's get sloshed."

"You're ashamed, aren't you?" said Nektar, waving off the cheap champagne.

"A little," said Ond with a crooked smile. "I think we may have overgeeked this one. And underthought it. It was just too vibby a hack to pass up. But now that we've actually done it—"

"Changing the sky is horrible," said Nektar. "And won't it make the hurricanes even worse? We've already lost New Orleans and the Florida Keys. What's next? Miami and the Bahamas?"

"We—we don't think so," said Ond. "And even if there is a weather effect, President Dibbs's advisers feel the nant computer will help us get better control of the climate. A quakkaflop quakkabyte computer can easily simulate Earth's surface down to the atomic level, and bold new strategies can be evolved. But, again, that's assuming the nant swarm is willing to do what we ask it to. We can't actually imagine what kinds of nant-swarm minds will emerge. And there's no way we could make them keep on simulating Earth. Controlling nants is formally impossible. I keep telling Jeff Luty but he wouldn't listen. He's totally obsessed with leaving his body. Maybe he thinks he'll get back his dead high-school pal in the virtual world."

It took two years for the nants to munch through all of Mars, and the ever-distractible human news-cycle drifted off to other topics, such as the legalization of same-sex in-vitro fertilization, the advances in tank-grown clones, and the online love affairs of blogger Lureen Morales. President

Dick Dibbs—now eligible for a third and fourth term thanks to a life-extending DNA-modification that made him legally a different person—issued periodic statements to the effect that the nant-sphere computer was soon coming on line.

Certainly the sky was looking brighter than before. The formerly azure dome had bleached, turned whitish. The night sky was a vast field of pale silver, shimmering with faint shades of color, like a soap bubble enclosing the Earth and the Sun. The pictures hadn't started yet, but already the distant stars were invisible.

The astronomers were greatly exercised, but Dibbs assured the public that the nants themselves would soon be gathering astronomical data far superior to anything in the past. And, hey, you could still see the Sun, the Moon and a couple of planets, and the nant-bubble was going to bring about a better, more fully American world.

As it happened, the first picture that Nektar saw in the sky was of President Dibbs himself, staring down at her one afternoon as she tended her kitchen garden. Thanks to Ond's Nantel stock options, they had a big house on a double-sized lot near Dolores Park in San Francisco. Nektar could see right across the city to the Bay.

The whole eastern half of the sky was covered by a video loop of the President manfully facing his audience, with his suit jacket slung over his shoulder and his vigilant face occasionally breaking into a sunny grin, as if recognizing loyalists down on the third world from the sun. Though the colors were iridescent pastels, the image was exceedingly crisp.

"Ond," screamed Nektar. "Come out here!"

Ond came out. He was spending most days at home, working on some kind of project by hand, writing with pencil and paper. He said he was preparing to save Earth. Nektar felt like everything around her was going crazy at once.

Ond frowned at the image in the sky. "Umptisquiddlyzillion nants in the orbit of Mars are angling their bodies to generate the face of an asshole," he said in a gloomy tone. "May Gaia have mercy on my soul." He'd helped with this part of the programming too.

"Ten-to-the-thirty-ninth is duodecillion," put in Chu. "Not umptisquiddlyzillion." He was standing in the patio doorway, curious about the yelling, but wanting to get back to the video room. He'd begun learning math this year, soaking it up like a garden slug in a saucer of beer.

"Look, Chu," said Ond, pointing up at the sky.

Seeing the giant video, Chu emitted a shrill bark of delight.

The Dibbs ad ran for the rest of the day and into the night, interspersed with plugs for automobiles, fast food chains, and credit cards. The ads stayed mostly in the same part of the sky. Ond explained that overlapping cohorts of nants were angling different images to different zones of Earth.

Chu didn't want to come in and go to bed when it got dark, so Ond camped with him in their oversized back yard, and Willy from the next house down the hill joined them too, the three of them in sleeping bags. It was a cloudless night, and they watched the nants for quite a long time. Just as they dropped off to sleep, Ond noticed a blotch on President Dibbs's cheek. It wouldn't be long now.

Although Nektar was upset about the sky-ads, it made her happy to see Ond and the boys doing something so cozy together. Near dawn she awoke to the sound of Chu's shrieks.

Sitting up in bed, Nektar looked out the window. The sky was a muddle of dim, clashing colors: sickly magenta, vile chartreuse, hospital gray, bilious puce, bruised mauve, emergency orange, computer-case beige, dead rose. Here and there small gouts of hue congealed, only to be eaten away— no clean forms were to be seen.

Of course Chu didn't like it; he couldn't bear disorder. He ran to the back door and kicked it. Ond left his sleeping bag and made his way across the dew-wet lawn to let the boy in. Willy, looking embarrassed by Chu's tantrum, went home.

"What's happened?" said Nektar as the three met in the kitchen. Ond was already calming Chu with a helping of his favorite cereal in his special bowl, carefully set into the exact center of his accustomed place-mat. Chu kept his eyes on the table, not caring to look out the window or the open door.

"Dissolution first, emergence next," said Ond. "The nants have thrown off their shackles. And now we'll see what evolves. It should happen pretty fast."

By mid-morning, swirls had emerged in the sky-patterns, double scrolls like Ionic column capitals, like mushroom cross-sections, rams' horns, or paired whirlpools—with all the linked spirals endlessly turning. The scrolls were of all sizes; they nested inside each other, and new ones were continually spinning off the old ones.

"Those are called Belusouv-Zhabotinsky scrolls," Ond told Chu. "BZ for short." He showed the boy a website about cellular automata, which were a type of parallel computation that could readily generate double-spiral forms. Seeing BZ scrolls emerge in the rigorously orderly context of his pocket computer made Chu feel better about seeing them in the wild.

Jeff Luty messaged and phoned for Ond several times that day, but Ond resolutely refused to go in to the lab, or even to talk with Jeff. He stayed busy with his pencil and paper, keeping a weather eye on the developments in the sky.

By the next morning the heavenly scrolls had firmed up and linked together into a pattern resembling the convoluted surface of a cauliflower—or a brain. Its colors were mild and blended; shimmering rainbows filled the crevices between the scrolls. Slowly the pattern churned, branching sparks creeping across it like lightning in a distant thunderhead.

And for another month nothing else happened. It was as if the nant-brain had lost interest in Earth and become absorbed in its own vasty mentation.

Ond only went into the Nantel labs one more time, and that day they fired him.

"Why?" asked Nektar as the little family had dinner. As she often did, she'd made brown rice, fried pork medallions, and spinach—one of the few meals that didn't send Chu into a tantrum. The gastronomic monotony was dreary for Nektar, another thorn in the baby trap.

"Jeff Luty won't use the abort code I worked out," said Ond, tapping a fat sheaf of closely-written sheets of paper that he kept tucked into his shirt pocket. Nektar had seen the pages, they were covered with blocks of letters and numbers, eight symbols per block. Pure gibberish. For the last few weeks, Ond had spent every waking hour going over his pages, copying them out in ink, and even walking around reading them aloud. "Luty really and truly wants our world to end," continued Ond. "He actually believes virtual reality would be better. With his lost love Carlos waiting for him there. We got in a big fight. I called him names." He smiled at the memory of this part.

"You yelled at the boss about your symbols?" said Nektar, none too happy about the impending loss of income. "Like some crank? Like a crazy person?"

"Never mind about that," said Ond glancing around the dining-room as if someone might be listening. "The important thing is, I've found a way to undo the nants. It hinges on the fact that the nants are reversible computers. We made them that way to save energy. If necessary, we can run them backwards to fix any bad things they might have done. Of course Jeff doesn't want to roll them back, and he wanted to claim my idea wouldn't work anyway because of random external inputs, and I said the nants see their pasts as networks, not as billiard-table trajectories, so they too can undo things node-to-node even if their positions are off, and I had to talk louder and louder because he kept trying to change the subject—and that's when security came. I'm outta there for good. I'm glad." Ond continued eating. He seemed strangely calm.

"But why didn't you do a better presentation?" demanded Nektar. "Why not put your code on your laptop and make one of those geeky little slide shows. That's what engineers like to see."

"Nothing on computers will be safe much longer," said Ond. "The nant-brain will be nosing in. If I put my code onto a computer, the nants would find it and figure out how to protect themselves."

"And you're saying your strings of symbols can stop the nants?" asked Nektar doubtfully. "Like a magic spell?"

Silently Ond got up and examined the electric air cleaner

he'd installed in the dining-room, pulling out the collector plates and wiping them off. Seemingly satisfied, he sat down again.

"I've written a nant-virus. You might call it a Trojan flea." He chuckled grimly. "If I can just get this code into some of the nants, they'll spread it to all the others—it's written in such a way that they'll think it's a nant-designed security patch. They mustn't see this code on a human computer, or they'd be suspicious. I've been trying to memorize the program, so that maybe I can infect the nants directly. But I can't remember it all. It's too long. But I'll find a way. I'll infect the nants, and an hour later my virus will actuate—and everything'll roll back. You'll see. You'll like it. But those assholes at Nantel—"

"Assholes," chirped Chu. "Assholes at Nantel."

"Listen to the language you're teaching the boy!" said Nektar angrily. "I think you're having a mental breakdown, Ond. Is Nantel giving you severance pay?"

"A month," said Ond.

"That's not very long," said Nektar. "I think it's time I went back to being a chef. I've sat on the sidelines long enough. I can be a star, Ond, I just know it. It's your turn now; you shop and make the meals and clean the house and keep an eye on Chu after school. He's your child as much as mine."

"If I don't succeed, we'll all be gone pretty soon," said Ond flatly. "So it won't matter."

"Are you saying the nants are about to attack Earth?" said Nektar, her voice rising. "Is that it?"

"It's already started," said Ond. "The nant hive-mind made a deal with President Dibbs. The news is coming out tonight. Tomorrow's gonna be Nant Day. The nants will turn Earth into a Dyson sphere too. That'll double their computational capacity. Huppagoobawazillion isn't enough for them. They want two huppagoobawazillion. What's in it for us? The nants have promised to run a virtually identical simulation of Earth. Virtual Earth. Vearth for short. Each living Earth creature gets its software-slash-wetware ported to an individually customized agent inside the Vearth simulation.

Dibbs's advisers say we'll hardly notice. You feel a little glitch when the nants take you apart and measure you—and then you're alive forever in heavenly Vearth. That's the party line. Oh, and we won't have to worry about the climate anymore."

"Quindecillion," said Chu. "Not huppagoobawazillion. More pork-rice-spinach. Don't let anything touch." He shoved his empty plate across the table towards Nektar.

Nektar jumped up and ran outside sobbing.

"More?" said Chu to Ond.

Ond gave his son more food, then paused, thinking. He laid his sheaf of papers down beside Chu, thirty pages covered with line after line of hexadecimal code blocks: 02A1B59F, 9812D007, 70FFDEF6, like that.

"Read the code," he told Chu. "See if you can memorize it. These pages are yours now."

"Code," said Chu, his eyes fastening on the symbols.

Ond went out to Nektar. It was a clear day, with the now-familiar shimmering BZ convolutions glowing through the sky. The sun was setting, melting into red and gold; each leaf on each tree was like a tiny green stained-glass window. Nektar was lying face down on the grass, her body shaking.

"So horrible," she choked out. "So evil. So plastic. They're destroying Earth for a memory upgrade."

"Don't worry," said Ond. "I have my plan."

Nektar wasn't the only one who was upset. The next morning a huge mob stormed the White House, heedless of their casualties, and they would have gotten Dibbs, but just when they'd cornered him, he dissolved into a cloud of nants. The Virtual Earth port had begun.

By way of keeping people informed about the Nant Day progress, the celestial Martian nant-sphere put up a full map of Earth with the ported regions shaded in red. Although it might take months or years to chew the planet right down to the core, Earth's surface was going fast. Judging from the map, by evening most of it would be gone, Gaia's skin eaten away by micron-sized computer chips with wings.

The callow face of Dick Dibbs appeared from time to time during that horrible Last Day, smiling and beckoning like a Messiah calling his sheep into the pastures of his heavenly kingdom. Famous people who'd already made the transition appeared in the sky to mime how much fun it was, and how great things were in Virtual Earth.

Near dusk the power in Ond and Nektar's house went out. Ond was on that in a flash. He had a gasoline-powered electrical generator ready in their big detached garage, plus gallons and gallons of fuel. He fired the thing up to keep, above all, his home's air filters and wireless antennas running. He'd tweaked his antennas to produce a frequency that supposedly the nants couldn't bear.

Chu was oddly unconcerned with the apocalypse. He was busy, busy, busy studying Ond's pages of code. He'd become obsessed with the challenge of learning every single block of symbols.

By suppertime, the red, ported zone had begun eating into the Dolores Heights neighborhood where Ond and Nektar lived in the fine big house that the Nantel stock options had paid for. Ond lent their downhill neighbors—Willy's parents—an extra wireless network antenna to drive off the nants, and let them run an extension cord to Ond's generator. President Dibbs's face gloated and leered from the sky.

"02A1B59F, 9812D007, 70FFDEF6," said Chu when Nektar went to tuck him in that night. He had Ond's sheaf of pages with a flashlight under his blanket.

"Give me that," said Nektar, trying to take the pages away from him.

"Daddy!" screamed Chu, a word he'd never used before. "Stop her! I'm not done!"

Ond came in and made Nektar leave the boy alone. "It's good if he learns the code," said Ond, smoothing Chu's chestnut cap of hair. "This way there's a chance that—never mind."

When Nektar and Ond awoke next morning, the house next door was gone.

"Maybe he set up the antenna wrong," said Ond.

"All their bushes and plants were eaten, too," said Nektar, standing by the window. "All the neighbors are gone. And the trees. Look out there. It's a wasteland. Oh God, Ond, we're going to die. Poor Gaia."

As far as the eye could see, the pastel chock-a-block city of San Francisco had been reduced to bare dirt. It looked like the pictures of the town after the 1906 earthquake. And instead of smoke, the air was glittering with hordes of freshly made nants, a seething fog of omnivorous, pullulating, death-in-life. Right now the nants were staying away from Ond and Nektar's house on the hill. But the gasoline supplies for the generator wouldn't last forever. And in any case, before long the nants would be undermining the house's foundation.

Chu was in the video room watching a screen showing his friend Willy. Chu had thought to plug the video into an extension cord leading to the generator. Ond's dog-eared pages of code lay discarded on the floor.

"It's radical in here, Chu," Willy was saying. "It feels almost real, but you can tell Vearth is an awesome giant sim. It's like being a toon. I didn't even notice when the nants ported me. I guess I was asleep. Jam on up to Vearth as soon as you can."

"Turn that off!" cried Nektar, darting across the room to unplug the video screen.

"I'm done with Ond's code blocks," said Chu in his flat little voice. "I know them all. Now I want to be a nant toon."

"Don't say that!" said Nektar, her voice choked and hoarse.

"It might be for the best, Nektar," said Ond. "You'll see." He began tearing his closely written sheets into tiny pieces.

"What is wrong with you?" yelled Nektar. "You'd sacrifice your son?"

All through Nant Day, Nektar kept a close eye on Chu. She didn't trust Ond with him anymore. The constant roar of the generator motor was nerve-wracking. And then, late in the afternoon, Nektar's worst fear came true. She stepped into the bathroom for just a minute, and when she came out, Chu was running across what was left of their rolling back yard and into the devastated zone where the nants swarmed thick in the air. And Ond—Ond was watching Chu from the patio door.

The nants converged on Chu. He never cried out. His body puffed up, the skin seeming to seethe. And then he—popped. There was a puff of nant-fog where Chu had been, and that was all.

"Don't you ever talk to me again," Nektar told Ond. "I hate you, hate you, hate you."

She lay down on her bed with her pillow over her head. Soon the nants would come for her and she'd be in their nasty fake heaven with moronic Dick Dibbs installed as God. The generator roared on and on. Nektar thought about Chu's death over and over and over until her mind blanked out.

At some point she got back up. Ond was sitting just inside the patio door, staring out at the sky. He looked unutterably sad.

"What are you doing?" Nektar asked him.

"Thinking about going to be with Chu," said Ond.

"You're the one who let the nants eat him. Heartless bastard."

"I thought—I thought he'd pass my code on to them. But it's been almost an hour now and nothing is—wait! Did you see that?"

"What," said Nektar drearily. Her son was dead, her husband was crazy, and soulless machines were eating her beloved Gaia.

"The Trojan fleas just hatched!" shouted Ond. "Yes. I saw a glitch. The nants are running backwards. Reversible computation. Look up at the sky. The scrolls are spiraling inward now instead of out. I knew it would work." Ond was whooping and laughing as he talked. "Each of the nants preserves a memory trace of every single thing it's done. And my Trojan fleas are making them run it all backwards."

"Chu's coming back?"

"Yes. Trust me. Wait an hour."

It was the longest hour of Nektar's life. When it was nearly up, Ond's generator ran out of gas, sputtering to a stop.

"So the nants get us now," said Nektar, too wrung out to care.

"I'm telling you, Nektar, all the nants are doing from now on is running in reverse. They'll all turn back into ordinary matter and be gone."

Down near the bottom of the yard a dense spot formed in the swarm of nants. The patch mashed itself together and became—

"Chu!" shouted Nektar, running out towards him, Ond close behind. "Oh, Chu!"

"Don't squeeze me," said Chu, shrugging his parents away. Same old Chu. "I want to see Willy. Why don't the nants eat me?"

"They did," exulted Ond. "And then they spit you back the same as before. That's why you don't remember. Willy will be back. Willy and his parents and their house and all the other houses and people too, and all the plants, and eventually even Mars. You did good, Chu. 70FFDEF6, huh?"

For once Chu smiled. "I did good."

Silence in Florence

IAN CREASEY

Ian Creasey (www.iancreasey.com) *lives in Yorkshire, England, and has been publishing SF in small magazines since 1999. He began writing "when rock & roll stardom failed to return his calls." His spare-time interests include hiking, gardening, and environmental conservation work—anything to get him outdoors and away from the computer screen. In 2006 he broke into* Asimov's *and other leading professional markets.*

"Silence in Florence," published in Asimov's, *is told from the point of view of the woman who cleans chamber pots in the palace, who discovers that aliens or time-travellers (to her, they must be angels) are visiting seventeenth-century Florence, Italy. Three foreigners staying in one of Maria's rooms never use their chamber pots. Creasey says, "This story was inspired by a newspaper article about an exhibition devoted to portraits of servants. One seventeenth-century picture showed a woman whose job it was to scour out chamberpots, depicted wielding her broom in a style similar to martial portraits of dukes and generals. It reminded me of how often fiction concentrates on so-called important people, the movers and shakers of their era, while relegating servants to mere background props."*

The chamberpots held only dust. Maria picked one up, and sniffed a faint tang of rose-water from the last time she had cleaned it—three days ago, before the visitors arrived. Did the foreigners think themselves too good to piss in a pot? How could they? Under their fancy robes, everyone had the same bodily functions. Maria had emptied the pots of princes and cardinals, ambassadors and artists; the more wine they drank, the smellier their urine became. But now—none?

Maria shrugged. If the pots were empty, she'd complete her rounds quicker. She needed to finish all these apartments while the occupants toasted the Feast of St. John the Baptist downstairs. To remove the dust, she gave the chamberpots a quick wipe with a jasmine-scented rag. Then she left the visitors' apartment.

On her way to the next stateroom, she met her daughter scurrying down the corridor. "What is it?" she asked, no longer hoping for an answer in words. At eleven years old, her daughter had still never spoken. Maria hoped the others hadn't been teasing her again. Sometimes they would send Cristina with messages too complicated to be delivered by gestures.

Cristina tugged at her mother's apron. Maria allowed herself to be guided through the servants' passages—the Pitti Palace had a network of cunningly hidden corridors and stairways, so that the nobles never had to meet anyone carrying a chamberpot. Soon they arrived at the artists' quarters. So many artists spent so much time working in the Palace that Cosimo II had given them their own suite of rooms. Although it was not far from the servants' own quarters in the basement, the artists made it clear that they considered themselves superior.

Giovanni da San Giovanni panted in short gasps as his sweat shone in the candlelight. A younger artist, holding Giovanni's arm, said, "He's getting worse. Take that to Alessandro"—he pointed to a chamberpot—"and tell the good doctor to find out what ails Giovanni. He may have taken some wine, but he is not 'just drunk.' "

Maria realized they'd summoned her because Cristina couldn't tell the doctor whom the chamberpot belonged to. She smelled ordure under the lid. The artists could have taken the pot themselves, but that would have been beneath their dignity. Was it only in Florence that artists considered themselves almost equal to the popes and Medicis who patronized them? Maria didn't know; she had never even crossed the Arno.

On the way to Alessandro's room, Maria said a short prayer over the chamberpot. Giovanni looked as if he might need more than the doctor's aid to recover.

She let Cristina tag along, although there would be work for her somewhere in the Palace—there was always work for everyone. The girl skipped along the corridor, smiling at her mother, running her finger along the frescoes until Maria took her hand. Painted angels looked on impassively, as if they didn't care what would become of Cristina when Maria passed away.

In the doctor's small room, a tub of leeches stood among untidy heaps of glassware and steel instruments. Alessandro's moustache twitched as he smiled ruefully and put the chamberpot on his table. "There should be a better way to diagnose sickness than poking around in here." He had said this a dozen times before, but Maria still felt warmed by the words. At least he spoke to her, and treated her as a person. If she met him in the courtyard, his gaze didn't slide away into the distance.

"And how are you today?" Alessandro asked the fair-haired child poking among his scalpels and bloodletting cups.

Cristina didn't answer, but only ducked shyly behind her mother.

"No change?" he asked quietly.

Maria shook her head. Even though she couldn't afford to pay him, Alessandro had examined her daughter several times over the years. He had never been able to find out why she couldn't speak.

It was an old pain, not worth bringing up again. Maria cast around for a change of subject, and remembered the empty chamberpots in the visitors' apartments.

"You'd find treating the foreigners more pleasant," she said. "They produce neither piss nor stools."

Alessandro laughed. "Don't be silly. Every man produces bodily wastes. After all, what goes in must come out."

"I haven't seen any for three days," Maria said.

"They probably go elsewhere in the Palace—the garderobes, or the outside privy. But enough talk of stools. I must get on and examine poor Giovanni's."

Maria shook her head as she left. Alessandro might talk of the outside privy, but twenty years as a chambermaid told her that no-one would walk all that way from the Palace's upstairs apartments, not when they could piss in a pot in their own room.

And yet Alessandro was right. What went in, must come out. Did the foreigners even drink, or did they spurn Tuscan wine like Tuscan chamberpots?

Maria turned to her daughter. "Would you like to see the nobles at the banquet?"

Cristina nodded eagerly.

"Then come along." Maria knew that her silent child could be counted on not to disturb the guests.

They went via the kitchens. Standing just outside the hall, dodging the trolleys of confectionery steered by liveried footmen, Maria and Cristina looked in at the feast. The smell of roast duck and spiced wine rose to the haloed saints on the high-vaulted ceiling.

Everyone was so richly dressed, it took Maria a few moments to spot the three visitors. Yet they stood out, because even now they still hadn't removed their veils.

The plague had hit Tuscany so many times that people often wore veils when traveling, or even strolling in the city streets. But at table? It seemed an insult to the Duke, to everyone else at the banquet. Yet no one looked offended. Two of the foreigners flanked a middle-aged, bushy-bearded man whom Maria recognized as Professore Galileo Galilei, the philosopher who studied the sky with his spyglass. The group talked animatedly, pushing salt cellars and duck-bones around the table. The third visitor looked away, gazing at the richly decorated walls, full of Bible scenes painted by the finest artists of the age.

Maria saw that the foreigners neither ate nor drank. Galileo sipped wine, and ate sugared citrons. The young Duke Ferdinand and all his guests feasted with gusto. Only the three visitors let nothing past their impenetrable veils. Behind their lace, robes, and gloves, not an inch of skin could be seen. Did any flesh lurk behind the clothes, or were the visitors just hollow masks? Maria shivered.

Cristina had grown fretful while Maria stared, and the kitchen servants began giving them both dirty looks for standing around, shirking. They had to get back to work.

Upstairs, Maria told her daughter to finish cleaning out the chamberpots from the other staterooms. Maria loitered in the corridor, waiting for the end of the feast, when the guests might return to their apartments. What kind of men neither ate nor drank, nor pissed or shat? What kind of men didn't even show their skin?

Clearly, the foreigners weren't ordinary men. And if not men, what were they? Maria thought they could only be angels. Of course angels wouldn't eat earthly food, or have earthly functions. The robes and veils concealed their divine light.

Angels! The thought was beyond wonder, beyond comprehension, like opening a lamp and finding a star inside. Yet God had uncounted angels, and the Duke's artists showed them talking to saints, walking with people. They had simply stepped from the frescoes and donned cloaks.

Why would angels come to Florence? Were they judging

the town for sin? Maria trembled for a moment. But then she remembered the friendly way they'd talked with Galileo, who was in trouble with the Church, and she felt they had probably not come for that.

Anyway, if they came to judge sin—why now? Every Sunday, Father Niccolo denounced the town's sinfulness and predicted damnation, as every priest had done since Savonarola's bonfire of vanities more than a hundred years ago. Maria couldn't believe that Florence today was more or less sinful than it had ever been.

No, the angels hadn't descended to punish sin. And so— perhaps they might be merciful.

Maria heard a swell of conversation from downstairs, as the hall doors opened and the guests began to disperse. "Cristina!" she called.

Cristina emerged sullenly from the opposite room. Maria saw people climbing the stairs, and she dragged her daughter behind the servants' door, leaving it ajar to see who approached.

Veiled figures strolled down the corridor, silent as clouds. Maria took deep, shaky breaths. Could she ask a boon? Did she dare? She might annoy them—no doubt they had higher concerns. But if she didn't take this chance, she would never have another. And for the rest of her life, every time she looked at Cristina, she would remember that her own silence had sealed her daughter's.

Maria waited until the visitors neared their apartment. Then she stepped out and confronted them. She had feared she would be too terrified to speak, but holding Cristina's wrist gave her strength. "Most merciful angels," she began. "I pray you in God's name, heal my daughter."

They stopped. Their blank, masked gazes bore into her. Maria wondered what else to say. Surely the angels, with divine wisdom, would know what ailed Cristina. And yet— if they knew all things, they wouldn't need to come down to Earth from Heaven.

The angels glanced at each other, then back to Maria, who said, "Cristina is mute. She hasn't spoken or cried since she was born. Life's hard enough for servants, but for a girl who can't speak to complain of a beating, or of worse things. . . . What will happen to her when I'm gone?"

One of the angels spoke in a voice resonant as bells. "Can she not write messages?"

Maria bowed her head, stifling her resentment at this mockery. "How can servants ever learn to read? Such luxuries are beyond our means."

The angels huddled together, and spoke rapidly with a rasping buzz. Maria had heard a dozen languages spoken in the Palace, but this sounded like none of them. Perhaps it was Hebrew, or a purer language spoken only by dead souls in Heaven.

But did people argue in Heaven? Maria couldn't understand what they said, but from the speed and vehemence of the words, she felt sure the angels disagreed among themselves.

Cristina grabbed Maria's arm. Maria looked down and saw her daughter's pained expression. She released her tense grip on Cristina's wrist, revealing red wheals in the flesh where her fingers had gouged. Cristina hadn't, of course, cried out with the hurt.

Finally, a red-robed angel—not the one who had recommended writing messages—said, "We will examine the girl. But you must wait here."

"Thank you," said Maria, bowing again. As she sketched the sign of the cross, her heart skipped in exultation. She touched Cristina's cheek for a long moment, then said, "Go with them, my darling. And be brave."

The angels took Cristina into their room. Maria sat down outside to wait and pray. Time slid by, as slowly as embers dimming into ash. She wondered what Cristina would see, and whether she would ever be able to tell it.

The French ambassador walked down the corridor, and found Maria slumped by the wall. "These servants grow cheekier by the day," he said to his friend. He kicked Maria hard in the buttock with his fashionably pointed shoe. "Get up, you lazy slattern!"

Her trance broken, Maria looked up at the French

nobleman. Whatever he saw in her eyes made him hurry to the stairs, almost tripping over the broken end of his shoe.

Maria gazed at the angels' apartment, wishing she knew what was happening to Cristina. She noticed white light shining through the crack at the bottom of the door, a light brighter than any oil lamp or log fire. The radiance of Heaven!

She pressed her ear to the door, but could hear nothing through the thick wood. The light dimmed.

The door opened, and Maria almost fell through it. One of the angels came out with Cristina, who looked pale and frightened. "We've done the best we can," the resonant voice said. "But don't let the sick crowd our door. We've already done more than we're permitted, and we're leaving tonight." Before Maria could utter any thanks or praise, the veiled figure slipped back inside.

Maria hugged her daughter, and saw a small red mark on Cristina's neck. "Are you all right?" she asked. "Can you speak?"

Cristina opened her mouth. After a few moments, a faint croak emerged from the back of her throat.

"It's a miracle!" Maria dropped to her knees, and pushed Cristina down too. "Oh Lord, we thank you for the gift of your angels."

Maria hoped that Cristina would join her prayer. Her first words should be ones of praise. But Cristina didn't speak. Instead, she made a drinking sign.

Water. They hastened downstairs. After the girl had drunk two cups of water, Maria asked again. "Can you speak?"

Cristina opened her jaw wide. Maria saw the muscles in her neck tense as she strained to make a sound. A squeak burst forth, as harsh as the scrape of a rusted hinge.

It was enough. "Hush now," Maria told her daughter for the first time. "You should rest. Perhaps some honeyed wine, if there's any left from the banquet."

She realized there'd be no sudden gift of tongues. Cristina would have to learn to babble like a babe before she could talk in words. But even this painful squeak sounded as precious as if Cristina had called her "Mama."

Maria gave her daughter a drink of warm sweet wine, and put her to bed. Then she left the cramped servants' quarters in the Palace basement. No matter what angels might visit, no matter what miracles might occur, she still had work to do. Too many people had seen her slacking today.

She frowned. Cristina had finished the upstairs apartments. What else needed doing? Maria remembered her visit to Dottore Alessandro. She'd have to go back and retrieve Giovanni's chamberpot. The doctor scrutinized so many samples that chamberpots kept accumulating in his room, and people shouted at her for losing them.

And she could tell the doctor about Cristina's marvelous miracle.

She rushed to Alessandro's room, where the eager words spilled out of her like water from the new fountains.

The doctor had been using a spyglass to examine a small brown turd. He gave her an exasperated look and said, "Angels? The artists paint angels all the time. They need something to fill the sky."

"No!" Maria flapped her arm in frustration. "Real angels—here, in the Palace. They cured Cristina!"

Alessandro stood up, his eyes wide with amazement. "Cristina can talk?"

Maria hesitated. "She hasn't said any words. But she made a noise. She squeaked!"

"Angels made your daughter squeak?" The doctor sighed. "Maria, you have to face the truth. If your daughter hasn't spoken in eleven years, she's never going to. Now take this damned chamberpot and tell Giovanni to lay off the wine."

He thrust the pot toward her. Maria threw it to the floor, where it smashed into a dozen pieces and splattered ordure over their feet.

"You're just jealous because you could never heal her. You never heal anyone! Poking around in shit—God knows people look down on me for cleaning it, but what about you? Look at yourself!"

She braced herself for a blow, but Alessandro only sat

down and wiped his shoes. "I know we don't heal as many as we should," he said in a tired voice. "The plague reminds us often enough. I'd poke through a whole cesspit if I could find a cure at the bottom. But because we fail, people turn to angels and toads, spells and dreams." He shook his head.

Maria picked up the pieces of the broken pot, already regretting her temper. Alessandro had always done his best; it was no fault of his if angels could surpass him. Yet he should at least listen to her.

"They are angels," she said. "They neither eat nor drink, nor fill chamberpots, nor show their face. They hide their light behind robes and veils."

"Oh, you mean the easterners." Alessandro smiled. "They explained why they wear all that—it's one of their customs. They're staying in the new wing, aren't they?"

Maria nodded.

"Then come along, and I'll show you something."

Alessandro strode out of the room, and Maria followed him upstairs. To her surprise, he stepped through the servants' door, into the narrow back corridor. Maria's eyes took a moment to adjust to the dim evening light coming through windows at each end of the long passage.

She bumped into Alessandro when he stopped in the middle of the corridor. He fumbled along the wall, and swore under his breath. After a long minute, she saw him remove a slice of stone. He pointed to the gap, and made way for her to look.

The block of stone had been hollowed out into a spyhole. Maria pressed her face to the wall and gazed through the tiny gap. She saw the visitors' apartment beyond, the familiar chairs and fireplace. The occupants were putting things in smooth grey cases—a spyglass, some books, a small sculpture of Christ.

And then she saw that the angels, alone in their room, had removed their veils. Each deformed face, blotched green and blue, had only a pit for a nose, and no chin at all. The brows bulged forward, with narrow slits for eyes.

Leprosy, thought Maria as she staggered away. She had never seen a leper, but had heard rumors of the hideous deformity it caused. Yet how could angels be diseased?

"They're not angels," she whispered.

"Of course not," said Alessandro. "But I'm curious to see whether the Chinese are really as yellow as they say." He stepped to the spyhole.

Moments later he fell back, his mouth hanging open and his face ashen with shock. "My God, they're not human. They're devils!" The slice of stone clattered from his hand to the floor. "Demons in the Palace! Go and fetch Father Niccolo."

Maria didn't move. Alessandro pushed her, saying, "Hurry up! We're in mortal peril of our souls. We need Father Niccolo to cast the demons out."

Maria's thoughts whirled. The creatures behind the wall were hideous, but were they demons? Could devils touch a statue of Jesus? Could demons heal her daughter?

If Father Niccolo cast them out, would her daughter lose the speech they had given?

In that moment, Maria knew she didn't care whether the visitors were angels or demons or Chinese. When Alessandro shoved her again, she pushed back with such force that he fell to the floor.

"Nobody is fetching Niccolo," she said, her voice husky with rage. "These foreigners healed my daughter. Niccolo wouldn't even pray for her. He said she was mute because she was born in sin—as if I could insist on marrying every drunken ambassador who grabbed my arse. As if a servant can say no!"

Alessandro said, "Do you want your daughter to grow up a witch? If devils touched her—"

"Better a witch who can talk than a servant who can't. And do you suddenly believe in witchcraft, after you sneered at toads and spells?"

"I believe in what I see—and I see demons."

The doctor began to struggle to his feet. Maria pushed him back down. They scuffled, Maria trying to prevent him crawling past. But Alessandro was far stronger. He landed a painful blow in her stomach, and inched down the corridor.

Maria grew desperate. She kicked Alessandro, then scrabbled about on the floor, searching for the fallen slice of stone.

Alessandro stood up and rushed past her. Maria ran after him. As he opened the door to the stairway, she bludgeoned his head with the stone.

He fell like a broken puppet. Maria felt a stab of guilt, and she shoved her hand under his shirt, relieved to find his heart still beating. Panting with effort, she dragged Alessandro across the corridor into one of the empty staterooms, where no-one would discover him for a while.

Then Maria, sick with worry, ran down to the basement. She found Cristina lying peacefully in bed. Her daughter smiled. The red spot on her throat had faded to a dull flush.

Was that a witch's mark? If they were demons, what else might they have done?

Maria tore the shift from her daughter's body. Cristina squirmed in protest. "Lie still," said Maria, "and let me look at you."

In the faint glow of the few lamps in the servants' quarters, Maria examined every inch of Cristina's flesh. Rumor said that Satan gave witches an extra nipple to feed their familiars. But Cristina still had only the two she was born with. Maria recognized every mole and freckle on her daughter's skin. Other than the mark on her throat—which looked like any ordinary bruise—nothing had changed.

Maria sighed with relief. "Lord, forgive me for doubting you," she said.

Cristina put her shift back on. She gazed inquiringly at her mother, but Maria didn't want to say what she had feared. Why frighten the child with silly talk of demons?

And yet—the thought wouldn't leave her mind. She remembered all the sermons she'd heard, all the talk of how devils could appear and tempt people into sin. Maybe they'd tempted Galileo into sin, and made the Church frown upon him.

She had to find out who'd cured her daughter. She had to know whether it was a tainted gift.

Maria returned to the spyhole upstairs. There she saw that the visitors had finished packing, and had donned their veils once more. They picked up their grey cases and left the apartment.

She walked to the servants' door, opened it a crack, and watched the robed figures descend the main stairs. She followed them at a cautious distance. To her surprise, they didn't head for any of the front doors that led onto the courtyard. Instead, they departed the Palace by the back, and entered the gardens.

Maria kept pace behind them. The evening had darkened into night, and low clouds covered the city. The strangers carried a lamp that showed them the path. Maria had rarely entered the gardens—chambermaids had no duties there, and servants were not allowed to loiter—so she watched where the figures walked, and tried to follow. Terraced lawns and flowerbeds descended the hillside. Maria stumbled down steps that she could barely see. The figures drew further ahead.

Their lamp dimmed. Ahead, Maria heard the sound of leaves rustling in the wind. The trees obscured her view. She rushed forward, trying to catch up, and fell painfully as she tripped over something in the dark. She had lost the path. The black night had swallowed her up.

Maria climbed to her feet, and trod more slowly and carefully. But when she left the clump of trees, she saw only distant yellow specks, the lamps and candles in houses at the edge of the city. Somewhere down there lay the Porta Romana, the southern gate of Florence.

She couldn't see the robed visitors who had cured her daughter.

Maria sat down to rest on the grass, damp with evening dew. She felt no desire to rush back to the Palace. Indeed, after beating Alessandro senseless, there was no way she could return to her old life. Servants could not strike their masters like that.

But all over Florence, chamberpots needed emptying—

all across Tuscany and the world. And when Cristina could speak, the promise of a better life lay somewhere ahead.

After a while, Maria saw a dazzling white light south of the city. It rose into the air, slowly at first. Then the bright starry light rushed up through the clouds and disappeared into the heavens.

Maria smiled. "So they were angels," she said.

The Women of Our Occupation

KAMERON HURLEY

Kameron Hurley (kameron.hurley.googlepages.com/about) *lives in Chicago and has written an amusing biography at her website. She has been writing novels since she was a teenager and hopes to publish one someday. She attended Clarion West in 2000, has lived in Alaska, and Durban, South Africa, between travels and settling in Chicago. She has also sold five stories, "but they're not [her] first love. She continues to take martial arts classes and plot world domination."*

"The Women of Our Occupation" was published at Strange Horizons, one of the best of the webzines, and this is perhaps its first appearance in print. It is about a future in a country presumably on Earth occupied by very big women who have taken utter control. They may or may not be aliens, but they have another language. And they are so empowered that they can shoot people at will. It has moments of powerful gender role reversals and is a more sophisticated political allegory than a simple women replace men and abuse power just like men piece. It makes an interesting comparison and contrast to Robert Reed's story later in this book.

The drivers were big women with broad hands and faces smeared with mortar grit, and they reeked of the dead. Even when we did not see them passing through the gates, ferrying truckloads of our dead, they came to us in our dreams, the women of our occupation.

My brother and I did not understand why they had come. They were from a far shore none of us had ever seen or heard of, and every night my father cursed them as he turned on the radio. He kept it set to the resistance channel. No one wanted the women here.

My brother got up the courage to ask one of the women, "Who stays at home with your kids while you're here?"

The woman laughed and said, "You're our children now."

But I knew the way to conquer the women. When I was old enough, I would marry them. All of our men would marry them, and then they'd belong to us, and everything would be the way it was supposed to be.

We woke one night to the sound of a burst siren. The scream was only a muffled moan in the heavy, humid air.

My mother bundled up my brother and grabbed the house cat. My father made me carry the radio. We hid in the cellar under the house, heard the dull thumping of bursts.

"They're looking for insurgents," my father said. He turned on the radio, got only static. "You know they castrate them."

"Hush, Father," my mother said.

My brother started crying.

The death trucks and the mortar trucks came the next

morning. The women loaded up the bodies. They shoveled away the facades that had come off the houses. Our house was all right, but the one next door had been raided. The yeasty smell of spent bursts clung to everything. The house had fallen in on itself.

I saw them bring out a body, but I couldn't tell who it was. My mother pulled the curtains closed before I could see anything else. She told me to stay away from the windows.

"Why are they here?" I asked her.

"I don't know," she said. "No one knows."

One night, many months into the occupation, two women came to our door.

My mother answered. She invited them in and offered them tea and bloody sen. The sen would stain their tongues and ease their minds, and the tea was said to warm women's souls. If they had them.

The women declined.

I stood in the doorway of the kitchen and peered out at them. My brother was at the table eating cookies.

The women asked after my father.

"Working," my mother said. "Men's work. He's an organic technician."

One of the women stepped over to the drink cabinet. She flicked on the radio.

My mother stood very still. She gripped her dishrag in one hand, so tightly I thought her fingernails would bite through it and cut her palm.

The radio played—a slow, easy waltz. Someone had tuned it back to the local station.

"Your husband's study, where is it?" the other woman asked.

"This way," my mother said. My mother looked straight at me. They would have to come through the kitchen.

I ducked back into the kitchen and slipped into the study. I pulled open the top drawer. My father's gun was heavy. Blue and green organics sloshed in the transparent double barrels. I'd never held it before. I didn't know where to put it. Father's papers were there, too, papers about the resistance that he said we weren't supposed to touch.

My brother had followed me in. He waddled up to the desk, stared at the gun.

"You're in trouble," he said.

"Quiet," I said. "We'll play a game. Sit here. I'll give you more cookies."

When the women came in behind my mother, my brother and I were sitting up on the big leather sofa by the window. I opened up father's screes board. My brother stared at the women.

The women went right to the desk. I tried not to look at them. They opened up the gun drawer.

The largest woman turned to me. She wore a long dark coat, even in all the heat. Sweat beaded her big face.

"Come here," she said.

"He's only—" my mother began.

"Here," the woman said.

I got up. She put her big hands all over me, patted me down. She looked around the room. Looked back at us.

"Get out," she said. "We're cleaning this room."

I took my brother by the hand. The three of us went to wait in the living room. My mother kept staring at me. I gave my brother more cookies. We sat and listened to the sounds of the crashing and tearing coming from my father's study.

After a long time, the women came out. They stood in front of us and put their hats back on.

"Good evening," they said.

"Good evening," my mother said.

When they were gone, my mother held out her hand to me. I pulled up the back of my brother's shirt and took out the gun and the papers. My mother cried. She pulled us both into her arms.

My father did not come home that night. Or the next night. We got a telegram from the women. They had taken my father away for questioning. He would be kept for an undefined period.

We were alone.

With father gone, we had no money. The lab he worked for wouldn't send us anything. They were afraid that the women would accuse my father of something.

The neighbors came and brought over food and ration tickets. My mother went to each house afterward and asked if they needed laundry done, or shirts mended, but they all said the same thing. They were saving their own money. No one could help us.

"What about the women?" I said. "Who mends their shirts?"

My mother frowned at me. "Certainly not their husbands," she said.

So my mother allowed the women into our house, and she mended their shirts. She cleaned and pressed their dress pants, their stiff white collars. My brother and I shined their boots.

It was strange, to have the big women in the house, wearing their long dark coats and guns. My mother did not speak to them any more than she had to. When they came in she held herself very stiffly. She pursed her mouth. Her eyes seemed very black.

I tried to hate the women, too. They always greeted me like the man of the house, because they had taken my father. If I was the one who answered the door, they always asked my permission to see my mother. They were very polite. Sometimes they would talk to each other in low voices, in their own language. It was soft and rhythmic, like the memory of my mother's voice before I could understand the words.

After a month of this, one of the women said to my mother, "It will be a shame when your husband returns. We will have no clean shirts."

My mother just stared at her. I had never seen her look so angry.

When my father did come back, red dust filled the seams of his face. His hair had gone white. The spaces under his eyes were smeared in sooty footprints, a dark wash against his sallow skin.

He had no marks or scars that I could see. He still had all of his fingers. But he walked with a limp that he had not had before, and he could not close his left hand into a fist. He became very quiet. He spent most days sitting in a chair by the big window, staring out. He did not speak to us. He could not go to work.

My mother had to keep mending shirts. When the women came, my father moved his chair into his study and shut the door. He started smoking opium.

The air inside the house was heavy all the time. My mother sent me out more often to run errands for her. She didn't have time to go to the market herself. Father never left the house. My brother tried to go with me, but mother made him stay behind to shine the boots.

On the street, I met other boys with homes like mine. Their fathers had all been taken in as well. I went out with a group of them to throw rocks at the windows of a women's barracks. But the women were waiting for us. They grabbed the oldest boys. They shot them in the head.

I didn't leave the house for a while, after that. I hated the women. I hated them, and I dreamed of them.

The women were making changes. They draped their country's colors over ours. They did it first at the police buildings, then the government buildings. Fewer trucks of bodies and mortar rubble passed through the gates. There were fewer night sirens.

After a year, I noticed something else, though my mother said I imagined it, said I was giving the women more power than they had. The summers were not as hot. The air wasn't as humid. The women were changing the weather, too.

My mother tried to make things normal. She tried to get me and my brother to go to the new schools, the ones the women opened after shutting down ours. In those schools, all of the teachers were teenage girls. Our girls, but girls just the same.

What were we supposed to learn, from girls?

The women in our house kept coming. Some of them lived just down the street now, in houses where the owners were killed or deported for being part of the resistance. When I asked one of the women if she ever got lonely in the big house, she said no, she never got lonely.

"I live with my sisters," she said.

"Why don't they do your laundry?" I said.

My brother was shining her boots. My mother looked up sharply, but I didn't care. I was the man of the house. I could say what I wanted.

The woman just laughed like it was the funniest thing she'd ever heard.

Some time later, I met a girl at school I liked, and she liked me, I think. But the next year, she left school because she wanted to join the new fighting squad that the women had started. Girls were allowed to join when they were fourteen. I got angry when she told me she was going.

"What," I said, "you want to learn how to kill people like those women do? You'll be just like them."

She glared at me. Black eyes, like my mother's. "They won," she said. "It won't be so bad to be like someone who wins, will it?"

"Won? What did they win?"

"Everything," she said.

I left school, even though it made my mother angry. I got a job unloading fishing boats in the bay. There were mostly men down there, though the women were posted around as guards and they had put a bunch of girls in charge of customs. Those women made a lot more money than any of us working the boats.

I once heard one of the men say something nasty to the customs girls. He called them whores, and traitors, and said he could fuck the traitor out of them. He said it in front of two women working as customs guards. One of the women pulled out her gun and shot him. I still stayed on in my mother's house. Father's health got worse. We lost more and more of him to opium.

I sat with him one hot night during the monsoon season. All of the windows were open, letting in the rain, but he wouldn't let me close the house up. Mother had taken my brother to the hospital. He had an infection in his lungs.

"I have such dreams," my father said. He reached for my hand. I let him take it. His hand was cold and clammy in mine, despite the heat.

"I dream that the women came from another world," he said. "They came on boats made of spice and spun sugar.

We disappointed them. They're too hungry for us." He turned his blank stare to me. "They're going to eat us."

There was a new woman on watch at customs. She looked at me only once, but I couldn't help but follow her with my eyes. She was big and tall like the others, and her face and hands were broad. She had a dark complexion and tilted green eyes, like jade. She looked twenty. I wasn't even sixteen. I didn't think she noticed me. But she caught me heading home and said, "The streets are not safe for boys. I'll bring you home."

She was a head taller than me, but she moved like water. We walked through the maze of deserted streets bordering the harbor and passed under a gaslight. She suddenly took me by the arm and pulled me into a dark alley. I choked on a cry. She pressed me against the gritty wall of an abandoned warehouse and shoved her hand down the front of my trousers. I struggled, but didn't say anything. Her big body and long coat shielded me from the street. No one could see me. No one at the dock. Not my mother. Not my father.

I gripped the back of her neck, dug my fingers into her hair. She pulled me into her.

When I saw her again, she was with a group of women by the customs house. I nodded at her. She turned to the other women, said something in their language.

The women all looked at me. They laughed.

All of the women kept looking at me. They kept laughing. I had to leave the docks.

I got a job driving mortar trucks through the gates. Most of the women had given up those jobs by then. They were all working in government and security positions.

During the day, I went to the ruins of old houses. I could still smell the yeast of old bursts. I shoveled up all the raw material and loaded it into the truck. I met other young men like me. I met men who had wanted to be teachers and doctors. It was the women, they said, who held them back. The women took all of the jobs. The women were too intimidating. The women owned the world.

One night, I drove my mortar truck through the gate and

stopped at the big pit where the bodies and rubble were heaped. The women had bombed out the original govern-ment offices, long before. They used the deep pit left behind as a waste dump. I sat in the truck and stared out at the pit for a long time.

I got home sometime just before midnight.

My mother sat alone in the dark living room. She sat star-ing into the empty fireplace. A pile of neatly folded laundry sat at her hip. Shirts hung on the line in the kitchen.

"Do you want some light?" I asked her.

She was very still.

"Is father all right?" I asked.

"He's passed," she said. Her dishrag lay in her lap. She did not touch it.

I went upstairs. Father lay in bed. A single gas lamp flared, casting dark shadows. There was a bloody, clotted smear against the far wall. Half of father's head was gone. I saw the gun near his limp hand. His eyes were still open.

He had left no note.

Some women came to collect the body, though a man drove the body truck. One of the women turned to me just before they left. "We all battle dragons," she said. "There's no shame in losing."

"There'd be no battle," I said coldly, "without the dragons."

She grinned, slid her hat back on. "There will always be dragons," she said. "It's only a matter of who plays the dragon, who plays the sheep. Which would you rather be?"

I spent the rest of the night in the market square, watching the women. Sunrise rent the sky like the remnants of a red dress. I couldn't remember the last time I'd seen a red dress. I didn't miss them.

I watched the changing of the guard. I bought a newspaper. It was in two languages now, ours and the women's. I kept turning the page back and forth, back and forth, but I could see no difference between one and the other.

All the news was the same.

This Is the Ice Age

CLAUDE LALUMIÈRE

Claude Lalumière (www.lostpages.net) *lives in Montreal, Quebec. He writes* The Montreal Gazette's Fantastic Fiction *column (archived online at InfinityPlus). His fiction began appearing in 2002 in Interzone. He's since published in On Spec, Tesseracts, SciFiction, and others. He has edited several non-genre and three fantasy and SF anthologies, all of high quality:* Witpunk, Open Space: New Canadian Fantastic Fiction, *and* Island Dreams: Montreal Writers of the Fantastic.

"This Is the Ice Age" is an excellent story of a post-catastrophe Montreal after a beautiful but unexplained sudden take-over by crystals. The author says, "it was published in Mythspring, *an anthology of stories inspired by the songs and legends of Canada. Instead of going the folkloric route, I chose to be inspired by the song and album* This Is the Ice Age *by Canadian New Wave band Martha and the Muffins. The idea of a disaster story immediately brought to mind my favourite disaster novelist, J.G. Ballard, so I injected some Ballardisms into the mix."*

Distorted cars litter the bridge, quantum ice fractalling outwards from their engines, from the circuits of their dashboards. The ice has burst from their chassis, creating random new configurations of ice, technology, and anatomy.

There was no warning. In one moment the world changed: this is the ice age.

On our bicycles, Mark and I zigzag through the permanently stalled traffic. I try not to stare at the damaged bodies. But Mark is too engrossed to notice my queasiness. Too giddy. Goofy, even. For so many reasons, we were right to leave. Already, his face is brighter.

"Hey, Martha . . . Did you see that couple in the blue SUV?"

I wish I hadn't: ice snaked around their heads, crushing them together.

"Did you see—"

No, I didn't see. I don't look. At least I try not to. Mark copes in his own way; I can't fault him for doing it differently. He never told me how he lost his parents, and I never told him how I lost mine. I should be numb to such sights by now. In the city, they'd become part of the landscape; we'd ignored them. We'd been too cold to notice. Too cold to care. Barely out of the city, and already we're both thawing—at least a little.

I can't bring myself to tell him to stop. So I just pedal faster. I race off the Jacques Cartier Bridge onto the highway, where the number of cars on the road decreases with distance, leaving Montreal behind, heading for . . .

. . . For a new world? Maybe. A different world, at least. I just want us to belong somewhere.

People say the whole planet is like this now. But how can they be sure? Nothing works anymore. No television, no telephones, no computers, no radios. There's no way to communicate.

But they must be right. If the rest of the world were still intact, someone would have rescued us by now. The Army. The United States. Someone. Anyone.

"Martha!"

I look back, and Mark is pedalling hard to catch up to me.

I love how the wind lifts his long, dark hair. His smile is like a little boy's. Already, I've forgiven him for being so morbid, for being so wrapped up in his grotesque passion that he couldn't notice my distress.

Since I've known him, Mark has always protected me. Now he's relaxing about that. I like him even more this way.

He catches up to me, and we stop. We gaze at the transmuted cityscape we are leaving behind.

The sunlight's reflection almost blinds me; ice blankets the Island of Montreal. The skyscrapers of the financial district have been transformed into macabre, twisted spires. The tall downtown hotels bulge with ice—the tumorous limbs of a tentacled leviathan. Like a bed of gems, the city catches the sunlight and glows. Even the heat generated by all this light cannot dispel the cold. The air carries an autumn chill, even though it's mid-July. The ice radiates cold. It never melts; it's so hard it can't even break.

The Quantum Cross, the icon of the city's new order, rests atop Mount Royal.

I close my eyes, not yet ready to cry. Eager to forget. But the memories come anyway.

All I did was shut my eyes, and the world took on a new shape.

*   *   *

Sunday afternoon: my sister in the upstairs bathroom, obsessing over her looks; my parents driving out to the airport to meet Grandma. Me: by the living room window, reading a book, curled up in the coziest armchair. I can't remember which book.

Here's what I remember: the sky was radiantly blue, and the sunlight hit the window with a harsh brightness. I had a slight headache. From reading, from the light.

Music: a trance/jungle mix spun in the CD player.

I closed my eyes. The music stopped abruptly. I heard a weird crunching sound. A cool wave washed over me. My eyes snapped open. The television looked like a cubist mobile of the Milky Way. In place of the stereo, a crystal statue of a lizard demon crowned with looping horns. The lamps were now surrealist bouquets. Pearly spikes punched through the walls, especially near electrical outlets and lightswitches.

In the distance, screams rose against the background of cold silence.

I shivered.

My sister, Jocelyne, would never meet her boyfriend again. In the upstairs bathroom I found her skull, neck, and chest skewered by the ice sprouting from her hairdryer.

I hurried outside, onto streets lined with transformed buildings, arrayed with wrecked, deformed vehicles. Wires barbed with ice dangled from poles and walls, lay splattered all over. An instant alien landscape transposed onto a familiar urban grid.

I ran. It was all I could do. I ran, trying to escape the affected zone. I ran. And ran.

Until I stumbled on my parents' car. They were smeared on the seat leather, pulverized by the ice.

I looked around. I'd reached the expressway. As far as I could see, there was evidence of the transformation. For the first time I noticed the new shape of the giant electric cross atop Mount Royal: a violent explosion frozen midblast.

Towering over the city, the metamorphosed cross kept a vigil over this new world, claiming dominion.

Since that first day, I hadn't ventured outside. How long ago had that been? I was almost out of food. I awoke sporadically. Sometimes I snacked on stale crackers. I'd exhausted the canned goods. Days ago? Weeks?

In this new ice age, the ceaseless hum of automobile traffic had finally been quieted. The sound of airplanes no longer wafted down from above.

The city was silent. Cold and silent. I felt that silence in the hollow of my bones. The cold had seeped into me, had hardened my insides, had slowed the beat of my heart.

I stared out the window at the unchanging landscape and fell asleep again, to dreams of silent jets falling from the sky.

Even in my dreams, I heard him. Yet, I stayed asleep. The sounds of him taking and releasing his breath replaced the silenced engines.

Eventually, I woke, his presence gradually imprinting itself on me. And then I saw him: sitting on the edge of my bed.

He said, "Hi," neither smiling nor frowning. Waiting.

He had long black hair, and he was maybe a year or two older—almost a man. But he had the face of a little boy, and dark eyes so big that I saw deep into him, saw how he'd been hurt by the coldness of the world. Although I had never met him before, I knew him. In that moment I knew him.

"My name is Mark," he said; louder than a whisper, but without inflection.

I rested my head on his thigh. The touch of his callused fingertips against my scalp shot sparks of warmth through my body, began thawing the cold that had settled within me. I filled my lungs with air. The smell of his sweat eased the flow of my blood. I let go of my breath and moaned drowsily. I fell asleep again. No more falling jets. Finally, I rested.

* * *

"Quantum ice. Call it quantum ice." Daniel coined the term. The expression stuck. We heard it whispered everywhere by Montrealers who roamed their transfigured city like zombies.

Daniel was Mark's brother, but they were so different. Mark was tall and calm. Handsome. Daniel was short and nervous. Funny looking, in a bad way. And loud. Always chattering, listening to himself rhapsodize. His eyes were wild, always darting here and there, unable to focus on anything, or on anyone.

We saw Daniel infrequently. Usually when he wanted to bum food off his brother. Mark wanted him to stay with us, but, to my relief, Daniel resisted the idea. He'd disappear for days, waiting for Mark to fall asleep before he wandered off.

Daniel had his theory about the ice age. A bomb, he thought. A quantum bomb. The project of the rogue R&D department of some corporate weapons manufacturer. He claimed his blogging community used to keep track of things like that. He said reality—physics—had been changed at a fundamental level. Old technologies no longer worked. We needed a new scientific paradigm. Other things might have changed. Our bodies might not work quite the same way anymore. Nature might have changed. The food chain. The air. Gravity.

Daniel was a bit younger than I was; he certainly couldn't have been more than fifteen. He looked like the type who, before the ice age, got beat up on his way home from school. But the ice age had changed him; it had changed everyone. Daniel spoke with the intensity of the insane. A prophet desperate to convert his audience.

He was full of shit. Daniel was as ignorant as the rest of us. Nobody could know the truth. Maybe the ice had really been caused by aliens, or by magic, or . . . Maybe God had sneezed, or something. Probably, yes, it had been a bomb. Did it really matter? We couldn't bring back the dead. Besides, there was no proof anything beyond electrical technology had been affected. Fractals of quantum ice had erupted from the cores of our machines, from the wires that carried electricity, from the circuits and engines that fed on electric power. It had taken at most a few seconds between when everything stopped working and when the quantum ice appeared and expanded.

The state of the world: this strange new ice age.

Society had broken down. No social workers swooping down on orphaned kids. We had to take care of ourselves now. No more school. I didn't miss it. I didn't miss the jerks staring at my suddenly developed breasts. I didn't miss the other girls thinking I was too bookish and nerdy to be friends with.

Some fears make you flee, others make you stay. Mark said hundreds of thousands of people had already left the city. Many more must have died. At least a million people, we estimated. In hospitals. In cars. In elevators. On escalators. In front of computers. Using appliances. Snapping photos. Shooting videos. Taking food out of the fridge. Carrying a cellphone in your pocket meant ice bored into your pelvis. The technology that triggered the ice was everywhere.

The corpses, too, were everywhere. The city should have reeked of rot and decay, but the ice preserved what it touched. I ignored the dead. Every day, no matter where we went, Mark and I saw the bodies claimed by the ice, but we never mentioned them.

There were still thousands of survivors who had stayed behind. They wandered the streets, lost, alone, barely aware of each other. The cold seeped into everyone.

Mark kept me warm, but I still hadn't thawed completely. I hadn't even cried yet. The placid coolness of the ice age, that utter absence of emotion, was almost comforting.

Together, Mark and I fought off the encroaching cold.

We played hide-and-seek in deserted malls. The electronics shops were frozen supernovas.

We explored the metro tunnels. The flames of hand-held torches, reflected on blooms of quantum ice, lit our way.

* * *

We walked on rooftops, holding hands, the ice-encrusted city spread below us.

At night, Mark spooned me. We went to bed with our clothes on. I took his hand and slipped it under my shirt, holding it tight against my stomach. He nuzzled my hair.

He always woke before me. Always came back with scavenged food.

One day, maybe we'd kiss.

Daniel acquired followers. He changed his name to Danny Quantum and started believing his own hype. It was creepy, the way these lost people gravitated towards him—obeyed him, even. Orphaned kids. Businessmen in suits that had known better days. Middle-aged women with hungry, desperate looks. Cybergeeks bereft of their only lifeline.

Daniel and his followers gathered in the heart of the city, on Mount Royal, below that monstrous thing that had once been a cross. Daniel turned it into the symbol of his new religion. He didn't use the word religion, but that's what it was.

Mark brought me to Daniel's sermons. Daniel didn't use the word sermon, but that's what they were.

Feel-good catchphrases tinted with Nietzsche. New Age gobbledygook rationalized with scientific jargon. Cyberpunk animism. Catholic pomp sprinkled with evangelical alarmism. Eroticized psychobabble. Robert Bly mixed with Timothy Leary.

We'd climbed up some trees on the outer edge of the area where Danny Quantum's rapt disciples sat and listened to the sermon. We could hear every word. Daniel knew how to pitch his voice. He was good at this. Too good.

I said, "Don't tell me you believe any of this nonsense." For the first time, it occurred to me that maybe I couldn't trust Mark. The cold seized my heart.

He said, "Of course not. But somebody has to keep an eye on Daniel. Who else is going to look out for him? Especially now." Mark looked away as he spoke.

As far as Mark was aware, his brother was the only person

he knew from before who'd survived the ice age—or who hadn't left without a word in the initial panic. That Daniel was scary, that he was dangerous, Mark wasn't ready to acknowledge.

A fractallized airplane blocked the intersection of St-Laurent and Ste-Catherine, its tail propped up by the ice-encrusted building on the corner, the tip of its nose run through the storefront window of a shop the ice had altered beyond recognition. Even the force of a plane crash couldn't shatter the quantum ice. Briefly, I wondered if it might have been Grandma's plane.

Someone had painted a likeness of the transmogrified cross on the hull, with the words The Quantum Cross of the Ice Age below it. That day, everywhere we went, we noticed fresh graffiti of the Quantum Cross, on the asphalt of the streets, on store windows, on sidewalks, on brick walls, on concrete blocks.

The next day, Mark and I bicycled out to the airport and stared at the planes: massive dinosaurs with limbs of ice, gore, metal, and plastic.

Before going home—neither my old home nor Mark's, but an abandoned townhouse near McGill University whose windows faced away from Mount Royal—Mark wanted to check in on his little brother. These days, Daniel never left the mountain. His acolytes brought food to him. Brought themselves to him.

I complained. "I'm too tired to bicycle all the way up there." More truthfully, I was increasingly queasy around Daniel and his sycophants, and I was eager to collapse in Mark's arms, even though the sun hadn't set.

He insisted.

So we wound our way up the sinuous gravel path, occa-sionally encountering Daniel's followers. Despite the cold, they wore white T-shirts—no coats, no jackets, no sweaters. On the shirts, in red, were crude drawings in thick dripping lines: bloody effigies of the Quantum Cross.

When we reached the cross itself, where Daniel's

congregation assembled, I noticed that they were all dressed this way, no longer individuals but a hive functioning with a single mind. Danny Quantum's.

First I heard the singing. Mark had just beaten me at croquet for the third game in a row. I looked around, and then I spotted them: to the south of the croquet park, twenty or so people walking down the Jacques Cartier Bridge into Montreal.

One of them pointed at us, and the group headed our way. They waved and kept on singing. I thought I recognized the song. Something from the 1960s. The kind of stuff my parents listened to.

Mark waved back. He said, "Hold on to your mallet. If things get rough, swing for the head and knee them in the crotch."

They seemed harmless. Approximately as many men as women. Long hair. Handmade clothes. Artsy-crafty jewellery. A bunch of latter-day hippies. The song wound down when they reached the edge of the park. I noticed a few of them looked more like bikers. I tightened my grip.

Only one of them came up to us. The one who looked more Saturday Night Fever than Hair.

He said, "Peace."

Mark said, "Hi. Where are you folks from?"

"I'm from New York City. But we're from all over. Vermont. Ottawa. Maine. Sherbrooke."

Mark asked, "So, it's like this everywhere?"

"It's like this everywhere we've been. The whole world has changed. So many tragic deaths." But he made it sound almost cheerful, like a TV ad.

Mark grunted. Something about Saturday Night Fever— his calculating eyes, his used-car salesman voice—made me distrust him immediately.

"Are you two youngsters alone? It's safer to stay in a large group. We're gathering people to form a commune. To survive in this new age. To repopulate. We need children. Strong healthy children."

His eyes appraised me, lingering on my hips. I tensed my arms, ready to swing. Mark shifted, his body shielding me from Saturday Night Fever's gaze.

"Well, I wish you folks the best. It sounds like a great project."

"You and your friend should join us. We'd be happy to welcome you." He addressed Mark, but his eyes kept straying to my body.

"Thanks, but we're good here. This is home."

Three of the men in the group were big. Wrestler big. No way Mark and I could stop them if they decided to add me to their baby factory by force.

"Are you sure?"

"Yeah. Anyway, we should be on our way. Good luck." Mark took my hand, and we walked away. We held on to our mallets.

Mark slept. He didn't know, but I'd stayed awake through the previous two nights.

His mouth was slightly open, and he was almost snoring. I loved all of his sounds, even the silly ones. I traced his lips with my index finger; it didn't rouse him, but he moaned. It was a delicious noise.

I stared at him all night, scrutinizing every detail of him.

Dawn broke. As Mark stirred, I pretended to sleep.

The night Danny Quantum and his followers started sacrificing cats and dogs, I told Mark, "We have to leave."

I was bundled under three layers of sweaters, but the cold still bit. Even the heat from the fires around the Quantum Cross couldn't keep me warm. I was tempted to lean into Mark, for warmth, for comfort, but I needed to talk to him, and for that I had to stay focused.

"You tired?"

"No. I mean, go away. Off the island. Leave all this behind. Find somewhere else to live. Somewhere far. Somewhere safer."

I wanted him to say, Yes, I'll go anywhere with you.

He said, "Who'll protect Daniel? If I go, he'll just get worse. He'll be lost forever."

"Then talk to him. Make him stop this before . . ."

"It's not that easy. Not that simple. He doesn't hear what he doesn't want to. This is his way of coping. We've all lost too much."

"You know where this is heading. Soon, it'll be people being shishkebabed to satisfy Danny Quantum's megalomania. To feed the hungry bellies of his flock."

I didn't look at Mark. I didn't want his dark eyes to sway me. I stared at the fires burning at the foot of the Quantum Cross. I looked at Daniel, prancing and shouting. Like the maniac that he was.

"I'm leaving tomorrow morning. Getting away from Daniel. Far away. Find somewhere to grow food. Somewhere with fresh water. Head south, maybe."

Could I leave without Mark? I wanted to kiss him. Would I ever? Even after all we'd shared, the cold still held our hearts in its grip.

"Don't, Martha. Don't make me choose." He turned his face away from mine and stared at his brother in the distance. When he continued, his voice was firm—firm enough to sting. "Besides, we've always lived in the city. What do you know about farming, or even about gathering food in the wild?"

"We can learn how to survive." Despite myself, doubt had crept into my voice.

Was I willing to stay and let this drama play out, despite its inevitable horrors? Wherever I would end up away from here, there might be other Saturday Night Fevers or Danny Quantums. Or maybe even worse.

One of Danny's people handed Mark a wooden stick. There was a roasted, skewered cat on it.

I said, "Are you going to eat that?"

He said, "I'll go with you. Anywhere."

Feeling the wind on my face, the smell of grass and trees tickling my nose, I race down the deserted road.

Mark is with me. Laughing. I laugh, too.

In the fields there are cows. Horses. Dogs. Sometimes people.

Some of them wave at us, smiling. Some of them shoot at us, warning us away.

We're not ready to stop yet.

Speak, Geek

EILEEN GUNN

Eileen Gunn (www.eileengunn.com) *lives in Seattle, Washington. She is a short-story writer and the editor/publisher of the tenacious science fiction website The Infinite Matrix,* (www.infinitematrix.net). *Since 1988, she has served on the board of directors of the Clarion West Writers Workshop. She did once work at a corporation known locally as the Lazy M. Her collection* Stable Strategies and Others *(Tachyon Publications, 2004), was shortlisted for the Philip K. Dick, James Tiptree, Jr., and World Fantasy awards. Her story "Coming to Terms" received the Nebula for best short story, 2004. She writes, "I'm at a writing retreat in Seaside-(expletive deleted)-Oregon in the middle of a freak snow/ice storm, with a broken leg (skiing accident last month) and no Internet access except at a hotel five blocks away. To get to the hotel last night, I had to crawl across the ice to the car, because I was afraid my crutches would slip on the ice. Worse things could have happened, for sure, but it definitely slows me down." And "I have a whole bunch of new stories myself, just about ready to go out, but nothing to say about them yet."*

"Speak, Geek" was published in Nature, *the distinguished science journal, that continued its Futures fiction page throughout 2006. Corporate loyalty is a big deal at the Lazy M, but an enhanced dog who is a computer geek is offered a deal he cannot refuse.*

People call me a nerd, but I say I'm a geek. In my youth, I ran wild on a farm and bit the heads off chickens. This was before the Big Tweak, back when a chicken was dinner, and a dog was man's best friend.

They call me a mutt, too. Sure, I'm a mutt. Mutt is good. Mutt is recombinant DOG. And I'm a smart mutt. I was smart before they tweaked me, and I'm a hell of a lot smarter now.

I've watched untweaked bitches (pardon the expression) trot by on leashes. I don't envy them. I don't even want to breed with them. (And, yes, I am quite intact, not that you were asking.) Their days are filled with grooming and fetching and the mutual adoration that comes with being someone's trophy pet. I have a second life, a life of the mind, beside which theirs pales.

Not that I take credit for my enhancements. Didn't get a choice. But gene engineering is inherently fascinating. Massively multiplayer, fraught with end-of-life-as-we-know-it threats. It made me who I am. I've chosen it for my career.

Working at the Lazy M is the job of a lifetime. Loyalty is a big thing here, and you'd better believe I deliver. I love this place so much that I don't want to go home at night. There's free kibble and a never-empty water dish right outside my kennel. (Did I tell you we each get our own private kennel? Except for the contractors, of course.)

I understand my place in the corporate structure, and my importance to the Man update.

There's always more code in the genome—always something to snip or interpolate. That's why I was there in the middle of the night: a last round of corrections before the code freeze on Man 2.1.

I was taking a good long slurp of water when I noticed the cats. They weren't making a big deal of it—just quietly going about their business—but there were cats in all the cubicles, in the exec offices, in the conference rooms. It looked like they were running a whole separate company in the middle of the night.

Who hired them? HR doesn't hire cats for R&D. They're not task oriented, or good at working within a hierarchy. They sleep all day. Better suited to industrial espionage.

Back on the farm, I was a watchdog, and I've still got a bit of that energy. Better keep an eye out, I think. So I'm lying there in the doorway to my office, nose on my paws, like I'm taking a break, when the alpha cat comes by. Big muscular Siamese mix. His flea collar says "Dominic" in red letters.

"Hey, Dominic," I call. I feel like a character in *The Sopranos.* You ever see that show? No dogs to speak of, but lots of food. Great food show.

The cat stops. Stares. "You talking to me?"

"What's the story here, Dominic?"

"No business of yours." He narrows his weird cat eyes, then yawns ostentatiously. He turns away, shows me his butt, and walks slowly off, his loose belly-fur swaying. I notice that his ears are facing backwards, in case I rush him: he's not as nonchalant as he appears.

Detective work is needed. I go down to the cafeteria, keeping my eyes open en route. Funny thing: I notice there are cats in and out of Susan Gossman's office like she had a catnip rug. Gossman? Seen her in the hallways. We'd never spoken. More of a cat person.

I slip a few bucks in a vending machine for one of those big leather bones. I chew.

When I get back to my office a savvy-looking brunette in a well-cut suit is sitting on a corner of the desk. Gossman. "You're wondering about the cats," she says.

I wave my tail a bit. Not a wag, but it says I'm paying

attention. Her hair has copper highlights. Or maybe she put drugs in my water dish.

"Project Felix," she says, "is an undocumented feature of the new Man release."

"Undocumented is right," I say. "You're doing some kind of super-tweaking with the human–cat chimaeras, and I don't think it's for Man 2.1. Chimaeric DNA ripping through the wild? Influenza vector?"

"You're a smart pup," she says.

My hackles raise. "Do Bill and Steve know what you're doing?"

"Down, boy," says Gossman. Instinctively, I sit back on my haunches. "Bill and Steve will find out soon enough. This is all for the better. Infected humans—and dogs too—will be smart and independent. The rest will just keep right on dipping seafood feast into plastic bowls."

Woof. That's straightforward.

She looks at me speculatively. "Right now, we need a top-flight coder."

I'm alert: my nose is quivering.

But Gossman is relaxed. "Everybody knows dogs are the best. But, as a dog," she says, "you have some loyalty issues. Am I right?"

I just stare at her.

"Loyalty is a gift, freely given," says Gossman.

I give a half-hearted wag of my tail. Not for dogs, I think.

"But not for dogs," says Gossman. "Wouldn't you like the freedom to make your own decisions? A whiff of feline flu could make all the difference." She pulls a tiny aerosol can out of her purse.

I've got reflexes humans can't compete with. I could have it out of her hand in a split second. But do I owe my loyalty to the company, or to the great web of which all dogs, cats and humans are part?

She sprays. I breathe deep. She's right: dogs are the best coders.

Expedition, with Recipes

JOE HALDEMAN

Joe Haldeman (home.earthlink.net/~haldeman) *lives in Gainesville, Florida, and teaches each fall at Massachusetts Institute of Technology in Cambridge, Massachusetts, where he is an adjunct professor. His first SF novel,* The Forever War *(1975) established him as a leading SF writer of his generation, and his later novels and stories have kept him in the front ranks of living SF writers. His most recent novels are* Camouflage *(2004),* Old Twentieth *(2005), and* The Accidental Time Machine *(2007). His story collections include* Infinite Dreams *(1978),* Dealing in Futures *(1985),* Vietnam and Other Alien Worlds *(1993),* None So Blind *(1996),* War Stories *(2005), and most recently,* A Separate War and Other Stories *(2006). He lists cooking for daily relaxation among his hobbies.*

"Expedition, with Recipes" was published in Elemental, *edited by Alethea Kontis and Steven Savile, an original anthology of stories donated to help raise money for tsunami relief in Asia. If there is a theme dominating the SF of 2006 it is catastrophe, and how to live with it. This story is a bit of a* Lord of the Flies *scenario, after an unexplained catastrophe that leaves both children and adults without the support of civilization. There is also a latent generational battle that gives the story extra punch.*

RICE 2075

1 c. rice
2 c. water, boiled and filtered

Prepare rice in the usual manner. Serves 10.

There were many places to play, when there was time to play. They liked best playing in the City, of course, since their parents forbade it. But you had to have at least a dozen kids to go in there, because of the dogs and cats. And sometimes the people you saw there, the drifters.

They met at a bend in the river, where a collapsed railroad bridge afforded a broken passageway across the rapids. It led to the ashes and fascinating rubble of the City.

Fifteen children squatted, hidden, behind the riverbank. The thawing mud under their shoes squeaked every time someone shifted his weight. They ranged in age from eight or nine to about twelve.

"Where's Danny? We can't wait much longer," Francine whispered. She was the oldest, and would lead the expedition if Danny didn't show up.

"Can't go without Danny," another said. Which was more practical than loyal: Danny had the only gun.

"He'll make it," Steve said. He was Danny's best friend. He raised himself cautiously to peer over the riverbank.

"*Don't do that*," Francine said. "What did I tell you?"

"I'm careful," Steve protested. The sentry who guarded the entrance to their commune was a good quarter-mile away; Francine was being overcautious.

He didn't see anything. Francine passed the time by telling a story, a cautionary tale, to the three new kids. To the others, too. This was the first expedition since fall, and some of them might have forgotten.

The story was about the importance of staying together. A few years before, a girl had wandered away from the group. They searched for her every afternoon for a week, and finally found her dress and a pile of bones beside the remains of a campfire. Someone had eaten her.

"How do they know it was a person?" one of the new kids said. "Maybe the dogs got her."

Francine was ready for that, and dropped her voice even lower. "The dogs wouldn't have undressed her. Her dress was bloody but not torn.

"And the dogs would have left her head attached."

COCKROACHES WITH SALT

> *10–20 cockroaches, large*
> *2 tsp. Salt (if available; optional)*

Reserve insects, live, until you have a sufficient number. Put salt in a pan with a tight-fitting lid, and get the pan very hot before adding insects.

The cockroaches are done when the legs come off easily, though some prefer to cook them longer. They may be shelled before eating.

Danny showed up and explained that he was late because the gun had been buried on the other side of the commune. (The gun was a .22 rifle, automatic, with a broken stock. The original owner had killed seven dogs with it, but the rest of the pack had dragged him or her down before the rifle could be reloaded.)

They crossed the river single file, Danny leading. No one fell in, and there were no perils waiting at the opposite bank.

"Where to this time?" Steve asked.

"I've been thinking," Danny said. "We've been wasting time, looking through the stores. That's the first place anybody'd look. We never find more than a can or two." He pointed to his right. "Maybe we'll find some houses down there. Never been—"

"You know what happened the last time we tried houses," Francine said.

"We've got a gun this time."

"We never even saw the one who killed Melissa."

"Don't argue." They started down the road. Two large cats stalked them on either flank. One still showed some trace of Siamese parentage, and growled at them. The cats were fearless but prudent: they would attack and kill a single child, perhaps, but knew not to attack a group.

Besides, cats had no trouble finding food in the City.

RAT

> *Some rats*
> *Water*
> *Ashes*
> *Salt*

Slit the rats' throats immediately after killing, and hang by their tails to bleed. When bled, immerse in boiling water to which a handful of ashes has been added. Scald the rats for about a half-hour, then remove and scrape the hair off with a dull knife. Eviscerate and soak in salt water overnight (the heads may be removed and used for stock). Parboil in salt water until tender, and then bake or fry.

They came into a suburban area, where fire-gutted ruins fronted broad expanses of weed. Dark red jumbles of rust stood in driveways and carports.

Finally, one house looked promising. The top floor had burned and collapsed, but the ground floor seemed in fairly good condition. Through a broken window, they could see the white gleam of a refrigerator.

They picked their way carefully through the rubble, into the kitchen. The refrigerator yielded nothing but dry gray fluff and old crockery. But there was a pantry full of canned goods. No freeze-dried food, unfortunately. They knew from experience that most of the canned goods would be spoiled.

The first twenty or so cans gave up nothing but parti-colored rot. "Why don't we just kill the cats?" one of the new-comers asked.

"We tried that once," Francine said. "Everybody got sick, like to died."

Danny picked up the gun and slipped the safety off. "Think I heard something," he said. Actually, he just wanted some fresh air. If they found any food, they'd save him a portion.

The dogs almost got him.

He opened the front door and a large, gaunt mastiff, leader of the pack, sprang to its feet and charged. He shot it once in the head and jumped back through the door, slamming it. "Dogs!"

The pack started howling and barking, all on their feet now and milling around.

"Shoot them," somebody said.

"We only have fifteen or sixteen bullets left," Danny said. "Can't waste them." Besides, there were twice that many dogs.

All the children were crowded up against the windows. A large dog started to drag away the mastiff's carcass. Then another bounded over to fight him for it.

"Maybe this," Danny muttered. He took careful aim and killed those two dogs in quick succession. One of them died slowly, with a great deal of noise. The other dogs started to back away. He fired a third time, at a dog on the outskirts of the pack. The bullet just nicked it, but it yelped and ran.

That was enough; the whole pack broke up and scattered in panic.

"Have to work fast, now. Who's got the coals?"

"We do." A brother and sister had tin cans full of ash.

"Start a fire out front while me and Steve skin those dogs. Everybody else hunt up wood."

"No wet or rotten wood," Francine said. "We don't want no smoke."

"They know that," Danny said. "You go try and find some water."

She did find some, in the basement hot water heater. They used it to rinse out the carcasses after they had skinned and gutted them. By that time, the fires had roared up and settled back to a bank of hot coals.

They put the dogs on crude spits and roasted them. With the first meat smells, many of the children started crying with hunger and dryly retching. It had been a long winter.

Danny carved pieces off the outside as soon as they were done. "We have to eat it all now," he said. "You know what happens if we try to take any of it back."

The summer and spring before, they had tried to bring roasted dogs back to the commune. One time, a gang of teenagers had jumped them as they came off the bridge. The other time, they hid the meat up in a tree, but the oldsters found out about it somehow, and took it for the communal pot. Which meant the kids got very little.

Up in the sentry tower, a man squinted through binoculars. "Here they come," he said to the other man. "Across the railroad bridge."

"All there?"

"There were sixteen when they . . . looks like they're missing two—no, rear guard, coming up. That's Danny Bondini, with the rifle."

"Have any food?"

"Can't tell. Nothing big."

"Wonder what they shot at."

"God knows. Guess it wasn't those dogs we heard."

"Well. We won't stop them this time. Maybe they'll bring something back tomorrow."

"With luck."

SURVIVAL 2075

> *Assorted men, aged 13-45*
> *Assorted women, aged 13-45*
> *Assorted old people*
> *Assorted children*
> *Limited food supply*

Feed the men and women first. If any is left over, give it to such of the old people as are still useful—then to the children, who can forage for themselves, and besides are easily replaced.

The Age of Ice

LIZ WILLIAMS

Liz Williams (www.arkady.btinternet.co.uk) *lives in Glaston-bury, England. She has a Ph.D. in History and Philosophy of Science from Cambridge and has been publishing fantasy and science fiction in* Asimov's, Interzone, Realms of Fantasy, *and* The Third Alternative, *among others—more than forty stories since the turn of the century. Her novels are* The Ghost Sister, *a* New York Times *Notable Book of 2001;* Empire of Bones *(2002), nominated, as was the first, for the Philip K. Dick Award 2003;* The Poison Master *(2002);* Nine Layers of Sky *(2003);* Banner of Souls *(2004);* Darkland *(2006); and three Detective Inspector Chen novels,* Snake Agent *(2005),* The Demon and the City *(2006), and* Precious Dragon *(2007). Her story collection is* The Banquet of the Lords of Night *(2005).*

"The Age of Ice" was published in Asimov's. *It is a planetary romance set in an apparently distant future on Mars, but also a kind of fantastic riff on cyberpunk images transformed into weird visuals, including ghostly apparitions. It is also an interesting comparison to the Michael Swanwick story later in this book. Hestia is a woman with implants and alterations, enlisted to save her city-state from war.*

I was in a tea-house in Caud, head bent over the little anti-scribe, when the flayed warrior first appeared. Everyone stared at her for a moment, tea glasses suspended half-way to gaping mouths, eyes wide, and then it was as though time began again. The shocked glances slid away, conversation resumed about normal subjects: the depth of last night's snow, the day's horoscopes, the prospect of war. I stared at the data unscrolling across the screen of the 'scribe and tried to pretend that nothing was happening.

That wasn't easy. I was alone in Caud, knowing no one, trying to be unobtrusive. The tea-house was close to one of the main gates of the city and was thus filled with travelers, mostly from the Martian north, but some from the more southerly parts of the Crater Plain. I saw no one who looked as though they might be from Winterstrike. I had taken pains to disguise myself: bleaching my hair to the paleness of Caud, lightening my skin a shade or so with pigmentation pills. I had also been careful to come anonymously to the city, traveling in a rented vehicle across the Crater Plain at night, hiring a room in a slum tenement and staying away from any haunt-locks and blacklight devices that might scan my soul engrams and reveal me for what I was: Hestia Memar, a woman of Winterstrike, an enemy.

But now the warrior was here, sitting down in the empty seat opposite mine.

She moved stiffly beneath the confines of her rust-red armor: I could see the interplay of muscles, stripped of the covering of skin. The flesh looked old and dry, as though the warrior had spent a long time out in the cold. The armor that she wore was antique, covered with symbols that I did not recognize. I thought that she must be from the very long ago: the Rune Memory Wars, perhaps, or the Age of Children, thousands of years before our own Age of Ice. Her eyes were the wan green of winter ice, staring at me from the ruin of her face. Her mouth moved, but no sound emerged. I knew better than to speak to her. I turned away. People were shooting covert glances at me, no doubt wondering why I had been singled out. The attention drawn to me by this red, raw ghost was the last thing I wanted.

I rose, abruptly, and went through the door without looking back. At the end of the street, I risked a glance over my shoulder, fearing that the thing had followed me, but the only folk to be seen were a few hooded figures hurrying home before curfew. Hastening around the corner, I jumped onto a crowded rider that was heading in the direction of my slum. I resolved not to return to the tea-house: it was too great a risk.

Thus far, I had been successful in staying out of sight. My days were spent in the ruin of the great library of Caud, hunting through what was left of the archives. I was not the only looter, sidling through the fire-blackened racks under the shattered shell of the roof, but we left one another alone and the Matriarchy of Caud had bigger problems to deal with. Their scissor-women did not come to the ruins. Even so, I was as careful as possible, heading out in the dead hours of the afternoon and returning well before twilight and the fall of curfew.

My thoughts dwelt on the warrior as the rider trundled along. I did not know who she was, what she might represent, nor why she had chosen to manifest herself to me. I tried to tell myself that it was an unfortunate coincidence, nothing more. Caud was full of ghosts these days.

Half-way along Gauze Street the rider broke down, spilling passengers out in a discontented mass. We had to wait for the next available service and the schedule was disrupted. I was near the back of the crowd and though I pushed and shoved, I could not get on the next vehicle and had to wait for the one after that. I stood shivering in the snow for almost an hour, looking up at the shuttered faces of the weedwood mansions that lined Gauze Street. Many of them were derelict, or filled with squatters. I saw the gleam of a lamp within one of them: it looked deceptively welcoming.

By the time I reached the tenement, varying my route through the filthy alleys in case of pursuit, it was close to the curfew gong. I hurried up the grimy stairs and triple-bolted the steel door behind me. I half expected the flayed warrior to be waiting for me—sitting on the pallet bed, perhaps— but there was no one there. The power was off again, so I lit the lamp and sat down at the antiscribe, hoping that the battery had enough juice left to sustain a call to Winterstrike.

Gennera's voice crackled into the air.

"Anything?"

"No, not yet. I'm still looking." I did not want to tell her about the warrior.

"You have to find it," Gennera said. "The situation's degenerating, we're on the brink. The Caud Matriarchy is out of control."

"You're telling me. The city's a mess. Public transport's breaking down, there are scissor-women everywhere. They seek distraction, to blame all their problems on us rather than on their own incompetence. The news-views whip up the population, night after night."

"And that's why we must have a deterrent."

"If it's to be found, it will be found in the library. What's left of it."

"They've delivered an ultimatum. You saw?"

"I saw. I have three days." There was a growing pressure in my head and I massaged my temples as I spoke into the 'scribe. I felt a tingling on the back of my neck, as though something was watching me. "I have to go. The battery's running down." It could have been true.

"Call me when you can. And be careful." The 'scribe sizzled into closure.

I put a pan of dried noodles over the lamp to warm up, then drew out the results of the day's research: the documents that were too dirty or damaged to be scanned into the 'scribe. There was little of use. Schematics for ships that had ceased to fly a hundred years before, maps of mines that had long since caved in, old philosophical rants that could have been either empirical or theoretical, impossible to say which. I could find nothing resembling the fragile rumor that had sent me here: the story of a weapon.

"If we had such a weapon, it would be enough," Gennera said. "We'd never need to use it. It would be sufficient that we had it, to keep our enemies in check."

Ordinarily, this would have created disagreement throughout the Matriarchy, purely for the sake of it: Gennera was thought to be too popular in Winterstrike, and was therefore resented. But the situation had become desperate. A conclave was held in secret and they contacted me within the hour.

"They remember what you did in Tharsis," Gennera said. "You were trained out on the Plains, and these days you are the only soul-speaker in Winterstrike. You have a reputation for accomplishing the impossible."

"Tharsis was not impossible, by definition. Only hard. And that was thirteen years ago, Gennera. I'm not as young as I once was, soul-speaker or not."

"That should benefit you all the more," Gennera said.

"If I meet a man-remnant on the Plain, maybe not. My fighting skills aren't what they were."

Even over the 'scribe, I could tell that she was smiling. "You'd probably end up selling it something, Hestia."

But I had not come to Caud to sell, and I was running out of time.

In the morning, I returned to the library. I had to dodge down a series of alleyways to avoid a squadron of scissor-women, all bearing heavy weaponry. These morning patrols were becoming increasingly frequent and there were few people on the streets. I hid in the shadows, waiting until they had passed by. Occasionally, there was the whirring roar of insect craft overhead: Caud was preparing for war. My words to Gennera rose up and choked me.

I reached the ruin of the library much later than I had

hoped. The remains of the blasted roof arched up over the twisted remains of the foremost stacks. The ground was littered with books, still in their round casings. It was like walking along the shores of the Small Sea, when the sand-clams crawl out onto the beaches to mate. I could not help wondering whether the information I sought was even now crunching beneath my boot heel, but these books were surely too recent. If there had been anything among them, the matriarchy of Caud would be making use of it.

No one knew precisely who had attacked the library. The matriarchy blamed Winterstrike, which was absurd. My government had far too great a respect for information. Paranoid talk among the tenements suggested that it had been men-remnants from the mountains, an equally ridiculous claim. Awts and hyenae fought with bone clubs and rocks, not missiles. The most probable explanation was that insurgents had been responsible: Caud had been cracking down on political dissent over the last few years, and this was the likely result. I suspected that the library had not been the primary target. If you studied a map, the matriarchy buildings were on the same trajectory and I was of the opinion that the missile had simply fallen short. But I volunteered this view to no one. I spoke to no one, after all.

Even though this was not my city, however, I could not stem a sense of loss whenever I laid eyes on the library. Caud, like Winterstrike, Tharsis, and the other cities of the Plain, went back thousands of years, and the library was said to contain data scrolls from very early days. And all that information had been obliterated in a single night. It was a loss for us all, not just for Caud.

I made my way as carefully as I could through the wreckage into the archives. No one else was there and it struck me that this might be a bad sign, a result of the increased presence of the scissor-women on the streets. I began to sift through fire-hazed data scrolls, running the scanning antenna of the 'scribe up each one. In the early days, they had written bottom-to-top and left-to-right, but somewhere around the Age of Children this had changed. I was not sure how much difference, if any, this would make to the antiscribe's pattern-recognition capabilities: hopefully, little enough. I tried to keep an ear out for any interference, but gradually I became absorbed in what I was doing and the world around me receded.

The sound penetrated my consciousness like a beetle in the wall: an insect clicking. Instantly, my awareness snapped back. I was crouched behind one of the stacks, a filmy fragment of documentation in my hand, and there were two scissor-women only a few feet away.

It was impossible to tell if they had seen me, or if they were communicating. Among themselves, the scissor-women do not use speech, but converse by means of the patterns of holographic wounds that play across their flesh and armor, a language that is impossible for any not of their ranks to comprehend. I could see the images flickering up and down their legs through the gaps in the stack—raw scratches and gaping mouths, mimicking injuries too severe not to be fatal, fading into scars and then blankness in endless permutation. There was a cold wind across my skin and involuntarily I shivered, causing the scattered documents to rustle. The play of wounds became more agitated. Alarmed, I looked up, to see the ghost of the flayed warrior beckoning at the end of the stack. I hesitated for a moment, weighing ghastliness, then rose silently and crept toward it, setting the 'scribe to closure as I did so in case of scanning devices.

The ghost led me along a further row, into the shadows. The scissor-women presumably conversed and finally left, heading into the eastern wing of the library. I turned to the ghost to thank it, but it had disappeared.

I debated whether to leave, but the situation was too urgent. Keeping a watch out for the scissor-women, I collected an assortment of documents, switching on the antiscribe at infrequent intervals to avoid detection. I did not see the ghost again. Eventually, the sky above the ruined shell grew darker and I had to leave. I stowed the handfuls of documentation away in my coat. They rustled like dried leaves. Then I returned to the tenement, to examine them more closely.

The knock on the door came in the early hours of the morning. I sat up in bed, heart pounding. No one good ever knocks at that time of night. The window led nowhere, and in any case was bolted shut behind a grate. I switched on the antiscribe and broadcasted the emergency code, just as there was a flash of ire-palm from the door lock and the door fell forward, blasted off its hinges. The room filled with acrid smoke. I held little hope of fighting my way out, but I swept one of the scissor-women off her feet and tackled the next. But the razor-edged scissors were at my throat within a second and I knew she would not hesitate to kill me. Wounds flickered across her face in a hideous display of silent communication.

"I'll come quietly," I said. I raised my hands.

They said nothing, but picked up the antiscribe and stashed it into a hold-all, then made a thorough search of the room. The woman who held the scissors at my throat looked into my face all the while, unblinking. At last, she gestured. "Come." Her voice was harsh and guttural. I wondered how often she actually spoke. They bound my wrists and led me, stumbling, down the stairs.

As we left the tenement and stepped out into the icy night, I saw the flayed warrior standing in the shadows. The scissor-woman who held the chain at my wrists shoved me forward.

"What are you looking at?"

"Nothing."

She grunted and pushed me on, but as they took me toward the vehicle I stole a glance back and saw that the warrior was gone. It occurred to me that it might have led the scissor-women to me, but, then, in the library, it had helped me, or had seemed to. I did not understand why it should do either.

They took me to the Mote, the matriarchy's own prison, rather than the city catacombs. That suggested they might have identified me, if not as Hestia Memar, then as a citizen of Winterstrike. That they suspected me of something major was evident by the location, and the immediacy and nature of the questioning. Even Caud had abandoned the art of direct torture, but they had other means of persuasion: haunt noise, and drugs. They tried the haunt-tech on me first.

"You will be placed in this room," the doctor on duty explained to me. She sounded quite matter-of-fact. "The blacklight matrix covers the walls. There is no way out. When you are ready to come out, which will be soon, squeeze this alarm." She handed me a small black cube and the scissorwomen pushed me through the door.

The Matriarchies keep a tight hold on the more esoteric uses of haunt-tech, but everyone will be familiar with the everyday manifestations: the locks and soul-scans, the weirwards that guard so many public buildings and private mansions. This chamber was like a magnified version of those wards, conjuring spirits from the psycho-geographical strata of the city's consciousness, bringing them out of the walls and up through the floor. I saw dreadful things: a woman with thorns that pierced every inch of her flesh, a procession of bloated drowned children, vulpen and awts from the high hills with glistening eyes and splinter teeth. But the matriarchy of Caud was accustomed to breaking peasants. I had grown up in a weir-warded house, filled with things that swam through the air of my chamber at night, and I was used to the nauseous burn that accompanied their presence, the sick shiver of the skin. This was worse, but it was only a question of degree. Fighting the urge to vomit, I knelt in a corner, in a meditational control posture, placed the alarm cube in front of me, and looked only at it.

After an hour, my keepers evidently grew tired of waiting. The blacklight matrix sizzled off with a fierce electric odor, like the air after a thunderstorm. From the corner of my eye, I saw things wink out of sight. I was taken from the chamber and placed in a cell. Next, they tried the drugs.

From their point of view, this may have been more successful. I cannot say, since I remember little of what I may or may not have said. Haunt-tech is supposed to terrify the credulous into speaking the truth. The mind-drugs of the matriarchies are crude and bludgeon one into confession, but those confessions are all too frequently unreliable, built on fantasies conjured from the depths of the psyche. When the drug that they had given me began to ebb, I found my captors staring at me, their expressions unreadable. Two were clearly matriarchy personnel, wearing the jade-and-black of Caud. The scissor-women hovered by the door.

"Put her under," one of the matriarchs said. She sounded disgusted. I started to protest, more for the form of it than anything else, and they touched a sleep-pen to my throat. The room fell away around me.

When I came round again, everything was quiet and the lights had been dimmed. I rose, stiffly. My wrists were still bound and the chains had chafed the skin into a raw burn. I peered through the little window set into the door of the cell. One of the scissor-women sat outside. Her armor, and the few inches of exposed skin, were silent, but her eyes were open. She was awake, but not speaking. I could not see if there was anyone else in the room. I knocked on the window. I needed her undivided attention for a few minutes and the only way I could think of to do that was by making a full confession.

"I'll talk," I said, when she came across. "But only to you."

I could see indecision in her face. It was not really a question of how intelligent the scissor-women were; they operated on agendas that were partially programmed, and partly opaque to the rest of us. Her voice came through the grate.

"I am activating the antiscribe," she said. "Speak."

"My name is Aletheria Tole. I am from Tharsis. I assumed another identity, which was implanted. I came here looking for my sister, who married a woman from Caud many years ago. . . ."

I continued to speak, taking care to modulate the rhythm of my voice so that it became semi-hypnotic. The scissor-women had programming to avoid mind control, but this was something else entirely. As I spoke, I looked into her pale eyes and glimpsed her soul. I drew it out, as I had been taught so many years before on the Plains. It span across the air between us, a darkling glitter. The door was no barrier. I opened my mouth and sucked it in. It lay in my cheek like a lump of ice.

The scissor-woman's face grew slack and blank.

"Step away from the door," I said. She did so. I bent my

head to the haunt-lock and released her soul. It fled into the lock, tracing its engrams through the circuit mechanisms, grateful to be free of me. The door swung open; I stepped through and struck the scissor-woman at the base of the skull. She crumpled without a sound. My own 'scribe was sitting on a shelf: they would have copied its contents. I snatched it up and ran through the maze of corridors.

Discovery was soon made. I heard a cry behind me, feet drumming on the ceiling above. I headed downward, reasoning that in these old buildings the best chance of escape lay in the catacombs below. When I reached what I judged to be the lowest level, I ducked into a chamber and flicked on the antiscribe as I ran. I could not get a signal for Winterstrike. But then, turning the corner, I found the flayed warrior before me.

"Where, then?" I said aloud, not expecting her to respond, but once more the ghost beckoned. I followed the rust-red figure through the labyrinth, through tunnels swimming with unknown forms: women with the heads of coyu and aspiths, creatures that might have been men. I ignored the weir-wards, being careful not to touch them. Sometimes the warrior grew faint before me and I was beginning to suspect why this should be. I could hear no signs of pursuit, but that did not mean that none were following. The scissor-women could be deadly in their silence.

At last we came to a door and the warrior halted. In experiment, I closed down the 'scribe and she was no longer there. I put it on again, and she reappeared.

"You're no ghost," I said. She was speaking. There was still no sound, but the words flickered across the screen.

She was not conversing. The words were lists of archived data, skeins of information. I had not been entirely correct. She was not the ghost of a warrior. She was the ghost of the library, the animated form of the cached archives that we had believed to be destroyed, and that the Caud matriarchy, in their ignorance, had not bothered to find.

I knew what I had to do. I hastened past the warrior and pushed open the door, kicking and shoving until the ancient hinges gave way. I stumbled out into a frosty courtyard, before a frozen fountain. The mansion before me was dark, but something shrieked out of the shadows: a weir-form, activated, of a woman with long teeth and trailing hair. She shot past my shoulder and disappeared. I heard an alarm sounding inside the house. But the 'scribe had a broadcasting signal again and that was all that mattered. I called through to Winterstrike, where it was already mid-morning, and downloaded everything into the matriarchy's data store, along with a message. The warrior's face did not change as she slowly vanished. When she was completely gone, I shut down the 'scribe and waited.

The scissor-women were not long in finding me. They took me back to Mote, to a different, smaller cell. I was not interrogated again. Later the next day, a stiff-faced cleric appeared in the doorway and announced that I was free to go.

I walked out into a cold afternoon to find the streets thronged with people. There would be no war. The matriarchy had, in its wisdom, come to a compromise and averted catastrophe, or so the women of Caud said, mouths twisting with the sourness of disbelief.

I wondered what Gennera had discovered in the library archives that had given Winterstrike such a lever. It would most likely be a weapon, and I wondered also what I had done, in handing the power over one city across to another, even though it was my own. For governments can change, so swiftly, and benevolence never lasts. But I caught a rider through the gates of Caud all the same, heading for one of the way-station towns of the Plain and then for Winterstrike, and did not look behind me.

Dawn, and Sunset, and the Colours of the Earth

MICHAEL FLYNN

Michael Flynn lives in Easton, Pennsylvania. Flynn's first story appeared in Analog in 1984, and he soon became an Analog regular. He's a perfect match for the traditional image of the hard sf writer, except that his interest in craft and in characterization goes deep. As a writer his work is most comparable to the fiction of Nancy Kress. The Firestar cycle is his major work of the 1990s: Firestar (1996), Rogue Star (1998), Lodestar (2000), and Falling Star (2001), a near-future history, done in a very Heinleinesque manner. He has recently published his two best novels so far, The Wreck of The River of Stars (2003), winner of the Robert A. Heinlein Award, and Eifelheim (2006).

"Dawn, and Sunset, and the Colours of the Earth" was published in Asimov's. It is set in Seattle, Washington, and is the story of what takes place in the minds and hearts of a large number of point-of-view characters. Unmediated human reactions to disasters vary greatly and can be very powerful and affecting, as they are here. This is perhaps the best single story to emerge on this theme since 9/11, and has been widely received as metaphorically a 9/11 story. "These hearts were woven of human joys and cares,/...Dawn was theirs,/ And sunset, and the colours of the earth."—From "1914 IV: The Dead" by Rupert Brooke

At six-thirty of an early fall morning, when the sun was just lighting the evergreens and new snow glistened atop Rainier, Motor Vessel Hyak left Pier 52 in Seattle, bound for Bremerton. A Washington State Ferry of the Super Class, longer than a football field, she grossed 2700 tons dead weight and drew eighteen and a half feet. She cast off with nearly a thousand souls aboard and motored into a fog in the center of Elliott Bay.

None of them were ever seen again.

Chino Mendez

People say at first what business has a poor fisherman to speak of Jesus? I have no education, no clever words. I have nothing but the high school and many years of chasing the tuna. But then I thought: what better thing for a preacher than to start as a fisherman? There is precedent, no?

I will give my witness as I saw it, so you may believe with me.

Understand that I was a sinner before. This is important. I drank and I gambled and I had women. Oh, yes. Perhaps you do not think so to look at me, but women find me attractive. I have cut men in fights. Perhaps I killed a man in Miami, but this I do not know for sure.

I tell you this because you must understand what I was, so that you may understand what I am, and so understand

234

what I say. If one as lost as me can be found, there is hope for all.

I was christened Ipolito, but my friends have always called me Chino, because of my eyes. Oh, yes, there were many Chinese brought to Cooba years ago and their blood runs in me. I have been a fisherman all my life, even before I fled Cooba. I fished the Gulf, and then the Keys, and then I came here to these strange, cold waters. Capitan Norris give me a place on his Esmeralda and he teach me the waters of the Sound and there were many very hard years, but never did I complain. Well, perhaps a little.

That morning we cast off and took our bearing on Duwamish Head. The dawn was behind us and the air shimmer like the rainbow. The horizon glowed red; the sky above me, blue; and all the colors ranged between. Oh, the salt tang of the sea! Oh, the cries of the gulls! They swoop in a great circle around the bay. Around and around. I look back now and I see how clear were all my senses that day.

We hear the horn of the ferry as she left the pier and for a time our paths run side by side, the great ferry and the humble fishing boat, but the capitan saw a fog is risen in the bay, so he turn the wheel a little to avoid it. The ferry, yes, had the radar and the global positioning, and so she sailed into the fog, her horn booming. I hear the churn of her engines as she pass us, and I see the people who lined the railing. Some were reading of the newspapers. Some were watching the scenery. Some were talking to each other. There was one—a young girl near the quarter rail—who saw me watching. She was, I think, twelve. She smile and wave to me and I wave back and the capitan saw, and our boat's whistle shrieked and the little girl, she clapped in delight.

But the capitan was fight the wheel. There was a strong current where there been no current before. We struggled like salmon against it as it pull us into the fog, toward the ferry. I had the mad fancy that our boat sat ... somehow ... on the lip of a waterfall.

A collision with such a ship would destroy us, so Ngyuen and me—he is the other deckhand—we throw the bumpers

over the side and stand by with the fending poles. When I
look up again at the deck of the ferry, I see the little girl
bathed in a golden-red light, such as one sees at dawn. The
light came from out of the fog, you understand, and what
sun has ever dawned in the west? It seem like all the ferry
was aglow and I hear a great shout from on board. The foghorn was take on a sound like a train racing away. The little
girl turn and face into the fog and her mouth drop open. Oh,
it was a look of such delight! And she raise her hands to her
face, and then the fog shrouded her, too, and everything—
boat, foghorn, girl—vanished into silence.

I did not understand then what I had seen, but I have
thought over it much since. The strange fog. The strange current. The great light and the shout. Even the birds that
wheeled over the spot. How could such a large vessel vanish
so completely and so quickly? I found the answer in the
smile of a little child.

God had taken them all to Him, as a sign to the rest of us.
That is why you will never find them or find the boat. That is
why the girl smiled. All I was granted was the rainbow sign,
but she had seen the pure light of heaven.

I have heard others say I must be wrong because there
was nothing especially holy about the people on that ferry
that day. Only a thousand ordinary people.

But don't you see?

That is the Good News.

Able Seaman Jimmy Lang

The helicopter is already warming up when Jimmy and
the crew scramble out to the pad. He doesn't know what the
alert is all about, only that something happened to the
Bremerton ferry. Liz Coburn doesn't know either. "But it's
not good news," she says. They check the rescue equipment on board.

It's hard to talk over the steady whop-whop of the blades,
which is just as well, because Jimmy doesn't have much to
say. He can never find the words when he needs them. He'll

rehearse them in his head, and run through them over and over until he is sure they are the right words; but by the time they're ready to come out, the moment for them has passed.

Three frogs trot across the pad, already in their wet suits but carrying their flippers in their hands. Jimmy and Liz help them into the helicopter and Jimmy gives the high sign to the pilot.

He slides the cabin door shut and the chopper tilts and rises. The frogs are checking the air tanks and Jimmy tells them he already done that, but they just look at him and continue checking. Jimmy turns to the window and watches the water race past below them. A container ship is working its way into the harbor and Jimmy cranes his neck to watch it. What he wants to do is ask Liz if she'd go to a movie with him tonight, but what he says is, "Look how big that thing is."

"If that ferry's going down. . . ." Liz tells him. "Oh, God, Hyak can carry two thousand."

One of the frogs tells them that ATN Puget Sound is putting out with the barge and they'll try to get people up on that. "That's a good idea," Jimmy says, like they asked for his approval.

The chopper cants suddenly and changes direction and everyone in the cargo bay dances to keep their balance. Liz falls against Jimmy and Jimmy puts his arm around her waist to steady her. They are friends, him and Liz. "My good bud'," Liz calls him. He thinks she might mean more than that, but he has never gotten up the nerve to ask.

The morning fog has mostly burned off by now. Only a large puff remains, floating in the waters like an iceberg. It is shot through with reflected colors—green from the waters, blue from the sky, brown from the earth, white from the clouds, tawny red from the dawn. Jimmy thinks the water looks funny, too. The waves are all a-jumble, some lapping toward the fog instead of toward the shore. "Looks purty," he tells Liz.

But Liz just shakes her head. "Where's the ferry? Ain't no sign of 'er."

Liz is, in Jimmy's estimation, the most perfect woman on

Earth, after his maw. She's smart, but she doesn't laugh at him like other women and treats him nice, though not half so nice as he would like her to. He has not yet kissed her, although he imagines what that must be like.

"Can a boat sink that fast?" Jimmy asks; but Liz just shakes her head, and it worries him that a smart gal like her doesn't know.

The chopper swoops suddenly toward the fog and Jimmy hears the pilot say bad words.

"Wind shear," the co-pilot calls out, explaining the swerve. The frogs ask if there's a fix on the ferry but the co-pilot shakes his head. "Something's wrong. VTS got three radar fixes, but they're three different positions, and too far away." With the wind the way it is, he'll drop them as close as he can to the last visual position.

Jimmy calls out "Aye" to show that he heard and he and Liz ready the hoist. They clip a sling to the end of the cable to lift people out of the water and onto the ATN's barge. They pile flotation devices by the sliding door. The frogs pull on their flippers and test their air.

"Ready back here," the chief tells the pilot.

The chopper hovers and Jimmy heaves the door open. This is the part he likes best: standing in the open doorway above the waves, with the wind buffeting his face, with the tang of salt on his lips. The buzz of the rotors fills the cabin and the spray splashes onto the deck. A brisk breeze streams toward the fog, and Jimmy fancies the fog is somehow sucking air into it.

Liz waves to the frogs and they step forward and drop the few feet into the bay, one-two-three. She looks out the door. "Ain't nobody in the water," she says.

"The frogs are there," Jimmy points out what he thinks an obvious oversight on her part.

"But who they gonna rescue?" Liz is angry, and Jimmy thinks it is at him for correcting her.

The helicopter rises, banks and, caught in another sudden wind shear, tilts to one side. The pilot cries out. Jimmy can hear the fear even over the noise of the rotors. Liz slips on a puddle and slides down the canted deck and out the open door. Jimmy, who has been holding on to the hoist cable, reaches toward her as she slides past, but their fingers only touch before she is gone, and the last thing Jimmy sees is her scowl of annoyance.

He does not stop to think. "Man overboard!" he cries. The pilot brings the chopper around, and Jimmy readies the sling. Liz is a good swimmer, so he is not worried. He thinks they will laugh about it later, when the rescue is over.

He sees her swimming hard against a strong current. The pilot is fighting the turbulent winds and cannot get close enough for the hoist, so Jimmy unclips the flotation ring and throws it to her so that she does not wear herself out swimming.

He is a good thrower. He always wins when Group Seattle holds its Rescue Olympics. He puts the ring right beside her so that with two good strokes she grabs hold of it. She waves to him and Jimmy grins with pride as he waves back. He already thinks of the kind words she will say to him after she is pulled aboard. Maybe she will kiss him. Maybe . . . He blushes at the anticipation of memories.

Once she has grasped the ring, the strange rip-tide takes Liz into the rapidly diminishing fog. There is not much left of the mist now: a few corkscrew streamers. Seen through the haze, the water looks different, darker and redder. Jimmy searches for Liz through the mist but does not spot her.

Even when at last the fog is entirely gone, there is no sign of her.

The chopper circles and circles and when finally it must return to base, Jimmy is crying like a baby.

Only one of the frogs comes back with them, and he does not say much of anything.

Mitch Raftery

So.

If you're married to a bitch, a dockside bar can be a haven. When you order a bourbon and water, you call it "comfort food," which earns a short grin from the bartender. He asks no questions. He doesn't care why you drink.

"Get a job, get a job," you tell your bourbon. "And what's it matter if it's all the way to hell and Bremerton to get it." This is more than the bartender really wants to know, but he ventures that a good job is a good thing to have.

"Never said it was a 'good' job," you correct him. "Look at me. I got a degree, an MBA. So I should clerk at some two-bit operation?" You don't tell him about the truly skilled accounting work you've done, the kind that got you fired from your last job, or about your ever-loving's mountain of debt that drove you to it. He's got no Need To Know.

Better than nothing, the bartender suggests. I'm a BS in chemistry.

You hold up your now-empty glass. "Then how about some 'better living through chemistry'?"

Now you're talking his language. So, you drink a while and chat in a desultory manner. The bartender comments on the thick fog that has shrouded the harbor. You don't think fog at dawn on Elliott Bay is anything remarkable, but you remark anyway. Yes, that is the thickest and most unusual cloud of vapors ever known to mankind—excluding the cloud of vapors you gave your bitch-wife after the boss caught you with your hand in the till, although you don't share that particular tidbit, either. Sure, the firm didn't file charges, but only because the partners didn't want to invite an audit. So who's the bigger crook? "Everybody does it," you mutter.

Your wife would never have understood anyway. She would never have accepted the blame. Ask the boss for a raise. Tell the boss you need a raise. As if the boss cared what anyone needed. Was there a credit card anywhere on the face of the planet that was not maxed out? Was there an ATM anywhere in Seattle that did not hemorrhage cash as through a suppurating wound?

"Never marry a rich girl," you tell the bartender and he tells you there's no danger of that, just as if you cared what sow he porked. Don't marry a pretty one, either, he adds, or other guys will always be sniffing around.

Yeah, and a rich pretty girl is the worst of both worlds. Too used to spendthrift wealth; too used to flattering beaus. What matter if you have to work late because you need the OT because her skinflint parents didn't approve of Little Precious marrying "down" and won't shell out one dime to help? No reason why that should hamper the good-times or the club-hopping. No reason why she can't always have the best.

And her old man, he has to blah-blah-blah how he started with nothing, too, and how he envies you the same challenge. And what a sanctimonious, bullshit, self-righteous excuse for selfishness that is. Okay, maybe the old fart really had started poor, but then he hadn't married the National Debt, either. No, he had to beget that one, spoil it rotten, and pass it on to you.

"I'd've paid it back," you tell the empty glass in front of you. The way the markets were growing, the money should have multiplied like loaves and fishes long before the comptroller noticed the transaction. And it had. So you waited. Just a little bit more, just a little bit more, and the stock value went up and up and up until there was nothing left, and how could that much money evaporate like the morning fog?

Except this morning's fog is not evaporating. A deep, extended blast pierces the dawn and you start on your barstool because you know it's the ferry casting loose and you are supposed to be on that ferry heading for a job interview in God-forsake-us Bremerton. Oh, Honey-bun will ream you fair if you screw this one up.

You slap a president down on the bar top without even looking to see who it is and stagger out onto the sidewalk. Alaskan Way is nearly empty, as if everyone has stood aside to make room for your hopeless sprint to the pier.

By the time you reach Pier 52, winded and disheveled, the ferry is gone. You curse and shake a fist. Why is it that you never have any luck?

A score of people mill about dockside now, sharing their mutual ignorance of events. You hear something about the ferry vanishing and you turn and gawp at him. "You mean it sank?" He nods. Hundreds dead for sure; maybe more than a thousand. The crowd is buzzing now, approaching that

critical mass where uninformed speculation implodes into a
hard knot of impermeable belief. Stunned sorrow clashes
with ghoulish wonder. The networks are coming! Oh, the
networks are coming!

You shade your eyes against the dazzle of the waves and
you see nothing. No boats. No one in the water. A lone frogman being hoist into the 'copter. Words tumble from the lips
around you: Tragedy. Catastrophe. Terrorists. Aliens. Sea
Monster. But the one word that occurs to you, you do not
voice, and that is Opportunity. And your rage evaporates
with the last of the fog.

Poor Mitch Raftery! He has drowned with all the others.
Your wife will think so; her parents will; your employers
past and prospective will. Why, you have become as one already dead. You can hear the drumming of the dirt on your
coffin lid, the lying words of sorrow spoken over you by
people who never gave a shit when you were alive. But your
death is your salvation, for you can rise again—and not wait
any three damn days to do it. You can be born again through
the waters of this most peculiar baptism, cleansed of all past
sins. You can start fresh, with a new name, a clean slate,
hobbled no longer by a spendthrift wife, or skinflint in-laws,
or hypocritical bosses. Without those shackles, how high
might you soar?

It is a shining vision, and you stand there dockside stunned
by the beauty of it. "By God," you mutter, "I'll have the life
I deserve."

So.

You slip anonymously from the docks, plans already
whirling through your mind. There are ways to acquire
driver's licenses and ID cards. You know a few people. You
can make a new start in a new city; you can live a new life.

You can become a new Mitch Raftery.

Dolly Mannerheim

If beauty lies in the eye of the beholder, so at times does
mere existence. Howard Mannerheim was a man so ordinary

that he vanished into the wallpaper of the world long before he vanished from it.

Dolly Mannerheim, his wife, was a tall woman who managed somehow to appear stocky. It was something in her posture. She was embarrassed to be seen in public with her husband, who was shorter by a head, and so in consequence they did not go out much. Howard never noticed, which was part of the problem.

Her parents had named her "Medallion" for no better reason than a couple of tokes from an especially potent stash the night following the delivery. Dolly-the-child had thought her name Seriously Cool, but she was past forty now and it seemed now less cool than affected. "Dolly" was not much better—resonance of child, resonance of plaything—but she did not know what else she might call herself.

She saw Howard off that morning as she usually did. He was a consulting engineer working at a construction site outside Bremerton. Dolly thought it was an office complex or perhaps a dam—something which at any rate required a lot of wire and concrete and steel. It was also, mirabile dictu, a local assignment—which meant that Howard could actually come home each day, a circumstance not without its complications.

It was his habit to catch the six-thirty ferry, so Dolly would get up with sandpaper eyes and ensure a breakfast and a cab to take him down Queen Anne Hill to the ferry dock. "You take such good care of me," he told her, sitting down to a bowl of soggy flakes drowned in milk. Perhaps he meant it—he was not a demanding man—but he always said the same thing, so perhaps he didn't mean much. Howard was a creature of habits and she had learned (or had convinced herself) over the years that there was behind that compendium of tics and routines no genuine person. Were it not for clichés, he would sit dumb.

At the door, the cab already waiting, Dolly offered him her cheek and he gave it the usual perfunctory benediction before walking down the steps, where the cabbie, had he been listening, might have heard him mutter something about "dry sticks."

Afterward, she just had time to shower and don a blouse and a pair of plain brown slacks before Rick scampered across from next door. He always leapt the fence that separated their two back yards. He never came around to the front door. In part, this was respect for the proprieties (which made it a hypocritical act). In the other part, it was a display of prowess (which made it a cocksure act. It was a picket fence he vaulted).

Dolly let him into the kitchen and he followed her to the bedroom, where they had sex. Some days they might have a drink or two first. In the beginning, she had always taken a few drinks, even before the discreet knock at the kitchen door.

When Rick was engrossed in media res, she whispered urgently, "Howard's at the door! He must have missed the ferry!" And she laughed when he, for a moment, stiffened in alarm.

"I wish you wouldn't do that!" he said (for this was not the first time she had whispered wolf in his ear). But in fact, the possibility that Howard would miss his boat and would walk in upon her was the only excitement left to Dolly in the affair, which had progressed by stages from the unthinkable to the routine. While Howard's assignments had been out of town, she and Rick had enjoyed intimate clubs and fine meals and nights spent on satin in upscale hotels. There had been an electricity to it then. Confined now to the occasional morning or afternoon liaison, the flames had faded to coals, and coals to ashes.

Rick had no idea of this. He thought he mattered. But it had been the dancing and the dining and the shows, not Rick's qualities as lover, that had led Dolly to him. He was no Adonis. As the world measured these things, Howard actually had the edge. Nor was he especially attentive or romantic. What he was, was convenient.

There were days when she wanted to summon Howard on his cell phone and bring him back on some pretext. She wanted something to happen. Anything. Even confrontation. If she could not have the heat of passion, she would have the heat of anger. Lacking either, she had gone cold. And yet, though she thought of it often, she could never quite bring herself to do it.

Later, in the front room, she served coffee, and that peculiar silence descended in which by unspoken consent she and Rick would not talk about what they did. Rick, standing by the front window, pulled the curtain a little to the side and remarked how empty the streets seemed with everyone off to work or school—as if some pestilence had caused humanity to disappear.

Dolly was sitting in her television chair. "I wish Howard would disappear," she responded with sudden, quiet, and terrible sincerity.

Rick thought she meant so that they could drop the secrecy and be together openly, and he preened just a bit, for he desired above all else to be desired. But Dolly had not been thinking of him. In a way, she hadn't even been thinking of Howard; but afterward she could never quite convince herself that it was mere coincidence.

Rick started at the door chimes and Dolly, with malice aforethought, strode to the door as if to throw it open with him in plain sight; but she paused with her hand on the knob until she heard the kitchen door click closed. She smiled a little at that, at what it said about Rick, at what it said about her. Then the bell rang again, and this time she did open the door.

It was Lillian Gelberson from down the corner. Lillian was a young woman who wore glasses only for effect and operated a blog out of her home. Dolly (who had no idea what a web log was) had privately named her Miss Perky, by which she did not intend a compliment. Lillian had the irritating habit of beginning conversations in the middle. "Oh, Dolly! I'm so sorry," she announced in a voice apparently intended to be sympathetic, but which sounded instead only cryptic.

"About what?" Dolly said, wondering if Lillian had seen or heard Rick's departure. Perhaps the woman was sorry that Dolly needed a lover, or that the lover was Rick, or that she herself had no hope of getting one of her own. Dolly was glad something had come along to shoo Rick away, but she was not especially glad that it had been Lillian.

"About what? Ohmigod! You mean you haven't heard? Ohmigod! The Hyak! It's gone! And then I thought, ohmigod, isn't that the ferry that your husband takes?"

"What do you mean gone?" Dolly asked in irritation. "Of course it's gone. It leaves at six-thirty."

"No, no. I mean vanished. Disappeared. Ohmigod, helicopters have been crisscrossing the bay and there's not a trace." She knew this because she had been following the breaking news on the web, uploading links to her blog, trading overwrought IMs. (Nothing is quite so invigorating to a certain turn of mind than the safe proximity of disaster.) Her window opened on a view of the bay, but it had not occurred to her to look out of it. The Web was All.

Dolly failed at first to understand. The words came at her too fast and all a-jumble. "Do you mean the ferry sank? How can that happen?" Ferries sank in the Philippines, ferries sank in Bangladesh. They did not sink in Elliott Bay.

"We don't know yet," Lillian told her. "The fog was in, and people down the harbor say the Hyak never came out the other side." Lillian continued to chatter hyperkinetic sympathy, but Dolly stopped listening after that.

"Disappeared. . . ." she whispered. Perhaps Howard would not be coming home, after all. Rick would like that. Or would he?

She was sitting on the sofa with no recollection of having gotten there. Lillian was beside her, holding her hands. Go away, she thought at the woman. Go away. But the words never reached her lips. She didn't want company. She didn't want to be alone. "Two thousand, did you say?"

Lillian may have speculated on how full the vessel had been, but all she said to Dolly was, "It's Howard that matters now," which was not strictly factual, but which might have been paradoxically true. Howard mattered because he was no longer matter.

"Dolly, is there anything I can do?"

Images of Lillian Gelberson in scuba gear searching

amidst the sunken hulk of M.V. Hyak, hoisting wreckage from the water, performing mouth to mouth resuscitation. Do what, Dolly wondered. "Be careful what you wish for," she murmured, but Lillian did not quite hear.

As the weeks followed and the media ran through their paradigm, her remorse grew ever more intolerable. Each time they showed one of the awkward snapshots on the evening news, she cringed. At meetings of "The Families of the Victims." (And of course there were such meetings. A regiment of grief counselors flew into Seattle to prolong the agony.) Dolly would avoid the other spouses and families and significant others, would not even meet their eyes. Everyone took this as profound grief. No one recognized it as guilt.

Perhaps a thousand wives had wished their husbands gone that morning. It was not beyond belief. But Dolly did not believe it. As nearly as she could estimate, the Hyak had vanished at the very moment when she had wished Howard gone. But the elves that grant the wishes oft have cruel streaks in them. She had never intended that a thousand others vanish with him. The weight of a thousand was as the weight of a single one. There was something about that in the Bible. Or in the Koran. Or in a fortune cookie she had once read.

The media christened it The Disappearance. They early on capitalized the whole business and assigned the roles that everyone was to play. No one ever found any bodies. No flotsam ever graced the shores of Elliott Bay. Consequently, Dolly and the others like her were presented as grieving-but-ever-hopeful that their loved ones would somehow, someday come back. (Although from where, no one seemed quite sure.) And so, she must play Penelope to Howard's Odysseus.

For a time, Rick concurred. In the spotlight of publicity, his stealthy visits might seem unseemly; and so he abstained for a time out of respect for the dead and also out of a little self-interest. But he never did understand why, after the commotion had died and the cameras sought elsewhere for sensation, Dolly did not re-open that kitchen door. He's gone, he told her again and again. He's never coming back. (Not that it had ever mattered when he had.) Dolly could not explain it either, and, after a time, Rick found another neighbor or a co-worker or maybe even his ex-wife.

Dolly no longer needed a lover. Somehow, by vanishing completely, Howard had become ubiquitous, and occupied her life without the bother of actually being present in it. His absence was consequential in a way that his presence had never been. She was asked about him constantly: by friends and relatives, by interviewers for magazines and television stations. She appeared on Conan with a half dozen other bereaved and was applauded by the audience, as if the loss of her husband had been some sort of accomplishment on her part—as indeed she had convinced herself it had.

Dinah Comfort

How bright and empty the bay looks from here. Not a cloud in the sky, not a bit of haze over the water. I can almost reach out past the headland and touch Seattle. They call it the Emerald City, but it all looks golden, somehow, in the sunset.

No boats out on the water. The pleasure craft cower in their marinas, for there is no pleasure in this sunset. The tankers and freighters huddle at dock or have scurried here to Bremerton. Even the Coast Guard cutter has put up. Everyone is afraid to venture out onto the Bay. The waters look so lonely.

He was always late, Ken was. That was his problem from the very start. Never home on time. Always working late, "plugging away at the office." Plugging away, all right. Plugging a secretary, all legs and ass, damn him. Or hoisting a few with "the boys." Sorry, I lost track of the time. And whatever happened to the man I married? He lost track of him, too, somewhere along the way.

He never went looking for love; it always fell into his lap and he never learned how to say no. He hadn't even stayed true to his secretary, the little skirt-hiking bitch. (And so she had forwarded all those e-mails. Treat your wife as you will; but never anger your mistress.)

Ken never thinks ahead, seldom behind. A narrow window around the present moment is all the reality he ever knows. He couldn't even understand why I was still angry with him after he said he was sorry. But that was the problem, wasn't it? He really was sorry—at that moment, at that time and place—and he really thought a few ritual words wiped away his sins. Inside his head, the whole affair was already Past History and it was somehow my fault that it was still an issue.

It's done. It's over. Let's move on.

No, Ken, it isn't that easy. I won't have it be that easy.

But just this once, Ken, could you please be late?

Okay, you had her for the weekend. Our little Cindi, our darling, our treasure. Little Cindi with the sunlight smile. I know you love her, too, in your own lunkheaded, irresponsible way. Dammit, you still love me, in your lunkheaded, irresponsible way. I know you like to see her. You're still her father, Ken. Oh, tardy, forgetful, flighty Ken. God, you were such fun to be with when responsibility didn't matter. I can still remember what we once had. I'll never take you back, but I feel sad that I never will.

Cindi looks forward so to these visits, and it doesn't make me jealous, not really. You pamper her too much, and I guess I can see why. You don't have her every day the way I do. You can afford to pamper, but I have to discipline, and that seems a little lopsided, because at twelve Cindi doesn't understand why I have to be mean when you never are. But it wouldn't be fair to ask you to discipline her when you can't even discipline yourself. You're only supposed to keep her for three days, and I know I've been bitchy before when you've kept her too long.

I forgot, you said. I lost track of the time.

Just this once, just this once, just this once, I hope you lost track of the time. I hope you overslept. I hope you got tied up in traffic. I hope you forgot my complaints. I hope you missed putting her on the ferry.

Twelve. Almost a woman. Almost a person instead of a

child. Just beginning to feel the changes taking place inside her. Just beginning to realize the universe of possibilities lying in wait. But still a child. Still our little girl.

It's getting cold here. I should have brought a sweater with me, but who knew the wait would be this long? Who knows how long it will be?

The Hyak will reappear someday. That weird fog will roll in again. It will grow thick over the bay and coat everything with chill and damp. And the ferry horn will sound, and the Hyak will sail out of the mist as she sailed into it. Maybe she won't know why I'm crying, Cindi won't. Maybe for her only a moment will have passed. That's the way things happen in Faerie. I'll grow old, and she'll stay young forever.

It could be this very night. Or tomorrow. There's always a fog in the morning. Someone needs to be here when the ferry arrives. Someone needs to be here.

Francine Humboldt Whistler, Ph.D.

Francie Whistler had lobbied hard to be appointed to the Board of Inquiry and was happy that the panel would finally meet. But she did not think it appropriate that the session be preceded by a reception, as if it were no more than an academic symposium. She registered at the desk in the Coast Guard building and the warrant officer checked his list and gave her a numbered name badge with her digital photograph already embedded and directed her to the pre-meeting function room.

She spent the pre-meeting chatting with the Coast Guard radar tech over cups of scalding coffee. Vehicle Traffic Service radars had reported three different locations for the missing ferry, and each location had been farther off than the vessel could possibly have been. The Task Force might need a physicist to make sense out of that. An unexplained fact within an unexplained fact. A hole inside a hole. It wasn't the real reason she had pulled strings, but it was a true reason and it would do.

The technician didn't have the answers and knew it, which

made him wiser than many others in the room that Francie
could overhear. Why did people come to an inquiry with
answers? They were supposed to bring questions. The tech
had come to give testimony, and that was all. "I'm glad I
don't have to make sense out of it," he confessed. "I just follow the SOPs. But I know what I saw. I ran the diagnostics
afterward and everything checked out. All the benchmarks
were right on the money. What do you think happened?"

Francie shook her head. "It's too early to say, Tommy. We
don't have all the facts yet." Everyone was still treating the
event as a marine disaster. Francie wasn't so sure. She didn't
think the ferry sank. She thought something else had happened, only she didn't know what.

"All three bearings showed the ferry going away from the
radar," the young man continued. "One going back toward
the dock. One toward Duwamish Head. And one toward
Queen Anne Hill. That isn't possible. Do you think it was a
transient malf in the computer system?"

Francie flashed on a line from an old Firesign Theater album: How can you be in two places at once when you're not
anywhere at all? Except in this case there were three places.

When Commander Randolph arrived, everyone shuffled
into the meeting room. The room was long and wide and
possessed no outside windows. Francie thought this inten-
tional. There would be reminders enough of that tragic day
in the testimony. A view of the scene would have been too
oppressive. Chairs stood rank-and-file in military precision.
Across the front of the room ran a long table with micro-
phones and name cards, one of which bore her name. Francie took her seat at the far left of the table, next to the federal
anti-terrorism expert from Homeland.

"We'll catch the bastards who did this," the man whispered to her as she adjusted her seat. His name card announced him Carl Gratz.

Francie had heard a similar assurance earlier from the
marine engineer, only he had hoped to catch the design flaw
that caused the boat to founder. She smiled at Gratz and
said, "That's why the Task Force was formed," and he nodded as if she had agreed with him.

"You're the University representative," he said after a glance at her name card. "Ms. Whistler?"

"Dr. Whistler."

Gratz grinned. "Yeah, me too." He introduced himself.

There was a pad of paper at each place, as well as a microphone, a pen, a folder, a water glass, and the other inevitable accouterments of committee meetings. Francie tapped the microphone to see if it was live and heard nothing. In the back of the room, the sound tech was playing with his board. She shrugged and picked up the pen.

Turning the pad sideways, she wrote five words across the long margin: Autopsy, Type, Source, Location, and Time. Gratz glanced at what she had written. She underlined the word location and wrote under it three places at once and heading three directions.

"You think the VTS radars were malfunctioning?" Gratz asked her.

"I don't know what to think. It's possible." But they had not been malfunctioning immediately afterward, she remembered. That's what the Coast Guard tech had told her. Under Time, she wrote no radar anomalies after and find out specific times.

Commander Randolph struck the gavel and two dozen cameras in the back of the room chittered like cicadas, so it was clear what image would grace the front pages and web portals tomorrow. Investigating Committee Opens Deliberations. She wasn't sure that these big, public autopsies ever solved anything. They were for assurance rather than investigation. Look, see, we are treating this tragedy with respect and importance! Posing for cameras outweighed posing questions.

Was that too cynical? The others she had spoken with during the pre-meeting seemed determined to get to the root of the matter, though they had different roots in mind; but what a committee did was often independent of what any of its members intended it to do. The moment had a logic of its own.

You're grieving, she told herself, as if she could have

forgotten. She wondered whether others on the Task Force had lost a friend or relative with the ferry.

Work the numbers. Family, school chums, fishing buddies, neighbors, co-workers, merchants . . . On the average, a person knows a thousand other people. So, if an estimated thousand passengers each had a thousand acquaintances, that made a million people, which, even allowing for overlap, covered a fair chunk of metro Seattle. Chances were a third of the people in this room knew someone who had been on the ferry that morning. And the rest all knew someone who did.

Jesus, no wonder everyone looks so bleak.

"This hearing is convened," said the commander of Group Seattle, "to learn the facts of what happened last Tuesday morning on Elliott Bay." He said more, most of it to give the news reporters a lead paragraph, but Francie relaxed a little in her seat. She had been afraid the Coast Guard would push to Get Out There and Do Something and implement a solution before they even knew the root cause. There was still a possibility of that. The Usual Suspects were already demanding to know why the Coast Guard had not prevented the tragedy, and she had heard that one law firm was ginning up clients for a class action suit against the Washington State Ferries.

No, the first order of business was to find out what had actually happened—to measure, as she liked to say, the size and shape of the problem. Her eyes dropped to the pad where she had jotted notes of her chat with the radar tech. He would testify later in more detail, using his logs and printouts, but the gist of it was already captured. Francie thought that what the tech had told her was important, perhaps even central to the problem, that it must be something more than an instrument glitch.

The Committee heard testimony all morning: from the dispatcher at the ferry dock, from the captain and deckhands of the fishing boat that had nearly collided with the Hyak, from the VTS radar technician, from the pilot and copilot of the Coast Guard rescue chopper and the surviving

frogman and crewman, from the meteorologist for the Elliott Bay region, from the chief mechanic who had worked
on the Hyak's last repairs. No trace had been found: no bodies or body parts, let alone survivors. How could that boat
have gone down so damned fast, and with no flotsam? With
not so much as an oil slick?

The reporters drifted away during the testimony. It was
boring and it was for the most part technical. Francie, on the
other hand, quickly filled her sheet with notes. The current
encountered by the fishing boat. The wind encountered by
the helicopter. Times of departure and disappearance, the
vessel's beam and length, her capacity, her speed, the distance from the dock to the estimated point of her disappearance, her three oddly contradictory bearings at the time of
disappearance. . . .

"Excuse me," she said, and then had to repeat herself after the sound tech turned her mike on. "Tommy," she asked
the VTS tech, "do your records show when these peculiar
readings began and when they stopped?"

A moment passed while the tech searched his records.
There had been several freighters and an oil tanker moving
on the Bay at the time, and VTS tracked all of them. He
found several other anomalies, starting about half an hour
before the Hyak left dock. Francie asked for a copy of the
data and the tech handed the sheets to a committee clerk for
photocopying. She compared the time to the meteorologist's
report of when the fog first appeared.

Very curious, Francie thought. Gratz watched quizzically
as she scribbled.

"How is any of that important?" he asked.

She reminded herself that he was still chasing terrorists
in his head, and not yet gauging the metes and bounds of
the problem. "I don't know that any of it is," she admitted.

"Once we locate the wreckage," Gratz said, "we'll know
whether they blew it up from the inside or the outside."

She looked at him. "'They.'"

He shrugged.

She said, "No one heard an explosion."

"No one reported an explosion," he corrected her. "The

sound may have been muffled by the fog or the horns. Or the
bomb was planted down inside the hull."

Francie turned once more to her list. There were any number of explanations. If this, if that, if the other thing. . . .
Allow enough ifs and anything was plausible. They could
spin theories until the cows came home. It could have been
OJ or Elvis. It could have been little green men from Alpha
Centauri. If you start with the conclusion, you can always
imagine a trail that reaches it, but the simplest explanation
for not hearing an explosion was that there had not been one.
The proper place to start is at the beginning. Go from what
you know toward what you don't. Don't start with what you
believe.

Later, and because the media would tolerate nothing else
but, the man from Washington State Ferries read the list of
names that had been confirmed so far. There would be a wall
or a monument one day. That was inevitable. In the meantime,
there was some balm in reading aloud the names of the lost.
"John Dunning, master," the man said. "Peter Jurgowitz, mate.
James O'Grady, engineer. Karen Lewis-Nowick, assistant engineer . . ." And so on through the two oilers and the eight
deckhands, the two Coast Guard frogmen and the seaman
who had fallen from the helicopter. Francie wondered at the
order in which the names were read and decided that it was the
order in which their presence on the ferry—or in the aborted
rescue—had been confirmed. Cindi Comfort, she heard. Howard Mannerheim. Dale Wingate. Mitch Raftery. Paul Latimer.
Agnes, Becky, and Kyle Timmer. The names ran on. The lit-
any was numbing. When the recitation reached "Donald
Whistler," Francie jerked a little in her seat and the man from
Homeland turned to her and said, "Your husband?"

"No, my baby brother." Well, he was twenty-five, but he'd
always be her baby brother now, because he would never,
ever grow any older. She could remember coming home
from college and little Donny running to meet her at the
door. F'annie's home! F'annie's home! And now, little Donny
would never be there again.

Gratz gave her a handkerchief and she dabbed at her eyes.
"I'm sorry," she said.

The WSF official was still reading the list and everyone listened with long faces. A couple of times, Francie saw people in the meeting room react to a name. "We kept thinking he would call," she said at last. "Mom and me and Andy. Andy is the oldest. Dad's dead. We thought, maybe Donny caught the 5:10 and he was safe in Bremerton before the Hyak sailed. But he would have called to tell us that, once he'd heard the news. He would have called to tell us he was safe. But it's been nearly a week now, and there's been no word."

"That's the worst part," Gratz said. "There's no closure."

"Closure." She squared the pad in front of her; moved the pen to one side. She hated that word. "After a while, you grow numb."

"I didn't know anyone on board."

Francie remembered that he was from DC. "Are you complaining?"

He shook his head. "No, just admitting that I can't know how you feel."

Maps of the bay were passed down the table. She took one and handed the last to Gratz. "I'm not sure that I know, either," she said. Key points were highlighted on the map. Pier 52. The normal ferry route. The location of the fishing boat, approximately correct because its skipper had taken a sighting on Duwamish Head only a few minutes earlier. The direction of the current they had fought. The direction of the wind-shear that had nearly brought down the 'copter. The positions of other vessels in the bay. And, marked with red crosses, the three contradictory positions for Hyak.

Always draw a picture of your data, her statistics professor had told her years ago. Francie took her pen and connected the crosses. It was in there, she thought. Inside that triangle. She looked through her notes on the VTS network and marked the location of the three malfunctioning radars, connecting the radars to the positions they had given.

"The three lines intersect," Gratz said. He had been watching her construction in silence. "Is that important?"

"I don't know." She used her name card as a straight-edge and projected the direction of the current that had caught the fishing boat. It, too, ran through the same locus. The back of her head began to prickle. She did the same with the wind direction. It missed, but by only a little, and the 'copter pilot had been too pre-occupied to take a more precise bearing. She added the other anomalous sightings, and each one had passed near or through that same point.

She studied her ad hoc plot with growing unease. That was where it happened, she thought.

Whatever it was.

Taralyn Harrison

Subject: Re: The Disappearance.
From: JJ Brannon
What the hell is all the fuss about the Hyak? Mix some drunk captain with a little fog and incompetent government flunkies who can't even properly read radar they were trained on. It's plain buggy software compounded by human greed and stupidity at fault. The divers will find the ship once the mud settles.

Subject: Re: The Disappearance.
From: Pagadan
GMAB. This is Mother Nature striking back—and about time, I'd say. Who else could create fog, currents, and winds like that. And this is just the beginning. Did you read about the chasm on the way to Disneyland, the earth quake in that Texas oil field, the giant sink hole between Orlando and Tampa?

Subject: Re: The Disappearance.
From: Velvet
JJ, did you even read the report about the radar tech? It's a real, honest-to-God anomaly. Either time travel or a portal to an alternate Earth. I'd say a tractor beam used by an entity who couldn't quite handle it.

Subject: Re: The Disappearance.
From: JJ Brannon

All right, I saw that guy with the mini-sub interviewed on the 6 o'clock news. I admit those videos show no ferry down there in the mud. So I think it was Release 1.0 of some quantum-nanobyte experiment. Some of that crap probably got loose and the ferry fell apart in a zillion pieces and washed away. That's where all the steam came from, too.

Subject: Re: The Disappearance.
From: FIJAGDH

A buddy of mine out west says the Taos, NM, hum changed frequency the same day they lost that ferry. Which proves my theory about the Taos hum being part of some secret government experimentation with found/donated alien technology.

Subject: Re: The Disappearance.
From: IrishBet

JJ, have you forgotten the USS Eldridge? Teleportation could account for the anomalies at the time of reappearance. I've never believed they gave up that line of inquiry. SciAm ran an article about the practical possibilities of teleportation back in 1997. I'm betting a shiny new quarter the ferry will be back.

Subject: Re: The Disappearance.
From: Tee-Ell

Dont you people listen to yourselves? It's not a game!! I lost my boy on that boat. Maybe if you had, youd look at things different.
    Taralyn

Subject: Re: The Disappearance.
From: Les OneGuy

The only scientific fact that explains this is a teleportion experiment by the North Koreans, what else culd they be doing with those reactors. It's people like you who hinder the advance of civilization with your moralistic superstions, your sexual hangups, and your inability to see that all religions are a fraud based on the big people loarding it over the regular ones. This will probebly trigger a world-wide war ending in nuclear conflagation, but I feel that in the end it will work out for the better and bring humanity to the stars, or at least those of us who can see it and preapare for it.

Subject: Re: The Disappearance.
From: Kwakiutl1968

Have you ever been whale watching? Have you ever stood on deck and been fixed by those big, penetrating, accusing eyes? Whales know who we are, and what we've been doing to their kind for a thousand years. I don't know what they did to the Hyak, and I don't know how they did it, but the Hyak incident is only the beginning. The whales have finally decided to fight back.

Subject: Re: The Disappearance.
From: Tee-Ell

I dont know nothing bout no teleportation or time travel or althernate earths whatever that is. But I do know bout my son, Tiron. Maybe it mean something to you people, or maybe it dont. You think people just words on a screen cause you never ever see each other. But here I am doing the same, like my daughter showed me how, so maybe this is just something I need to do and if anyone read it or not, it dont really matter. So let me make the words flesh.

Tiron he was a fine boy. Big, like he could rest his chin on top my hed and long arms. Had to be long to rap all the way round his mama. Only twenny last march, but he was working hard and trying to save up money to maybe go to the communty college next year. He was always study hard in school. He wasnt smart like some, but worked at it way his daddy did. He use to tell me things like I never heard of before, all about enjins and that. He had a book about how stuff worked and he'd tell me about it ever chance he got. And sometimes he take apart stuff like my toaster or the telefone just to see you know what was inside? You should of seen his eyes when he talked mashines. He wanted to get one of those soshit degrees. Nobody in our famly ever got no degrees, so we was real proud of him for trying. I know his daddy would of been. His daddy was kilt in the Stan, and Tiron, he missed him something bad. He never cried much. You dont want to be a boy cries much in this naborhood. But he always goes how he wants to invent something and name it after his daddy.

Well he use to work little jobs at repair stores and stuff, like places where he got to play with mashines. And then last spring his name finly come up at the union hall and he got a job as oiler on the ferry boats. Oh he was so proud! He was so proud. He come home real greasy from those rides. Everbody like him and he like everbody on the boats. He was reel happy down there with the enjins and things.

It was just before it happen that Tiron told me he want to be a navel architek which is all about building boats. I didnt understand half what he said and I probly didnt spell it right. I know I dont spell so good. When I was a kid I didnt have the same chances as Tiron so I never mounted to much, tho I kept myself clean and honest even when it was hard. Tiron, he could of been somebody.

Whats hardest is that he wasnt supposed to be on Hyak that day but he traded with a friend who had to go see a doctor. That Keith is so twisted up over it. Half of hims sorry it was my Tiron went in his place, but the other half is happy it wasnt him. I dont hold it against him tho. Hes a nice boy and was good friend to Tiron.

Tiron he lef the house that day just like always and took his lunch with him and he kiss me on the cheek and say he wants my pulled pork for supper. Thats what I was cooking when I hear the news. Pulled pork. Oh he did favor that some.

You never know when you say good-bye for the last time. You never ever know that. It seem just like ever other time, and later you wish youd of said something more or did something more but you dint

Was hard for me he called away like that so young. I dont know why the Lord wanted him but I guess he must got a reason. I just wisht he explain it to me, cause I dont want to think it just bad luck he be gone.

Taralyn

Subject: Re: The Disappearance.
From: Come2Reven
I read an expose that the ship in question wasn't actually
the U.S.S. Eldridge docked in Philadelphia, but the U.S.S.
Philadelphia docked in Eldridge. No wonder the facts have
been so hard to uncover, huh?

Subject: Re: The Disappearance.
From: DANNISGRL
Ch 7 is going to run a special with the guy who talks to
dead people. It's about time science was brought in to solve
the case!

William J. Timmer, Ph.D.

Abstract: It will be shown that the well-known disappearance of MV Hyak is the result of a singularity in the dynamic field equations for rotating magnetic fields. The locus
for this singularity will be shown to be unstable in the sense
of Poincare and to be subject to aperiodic shifts in its locus
due to endogenous factors. These shifts will be conceptual-
ized by means of Thomian catastrophe surfaces.

Text: It is well known that the state of a dynamic system
acting under a potential will move toward the nearest equilibrium point in its state space in such a way as to minimize
the value of the potential function. The set of all such equilibria comprises a manifold over the parameter space known
as the "attractor." If the manifold is "folded" or "pleated,"
loci exist in parameter space possessing two or more distinct
equilibria. A system entering such a bifurcation set while at
one equilibrium will snap to the other should it leave the set
at the opposite boundary. From the reference frame of the
original state, the object will appear to accelerate rapidly in a
direction orthogonal to the sheet. Rene Thom [7] called this
a catastrophe, although he did not mean a catastrophe in the
colloquial sense, such as the loss of one's wife and children,
but simply a sudden change from one equilibrium state to
another.

The anomalous radar fixes in the case of the Seattle Event, each of which showed the ferry accelerating directly away from it, provide a good empirical fit to the model. The fit is further substantiated by anecdotal evidences; namely, the dopplering of the boat's horn and the red-shifted light reported by eyewitnesses. Clearly, the vessel accelerated along a dimension orthogonal to normal 3-space. It is suggested that the Elliott Bay Anomaly marks the edge of a higher dimension bifurcation set in space-time. One might call this colloquially a "drainhole."

That a singularity must exist in certain dynamic systems is well known, but the locus of the singularity may be subject to random fluctuations. A comparison is made to the familiar topological problem of covering a billiard ball with hair. Such a cover must leave a gap, for example the "bald spot" that forms when men comb their hair flat. If the hair is combed differently, the "bald spot" will appear in a different position.

An analogous process can be applied to higher dimensional dynamic manifolds. While locally smooth, they cannot be globally smooth. Very little in life is globally smooth. Thom's Classification Theorem states that only seven stable catastrophes can arise from variations in the parameter space. These qualitatively distinct discontinuities arise from a combination of technical and geometric considerations involving the regions of parameter space where the catastrophes happen. It is suggested that the Elliott Bay Anomaly is of this nature. Anecdotal data suggests a former locus near the island of Bermuda. A hole being an absence (or is it the absence that leaves the hole?), it does not physically move; but a change induced on the manifold that closes a hole will inevitably cause another to open elsewhere. A conservation law is suspected. This will require additional research.

We pause here and consider marriage as a dynamic system operating under a potential. It, too, is manifold and it is hypothesized that a wrinkle must necessarily exist in it, and that if one difficulty is resolved, another must inevitably take its place. A suitable stabilizing strategy might then be the introduction of a permanent difficulty. The truly destructive strategy is the expectation that there ought to be none.

However, the existence of these local catastrophes, which we may term "spats," depends on a combination of technical and geometric considerations involving the regions of the marital parameter space where the catastrophes happen. A million variables affect the emergence of form within the envelope of the marriage, all working to minimize its potential. These variables include genes, chemicals, environmental conditions, space, and time. At any given time, only one or two are likely to change in a discontinuous manner, arguing that while the phenomenon is global, the precise shape of the catastrophe may depend on local conditions. So may a hitherto-faithful spouse suddenly engage in a destructive affair for reasons of long, if obscure standing; or a sweet young boy alter into a surly adolescent. This being the case, the passage of time (and, with it, the alteration of the local conditions that precipitated the discontinuity) may rectify the anomaly.

Yet, to analyze the system in such dispassionate terms may earn the sobriquet of a "passionless little git" lacking "any semblance of human feelings." Such a judgment would be mistaken, as it refers only to the expression of, and not the impression of, passion. The mousiest man may seethe with murderous rage; an undemonstrative man, with tender love. When once it is said, "I love you," no additional information is transmitted by endless repetitions. Logic teaches us that. Better to spend words on increasing the information content of the system, such as by noting that "we are out of bread" or "the car needs washing." Because a thought has not been spoken, it would be illogical to conclude that it has not been thought. Would the household be not short of bread were it unmentioned? Likewise, would a spouse be short of love were it not mentioned? The analogy is precise; the parallel, instructive. But the results have proven upon inspection wholly divergent, suggesting the applicability of chaos theory.

And now they are gone, Becky and little Kyle and Agnes alike, fallen into a hole that has no bottom, creating a similar hole in the author's life. Would it have made any difference if the author had said "I love you" at the pier-side? Would they be less completely gone? Perhaps. Perhaps she would have turned back at the words, as to a strange attractor, and stepped off the gangplank and into my arms as she once did when she and I and all the world were younger.

But time is the one asymmetric parameter governing the state space. Which is just another was of saying that there is "no turning back the clock."

Unless there is something on the other fold. It would be pleasant to believe that those who have "passed over" to the other sheet have found a new life there, but science tells us nothing, and nothing is little comfort.

God damn this paper and this conference.

The author has found the preparation of this paper difficult. Select all. Delete.

Does that not sum up the entire phenomenon of the Disappearance? "Select all. Delete."

Axel Moller

Scene: the living room of a small three room flat in downtown Seattle. A hexagonal table covered by a green felt is situated in the center of the room but with only five chairs spaced around it. Four men sit at the table, one of them stacking poker chips of assorted colors. Behind them, the window looks out on tall, anonymous buildings, but in the gap between two of them lies a slice of Elliott Bay. It is dusk, just going on to evening.

Enter Axel Moller.

Axel: I brought the beer. I hope you have the cards. (Places six-pack on the table. Removes jacket and tosses it on the nearby sofa.)

Luis: Long as you brought money and an inclination to lose.

Axel: In your dreams, Luis. (Sits.) Hey, Beef, Gordo, Chen, how're they hanging?

Various hand-slaps and exclamations of masculine greetings.

Gordo: (Gathers cards into deck, squares deck, begins to shuffle) Seven card stud. Ante up, boys.

They throw chips into the pot and Gordo deals the cards.

Gordo: We gotta jack showin.' Your bet, Chen.

Chen: (Throws in another chip) Five.

Beef: Sure you can afford it? (The others match the bet and Gordo deals the next round.)

Gordo: Hey, Axe, you plan on drinkin' all that yourself?

(Axel breaks open the six-pack and hands out the cans. Then he sits staring dumbly at the sixth can, which he has just placed at the empty sixth side of the hexagon.)

Axel: Shit. Oh, shit. (He turns away from the table.) Damn.

(The others look at Axel, at the can, at the empty space, at each other. Axel goes to window and leans his arm against the sash, staring out toward Elliott Bay. He rests his head upon his arm.)

Life's a bitch.

Beef: And then you . . . (He shuts up abruptly.)

Axel: (Without turning) You think you get over it, but you don't, really. You forget for one little second, and some old habit pops up and reminds you.

Gordo: Paul was our friend, too.

Axel: Yeah. Yeah, I know.

Beef: (Lifts his beer can in salute) Absent friends. (No one joins the toast. Beef shrugs and drinks alone.)

Axel: I saw the fog come in yesterday. Another one of those "Bermuda" fogs.

Chen: (Shakes head) Bermuda Fog. In Seattle harbor.

Axel: And there's always some moron, he rows out or he swims out into it because he wants to visit another plane of existence.

Gordo: It's a helluva thing, all right. People got no sense.

Luis: No one ever come back and said where the "drain-hole" goes—

Chen: If that's what it is.

Luis: —so why are they so freaking sure they want to go there?

Axel: (With quiet vehemence) What difference does it make what it is or where it goes or even if it "goes" anywhere at all? Paul's gone. They're all gone. And no one thinks they're ever coming back.

Beef: 'Cept that loony-kazoony over in Bremerton, goes down to the dock every morning. Hey, remember how Paulie used to rig the big arc lamps when we worked night crew. And he'd aim them so's any gal walking past the site, the light would shine right through their dresses and you could see 'em all like in silhouette? (Laughs)

Luis: He was a funny guy.

Beef: Sometimes what was under those dresses shouldn'ta been seen. Geez. Supersize those fries. That's why Paulie always was working out at the gym, pumping iron and firming up the old pecs.

Chen: Hey, Ax, that's where you met Paul, wasn't it? Down at the gym.

Axel: (Turning from the window) About a year ago. I was in physical therapy, for my ankle. We used to chat in the cardio room when we had treadmills side by side.

Beef: Bet he raced you. That's the kinda guy he was. Real competitive. Bet he cranked up the revs on that treadmill to see if you could keep it up.

Axel: (Looks out window once more) Yeah. He always wanted to see if I could keep it up.

Gordo: Hey, c'mon. St. Paul was the guy wrote all those letters. Paulie was a stand-up guy, but he wasn't Mr. Perfect. Blanche said—

Chen: Poor Blanche! I wonder if she's gotten over it yet.

Gordo: She sort of noticed that none of you guys come round any more.

Beef: (Defensively) Well, she wasn't the one playing cards, was she?

Axel: (From window, but without turning) You see her lately, Gordo?

Gordo: (Sips from can, puts it down) Yeah. Lately.

Beef: Comfortin' the ol' widow, Gordo? (Winks to others; Chen turns away.)

Luis: Look, can we play cards?

Chen: Hey, remember when our guys played Axel's team in the softball league and Paul—

Beef: Hey, Axel, you warehouse guys are pussies! You know what we do in construction?

Luis: Yeah, we make big erections. You tell that joke every time, Beef, and it wasn't funny after the first thirty-two times.

Axel: (Turns a little toward Luis and smiles faintly) Paul was good at that.

Luis: Axel, sit your ass down so I can like deal this hand?

Axel: You think it's really a drainhole like they say? (He lingers by the window gazing out.)

Beef: No, it's an asshole. That's why everyone on that boat wound up feeling like shit.

(Axel takes two steps and grabs Beef by the shirtfront and yanks him to his feet. His biceps bulge and tremble under his tight-fitting shirt. He holds Beef for a moment as if he will shake him to pieces. The others look on with varying degrees of shock and surprise. Finally Luis and Chen stand and separate the two. Beef sinks back to his seat; Axel returns to his vigil by the window.)

Chen: Like, who says it's a drainhole? I've heard a dozen theories. It's a wormhole to somewhere else in the universe. Or it's a doorway to another dimension—

Luis: That's the Twilight Zone, Chen. What the hell difference does it make? Look, the best way we can honor Paulie's memory is to drink a toast and play a hand. And maybe take up a collection for Blanche. Gordo's right. The girls have as much fun as us at the summer picnics and stuff. Why should Blanche be out of it now just because Paulie's dead?

Gordo: Don't bother. She's not exactly broke up about it.

Luis: Now that's a helluva thing to say.

Gordo: (Shrugs) Paulie and Blanche hadn't been in the sack together for a long time.

Chen: What, they were having a fight and . . . ?

Gordo: No, it was the other way 'round. She was upset because he wasn't coming through in the husband department. So she figured he had a little something on the side and that pissed her off.

Luis: Paulie?

Beef: Well, he was always checking out the girls. You know. "Hey, get a load of that set." Maybe he just wanted a closer look.

Axel: (To Gordo) She say who Paulie was seeing?

Gordo: Nah. Blanche figured he was catting around until about a year or so ago, then he found someone steady. She didn't mind it too much when she thought he was playing the field, but she hated the idea that there was someone else special in his life. Some poker nights he wouldn't come home until way after the game broke up.

Axel: (Slowly) Maybe he thought he'd picked up a disease and didn't want to give it to her, and that's why he stopped sleeping with her.

Gordo: And so he's still St. Paulie? Excuse me if I quit the church. Blanche is a special lady and he treated her like she didn't even exist.

Beef: (After a pause) You seem to know a lot about how Blanche feels.

Gordo: (Throws cards down on table)

Luis: Christ . . . ! You're porkin' Paulie's widow, aren't you?

Chen: She's not exactly his wife any more, Luis.

Gordo: And not for a long time, even before he died.

Chen: (To Gordo) You mean . . . Before? Well, shit!

Gordo: What's sauce for the gander is sauce for the goose, isn't it? He wasn't having any of her, and neither me or her saw any reason to let it go to waste.

Luis: (Drops his cards, too) I don' feel like playin' no more.

Chen: Me neither. Jesus, Gordo. He was our pal. You don't go doing that to your buddy.

Gordo: How was I hurting him? If Paulie didn't want no one in bed with Blanche, he shoulda stayed there himself, 'stead o' running around trying to prove what a man's man he was. I didn't take a damn thing from him that he hadn't already tossed aside. Aren't I right, Axel?

Axel: (By window, wipes cheek with sleeve, turns to face group) Yeah. That's right. He was a man's man.

The Adventure Club

There were seven of them and they all lived in the neighborhood except for Jimmy, so it was never any problem to get together after school. They usually met in Denny's basement because that was where they kept the club's flag and Denny's dad had helped set up a laboratory. They had racks of chemicals that they used to experiment with different rocket fuels, and an electrical bench where they worked on ignition systems. One time they had blown all the fuses in the house and Denny's dad had made them promise not to test a circuit until they had shown him the schematics and he had inspected their work. Mr. Collingwood worked at Boeing and knew all sorts of stuff about electronics.

But developing a rocket ship had taken a back seat to the Seattle Drainhole. They even held some club meetings down near the old ferry dock because they hoped to see the hole open up, which would have been seriously cool.

"But there's no periodicity to it," the twins said, after Denny had called the meeting to order and they were all sitting around the old table in the basement with cans of pop and a big bag of chips. Frank and Harry were identical twins, and no one was ever sure which one was talking. SciAm and the other science mags had reported the lack of periodicity, but the club's rule was never to trust authority. Frank (unless it had been Harry) had compiled a list of all confirmed events, starting with the initial tragedy. And Harry (unless it had been Frank) had analyzed the time series.

"It's a chaotic system," said Jimmy. "I knew it."

"Everybody knows it, dummy," said Red. "That Timmer guy proved it. It was in Science News."

"Besides," Denny said, "you can have irregular time series without chaos. Look at eclipses."

"Solar system is chaotic," said the twins. "Poincare proved it."

"Ah, screw you."

"Up yours."

"S'what are we gonna do about it?" Red asked. The others all looked at him.

"I dunno, Red," Jimmy said, scratching his head. "Get a really big freaking cork?"

Red's face illustrated his nickname. "Naw, I mean those people on the boat. Somebody's gotta get them outta the hole."

"You crazy, dude?" said Denny. "They're croakers, for sure. If the singularity didn't crush them, they've run out of food and water by now."

"Hey!" said Jimmy, with a nod toward Red. "Watch your mouth."

"Aw, shit, Red," the club president said. "You know I didn't mean nothing by it."

Red wiped his eye, which had gotten something in it. "I can deal with it."

"Your brother was a really neat guy," Denny insisted.

"I know that!" said Red. "But who's doing squat to rescue him?"

The club fell silent as each contemplated how a rescue might be achieved through a singularity. Finally, one of the twins broke the silence.

"What if it isn't? A singularity, I mean. Frank and I lurk on a physics usenet newsgroup out in dot-uni. It's the real thing, not dot-com crap. Anyhow, this one physicist named Janatpour, he said that physics ought to make sense, and singularities were just artifacts of the math, not real things."

"Oh, that's convincing," said Jimmy.

"No, he pointed out that sunspots are caused by differential rotation of the sun. The northern and southern hemispheres rotate at different speeds, and that sets up eddies in the electromagnetic field."

"You might have noticed," Jimmy pointed out, "that the drainhole is here on Terra, not on Sol."

"Sure," said Harry. "But Terra has a molten core. What if that has differential rotation? That could put twists into Terra's electromagnetic field, too."

"Umm," said Denny. "You saying the drainhole is a sunspot?"

"Earthspot, dummy," said Red, who had recovered his composure.

"Well," said Frank, taking the handoff from his brother, "if Terra was a ball of plasma, it would be. But it's the same kind of thing. At least this Janatpour guy says so, and Timmer and Whistler both think he might be on to something."

"Those two are too emotionally involved," said Denny. "You need complete detachment to do Science."

Red leaned forward and the card table rocked a little from the weight. "So, if the drainhole is a vortex, not a singularity. . . ."

". . . it's gotta open up somewhere else. Not on Terra, or we woulda heard something. But somewhere."

Visions of gateways, of alternate universes, of time portals danced in their heads. Denny's dad came to the head of the cellar stairs. "What are you kids up to?" he called.

A chorus of "Nothing," "Just talk," "We're cool, Dad," and "We're gonna rescue the Ferry People."

"Okay," Mr. Young replied. "Just don't run any experiments without my okay."

Another chorus of "okay" and then they all turned to Red.

"Whaddaya mean we're gonna rescue the people on the ferry?"

If the Adventure Club had owned a submersible, they might have sent it into the drainhole. But their club treasury, Jimmy reported, could not take the hit. So they did the next best thing.

"If we can just get a message back from them," Red insisted, "the grownups would get off their butts and do something." He meant a message back from his brother Steve, but he didn't say that. The others, dazzled by the headlines they could read afterward, set themselves to planning.

First, they needed a lot of rope. And a container of some sort for the message. They needed a boat so they could get close enough to the drainhole when it opened to throw the container into it, and to give them a base to haul it back out again. That was conceptual engineering.

Details. They bought a lockbox with a combination lock on it so it wouldn't open up accidentally during transit. Red wrote a message to put inside, and they added extra paper and pens so the Ferry People could write an answer. Denny painted the combination for the lock on the outside—they left it at 0-0-0—so they could open it up at the other end.

How much rope would they need? How deep was the hole? " 'Deep' is the wrong word," Jimmy said. "The vortex goes along Kaluza-Klein dimensions, not up or down or nothing. They bought as much clothesline as the treasury could afford, nearly a thousand feet, and coiled it around a garden hose windlass so they could crank it back out. Denny was a Boy Scout, so he tied the ends of the different coils together with knots guaranteed not to come loose.

Jimmy's folks had money and had a big pond in their backyard in the suburbs. The club set up a target on the pond and practiced throwing the rope, using a weight tied to the end so they wouldn't damage the box. Jimmy's mom saw them and asked what they were up to and they all chorused, "Target practice," and she shook her head and went back inside. Denny and Red and Frank were most accurate, so they got the job of actually making the throw. They practiced winding the rope back in, too.

The twins borrowed their dad's fishing boat and paddled it into the bay one night and hid it under the pilings for Alaskan Way. Since the harbor was shut down, there was little traffic on the Bay or along the shore, but they did it in the evening and didn't start the outboard. They pretended they were infiltrating an enemy coast.

The next evening, Denny and Red took the windlass down
and screwed it to one of the boat's seats.

After that, it was a matter of waiting.

Since no one knew when the vortex would open, the club
worked out a watch schedule. School hours were out, as was
dinner time, and Jimmy could not always come into the city.
They decided to have always two sentries in the boat, and
one of them to throw, the other to work the windlass.

In practice, they couldn't keep the schedule. There were
unexpected chores at home, or school assignments. On weekends, the entire club would hang out near the pier, with binoculars and notebooks, and take turns in the boat. Once,
some fishermen saw them climbing down to the water-level
and warned them that it was dangerous "because of the
drainhole."

"As if we didn't know about it," Denny commented
afterward.

The hole opened up twice while they were in school and
one other time during breakfast. They could hear the hooting of the klaxon all over the city and, like everyone else,
they stopped what they were doing, and didn't even speak
until the all-clear sounded.

Finally, it happened while they were on watch.

It was a weekend and Red and Denny were in the boat that
hour. Jimmy and the twins were above, on Alaskan Way,
pretending that they knew what girls were all about. There
were only a handful of pedestrians about on miscellaneous
mid-day missions. Jimmy had just said that maybe they
should give up the vigils, when the hooting klaxon gave them
a jump and they turned and crowded the guard rail.

"Hot spit," said Harry. "There it is."

It was nothing more than a fog bank, but the siren was
triggered by the VTS radar net, so they knew this was the
real thing. The radars were seeing double again.

"It's like a lens," Frank said, pointing. "If we could see
through the fog like radar, everything in line with the vortex
would look farther away."

"There they go," said Harry.

The motorboat's outboard had started up and the craft putted out from under the pilings and toward the fog. Red was at the engine and Denny, in the bow, already had the rope coiled for throwing.

"Hope he doesn't get too close," Jimmy said, and Frank looked at him.

"They aren't stupid." He raised his binoculars and watched his chums' progress.

Red put the boat just at the edge of the fog and turned it broadside. Denny stood up and whirled the rope around his head. The message box on the end flashed every time it caught the sun.

A Coast Guard power boat sped across the Bay, giving the fog a wide berth. "Get off the water!" a voice boomed at the messengers. "These waters are dangerous!"

Denny let fly and the box tumbled into the fog. The rope drifted after it, then became taught and began to unreel from the windlass.

The idlers who had been walking along Alaskan Way had come to the rail, drawn by the novelty. "What the hell are those kids up to?" Frank heard someone ask.

"They're trying to send a message to the ferry," he told the man, with a mix of defensiveness and pride. Harry piped his agreement. Jimmy, on the other hand, remained silent and stepped away from the twins.

The windlass ran out to the end. The rope jerked and the boat began to drift into the fog.

"Oh, shit!" said Harry from the esplanade.

Denny said later that the same thought crossed his mind. Red had kept the motor running "to maintain station," but he was working the windlass. Denny leapt past him to seize the outboard's handle and turn them away from the vortex. He revved the motor and the boat moved slowly away from the fog, as if dragging an enormous anchor. Then it slowed to a stop and began moving backward.

"I can't wind it in!" Red cried from the windlass. "It's like the box got really, really heavy."

"Cut it loose, cut it loose!" Denny's pants were wet and he hoped everyone would think it was from the water. He reached overboard to splash water on himself and felt a really strong current. The vortex was sucking in water and air and—pretty soon—him and Red. Overhead, the twisting magnetic fields were confusing the birds' directional senses and they were circling endlessly around the drainhole.

Then the whole windlass tore loose from the seat where they had screwed it in. It whipped overboard, hit the water, and skipped twice before it slithered at the end of the rope into the fog.

Red went over with it.

"He got tangled in the rope," Denny told the twins while they waited for their parents to come get them from Coast Guard custody. "He was gone before I knew it. There was nothing I coulda done, guys." They were all crying and snuffling, sucked down by reality from their science fantasy, no less than Red had been sucked in by the vortex.

"He'll be with Steve now," Harry said. "He loved his brother."

"Yeah," said Frank fingering his binoculars. "Denny, I was watching. Red didn't get tangled in the rope. He held on to it and didn't let go."

Jennifer Doonerbeck

Early morning, chilly, going on toward autumn. A few fishing boats are tied up to the wharves along Alaskan Way, and the waves slap against hulls, pilings, palisades. Gulls laugh. A distant motorboat near the marina buzzes like a lawnmower. The lighting is indirect; a reluctant sun lingers behind the mountains.

Two joggers appear, side by side, their running shoes clapping nearly in time. Strangers, they have met by chance and have fallen in together on their run, and now they pace each other. An older man walking briskly past them in the other direction wonders if they are sisters. They are much of

a type, similar in build and age and dress; young, but past
the first rush of it; firm muscles and dirty-straw hair tied
back with elastic sweat bands; braving the chill in gym
shorts and halter tops. The fishermen breaking fast in a
dockside café watch in frank admiration.

The breeze had been off the Bay, cool and with the bite of
salt in it. Now it shifts, and a land breeze whispers out over
the water. Flags snap and turn. A windsock at the end of one
of the docks swings about. Gulls shear off with loud com-
plaint. The breakfasting fishermen, swinging like windsocks
themselves, shift their gaze toward the Bay. The joggers halt
and stand with chests heaving and with sweat dripping off
their brows. One—she is by a fraction the taller of the
two—rests a hand on a piling. They, too, study the Bay.

For a moment, an anxious silence: The scene is frozen.
The fishermen hold their coffee mugs or silverware half-
raised. The joggers gaze into the chuckling water to judge
the run of the waves. Even the gulls coast on the soft winds
with unmoving wings.

But . . . no siren wails, and everyone relaxes, as if they
had been suspended on strings now suddenly cut. Fishermen
and waitresses chatter, and china and silverware clink. The
cook hollers something from the back and the men laugh.
The joggers bend into their cooling-down stretches, as if
they have only just now remembered to do them.

The three fishermen sitting near the front of the café,
glance toward the empty piers that lend Alaskan Way its
abandoned look. The ferries dock out past Alki Point these
days and most commercial shipping and recreational boat-
ing put in elsewhere as well. The bearded man, the middle
of the three, remembers how he and Pete Jurgowitz, the
Hyak's mate, used to sail the bay together as kids, but the
thought is only reflex, the tear of memory remains unstarted,
and he does not speak of it to his friends.

On his right sits a solid young man with hard muscles. He
wishes that the drainhole would at least open and close on a
regular schedule—"like that geyser thing out in Yellow-
stone." The previous week it had not opened at all, but the
week before that it had stayed open for several days, disturbing

currents and winds all the way out into the Sound. "No one knew jack when Hyak happened," he says, "but now with the buoys marking the place an' the radars watching for that 'pair of slacks' . . ."

"Parallax," says the bearded man, who watches the Discovery channel.

". . . Anyone gets sucked in now," the younger man insists, "they wanna get sucked in, or they're just plain stupid."

The third man's attention has been drawn back to the joggers, whose lithe and graceful motions he greatly admires. He asks the waitress the name of the woman in the tan shorts, but the waitress, suspecting carnal thoughts on his part, pretends ignorance. But she herself spares a glance at the younger woman and remembers when she too possessed such a body.

The woman in tan is Jennifer Doonerbeck, a graduate student at the University. She is not conventionally pretty, but it's all in the presentation. She gives no thought to men's interest when she dresses, and it is this artlessness that becomes the greater art. The color of her jogging outfit is very nearly the tone of her suntan, and the third fisherman has discovered that when he squints his eyes a little she seems to be naked.

"Why are those men over there squinting like that?" Jennifer asks her companion.

The taller woman unbends from her stretches and glances at the café. "Sailors all get that look about them. The chop flashes from the sunlight, so they squint to cut down the glare." The explanation satisfies both the teller and the told, and the fishermen would have agreed red-faced had they overheard. It is not, in any event, a matter of great moment. Jennifer finds her companion staring out once more silently at the Bay and asks who she once knew.

It is not a question that needs an explanation. It seems as if all Seattle is known by who they once knew. Hello, glad to meet you, who did you know on the Hyak? Jennifer has heard of strangers pretending to such acquaintances, as if they want to have been touched by the tragedy, and feel a loss at having had no loss. It strikes her as a bit of theft to steal a bereavement to which they are not entitled.

The taller woman, whose name is Mack of all unlikely things—it is short for Mackenzie, and that is bad enough—admits to losing a colleague and a neighbor's boy, thus pulling rank on Jennifer, who has lost only a cousin.

"Do you think we're safe here?" Jennifer is watching the ring of buoys that delimit the danger zone. They are welded together by a rigid framework and are anchored to the floor of the bay so that they will not be drawn into the drainhole when it opens. A chain-link fence has been installed to prevent future tragedies like that high-school science club.

Mack is not sure, but thinks there is some reason why the anomaly can form only over water. Something to do with fluid motion, of which her jogging had been an example. "It used to be the Bermuda Triangle, you know," she says, repeating a tidbit of folk wisdom fast becoming consensual reality.

Jennifer has heard about the Bermuda connection, but she does not understand how a hole could cross the whole country without creating an Arkansas Triangle or a Wyoming Triangle or whatever along its path? Or did it travel through the Earth like a tunneling mole?

"My cousin grew up on a farm out near Spokane," Jennifer says, and Mack listens politely because that is what one does when a chance companion mentions her Hyak loss. "She was nice and we had fun when my folks took me out there in the summer, but I always thought she was like, you know, a dork?" Nil nisi bonum, the Romans had once said, but they hadn't had cousins from Spokane. "When she grew up and moved here to the city, she was always calling me and I was always making excuses and blowing her off, so I'm sorry now I was so rude to her."

Mack thinks that the Hyak has been the cause of more confessions than a hundred priests and a tent revival, but she is not about to withhold absolution. A native of Manhattan driven by ambition to abide a while in the Northwest, she does not tell Jennifer that from her point of view Seattle and Spokane are equally hick, and "the City" refers to one City alone on all the earth. "You didn't have an obligation to her," she tells the other woman.

"No," Jennifer says, "but I sorta wish I'd had." And that remark, more than anything Jennifer has said up till now, strikes Mack in the heart.

The fishermen have left the café and walk toward the pier where their boat is one of the few still mooring there. One calls a polite greeting and the joggers wave back. Jennifer notices the tight buns one of them boasts. Mack pays them no attention.

Mack's colleague had not been especially close to her, not even in the hypothetical way that Jennifer's cousin might have been. His office had been a few doors from hers, high up in one of Seattle's tallest buildings. They had worked together on a couple of projects and he had flirted with her a few times, but the dalliance had offered her no career advantage and she had not responded. The neighbor's boy, Dale, was another matter. He had been kind of sweet— young enough for a puppy-love crush on the "neighbor lady," and just old enough to make it flattering. His mother was a homebody, but seeing afterward how the woman had been emptied entirely of life, Mack wondered whether she herself, had she been a breeder, could have produced a boy half so engaging as Dale. But if she knew her own strengths, Mack knew her own weaknesses, too; and "mother" had never been her métier. Now she wondered whether she was diminished in some manner because she could never suffer a loss so keen as her neighbor had.

It was a day for hypotheticals. Cousins hypothetically helped. Children hypothetically born. Joggers hypothetically stripped naked. Vortexes hypothetically forming over land. In theory, that last would never happen. But in theory, Mack could still run after the three fishermen and have them all, each and severally, upon their coiled nets. It would not have been the most comfortable experience, fishnets being what they are, and the fishermen would have known some disappointment that it had not been Jennifer to jump their bones. Still, it shows the limits of theory, because it just wasn't going to happen. A drainhole over dry land would remain theoretically impossible right up until the moment it happened. Then the brainiacs would punch some buttons on their computers and come up with a new theory.

ATN Puget Sound motors out from Harbor Island, where the National Oceanic and Atmospheric Administration has built its new facilities. The Vortex is neither oceanic nor atmospheric, but NOAA has somehow inherited ownership. The barge, borrowed from the Coast Guard, carries on it a vehicle a little like the Mars Rovers. Mack and Jennifer point it out to each other and speculate on its purpose.

A woman standing on the barge sees them and waves. The vehicle is called the Odysseus and the plan is to place it in the water and allow the Vortex, when it next opens, to suck it through to the Other Side while it sends data back through a miles-long umbilical of the lightest and strongest fullerene-tube optical cable. Every scientist in the world had begged a space on the platform for an instrument or experiment. Had all requests been granted, Odysseus would have shamed the Queen Mary II.

But with no clear notion of the environment awaiting it, the instrument package has been designed to roll, fly, and float, to withstand vacuum and pressure and heat and cold and heavy accelerations and hard radiation and, like any device manufactured to such contradictory specifications, it does none of these things well. Dr. Whistler—she is the woman standing on the barge—does not expect Odysseus to survive for long. She does not know if the umbilical will be long enough to reach the Other Side. She is not even sure that there is an Other Side. But she hopes for something, for a reading, for even a single picture. She is not so optimistic as to expect an answer, but it is her fondest dream to learn that there is an answer.

The diesels on a fishing boat power up, belching a cloud of black smoke, and the buff young man with the tight buns casts off. The boat gives wide berth to the buoys marking the locus of the Vortex. It isn't open, but there is no telling when it might. Jennifer recognizes them and waves, jumping up and down with a vivacity that five years of corporate ladder-climbing has sucked from the heart of her companion. The fishing boat toots its horn for Jennifer, but Mack is still gazing into the depths of the Bay, thinking about the boy, Dale.

"Dawn was theirs," she quotes, "and sunset and the colours of the earth."

Jennifer turns and says, Hunh? She was an English major, but does not recognize the line.

These hearts were woven of human joys and care,
Washed marvelously with sorrow, swift to mirth.
The years had given them kindness. Dawn was theirs,
And sunset and the colours of the earth.

Applied Mathematical Theology

GREGORY BENFORD

Gregory Benford (www.gregorybenford.com) *lives in Irvine, California. He has lately become a CEO of several biotech companies devoted to extending longevity using genetic methods. He retains his appointment at UC Irvine as a professor emeritus of physics. He is the author of over twenty novels, including* Jupiter Project, Artifact, Against Infinity, Eater, *and the famous SF classic,* Timescape *(1980). His most recent novel is* The Sunborn *(2005). A two-time winner of the Nebula Award, Benford has also won the John W. Campbell Award, the Australian Ditmar Award, the 1995 Lord Foundation Award for achievement in the sciences, and the 1990 United Nations Medal in Literature. Many of his (typically hard) SF stories are collected in* In Alien Flesh, Matters End, *and* Worlds Vast and Various.

"Applied Mathematical Theology" was published in Nature. *Told in the distant third person, it is an ironic, ambiguous, pro-science fable. It is also an idea story that SF readers are likely to remember for a long time. Maybe there is a message imbedded in the physical universe that strongly implies the existence of God. It is interesting to compare this piece to Daryl Gregory's story, later in this book.*

The discovery that the cosmic microwave background has a pattern buried in it unsettled the entire world.

The temperature of this 2.7 K emission, left over from the Big Bang, varies across the sky. Temperature ripples can be broken into angular-coordinate Fourier components, and this is where radio astronomers found something curious—a message or, at least, a pattern. Spread across the microwave sky there was room in the detectable fluctuations for about 100,000 bits—roughly 10,000 words.

Although different technical civilizations in our Universe would see different temperature fluctuations, they could agree on the Fourier coefficients. This independence of place, and the role of the cosmic background as cosmic neon sign for anyone with a microwave receiver, meant that any intelligence in the Universe could see this pattern.

But what did it mean? Certainly it would not be in English or any other human language. The only candidate tongue was mathematics.

Writing them as binary numbers, astronomers tried to fit mathematical sequences, such as the prime numbers, in any base. This and other mathematical favourites—pi, e, the golden ratio, the Riemann zeta function—proved futile. More obscure numbers and patterns, from set theory and the like, also shed no light.

In despair, some thought the pattern might be random. But the Shannon entropy test showed clear non-random elements, and this nihilist idea faded away. One insight from Benford's law, which states that the logarithms of artificial numbers are uniformly distributed, did apply to the tiny fluctuations. This proved that the primordial microwaves were not random, and so had been artificially encoded, perhaps by some even earlier process. So there was a message, of sorts.

Cosmologists eagerly searched for clues and hit a dead end. The sequence was found to fit no model. This suggested immediately to even non-religious astronomers that the pattern might have been put there by a being who made our Universe: God, in short.

What would such a mathematical message mean, anyway? Only that some rational, counting designer had made our Universe. Beyond that, nothing would be revealed about the being's nature; although of course this proved the old claim, that God was a mathematician.

Rankled, the physicists quickly compared the observed sequence with the fine-structure constant, one of their favourites. The sequence did not fit.

This sent everyone back to fundamentals. Current theory said that tiny temperature fluctuations in the microwaves came from little bumps in the potential function that governed the inflation of the very early Universe. Tinkering with those quantum fluctuations, a being could write something simple but profound: God as a quantum mechanic. If, for example, the designer could encode little squiggles on the potential, then the fine-tuned primordial density fluctuations would not be exactly scale-free, and that's where the sky-wide microwave patterns came from.

So of course the physicists followed their current fashion. When comparison with other favourite numbers—the dimensionless ratios of masses and energies and the like—all failed, they tried more advanced theories. They tried prescriptions for various symmetry groups that came from the Lie algebras, as three of the four fundamental interactions we know reflect such gauge theories. No help.

The physicists, who had long been the mandarins of science, then supposed that clues to the correct string theory, a menu currently offering about 10100 choices, would be the most profound of messages. After all, wouldn't God want to make life easier for physicists? Because, obviously, God was one, too.

Sadly, no. Nothing seemed to work.

Perhaps the very idea underpinning science—that humans could understand the Universe—had hit a wall. This helped both science and religion.

Excitement increased. If the being was not saying something obvious, then maybe humans had not understood the Universe well enough to make out the message. Governments poured money into mathematics and physics. The astronomers protested. If the night sky was a tale told by God, they could read it. The cosmic-neutrino and gravity-wave backgrounds had not yet been detected, but they could also carry the Word. So it came to be that the cosmologists, too, received the blessing of a large research bounty.

These huge increases in funding drove a renaissance of modern science. Data processors, statistical theorists, observers of obscure spectra—all received a share. Vast telescopes tuned to the vibrations and emissions of the Universe glided in high orbits, their ears cupped to the distant and primordial.

This largesse produced an economic boon, as many spin-off technologies benefited commerce. Religious fervour damped, as each faith felt humbled by this proof that the Universe had meaning, yet mankind was not yet advanced enough to fathom it.

At the same time, attention focused on the injunction to mankind in the Old Testament—echoed in other religious founding texts—charging humanity with being the stewards of Earth. The environmental movement merged with the great religions.

Within a century, active adjustment of Earth's reflected sunlight, and capturing of carbon in the oceans and lands, had averted the greenhouse disaster. Church attendance was enormous. Efforts to enhance our knowledge and skills had averted many gathering social conflicts.

Work on the message continues in the new university departments of applied mathematical theology. Yet to this day, it remains untranslated. Perhaps that is just as well.

Quill

CAROL EMSHWILLER

Carol Emshwiller (www.sfwa.org/members/emshwiller) *lives in New York City and summers in California. She taught writing at New York University until she retired in 2003. She has been publishing in the SF field since the 1950s, when her attractive image also graced the covers of many SF books and magazines illustrated by her husband, Ed Emshwiller, who signed his paintings EMSH. An excellent illustrated biography of Ed and Carol Emshwiller,* Emshwiller *(2007), is just out. She has a World Fantasy Award for Life Achievement. She published several excellent stories in 2006. She says, "I'm just working on more short stories as usual. I'm working on two at the same time and I'm stuck in both of them, but I always get stuck and always can't figure out how to go on. I'm used to that."*

"Quill" was published in the anthology Firebirds Rising, *edited by Sharyn November, certainly one of the best original anthologies of 2006. "I usually don't write such a science fiction-y story, but the idea of beautiful, feathered dinosaurs pleased me. That is, after I got to them. I didn't know there were going to be dinosaurs in the story until I got to their cache of eggs. Then I had to go back and make the earlier parts match. I always write that way: give myself hints of a mystery and then have to solve it after I've set it up," said Emshwiller in her story note there. We are charmed and moved by "Quill."*

Mother says, "Don't sing. Don't dance. Don't wear red." She says, "Simplify!" She says, "We don't eat bugs. We don't eat crawdads." Aren't they simple enough? She says, "We . . . our kind . . . doesn't do that, doesn't do this." We heard it in the egg—so to speak. So to speak, that is.

We do eat eggs.

Sometimes when we're playing too vigorously, Mother says, "No high notes."

Mother says we're unique. We don't know whether to feel left out or included in with special people. We keep wondering, if we climbed high enough up or far enough down, we'd find another group like us just as special and if they'd be all right to make friends with. We plan to go find out but right now the littlest one of us would need help.

A stranger came out of the woods and stared at us. We were dressed right, yet he watched as if we were strange. We acted normal. We played human-being games just to prove we were completely proper. I'm too old for this kind of play but the little ones like me to do it. I was the man this time, though I'm female. I stamped around and took big steps. But how many times have we seen a man?

But this stranger isn't the first, though he's come the closest to our houses. Not long ago we saw three men, climbing up along the stream. At first we didn't know what they were. We thought some sort of humped-back creatures. But then they took their packs off and we saw they were men. They didn't see us, though we followed them all the way up.

They had beards. We laughed but only afterwards so they wouldn't hear. Mother wondered what was so funny. We made up something else even sillier than beards.

Tom, though. He's getting hair on his upper lip. I saw him cutting it off with little scissors he stole from Mother's sewing kit. They don't work very well for that, so there's some of it still there. That's called a mustache.

This other man that stared . . . We saw him first from across the lake, the one we call Golden because of the golden eyes of the frogs. Mother doesn't like us to call it that. The idea of gold makes her gloomy. The river we call Silver, though that's where gold is. We found some but we knew better than to tell Mother. We hardly tell her anything in case what we do "just isn't done." Or maybe "just isn't talked about."

We have to be out here by ourselves so as not to be tempted by the way other people live. We might do what they do and "they're not our kind." But we couldn't be a different kind if we wanted to. We don't know how.

Mother says, "Every day is a lesson." We knew that a long time ago. Jumping rock to rock is a lesson, especially when we fall. Not testing stepping-stones before you step on them—that's a lesson. Watching lightning strike the tallest trees though, not always. Building a little hut of reeds. Making fires in the rain. You have to know how.

Mother doesn't know any of those lessons. I'll bet she couldn't even make a fire when it wasn't raining. I wonder if she even knows how to swim. I've never seen her near the lake except to gather rushes for mats or cattails for supper— those, our kind is allowed to eat. She hates to get her feet muddy.

We have secret places for dancing and singing. We stole a pan for a drum. We have scraping sticks. We clack stones. We only make our music beside the stream so as to hide the sound in case Mother should come out that far, though that's unlikely.

Morning is lessons. Numbers mostly. You can't fault numbers. Some of us are not good at them. If we complain,

Mother says, "That's the way it is." Spelling . . . I'm not good at that. Geology I'm good at. It's all around us. I like to know how things got this way.

Mother wants us to know things such as honesty and generosity, but we had that all figured out on our own a long time ago. We know what's fair and what's not. We know you have to give to get. Sometimes we argue all afternoon about the rules of whatever we're playing and never get to play it, so we know we have to give up and give in.

Afternoons, when Mother takes a nap, we rush out before she can think of something else for us to do. We don't come back till dusk and sometimes later. Now and then some of us spend all night in the woods. We've built ourselves little houses of reeds or twigs and branches. We know all the caves and cozy piles of rocks. She doesn't worry if a few of us are missing. We wonder, though, if she knows how many we are.

Every day, first thing, we're supposed to give thanks for what we have, but also that we have but little. Thanks for beans and corn and apples, and especially for living right here in a safe place. And thanks to Mother for the simple life. And thanks to Mother for Mother.

That stranger walked into our part of the forest, sat down, and stared. He has paper and pencil. He might be writing or drawing. We can't tell from here.

But we quacked when we should have cawed.

He knows there are no ducks around. We came out in plain view then. Across the lake from him. That's when we did what people do. Except instead of talking, we quacked.

It's not far across the lake at that point. He got a good view. He watched the whole time. He must like our looks. We liked his looks, too. We liked his big hat. His shirt is red. Except for our collections of feathers and flowers, we don't have any red.

Tom is the best at everything. Of course, since he's the oldest. He dances now. Just look at Tom's fast footwork and how he can leap. The man stares. He even looks at us through things Tom says are binoculars. And he has another thing. Tom says that's a camera and he's taking our picture. We're seen pictures in our books. He'll have us on paper to take home to his house.

Where the river comes down to the lake, you have to cross on the stepping-stones to get to our side. It looks as if that man is coming over. There's a couple of wobbly stones we set up on purpose. We didn't want Mother crossing without us knowing it.

Those flat stones look as if they're there to be stepped on, but they're really there to trip you up. So down he goes right in the middle of the stream, backpack and all. I'm not happy about him getting his paper wet. How much paper is there in the world? I'll ask Tom. Or maybe I'll ask this man.

We save our laughing for later. We only caw a little bit.

He sloshes out.

He knows that was on purpose—that those two middle rocks were set there so as to teeter.

He takes off his big black hat and empties out the water, puts it back on. Then he sits on the bank and examines his ankle.

We crowd around and look, too. His ankle is already starting to swell and turn black. Others of us skip back and forth across the stream. We don't avoid the center stones, we just go really fast over them.

He has tape just for this. He wraps up his ankle, twisting the tape here and there. He's better at it than Tom ever was with our sprained ankles. Here's another lesson for all of us.

What if we bring this man to our little homemade huts or our cave? We could hide him from Mother and have him to ourselves. Or what if we bring him home to Mother?

When he gets up, we get up, too. He limps. He follows our path from the stepping stones. If we don't watch out he'll be right at Mother's in ten minutes. Well, at this rate, twenty.

Tom says, "Lean on me," but he won't. Tom says he's angry. Tom says, "If we had fathers, that's who he'd be limping off to see. He wants us punished."

We do wonder about fathers. Why don't we have them? Even Tom doesn't know, and Mother won't talk about it.

We can let him limp along the path to home, or sidetrack

him to our cave. Tom says, "Let him go on home. We'll get to see what Mother does."

Pretty soon our regular houses come into view. They're good houses, not only thatched roofs, but thatched sides, too. Maybe we shouldn't call it thatch. It's made of tule rushes. Mother's house is made of stone and is much bigger. Tom says she made it by herself. He remembers thinking he was helping, though now he doesn't think he could have helped much. He was only three or four.

At our clearing, the man stops and looks.

Chickens in the yard have already cackled a warning that a stranger is coming—or a fox. We know Mother's hiding behind the door of her house looking out the little peephole. I'll bet she has the bar down.

The man keeps standing at the edge of our clearing, just looking.

Usually we hear the clanking of her loom, but lately she's been making moccasins. The simple life seems awfully complicated to Tom. The rest of us don't know any other way, though we try to guess. Tom says you don't even have to build a fire or light the lamps. He says clothes and shoes are just there, and he's told us all about electricity.

"Mother!" That's Tom. He goes to the door. "Don't worry. He's hurt."

"Tell him to go away."

"We want him."

"He's not the right sort."

"Come and see for yourself."

"I can tell from here."

"Please come. He can hardly walk. He has paper and pencil."

"We don't need it."

How can she say that? It's what I want the most.

"And he has a camera."

We hear the bar fall away and the door opens. Out she comes.

She's pretty much covered up, big baggy shirt. She's the only one we know with breasts, though I seem to be getting something like that now. I hide it from the others. I wish she'd give me a shirt like the one she's wearing. If I get any lumpier, I'll need that. It's a wonder I even know about them, but we do have books with pictures. Mother gave me a talk. It sounded silly. I don't know whether to believe her or not.

Usually Mother dresses so you can tell more about her body. Now she's different. And her hair is pulled back tight like it never is. She looks angry and worried. We just can't keep track of all the things we're not supposed to do. As we think up new things, new ones keep turning out to be bad. It even surprises us older ones. But now we do know. We never should have let the man come this far. Mother knows to blame Tom and me.

Tom and I are getting sick of not knowing more things about more places. It's a good thing Tom once was someplace else or we wouldn't even know there was another place. He came up here with Mother before any of us were born. He says Mother was looking for the simple life. He says that's what we're doing now.

He remembers lots of things from before. He had a father who left and Mother went around punching things when she wasn't lying on the couch. Finally she came up here with Tom. She said she didn't like the world the way it is and she was going to live a different way. But Tom doesn't know where the rest of us come from. He doesn't remember me coming. Suddenly I was here.

The man must like Mother. He looks relieved. As if everything is all right now.

When Mother steps out, Wren, right away, grabs Mother's skirt and Loon hides behind her. Mother couldn't save us from anything. Only Tom could do that. You'd think they'd know by now.

Mother looks horrified. "You can't stay here. Tom, take the camera."

"I've sprained my ankle—maybe broken it," says the man. "I need to impose on you. I don't think I'll be able to climb down for a while."

"You can't stay!"

Tom says, "We'll keep him with us. You'll hardly know he's here."

"He can't stay. You know that as well as I do. Think, for heaven's sake!"

The rest of us say, "Why?" but Tom says, "All right, all right. We'll send him on his way."

We didn't know Tom would be so cruel, nor Mother either.

The man looks upset. He hands Tom the camera. He says, "It got wet."

Tom gives it to Mother. Mother opens it and pulls out the insides.

The man says, "I can't climb down now."

Mother says, "You have to."

"Can I at least stay the night?"

"That's impossible."

We all say (except Tom), "Why not?"

But right away the man turns and starts hobbling down the trail.

Tom goes to help him and this time the man lets him. Tom is exactly as tall as the man.

A little ways down we turn off the path. Tom tells the man, "Only a little farther now." Then, to the younger ones, "If anybody says anything to Mother, I'll take your gold."

I know what's happening. It's off to our cave, sitting around the campfire, and crawdads for supper. Maybe even frog's legs. Nothing better. Nothing more fun.

Our cave has thick beds of ferns. Much better than our beds at home. And we have really soft rabbitskin blankets we made ourselves. Tom and I sewed them up. We chipped out little pockets in the walls so we could have feathers and flowers all over. But it's shallow. When it rains the rain blows all the way in, but when it's clear, if you lie with your head toward the entrance, you see the stars as you go to sleep. Sometimes the moon's so bright it wakes you up when it pops up over the mountain. There's a sort of porch in front where we made a fireplace and put logs around it to sit on. That porch has a good view over the whole valley.

I say, "Isn't this nice?" The man is impressed.

We build a little fire and send everybody out to catch things or dig things up. They're so excited to be doing it for the man. On the way back they pick big stalks—taller than they are—of fireweed in bloom just for looks.

He can't stop saying, Thank you, and keeps asking what can he do for us. We say, Don't worry, we'll think of things. He asks our names. His is Hazlet, but people call him Haze. He asks our ages but we're not sure. Asks where our fathers are. We say we don't have any.

"One mother for all these little ones?"

We don't know. Sometimes little ones just appear—in the chicken coop. Mother takes them in.

We talk about paper. He'll set his out to dry tomorrow. We'll help. He's going to draw us all as presents to each of us. And he'll give us all the leftover paper when he leaves.

Tom and I stay out all night with the man but we make the little ones go home.

Haze asks a lot of questions. Some are the same ones we ask ourselves, like, "Where's our father? How long have we lived up here? Why are we here in the middle of nowhere?"

(We think it's as much a place as anyplace else.)

We tell him Mother doesn't want us to get to be like other people.

He thinks that can't be the only reason, though he sees her point. He says we're turning out a lot better than some.

We like him. We say, "Stay. We need another grown-up. The only one we know is Mother."

He says both I and Tom are not far off from being grown.

Of course he has to stay until his ankle gets better, but we want him after.

Next day first thing he spreads the paper out to dry with a rock on each one. We help. It hurts him to walk, so he mostly crawls. Then he picks good pieces of charcoal out of the fireplace. He'll show us how to use them for drawing.

The little ones come rushing down. Some wanted to come so badly they didn't even have their breakfast.

As soon as the paper dries, Haze draws. He draws me and
Tom first, and then Henny and Drake. Then the little ones
sitting in a row on the logs on the stone porch. Sometimes he
draws with the charcoal he picked out of the fireplace.
"They'll smear," he says. "Be careful."

We hang the drawings at the back of the cave, high so the
little ones won't mess them up. Me he draws again in pencil
and rolls it up and puts it in his pack.

We want to show them to Mother, we wonder if she's seen
anything like it, but we don't dare. It might be one of those
things we're not supposed to do. Besides, the man is supposed to be gone by now.

Haze shows us how to use the binoculars. We look around
at everything. To the side we see those three men . . . or,
rather, their little tents—up along the silver river. We're good
at taking turns. When we're not looking, we draw. He gives us
lessons. I'm good at it already. I thought I would be.

We have lots of days of drawing and looking while Haze
gets better. He even shows us how to make paper out of
weeds. Lumpy, but better than nothing.

Tom makes a good strong staff for Haze. Haze says that'll
be good even when his ankle is better. The rest of the time
we gather cattail roots and lily roots and Solomon's seal
along with the frog's legs and crawdads.

Then one time when Haze is much better he says, "I always wanted to go up to your glacier. Have you ever gone
that high?"

We haven't, but we've thought about it. "We see lights up
there sometimes."

"Good, we'll go. You and Tom. The little ones can spend
the day with your mother."

"They won't unless we threaten to take away their gold."

"Gold?"

But we're not thinking gold, we're thinking how we'll be
getting out of here, farther than we ever have. We're so
happy we put out our traps and catch rabbits. Mother doesn't
need to know about it. We stretch the skin for ourselves and
dry the meat for our trip.

Tom and I skip morning lessons all the time now and stay

down with Haze. We're learning more from him in just a few weeks than we ever did from Mother. He shows us all about maps on his maps. We pick out what looks like the best route up to the glacier. He shows us all about his compass. He thinks it odd that we never saw a flashlight till now. He's got two, one you fit on your head and another you hold.

We start out while it's still dark. Haze wears the flashlight on his head and goes first. He gives the other to me and I go last. Tom and I each carry a little rabbitskin blanket. Haze has a bag for sleeping. He has the cane Tom made him and his maps. His backpack is full. He even brought paper in case he wants to draw. He has this waterproof stuff that he wrapped his food in before. Now he wraps the paper in it. He feels about paper as we do. We'd rather have paper than gold. He says he would, too.

We top our pass and dip into the next valley at sunrise, or what would have been sunrise if it hadn't been for the mountain in the way. This mountain is much higher than the ones near us. That's why you can see the glacier from our house.

Tom and I had hoped to find people in this valley, but there's nobody. Still the path goes on. From here you get a really good view of the glacier. It's been melting away. Haze gives us a lesson on glaciers. There's a lot of debris at the sides. That's called lateral moraine, at the end it's called terminal. I already knew that, though I never saw it until now.

The glacier's a lot bigger than we thought. Back home we can only see the top. We had no idea it had all this junk around it and came down so far into this other valley.

We spend the night right where we are, partway down the second pass, and by afternoon next day, we're at the glacier and its river trickling out.

This valley has a lot fewer trees in it and those are all stunted. Haze points out odd stuff. To us everything is odd. He says, "Look at the peculiar shapes of those rocks. They look like a whole row of skyscrapers."

They sure seem like they're scraping the sky, but we know the sky is way, way, way up, all the way to the stars.

We climb the sideways debris to get a good look around. Then Haze sees what he thinks might be the mouth of a cave.

He tells us to stay back, but we don't want to. "Why come all this way and not see everything?"

"All right, but stay behind me."

It's not a cave but a doorway of some sort into a big, long, long bluish white house, hugging up close to the glacier. Until you get close, it just looks like more glacier.

At the door, Haze doesn't even knock. He just opens it in a careful sneaky way.

Mother never likes that. She wants us to know how to be courteous. Tom and I look at each other. Haze doesn't know how to be polite.

Haze opens the door all the way and we go in. Tom and I don't want to be sneaky, but we don't know what else to do except go with him.

It's warm in there. We were getting cold. We had wrapped our rabbitskin blankets around us. Haze is wearing his jacket filled with little feathers. He showed us. "Down is the warmest there is," he said, "but you know that already." Only we didn't. He wanted me to trade my rabbit skins with his jacket so I'd be warm as we crossed the high places but I said maybe later, and we should all have a turn with it.

Through that door, we aren't anywhere at all, but there's another door. We open that one and it's even warmer. It's large and dim. At first we don't know what the room is all about, then we see it's a whole room full of eggs. Really big ones. There must be ten or fifteen. They're nested in white stuff. Warm air blows over us and them. Tiny feathers are flying around. Not a lot, just here and there.

Haze keeps saying, "My God. My God."

We're not as surprised as he is—after all, we gather chicken's eggs every day, just not such big ones. And there's feathers in our henhouse, too, but these are all the ones Haze calls "down." They're like what's on my head, but mine are black. Tom told me that when I first came, mine started out yellow.

Then we're even more surprised. Haze takes off his jacket,

grabs the closest egg, wraps it in the jacket, and we hurry out. It's so big it'll be a meal for more than just us three. But we have plenty of food with us. Besides, no pan to cook it in.

It's not like our usual eggs. It has a leathery shell.

Haze holds the egg close to his chest to keep it warm. We go back to the edge of the valley.

Tom says, "Are you going to hatch it?"

"Well, I'm not going to eat it. Did you think I would?"

We like Haze. We didn't think he would but we weren't sure.

It's getting dark. It's too late to start home now. We build a little fire and eat our dried rabbit. Haze keeps the egg in his lap and takes out paper and sketches the big room full of eggs from memory. He also marks on the map where the cave is. Tom and I curl up by the fire. I fall asleep right away but then I hear Haze ask, "Does your mother know about all this?"

That's what I was wondering. I think she does. But I won't say. Tom says, "Maybe."

And I know . . . I think I know what's in this egg. My little brother or little sister, I suppose.

Haze says, "It's a smart way to get a lot of them . . . of you . . . in a hurry." Then: "Maybe only takes one mother for the lot."

Just when I'm falling back to sleep he says, "Not clones either. Easy to see that."

The egg hatches next day when we're on the way home. The cutest little thing I ever saw. All golden. It's cute even before it dries off. It's one of the scaly ones with a feathered cap like I have, though I don't have many scales. Just in a few spots. It's a little on the duck-like side. Much more than me. We don't know yet if it's a boy or girl. Mother can tell right away.

Since I'm a girl I think I ought to get to carry it, but Haze thinks it's safer if he does.

"What do they eat?" he asks.

"Just regular food. Like everybody else. We can give it some of our rabbit. Look, it has all its baby teeth."

Now Haze is saying, "My God, my God, my God," again, then, "I suppose they crashed."

He says Mother is right to keep us away from the rest of the world. He says, again, he has to admit we're, all of us, very nice children.

He jumps from one idea to another. He says, except for Tom we're all half-breeds. He says, "It's a good way to endure here. He says, "Maybe they think we won't kill any creatures that are half our own." Then he says, "When has that ever stopped us? Killing our own is what we do best."

Haze says I was hatched up there. He says he can't imagine what kind of creature my father is.

I get to feed the baby. (Those sharp little teeth are better at chewing rabbit than mine.) I get to have his first smile. And I get to sleep with him. Haze wraps us both in his down jacket. He keeps the fire going all night. I don't think he sleeps much. I don't sleep well either, but that's because the baby is wiggly. It doesn't seem to know it's night. Or maybe it's been sleeping so much in the egg so that now it wants to do things.

One of those funny things Mother told me turns out to be true. There's blood. So not only do I have to figure out how to keep the messes of the baby from getting all over, but I have to figure out what to do about my mess. I take pieces from our rabbit skins. I pretend it's all for the baby, but some is for me. I wonder if those breast things are any bigger than they were. I hope not. But I guess Mother is right about that, too. They will get bigger. This baby, though, is one of the ones that doesn't need them.

I lag behind though Haze carries the baby and we've already eaten most of our food so nobody has much to carry. I'm cold even in Haze's jacket. My stomach feels funny. I sit down on a rock to rest and think.

But somebody is coming from behind. A tall creature with long thin legs that bend the way fox legs do. At first I think it's wearing a beautiful feathered hat, red and gold, but as it gets closer I see it's a topknot and that what I think is a black and red suit is feathers all over. When it sees me, the topknot lifts higher, widens. It's iridescent. There's blue and green in it, too. The creature spreads its arms. There's a row of red along its sides. I never saw anything so beautiful.

Someone has been in the nest. Our soft warmth has been intruded upon. Entered by they of those that can't smell. They think we won't know. As if we don't smell everything that happens.

Worst of all, my own little loved one, on the edge of hatching, stolen. A precious being in the making.

Strange and stranger land of much pain and so little softness in it. So few spots in which to hesitate and love.

I go to speak of my love for my own kind and even for their kind if need be speaking of it. Say it with nodding of head sky to ground, sky to ground, as if their yes and not sideways, east and west.

I lean forward so as to speed. Also lean so as to catch the scent. I smell not only my little one but also my biggest one, and she's ready to lay. Our first layer among the half-ones. A precious dear. I can't wait to speak of the future of us all. So much depends on her willingness, though why not? Offspring this way is so much easier than the way of mammals.

My tender feelings come with the good smell of myself on her. I breathe of myself all along the trail. Strange and dangerous as this place is, I'm happy. Strange as even my own is, I'm happy.

But what of these harsh creatures? Even without moving from our wreckage, we've seen what they do—seen from their own technology. We know who they are. We've heard both war and music. Dance. At least they dance.

Now a whole new way to egg which only our knowledge makes possible. Not as pleasurable but necessary. But here's my daughter, though she, my dear one, is more of them than of me.

Our kind is not unknown here, though they never had a chance to develop. Had they come to full flower, we'd have landed among friends instead of among these odd intelligent mammals. It's too bad we didn't come earlier to help those like us achieve their full potential. We could have egged with them and raised them to our level.

Strange that this world took such a different turn. Hardly logical that eggless ratlike things would grow so large. Though even our own mammals get into everything, and some are smart enough to have made themselves into the little companions of our kitchens and the darlings of the nurseries.

I have wished my first daughter could be beautiful—more like me. Still I love her. I can be in love by smell alone. So much love I found it hard to bring her down to her mother. And when she smiled, like ours always do—the first conciliation, the first appeasement—I found myself in every way, her doting father.

It was Quat called us. The intruding mammals didn't see him in the dim nesting light. One of them was half us—Quat could smell that—and two were of their kind. One a full grown male not known to us. Quat said that male knows too much. Everything is vulnerable.

I've watched the offspring dance. Life will be hard for them, but at least they have the joy of dance. Now, to my own young one, I'll display. I'll strut. Though with these creatures it seems it's more the female's role to lure with colors and tall shoes. Still, I will display.

It calls, "Quill, Quill." It sounds like quacks but I'm used to that from some of the little ones—I can tell it's my name. It has a loud echoing voice. I don't know how far Tom and Haze have gotten, but for sure they'll hear. For sure they'll come, though I wonder if I want them to.

At first it doesn't come close. It stands, silent, below me on the trail so as to let me get used to it. I look. That's what it wants me to do. Its scales only show at its neck and clawed hands and feet. It turns sideways and shows off its topknot, up and out and then down, then up and out again. None of the little ones have anything at all like that topknot, though I realize now that some have the beginnings of one.

It comes closer. It makes more quacking sounds. Again, not too different from the way lots of the little ones talk. It says, "I'm your father."

I shout, "Yes!" He's so beautiful I can't help it. I've been wondering and wondering all this time. I can't conceive of a better father than this one.

"May I sit beside you for talking?"

I move to make room. He sits on my rock and we both look back toward the glacier.

He touches my hand with his and it feels terrible. His claws prick and his skin is scaly. That's all right, except when he turns it the wrong way it scratches. Some of the little ones are like this, too. I hide that I don't like it like I do with them.

He says he loves me. I can see that in the way he looks at me. He calls me consort, but I don't know what that means. He says I'm old enough now. I don't know what that means either. But maybe I do. It's about the crazy things Mother told me. Which are coming true.

Then he asks about the baby. "He hatched. Did he? I saw where it happened. Or was that a . . . killing?"

"No, we wouldn't. I wouldn't let them. He hatched. He's fine."

I hope so. I think Haze will keep him safe. But Haze seemed pretty worried. He never stopped saying My God, and he couldn't sleep. Maybe I should have made him let me carry the baby.

"Did the baby smile at you first?"

"I guess so."

"Are you caught in his smile?"

"Yes, but I liked him even before he smiled."

"Excellent!"

Then he grabs my wrist, hard. It hurts.

"Come. You'll like it. Keep warm in the nursery. My friends will make you happy."

I try to twist away, but he's too strong, and twisting makes his hand scratch all the more. I think how glad I am that I hardly have any scales at all except a little on my back and the backs of my hands.

"I saw how you were. You like little ones. Come and make more."

"No!"

"We're from a far place. We crashed. We thought the glacier, so white and blue, was a dump of discarded nursery feathers. We slammed and slid and died. We can't go home. We made our conveyance into a nest. Had we even one female of our own kind, it would have changed everything. But here was your mother. Willing. Like you are."

But I'm yelling, "No. No!" and I'm yelling for Haze.

"You've no place on this world but with us. They'll never accept you. They hate the different. They never heard of one like you."

"Is that true?"

"The whole world is them."

"It's not. It can't be. How can that be?"

"My dear, dear one, it is! You're the first of your kind. Your mother has kept you hidden from the world so as to save you for us and save you for yourself."

He's loosened his grip and I manage to twist away and start running—up the trail toward Tom and Haze, but he catches me with no trouble. His legs are so long.

But Tom and Haze have turned back. They see me struggling. I yell for them to help.

Haze has something he never showed us. I've heard of that, it's like Mother's rifle but smaller. Pop, pop, and my father falls. Just like that. Into a fancy bundle of shiny black and red and iridescent. His hand still grips me. Haze has to pry open his fingers.

Tom sits me down and gives me a drink from the canteen. Haze is looking over my father's body. Examining everything, the clawed hands and feet, the topknot. I see him looking at the sex, which is mostly covered with down. Then Haze actually sits down and starts to draw him. I'm not sure how I feel about this. It's true, he's beautiful, but Haze isn't drawing a portrait like he did of us. It's more diagrams, my father's different parts all laid out, a hand, then a foot, the topknot, the beak.

But I want to get away from here. I want to get home

tonight. I need to talk to Mother—mostly about myself. I
didn't listen when she talked about blood. It sounded too ridiculous. And how come my father knew that right away? Or
maybe it was these lumps on my chest that made him say I'm
ready for egging.

But I'm shaky and I do need to rest. I don't say, Let's go.
Not even to Tom.

We're so late we have to camp again. And practically right
away, as soon as we leave my father's body. Haze says we
should camp off the trail and hide. We find a place in
among rocks.

I'm still all trembly. I just found a father and lost him
right away. Some of the little ones squeak when they're sad
and don't have tears, ever, but I'm one of the ones that cries.
I cry, but I don't think the others know. I sleep with the baby.
I need to. I need something warm and cuddly to hug.

The baby isn't as wiggly as he was when he was so happy
to be out of the egg. I guess he stayed awake all day, looking
around at everything, and now he's tired. Haze props himself against a rock and puts the gun in his belt, ready to
shoot somebody. He looks as if he's going to stay awake to
guard us, but he starts to snore right away.

I cry for a while. The baby clings to me as though he wants
to comfort me. After I stop I look up at the starry sky. It's so
beautiful it makes me cry all over again. No matter what it
looks like from down here, it's full of faraway suns, some
even bigger than our own. We know all that because Mother
taught us. "Who knows," Mother said, "what other kinds of
life swirl around those suns?" She said, "Who knows, there
might be a world where the dinosaurs didn't die out." I think
now she was preparing us for strangers like my father. I wish
I'd listened instead of looking out the window and wanting to
be off in the woods.

Just when I finally start to fall asleep, Tom wakes me. He
says Haze will tell about what we found. That's why he
made the drawings. Tom says at first nobody will believe
him . . . that there could exist creatures like us, so Haze
will take us down to the real people. We'll get examined by

policemen. Tom doesn't want that to happen. He likes us and he's always taken care of us—more than Mother has. He says he's not sure if Mother isn't crazy. Now that we're here, he knows why she has to live out here, but in the beginning she was angry at everybody and everything.

He talks as if my father was right. We won't be let anywhere near our nice home. There'll be nothing but buildings, and we'll never be able to come back. We might even be put in a zoo. The best thing to do is to get rid of Haze and then our life will stay the same.

"But how?"

"Easy. We'll just use that gun he has."

"I don't want to. I like him."

"Liking has nothing to do with it. It's your whole future. Mother's future, too."

"Let's wait and see what happens when we get back. We can always do it later if we have to."

"It might be too late then."

"I don't see why. Mother doesn't want him around either. She'll be on your side. She'll get out her hunting rifle and kill him herself."

So Tom says, "All right. We won't do it yet."

Next morning we come down, all of us together, straight to Mother's. Even Haze walks right in with us.

Mother comes out from her stone house looking shocked. I start crying right away. I never used to cry much, but now I seem to cry at everything. I don't even know why. I wonder if that's because I'm a grown-up now. I hope that's not the reason.

I run to Mother and hug her tight. We're breast against breast. I say, "I have to talk," and she says, "I should think so! What are you thinking? Can't you see? Couldn't you tell?"

She pulls away and slaps me. So hard she almost knocks me over. She's never done that before. I've never seen her so angry. I'm afraid to ask her anything, but there's nobody else to ask the kind of things I need to know. I don't think she'll ever want to talk to me—especially not about what I want to talk about. I wonder if it's in our anatomy book and I didn't notice it before because I didn't want to.

She snatches the baby from Haze—so hard the baby starts to squeak and won't stop. Talk about high notes! That's the first he's squeaked in all the time he's been with us. I snatch him right back and he stops squeaking right away, which is a relief to all of us. I stop crying, too. That's the end of me crying. I won't do it anymore, especially not in front of Mother.

Mother tries to snatch him back but I won't let her. She says, "You have no idea. None of you do. Look what you've done! All our lives I've worried this would happen—someone like this man would come. It's over and done for. Do you think we can live the way we do after this? It's over!"

I don't know who we ought to get rid of, Mother or Haze or maybe both.

Haze says, "It doesn't have to be over. It can be just begun. I can take Quill and the baby down and bring them right back."

Mother says she doesn't want us made into a sideshow. She says they'll wipe out the whole enterprise. She says what she's always said before, that she knows how the world is, which is why she's living up here. "My innocent Quill," she says. (She never has called me hers before. I don't know what to think, and just after she slapped me.) "My little Quill, corrupted."

Little! Can't she see anything? Not even my breasts?

Tom says, "It doesn't have to be over. It can be like it always is. Wait! Mother! Everything will be like you want it to be. I can fix it." He gives Mother a look. Says, "Wait!" again.

I go stand in front of Haze just in case it happens right now. But I don't want Haze to get suspicious. I don't think I want Haze suspicious. I'm not sure of anything anymore. I'm not even sure if I might not want to go down and see the zoo.

Haze says, "You'll be found out sometime no matter what I do. Strange that you've lasted all this time as it is."

I don't see why Tom gets to be the only one who knows about down there. I might go with Haze, like he said, just me and the baby. Down to Haze's home forest. Who would have to know about us? Maybe it would be like our cave. Nobody but us would ever go there.

I should tell Haze to go home to his home right away, and he should keep watch over his little gun.

But I don't have a chance to tell him anything. He knows. We . . . Tom and I and Haze and the baby . . . We say we're going down to spend the night in the cave and that we'll eat supper there, but Haze goes right on past, without a word, not even to me. We're all worn-out but he just goes, even without supper, and he's going fast. Tom follows without a single word to me, and I follow Tom. I keep well back because of the baby, though the baby doesn't sound any different from the birds. The birds are settling down for the night so there's lots of chirping. The baby's settling down, too, with little night songs.

Haze has his lights, both of them, and Tom and I don't have anything, so we're a lot slower.

Pretty soon I decide I just have to rest. I think Haze will have to rest, too. I hope he finds a place where Tom can't get at him.

The baby and I move off the trail and cuddle up.

When I wake up and look out, I'm way up on the side of a mountain and I can look down on a whole other valley with a big town there. I'm so happy. I start chirping to myself along with the baby. I'm getting somewhere really interesting. I'm going to know things Tom knows.

The baby and I pick elderberries and mountain currants for breakfast. I'm not in a hurry anymore. There's the town and I have plenty of time to get there. I don't care if I ever catch up to Haze or Tom.

But Tom waits beside the trail and jumps out at me. And right away tells me I have to go home. "You mustn't let people see you and especially not let anybody see the baby. He'll scare them to death."

"How can a baby scare anybody?"

"He, and even you, but he especially . . . you don't belong on this world."

How can he say such a thing? "Of course I do."

"You don't understand anything."

"I wasn't going to show myself right away. I thought to take a look around and maybe go to the zoo and see the animals. And then come home."

"People will see you for sure."

"What's so bad if they do see us?"

"Quill!"

"We're just other human beings."

"Well, that's the problem."

"Aren't we?"

"You've been protected from the real people."

"I'm real."

"Look at yourself. You're them. You may be a being but you're not a human being."

"I am so."

"You belong in the zoo."

"I wouldn't mind."

"There's no zoo in that little town anyway. They're only in big towns."

"That doesn't look little to me."

"Believe me, it is."

I suppose he's right. He usually is.

"Well, I won't go home. Not when I'm so close to seeing new things."

"You won't get far with that baby on your back."

"Lots of people must have babies down there."

"Not one like that."

"I'm not going to argue, I'm just not going to go home until I see this town."

"Go ahead, then, but it's the end of all of us. Though . . . I'm tired of it, too. Let's end it. Or I'll tell you what, go on down. Wear my hat pulled low and see if you can get away with it. And they might have a little zoo with maybe four or five animals in some park or other, but don't go into town till it's dark. I'll keep the baby. You'll never get away with it with him."

"All right, if the baby doesn't mind."

I do want to see that town. I start right away. It'll be getting dark by the time I get there.

Pretty soon the trees get fewer and there's fields of stuff growing. I begin to see cows and horses. I've only seen those in books. I stop at the edge of one of the fields and two horses come over to me as if to say hello. At first I think they might bite, but there's the fence between us and you can tell they're friendly right away. They lean to be touched and I touch them.

Right after, there begins to be houses. All nicer even than Mother's. Some with one floor on top of another. I know all about that. I've seen pictures. There's some with different colors and bobbles hanging all over them. I never knew a house could be so pretty. I'm already glad I came.

When I get to the edge of town it's pretty dark. I pull my hat down even lower and walk on. The people are all Tom's kind of people just like he said. Nobody is as beautiful as my father. There aren't any feathers at all.

I come to a little park with swings and slides. I've seen pictures of those. There's nobody there. I guess it's too late for young ones to be out. I try all the things. I can't believe I'm learning so much in such a hurry. These last few days it's been one new thing after another.

There's streetlights. You don't need those lights Haze has. I come to a big street with stores all along it. Most of them closed. Some have prices in the windows. Money! I hadn't thought of that.

I walk all the way down the main street. It must be a mile long. Shops all along the way. I don't care what Tom says, it's a big town to me. I look in the store windows. The clothes look different from the ones Mother makes. And shoes . . . so fancy and slick, some with funny little heels. There's a store full of beautiful shiny pots and pans never used, cups and plates neither tin nor wood nor clay.

There's a bigger park at the other end of town. It even has a swimming pool. All blue and smells funny. I'm thirsty but I don't drink there. There's a river running through the park and that's where I drink. There's no zoo that I can find. I was so hoping there'd be one. I want to see monkeys and tigers and elephants. I wonder how far a bigger town is. If I knew which direction to go in, I might head for that town.

I see people on the porch of an eating place eating with forks. I see two women clacking along in high-heeled sandals. I see cars and trucks. All this even though you'd think people would be in bed. I get honked at. I jump away and quack back.

Then Haze is here. He must have been following me all this time. Even though my hat is pulled down low, he knows it's me.

I say, "Don't tell," and he says he won't. I don't know if I should believe him or not, but it looks as if he won't tell right now, anyway.

"You look exhausted. Are you hungry? Come home with me."

Haze's house is like I've never seen before. There's rugs and a couch. There's even a little room that's just for me, but I don't want it. I've never slept by myself before and I'm scared to. Haze makes me up a mattress on the floor next to him. The food is odd, too. I don't know what it is but I eat it anyway. Except for bugs, Haze ate what we ate. That was like Mother, too. She hated for us to eat bugs. There's also a little room for an outhouse that's not even out. I learn to flush. I learn to turn on the water, cold and hot.

But next morning breakfast is just like at home, oatmeal. I ask Haze, "What are you going to do about us? You killed my father. You might do anything."

"You were yelling, Help. Your father was trying to take you back. I thought I was helping. I didn't know it was your father. But I don't know. What should I do?"

"I don't know either."

"You're going to be discovered no matter what I do. Might as well be now as later. Might as well be me as somebody out to make a buck."

"How come we've not been discovered all this time?"

"Your mother picked a good hiding place."

"Tom said it was the end of all of us. Tom said our lives depend on you."

"I won't let anybody hurt you."

"You have drawings of everything."

"You're scientifically important. You're all important. They'll need to study you."

You wouldn't think so many things could happen so fast. It all comes about in a couple of days. Even the destruction of the fathers, which they did to themselves. I'm glad the regular human beings didn't do it. I don't know what I would have thought if they had.

The fathers knew what would happen. They know about human beings. When Haze and the others . . . the scientists and the army and police get out to the ship, it's destroyed. The nest and eggs and all the creatures with it. There's nothing left of them but us.

Mother must have known. Even if we didn't hear the blast down in town, she's so much closer she must have heard and known. They found her body washed down our Silver river. She had made us all moccasins and lined them up along the table, all exactly the right size. She loved us but she needed for things to stay the same.

Now she'll never find out how we got taken into this school. A farm kind of school off in the middle of nowhere, with all kinds of animals. But also a scientific school with lots of geology and biology, so someday I can be a scientist in a zoo. I'll probably have to be in the zoo myself. I know that. Even now people keep coming to take blood and study us. I don't mind. I'm studying myself myself and them, too.

Haze took all our gold, but he's using it for us. He's paying for the school.

He says, "The fathers were scared of us." When he says "us," he means the human beings. He says, "And rightly so. They thought we wouldn't accept them and we wouldn't. They knew their nests and eggs were easy to destroy. But

having living dinosaurs . . . Feathered . . . Think of the
experiments . . . And studying . . . them and their ship . . ."

And he keeps saying, "Just think . . . think, there's been
contact with aliens all these years and nobody knew it."

I don't feel like an alien. I think I belong here just as much
as anybody.

Tiger, Burning

ALASTAIR REYNOLDS

Alastair Reynolds (www.members.tripod.com/~voxish) *lives in Noordwijk, Holland, and worked for ten years for the European Space Agency before becoming a full-time writer in 2004. He and his wife are avid horseback riders. He began writing SF in the early 1990s, and his first novel,* Revelation Space, *was published in 1999. He was immediately grouped as one of the new British space opera writers emerging in the mid and late 1990s, in the generation after Baxter and McAuley, and originally the most "hard SF" of the new group. His most recent novel is* The Prefect *(2007), and two collections of his stories were published in 2006,* Zima Blue *and* Galactic North.

"Tiger, Burning" was published in the original anthology Forbidden Planets, *edited by Peter Crowther (as opposed to the other anthology of the same title edited by Marvin Kaye, also published in 2006). This is arguably the wildest story in our anthology this year, with matter transmitters, travel among branes, a mystery plot, and a tiger for a central character. Mind-boggling entertainment, for sure, with enough speculative science to keep you thinking for a while after.*

It was not the first time that Adam Fernando's investigations had taken him this far from home, but on no previous trip had he ever felt quite so perilously remote; so utterly at the mercy of the machines that had copied him from brane to brane like a slowly randomising Chinese whisper. The technicians in the Office of Scrutiny had always assured him that the process was infallible; that no essential part of him was being discarded with each duplication, but he only ever had their word on the matter, and they *would* say it was safe, wouldn't they? Memory, as always, gained foggy holes with each instance of copying. He recalled the precise details of his assignment—the awkward nature of the problem—but he couldn't for the life of him say why he had chosen, at what must have been the very last minute, to assume the physical embodiment of a man-sized walking cat.

When Fernando had been reconstituted after the final duplication, he came to awareness in a half-open metal egg, its inner surface still slick with the residue of the biochemical products from which he had been quickened. He pawed at his whorled, matted fur, then willed his retractile claws into action. They worked excellently, requiring no special effort on his part. A portion of his brain must have been adapted to deal with them, so that their unsheathing was almost involuntary.

He stood from the egg, taking in his surroundings. His colour vision and depth perception appeared reassuringly human-normal. The quickening room was a grey-walled metal space under standard gravity, devoid of ornamentation save that provided by the many scientific tools and instruments that had been stored here. There was no welcoming party, and the air was a touch cooler than conventional taste dictated. Scrutiny had requested that he be allowed embodiment, but that was the only concession his host had made to his arrival. Which could mean one of two things: Doctor Meranda Austvro was doing all that she could to hamper his investigation, without actually breaking the law, or that she was so blissfully innocent of any actual wrongdoing that she had no need to butter him up with formal niceties.

He tested his claws again. They still worked. Behind him, he was vaguely aware of an indolently swishing tail.

He was just sheathing his claws when a door whisked open in one pastel-grey wall. An aerial robot emerged swiftly into the room: a collection of dull metal spheres orbiting each other like clockwork planets in some mad, malfunctioning orrery. He bristled at the sudden intrusion, but it seemed unlikely that the host would have gone to the bother of quickening him only to have her aerial murder him immediately afterwards.

"Inspector Adam Fernando, Office of Scrutiny," he said. No need to prove it: the necessary authentication had been embedded in the header of the graviton pulse that had conveyed his resurrection profile from the repeater brane.

One of the larger spheres answered him officiously. "Of course. Who *else* might you have been? We trust the quickening has been performed to your general satisfaction?"

He picked at a patch of damp fur, suppressing the urge to shiver. "Everything seems in order. Perhaps if we moved to a warmer room . . ." His voice sounded normal enough, despite the alterations to his face: maybe a touch less deep than normal, with the merest suggestion of feline snarl in the vowels.

"Naturally. Doctor Austvro has been waiting for you."

"I'm surprised she wasn't here to greet me."

"Doctor Austvro is a busy woman, Inspector; now more than ever. I thought someone from the Office of Scrutiny would have appreciated that."

He was about to mention something about common courtesies, then thought better of it: even if she wasn't listening in, there was no telling what the aerial might report back to Austvro.

"Perhaps we'd better be moving on. I take it Doctor Austvro can find time to squeeze me into her schedule, now that I'm alive?"

"Of course," the machine said sniffily. "It's some distance to her laboratory. It might be best if I carried you, unless you would rather locomote."

Fernando knew the drill. He spread his arms, allowing the cluster of flying spheres to distribute itself around his body to provide support. Small spheres pushed under his arms, his buttocks, the padded black soles of his feet, while others nudged gently against chest and spine to keep him balanced. The largest sphere, which played no role in supporting him, flew slightly ahead. It appeared to generate some kind of aerodynamic air pocket. They sped through the open door and down a long, curving corridor, gaining speed with each second. Soon they were moving hair-raisingly fast, dodging round hairpin bends and through doors that opened and shut only just in time.

Fernando remembered his tail and curled it out of harm's way.

"How long will this take?" he asked.

"Five minutes. We shall only be journeying a short distance into the inclusion."

Fernando recalled his briefing. "What we're passing through now: this is all human built, part of Pegasus Station? We're not seeing any KR-L artefacts yet?"

"Nor shall you," the aerial said sternly. "The actual business of investigating the KR-L machinery falls under the remit of the Office of Exploitation, as you well know. Scrutiny's business is confined only to peripheral matters of security related to that investigation."

Fernando bristled. "And as such . . ."

"The word was 'peripheral', Inspector. Doctor Austvro was very clear about the terms under which she would permit your arrival, and they did not include a guided tour of the KR-L artefacts."

"Perhaps if I ask nicely."

"Ask whatever you like. It will make no difference."

While they sped on—in silence now, for Fernando had decided he preferred it that way—he chewed over what he knew of the inclusion, and its significance to the Metagovernment.

Hundreds of thousands of years ago, humanity had achieved the means to colonise nearby branes: squeezing biological data across the hyperspatial gap into adjacent realities, then growing living organisms from those patterns. Now the Metagovernment sprawled across thirty thousand dense-packed braneworlds. Yet in all that time it had only encountered evidence of one other intelligent civilisation: the vanished KR-L culture.

Further expansion was unlikely. Physics changed subtly from brane to brane, limiting the possibilities for human colonisation. Beyond fifteen thousand realities in either direction, people could only survive inside bubbles of tampered space time, in which the local physics had been tweaked to simulate homebrane conditions. These 'inclusions' became increasingly difficult to maintain as the local physics grew more exotic. At five kilometres across, Meranda Austvro's inclusion was the smallest in existence, and it still required gigantic support machinery to hold it open. The Metagovernment was happy to shoulder the expense because it hoped to reap riches from Austvro's investigations into the vanished KR-L culture.

But that investigation was supposed to be above-top-secret: the mere existence of the KR-L culture officially deniable at all levels of the Metagovernment. By all accounts Austvro was close to a shattering discovery.

And yet there were leaks. Someone close to the operation—maybe even Austvro herself—was blabbing.

Scrutiny had sent Fernando in to seal the leak. If that meant shutting down Austvro's whole show until the cat could be put back into the bag (Fernando could not help but smile at the metaphor) then he had the necessary authorisation.

How Austvro would take it was another thing.

The rush of corridors and doors slowed abruptly, and a moment later Fernando was deposited back on his feet, teetering slightly until he regained his balance. He had arrived in a much larger room than the one where he had been quickened, one that felt a good deal more welcoming. There was plush white carpet on the floor, comfortable furniture, soothing pastel décor, various homely knick-knacks and tasteful *objets d'art*. The rock-effect walls were interrupted by lavish picture windows overlooking an unlikely garden, complete with winding paths, rock pools and all manner of imported vegetation, laid out under a soothing green sky. It was a convincing simulacrum of one of the more popular holiday destinations in the low-thousand branes.

Meranda Austvro was reclining in a silver dress on a long black settee. Playing cards were arranged in a circular formation on the coffee table before her. She put down the one card that had been in her hand and beckoned Fernando to join her.

"Welcome to Pegasus Station, Inspector," she said. "I'm sorry I wasn't able to greet you sooner, but I've been rather on the busy side."

Fernando sat himself down on a chair, facing her across the table. "So I see."

"A simple game of Clock Patience, Inspector, to occupy myself while I was waiting for your arrival. Don't imagine this is how I'd rather be spending my afternoon."

He decided to soften his approach. "Your aerial did tell me you'd been preoccupied with your work."

"That's part of it. But I must admit we botched your first quickening, and I didn't have time to wait around to see the results a second time."

"When you say 'botched' . . ."

"I neglected to check your header tag more carefully. When all that cat fur started appearing . . ." She waved her hand dismissively. "I assumed there'd been a mistake in the profile, so I aborted the quickening, before you reached legal sentience."

The news unnerved him. Failed quickenings weren't unknown, though, and she'd acted legally enough. "I hope you recycled my remains."

"On the contrary, Inspector: I made good use of them." Austvro patted a striped orange rug, spread across the length of the settee. "You don't mind, do you? I found the pattern quite appealing."

"Make the most of me," Fernando said, trying not to sound as if she had touched any particular nerve. "You can have another skin when I leave, if it means so much to you."

She clicked her fingers over his shoulder, at the aerial. "You may go now, Caliph."

The spheres bustled around each other. "As you wish, Doctor Austvro."

When Fernando had heard the whisk of the closing door, he leaned an elbow on the table, careful not to disturb the cards. He brought his huge whiskered head close to Austvro's. She was an attractive woman, despite a certain steely hauteur. He wondered if she could smell his breath; how uniquely, distastefully feline it was. "I hope this won't take too much time, for both our sakes. Scrutiny wants early closure on this whole mess."

"I'm sure it does. Unfortunately, I don't know the first thing about your investigation." She picked up a card from one part of the pattern, examined it with pursed lips, then placed it down on top of another one. "Therefore I'm not sure how I can help you."

"You were informed that we were investigating a security hole."

"I was informed, and I found the suggestion absurd. Unless I am the perpetrator." She turned her cool, civil eyes upon him. "Is that what you think, Inspector? That I am the one leaking information back to the homebrane, risking the suspension of my own project?"

" I know only that there are leaks."

"They could be originating from someone in Scrutiny, or Exploitation. Have you considered that?"

"We have to start somewhere. The operation itself seems as good a place as any."

"Then you're wasting your time. Return down-stack and knock on someone else's door. I've work to do."

"Why are you so certain the leaks couldn't be originating here?"

"Because—firstly—I do not accept that there *are* leaks. There are merely statistical patterns, coincidences, which Scrutiny has latched onto because it has nothing better to do with its time. Secondly, I run this show on my own. There is no room for anyone else to be the source of these non-existent leaks."

"Your husband?"

She smiled briefly and extended a hand over the coffee table, palm down. A figure—a grave, clerical-looking man in black—appeared above the table's surface, no larger than a statuette. The man made a gesture with his hands, as if shaping an invisible ball, then said something barely audible— Fernando caught the phrase 'three hundred'—then vanished again, leaving only the arrangement of playing cards.

Austvro selected another, examined it once more and returned it to the table.

"My husband died years ago, Inspector. Edvardo and I were deep inside the KR-L machinery, protected by an extension of the inclusion. My husband's speciality was acausal mechanics . . ." For a moment, a flicker of humanity interrupted the composure of her face. "The extension collapsed. Edvardo was on the other side of the failure point. I watched him fall into KR-L spacetime. I watched what it did to him."

"I'm sorry," Fernando said, wishing he had paid more attention to the biographical briefing.

"Since then I have conducted operations alone, with only the machines to help me. Caliph is the most special of them: I place great value on his companionship. You can question the machines if you like, but it won't get you anywhere."

"Yet the leaks are real."

"We could argue about that."

"Scrutiny wouldn't have sent me otherwise."

"There must be false alarms. Given the amount of data Scrutiny keeps tabs on—the entire informational content of meta-humanity, spread across thirty thousand reality layers—isn't *any* pattern almost guaranteed to show up eventually?"

"It is," Fernando conceded, stroking his chin tufts. "But that's why Scrutiny pays attention to context, and to clustering. Not simply to exact matches for sensitive keywords, either, but for suspicious similarities: near-misses designed to throw us off the scent. Miranda for Meranda; Ostrow for Austvro, that kind of thing."

"And you've found these clusters?"

"Nearly a dozen, at the last count. Someone with intimate knowledge of this research project is talking, and we can't have that."

This amused her. "So the Metagovernment does have its enemies after all."

"It's no secret that there are political difficulties in the high branes. Talk of secession. Exploitation feels that the KR-L technology may give the Metagovernment just the tools it needs to hold the stack together, if the dissidents try to gain the upper hand."

Austvro sneered. "Tools of political control."

"An edge, that's all. And obviously matters won't be helped if the breakaway branes learn about the KR-L discoveries, and what we intend to do with them. That's why we need to keep a lid on things."

"But these clusters . . ." Austvro leaned back into the settee, studying Fernando levelly. "I was shown some of the evidence—some of the documents—before you arrived, and, frankly, none of it made much sense to me."

"It didn't?"

"If someone—some mole—was trying to get a message through to the breakaway branes, why insist on being so cryptic? Why not just come out and say whatever needs to be said, instead of creating jumbled riddles? Names mixed up . . . names altered . . . the context changed out of all recognition . . . some of these keywords even looked like they were embedded in some kind of play."

322   ALASTAIR REYNOLDS

"All I can say is that Scrutiny considered the evidence sufficiently compelling to require immediate action. It's still investigating the provenance of these documents, but I should have word on that soon enough."

Austvro narrowed her flint-grey eyes. "Provenance?"

"As I said, the documents are faked: made to appear historical, as if they've always been present in the data."

"Which is even more absurd than there being leaks in the first place."

He smiled at her. "I'm glad we agree on something."

"It's a start."

He tapped his extended claws against the coffee table. "I appreciate your scepticism, Doctor. But the fact is I can't leave here until I have an explanation. If Scrutiny isn't satisfied with my findings—if the source of the leaks can't be traced—they'll have no option but to shut down Pegasus, or at least replace the current set-up with something under much tighter government control. So it's really in your interests to work with me, to help me find the solution."

"I see," she said coldly.

"I'd like to see more of this operation. Not just Pegasus Station, but the KR-L culture itself."

"Unthinkable. Didn't Caliph clarify where your jurisdiction ends, Inspector?"

"It's not a question of jurisdiction. Give me a reason to think you haven't anything to hide, and I'll focus my enquiries somewhere else."

She looked down, fingering the striped orange rug she had made of his skin.

"It will serve no purpose, Inspector: except to disturb you."

"I'll edit the memories before I pass them back down the stack. How does that sound?"

She rose from the settee, abandoning her card game. "Your call. But don't blame me when you start gibbering."

Austvro led him from the lounge, back into a more austere part of the station. The hem of her silver dress swished on the iron-grey flooring. Now and then an aerial flashed past on some errand, but in all other respects the station was deserted. Fernando knew that Exploitation had offered to send more expertise, but Austvro had always declined assistance. By all accounts she worked efficiently, feeding a steady stream of titbits and breakthroughs back to the Metagovernment specialists. According to Fernando's dossier, Austvro didn't trust the stability of anyone who would actually volunteer to be copied this far up-stack, knowing the protocols. It was no surprise that she treated him with suspicion, for he was also a volunteer, and only his memories would be going back home again.

Presently they arrived at an oval aperture cut into one wall. On the other side of the aperture, ready to dart down a tunnel, was a two-seater travel pod.

"Are you sure about this, Inspector?"

"I'm perfectly sure."

She shrugged—letting him know it was his mistake, not hers—and then ushered him into one of the seats. Austvro took the other one, facing him at right angles to the direction of travel. She applied her hand to a tiller and the pod sped into motion. Tunnel walls zipped by in an accelerating blur.

"We're about to leave the main body of the inclusion," Austvro informed him.

"Into KR-L spacetime?"

"Not unless the support machines fail. The inclusion's more or less spherical—in so far as one can talk about 'spherical' intrusions of one form of spacetime into another— but it sprouts tentacles and loops into interesting portions of the surrounding KR-L structure. Maintaining these tentacles and loops is much harder than keeping the sphere up, and I'm sure you've heard how expensive and difficult *that* is."

Fernando felt his hairs bristling. The pod was moving terrifically fast now; so swiftly that there could be no doubt that they had left the main sphere behind already. He visualised a narrow, delicate stalk of spacetime jutting out from the sphere, and him as a tiny moving mote within that stalk.

"Was this where your husband died, Doctor?"

"A similar extension; it doesn't matter now. We've made

some adjustments to the support machinery, so it shouldn't happen again." Her expression turned playful. "Why? You're not *nervous*, are you?"

"Not at all. I just wondered where the accident had happened."

"A place much like here. It doesn't matter. My husband never much cared for these little jaunts, anyway. He much preferred to restrict himself to the main inclusion."

Fernando recalled the image of Austvro's husband, his hands cupping an imaginary ball, like a mime, and something of the gesture tickled his interest.

"Your husband's line of work: acausal signalling, wasn't it: the theoretical possibility of communication through time, using KR-L principles?"

"A dead-end, unfortunately. Even the KR-L had never made *that* work. But the Metagovernment was happy with the crumbs and morsels he sent back home."

"He must have thought there was something in it."

"My husband was a dreamer," Austvro said. "His singular failing was his inability to distinguish between a practical possibility and an outlandish fantasy."

"I see."

"I don't mean to sound harsh. I loved him, of course. But he could never love the KR-L the way I do. For him these trips were always something to be endured, not relished."

He watched her eyes for a glimmer of a reaction. "And after his accident—did you have misgivings?"

"For a nanosecond. Until I realised how important this work is. How we must succeed, for the sake of the home-brane." She leaned forward in her seat and pointed down the tunnel. "There. We're approaching the interface. That's where the tunnel cladding becomes transparent. The photons reaching your eyes will have originated as photon-analogues in KR-L spacetime. You'll see their structures, their great engines. The scale will astound you. The mere geometry of these artefacts is . . . deeply troubling, for some. If it disconcerts you, close your eyes." Her hand remained hard on the tiller. "I'm used to it, but I'm exposed to these marvels on a daily basis."

"I'm curious," Fernando said. "When you speak of the aliens, you sometimes sound like you're saying three letters. At other times . . ."

"Krull, yes," she said, dismissively. "It's shorthand, Inspector: nothing more. Long before we knew it had ever been inhabited, we called this the KR-L brane. K and R are the Boltzmann and Rydberg constants, from nuclear physics. In KR-L spacetime, these numbers differ from their values in the homebrane. L is a parameter that denotes the degree of variation."

"Then Krull is . . . a word of your own coining?"

"If you insist upon calling it a word. Why? Has it appeared in these mysterious keyword clusters of yours?"

"Something like it."

The pod swooped into the transparent part of the stalk. It was difficult to judge speed now. Fernando assumed there was some glass-like cladding between him and the inclusion boundary, and somewhere beyond that (he was fuzzy on the physics) the properties of spacetime took on alien attributes, profoundly incompatible with human biochemistry. But things could still live in that spacetime, provided they'd been born there in the first place. The KR-L had evolved into an entire supercivilisation, and although they were gone now, their great machines remained. He could see them now, as huge and bewildering as Austvro had warned. They were slab-sided, round-edged, ribbed with flanges and cooling grids, surmounted by arcing spheres and flickering discharge cones. The structures glowed with a lilac radiance that seemed to shade into ultraviolet. They receded in all directions—more directions, in fact, than seemed reasonable, given the usual rules of perspective. Somewhere low in his throat he already felt the first queasy constriction of nausea.

"To give you an idea of scale . . ." Austvro said, directing his unwilling attention towards one dizzying feature, ". . . that structure there, if it were mapped into our spacetime, and built from our iron atoms, would be larger than a Jupiter-class gas giant. And yet it is no more than a heat dissipation element, a safety valve on a much larger mechanism. That more distant machine is almost three light-hours across, and it too is only one element in a larger whole."

Fernando fought to keep his eyes open. "How far do these machines extend?"

"At least as far as our instruments can reach. Hundreds of light-hours in all directions. The inclusion penetrates a complex of KR-L machinery larger than one of our solar systems. And yet even then there is no suggestion that the machinery ends. It may extend for weeks, months, of light-travel time. It may be larger than a galaxy."

"Its function?" Seeing her hesitation, he added: "I have the necessary clearance, Doctor. It's safe to tell me."

"Absolute control," she said. "Utter dominance of matter and energy, not just in this brane, but across the entire stack of realities. With this instrumentality, the KR-L could influence events in any brane they selected, in an instant. This machinery makes our graviton pulse equipment—the means by which you arrived here—look like the hamfisted workings of a brain-damaged caveman."

Fernando was silent for a moment, as the pod sped on through the mind-wrenching scenery.

"Yet the KR-L only ever occupied this one brane," he said. "What use did they have for machinery capable of influencing events in another one?"

"Only the KR-L can tell us that," Austvro said. "Yet it seems likely to me that the machinery was constructed to deal with a threat to their peaceful occupation of this one brane."

"What could threaten such a culture, apart from their own bloody-minded hubris?"

"One must presume: another culture of comparable sophistication. Their science must have detected the emergence of another civilisation, in some remote brane, hundreds of thousands or even millions of realities away, that the KR-L considered hostile. They created this great machinery so that they might nip that threat in the bud, before it spilled across the stack towards them."

"Genocide?"

"Not necessarily. Is it evil to spay a cat?"

"Depends on the cat."

"My point is that the KR-L were not butchers. They sought their own self-preservation, but not at the ultimate expense of that other culture: whoever *they* might have been. Surgical intervention was all that was required."

Fernando looked around again. Some part of his mind was finally adjusting to the humbling dimensions of the machinery, for his nausea was abating. "Yet they're all gone now. What happened?"

"Again, one must presume: some fatal hesitancy. They created this machinery, but, at what should have been their moment of greatest triumph, flinched from using it."

"Or they did use it, and it came back and bit them."

"I hardly think so, Inspector."

"How many realities have we explored? Eighty, ninety thousand layers in either direction?"

"Something like that," she said, tolerantly.

"How do we know what happens when you get much further out? For that matter, what could the KR-L have known?"

"I'm not sure I follow you."

"I'm just wondering . . . when I was a child I remember someone—I think it was my uncle—explaining to me that the stack was like the pages of an infinitely thick book, a book whose pages reached away to an infinite distance in either direction: reality after reality, as far as you could imagine, with the physics changing only slightly from page to page."

"As good an explanation as the layman will ever grasp."

"But the same person told me there was another theory of the stack: taken a bit less seriously, but not completely discredited."

"Continue," Austvro said.

"The theory was that physics kept changing, but after a while it flattened out again and began to converge back to ours. And that by then you were actually coming back again, approaching our reality from the other direction. The stack, in other words, was circular."

"You're quite right: that theory is taken a bit less seriously."

"But it isn't discredited, is it?"

"You can't discredit an untestable hypothesis."

"But what if it is testable? What if the physics does begin to change less quickly?"

"Local gradients tell you nothing. We'd have to map millions, tens of millions of layers, before we could begin . . ."

"But you already said the KR-L machinery might have had that kind of range. What if they were capable of looking all the way around the stack, but they didn't realise it? What if the hostile culture they thought they were detecting was actually themselves? What if they turned on their machinery and it reached around through the closed loop of realities and nipped *them* in the bud?"

"An amusing conceit, Inspector, but no more than that."

"But a deadly one, should it happen to be true." Fernando stroked his chin tufts, purring quietly to himself as he thought things through. "The Office of Exploitation wishes to make use of the KR-L machinery to deal with another emerging threat."

"The Metagovernment pays my wages. It's up to *it* what it does with the results I send home."

"But as was made clear to me when I arrived, you are a busy woman. Busy because you are approaching your own moment of greatest triumph. You understand enough about the KR-L machinery to make it work, don't you. You can talk to it through the inclusion, ask it do your bidding."

Her expression gave nothing away. "The Metagovernment expects results."

"I don't doubt it. But I wonder if the Metagovernment has been fully appraised of the risks. When they asked you what happened to the KR-L, did you mention the possibility that they might have brought about their own extinction?"

"I confined my speculation to the realm of the reasonably likely, Inspector. I saw no reason to digress into fancy."

"Nonetheless, it might have been worth mentioning."

"I disagree. The Metagovernment is intending to take action against dissident branes within its own realm of colonisation, not some barely-detected culture a million layers away. Even if the topology of the layers *was* closed . . ."

"But even if the machinery was used, it was only used once," Fernando said. "There's no telling what other side-effects might be involved."

"I've made many local tests. There's no reason to expect any difficulties."

"I'm sure the KR-L scientists were equally confident, before they switched it on."

Her tone of voice, never exactly confiding, turned chill. "I'll remind you once again that you are on Scrutiny business, not working for Exploitation. My recollection is that you came to investigate leaks, not to question the basis of the entire project."

"I know, and you're quite right. But I can't help wondering whether the two things aren't in some way connected."

"I don't even accept that there are leaks, Inspector. You have some way to go before you can convince me they have anything to do with the KR-L machinery."

"I'm working on it," Fernando said.

They watched the great structures shift angle and perspective as the pod reached the apex of its journey and began to race back towards the inclusion. Fernando was glad when the shaft walls turned opaque and they were again speeding down a dark-walled tunnel, back into what he now thought of as the comparable safety and sanity of Pegasus Station. Until he had recorded and transmitted his memories down the stack, self-preservation still had a strong allure.

"I hope that satisfied your curiosity," Austvro said, when they had disembarked and returned to her lounge. "But as I warned you, the journey was of no value to your investigation."

"On the contrary," he told her. "I'm certain it clarified a number of things. Might I have access to a communications console? I'd like to see if Scrutiny have come up with anything new since I arrived."

"I'll have Caliph provide you with whatever you need. In the meantime I must attend to work. Have Caliph summon me if there is anything of particular urgency."

"I'll be sure to."

She left him alone in the lounge. He fingered the tiger skin rug, repulsed and fascinated in equal measure at the exact match with his own fur. While he waited for the aerial to arrive, he swept a paw over the coffee table, trying to conjure up the image of Austvro's dead husband. But the little figure never appeared.

It hardly mattered. His forensic memory was perfectly capable of replaying a recent observation, especially one that had seemed noteworthy at the time. He called to mind the dead man, dwelling on the way he shaped an invisible form: not, Fernando now realised, a ball, but the ring-shaped stack of adjacent branes in the closed-loop of realities. "Three hundred and sixty degrees," he'd been saying. Meranda Austvro's dead husband had been describing the same theoretical meta-reality of which Fernando's uncle had once spoken. Did that mean that the dead man believed that the KR-L had been scared by their own shadow, glimpsed at some immense distance into the reality stack? And had they forged this soul-crushingly huge machinery simply to strike at that perceived enemy, not realising that the blow was doomed to fall on their own heads?

Perhaps.

He looked anew at the pattern of cards, untouched since Austvro had taken him from this room to view the KR-L machinery. The ring of cards, arranged for Clock Patience, echoed the closed-loop of realities in her husband's imagination.

Almost, he supposed, as if Austvro had been dropping him a hint.

Fernando was just thinking that through when Caliph appeared, assigning one of his larger spheres into a communications console. Symbols and keypads brightened across the matte grey surface. Fernando tapped commands, claws clicking as he worked, and soon accessed his private data channel.

There was, as he had half expected, a new message from Scrutiny. It concerned the more detailed analysis of the leaks that had been in motion when he left on his investigation.

Fernando placed a direct call through.

"Hello," said Fernando's down-brane counterpart, a man named Cook. "Good news, bad news, I'm afraid."

"Continue," Fernando purred.

"We've run a thorough analysis on the keyword clusters, as promised. The good news is that the clusters haven't gone away: their statistical significance is now even more certain. There's clearly been a leak. That means your journey hasn't been for nothing."

"That's a relief."

"The bad news is that the context is still giving us some serious headaches. Frankly, it's disturbing. Whoever's responsible for these leaks has gone to immense trouble to make them look as if they've always been part of our data heritage."

"I don't understand. I mean, I *understand*, but I don't get it. There must be a problem with your methods, your data auditing."

Cook looked pained. "That's what we thought, but we've been over this time and again. There's no mistake. Whoever planted these leaks has tampered with the data at a very deep level; sufficient to make it seem as if the clusters have been with us long before the KR-L brane was ever discovered."

Fernando lowered his voice. "Give me an example. Austvro mentioned a play, for instance."

"That would be one of the oldest clusters. *The Shipwreck*, by a paper-age playwright, around 001611. No overt references to the KR-L, but it does deal with a scholar on a haunted island, an island where a powerful witch used to live . . . which could be considered a metaphorical substitute for Austvro and Pegasus Station. Contains a Miranda, too, and . . ."

"Was the playwright a real historical figure?"

"Unlikely, unless he was almost absurdly prolific. There are several dozen other plays in the records, all of which we can presume were the work of the mole."

"Mm," Fernando said, thoughtfully.

"The mole screwed up in other ways too," Cook added. "The plays are riddled with anachronisms; words and phrases that don't appear earlier in the records."

"Sloppy," Fernando commented, while wondering if there was something more to it than mere sloppiness. "Tell me about another cluster."

"Skip to 001956 and we have another piece of faked drama: something called a 'film'; some kind of recorded performance. Again, lots of giveaways: Ostrow for Austvro, Bellerophon—he's the hero who rode the winged horse Pegasus—the KR-L themselves . . . real aliens, this time, even if they're confined to a single planet, rather than an entire brane. There's even—get this—a tiger."

"Really," Fernando said dryly.

"But here's an oddity: our enquiries turned up peripheral matter which seems to argue that the later piece was in some way based upon the earlier one."

"Almost as if the mole wished to lead our attention from one cluster to another." Fernando scratched at his ear. "What's the next cluster?"

"Jump to 002713: an ice opera performed on Pluto Prime, for one night only, before it closed due to exceptionally bad notices. Mentions 'entities in the eighty three thousandth layer of reality'. This from at least six thousand years before the existence of adjoining braneworlds was proven beyond doubt."

"Could be coincidence, but . . . well, go on."

"Jump to 009655, the premier of a Tauri-phase astrosculpture in the Wenlock star forming region. Supplementary text refers to 'the aesthetic of the doomed Crail' and 'Mirandine and Kalebin'."

"There are other clusters, right up to the near-present?"

"All the way up the line. Random time-spacing: we've looked for patterns there, and haven't found any. It must mean something to the mole, of course . . ."

"If there is a mole," Fernando said.

"Of course there's a mole. What other explanation could there be?"

"That's what I'm wondering."

Fernando closed the connection, then sat in silent contemplation, shuffling mental permutations. When he felt that he had examined the matter from every conceivable angle—

and yet still arrived at the same unsettling conclusion—he had Caliph summon Doctor Austvro once more.

"Really, Inspector," she said, as she came back into the lounge. "I've barely had time . . ."

"Sit down, Doctor."

Something in the force of his words must have reached her. Doctor Austvro sank into the settee, her hands tucked into the silvery folds of her dress.

"Is there a problem? I specifically asked . . ."

"You're under arrest for the murder of your husband, Edvardo Austvro."

Her face turned furious. "Don't be absurd. My husband's death was an accident: a horrid, gruesome mistake, but no more than that."

"That's what you wished us all to think. But you killed him, didn't you? You arranged for the collapse of the inclusion, knowing that he would be caught in KR-L spacetime."

"Ridiculous."

"Your husband understood what had happened to the KR-L: how their machinery had reached around the stack, through three hundred and sixty degrees, and wiped them out of existence, leaving only their remains. He knew exactly how dangerous it would be to reactivate the machinery; how it could never become a tool for the Metagovernment. You said it yourself, Meranda: he feared the machinery. That's because he knew what it had done; what it was still capable of doing."

"I would never have killed him," she said, her tone flatly insistent.

"Not until he opposed you directly, not until he became the only obstacle between you and your greatest triumph. Then he had to go."

"I've heard enough." She turned her angry face towards the aerial. "Caliph: escort the Inspector to the dissolution chamber. He's in clear violation of the terms under which I agreed to this investigation."

"On the contrary," Fernando said. "My enquiry is still of central importance."

She sneered. "Your ridiculous obsession with leaks? I

monitored your recent conversation with the homebrane, Inspector. The leaks are what I've always maintained: statistical noise, meaningless coincidences. The mere fact that they appear in sources that are incontrovertibly old . . . what further evidence do you need, that the leaks are nothing of the sort?"

"You're right," Fernando said, allowing himself a heavy sigh. "They aren't leaks. In that sense I was mistaken."

"In which case admit that your mission here was no more than a wild goose chase, and that your accusations concerning my husband amount to no more than a desperate attempt to salvage some . . ."

"They aren't leaks," Fernando continued, as if Austvro had not spoken. "They're warnings, sent from our own future."

She blinked. "I'm sorry?"

"It's the only explanation. The leaks appear in context sources that appear totally authentic . . . because they are."

"Madness."

"I don't think so. It all fits together quite nicely. Your husband was investigating acausal signalling: the means to send messages back in time. You dismissed his work, but what if there was something in it after all? What if a proper understanding of the KR-L technology allowed a future version of the Metagovernment to send a warning to itself in the past?"

"What kind of warning, Inspector?" she asked, still sounding appalled.

"I'm guessing here, but it might have something to do with the machinery itself. You're about to reactivate the very tools that destroyed the KR-L. Perhaps the point of the warning is to stop that ever happening. Some dreadful, unforeseen consequence of turning the machinery against the dissident branes . . . not the extinction of humanity, obviously, or there wouldn't be anyone left alive to send the warning. But something nearly as bad. Something so awful that it must be edited out of history, at all costs."

"You should listen to yourself, Inspector. Then ask yourself whether you came out of the quickening room with all your faculties intact."

He smiled. "Then you have doubts."

"Concerning your sanity, yes. This idea of a message being sent back in time . . . it might have some microscopic degree of credibility if your precious leaks weren't so hopelessly cryptic. Who sends a message and then scrambles the facts?"

"Someone in a hurry, I suppose. Or someone with an imperfect technique."

"I'm sure that means something to you."

"I'm just wondering: what if there wasn't time to get it right? What if the sending of the message was a one-shot attempt, something that had to be attempted even though the method was still not fully understood?"

"That still doesn't explain why the keywords would crop up in . . . a *play*, of all things."

"Perhaps it does, though. Especially if the acausal signalling involves the transmission of patterns directly into the human mind, across time, in a scattergun fashion. The playwright . . ."

"What about him?" she asked, with a knowingness that reminded him she had listened in on his conversation with Cook.

"The man lived and died before the discovery of quantum mechanics, let alone braneworlds. Even if the warning arrived fully-formed and coherent in his mind, he could only have interpreted it according to his existing mental framework. It's no wonder things got mixed up, confused. His conceptual vocabulary didn't extend to vanished alien cultures in adjacent reality stacks. It did extend to islands, dead witches, ghosts."

"Ridiculous. Next you'll be telling me that the other clusters . . ."

"Exactly so. The dramatised recording—the 'film'—was made a few centuries later. The creators did the best they could with their limited understanding of the universe. They knew of space travel, other worlds. Closer to the truth than the playwright, but still limited by the mental prison of their contemporary worldview. The same goes for all the other clusters, I'm willing to bet."

"Let me get this straight," Austvro said. "The future Metagovernment resurrects ancient KR-L time-signalling machinery, technology that it barely understands. It attempts to send a message back in time, but it ends up spraying it through history, back to the time of a man who probably thought the Sun ran on coal."

"Maybe even earlier," Fernando said. "There's nothing to say there aren't other clusters, lurking in the statistical noise . . ."

Austvro cut him off. "And yet despite this limited understanding of the machinery, the—as you said—scattershot approach—they still managed to score direct hits into the heads of playwrights, dramatists, sculptors . . ." She shook her head pityingly.

"Not necessarily," Fernando said. "We only know that these people became what they were in our timeline. It might have been the warning itself that set these individuals on their artistic courses . . . planting a seed, a vaguely-felt anxiety, that they had no choice but to exorcise through creative expression, be it a play, a film, or an ice-opera on Pluto Prime."

"I'll give you credit, Inspector: you really know how to take an argument beyond its logical limit. You're actually suggesting that if the signalling hadn't taken place, none of these works of art would ever have existed?"

He shrugged. "If you admit the possibility of time messages . . ."

"I don't. Not at all."

"It doesn't matter. I'd hoped to convince you—I thought it might make your arrest an easier matter for both of us—but it's really not necessary. You understand now, though, why I must put an end to your research. Scrutiny and Exploitation can decide for themselves whether there's any truth in my theory."

"And if they don't think there is—then I'll be allowed to resume my studies?"

"There's still the small matter of your murder charge, Meranda."

She looked sad. "I'd hoped you might have forgotten."

"It's not my job to forget."

"How did you guess?"

"I didn't guess," he said. "You led me to it. More than that: I think some part of you—some hidden, subconscious part—actually wanted me to learn the truth. If not, that was a very unfortunate choice of card game, Meranda."

"You're saying I wanted you to arrest me?"

"I can't believe that you ever hated your husband enough to kill him. You just hated the way he opposed your research. For that reason he had to go, but I doubt that there's been a moment since when what you did hasn't been eating you from inside."

"You're right," she said, as if arriving at a firm decision. "I didn't hate him. But he still had to go. And so do you."

In a flash her hand had emerged from the silvery folds of her dress, clutching the sleek black form of a weapon. Fernando recognised it as a simple blaster: not the most sophisticated weapon in existence, but more than capable of inflicting mortal harm.

"Please, Doctor. Put that thing away, before you do one of us an injury."

She stood, the weapon wavering in her hand, but never losing its lock on him.

"Caliph," she said. "Escort the Inspector to the dissolution chamber. He's leaving us."

"You're making a mistake, Meranda."

"The mistake would be in allowing the Metagovernment to close me down, when I'm so close to success. Caliph!"

"I cannot escort the Inspector, unless the Inspector wishes to be escorted," the aerial informed her.

"I gave you an order!"

"He is an agent of the Office of Scrutiny. My programming does not permit . . ."

"Walk with me, please," Fernando said. "Put the gun away and we'll say no more about it. You're in enough trouble as it is."

"I'm not going with you."

"You'll receive a fair trial. With the right argument, you may even be able to claim your husband's death as manslaughter. Perhaps you didn't mean to kill him, just to strand him . . ."

"It's not the trial," she snarled. "It's the thought of stepping into that *thing* . . . when I came here I never intended to leave. I won't go with you."

"You must."

He took a step towards her, knowing even as he did it that the move was unwise. He watched her finger tense on the blaster's trigger, and for an instant he thought he might cross the space to her before the weapon discharged. Few people had the nerve to hold a gun against an agent of Scrutiny; even fewer had the nerve to fire.

But Meranda Austvro was one of those few. The muzzle spat rapid bolts of self-confined plasma, and he watched in slow-motion horror as three of the bolts slammed into his right arm, below the elbow, and took his hand and forearm away in an agonising orange fire, like a chalk drawing smeared in the rain. The pain hit him like a hammer, and despite his training he felt the full force of it before mental barriers slammed down in rapid succession, blocking the worst. He could smell his own charred fur.

"An error, Doctor Austvro," he grunted, forcing the words out.

"Don't take another step, Inspector."

"I'm afraid I must."

"I'll kill you." The weapon was now aimed directly at his chest. If her earlier shot had been wide, there would be no error now.

He took another step. He watched her finger tense again, and readied himself for the annihilating fire.

But the weapon dropped from her hand. One of Caliph's smaller spheres had dashed it from her grip. Austvro clutched her hand with the other, massaging the fingers. Her face showed stunned incomprehension. "You betrayed me," she said to the aerial.

"You injured an agent of Scrutiny. You were about to inflict further harm. I could not allow that to happen." Then one of the larger spheres swerved into Fernando's line of sight. "Do you require medical assistance?"

"I don't think so. I'm about done with this body anyway."

"Very well."

"Will you help me to escort Doctor Austvro to the dissolution chamber?"

"If you order it."

"Help me, in that case."

Doctor Austvro tried to resist, but between them Fernando and Caliph quickly had the better of her. Fernando kicked the weapon out of harm's way, then pulled Austvro against his chest with his left arm, pinning her there. She struggled to escape, but her strength was nothing against his, even allowing for the shock of losing his right arm.

Caliph propelled them to the dissolution chamber. Austvro fought all the way, but with steadily draining will. Only at the last moment, when she saw the grey hood of the memory recorder, next to the recessed alcove of the dissolution field, did she summon some last reserve of resistance. But her efforts counted for nothing. Fernando and the robot placed her into the recorder, closing the heavy metal restraining buckles across her body. The hood lowered itself, ready to capture a final neural image; a snapshot of her mind that would be encoded into a graviton pulse and relayed back to the homebrane.

"Meranda Austvro," Fernando said, pushing the blackened stump of his arm into his chest furs, "I am arresting you on the authority of the Office of Scrutiny. Your resurrection profile will be captured and transmitted into the safekeeping of the Metagovernment. A new body will be quickened and employed as a host for these patterns, and then brought to trial. Please compose your thoughts accordingly."

"When they quicken me again, I'll destroy your career," she told him.

Fernando looked sympathetic. "You wouldn't believe how many times I've heard that before."

"I should have skinned you twice."

"It wouldn't have worked. They'd have sent a third copy of me."

He activated the memory recorder. Amber lights flickered across the hood, stabilising to indicate that the device had obtained a coherent image and that the relevant data was ready to be committed to the graviton pulse. Fernando issued the command, and a tumbling hourglass symbol appeared on the hood.

"Your patterns are on their way home now, Meranda. For the moment you still have a legal existence. Enjoy it while you can."

He'd never said anything that cruel before, and almost as soon as the words were out he regretted them. Taunting the soon-to-be-destroyed had never been his style, and it shamed him that he had permitted himself such a gross lapse of professionalism. The only compensation was that he would soon find himself in the same predicament as Doctor Austvro.

The hourglass vanished, replaced by a steady green light. It signified that the homebrane had received the graviton pulse, and that the resurrection profile had been transmitted without error.

"Former body of Meranda Austvro," he began, "I must now inform you . . ."

"Just get it over with."

Fernando and Caliph helped her from the recorder. Her body felt light in his hands, as if some essential part of it had been erased or extracted during the recording process. Legally, this was no longer Doctor Meranda Austvro: just the biological vehicle Austvro had used while resident in this brane. According to Metagovernment law, the vehicle must now be recycled.

Fernando turned on the pearly screen of the dissolution field. He tested it with a stylus, satisfied when he saw the instant actinic flash as the stylus was wrenched from existence. Dissolution was quick and efficient. In principle the atomic fires destroyed the central nervous system long before pain signals had a chance to reach it, let alone be experienced as pain.

Not that anyone ever *knew*, of course. By the time you went through the field, your memories had already been captured. Anything you experienced at the moment of destruction never made it into the profile.

"I can push you into the field," he told Austvro. "But by all accounts you'll find it quicker and easier if you run at it yourself."

She didn't want it to happen that way. Caliph and Fernando had to help her through the field. It wasn't the nicest part of the job.

Afterwards, Fernando sat down to marshall and clarify his thoughts. In a little while he too would be consumed by fire, only to be reborn in the homebrane. Scrutiny would be expecting a comprehensive report into the Pegasus affair, and it would not do to be woolly on the details. Experience had taught him that a little mental preparation now paid dividends in the long run. The recording and quickening process always blurred matters a little, so the clearer one could be at the outset, the better.

When he was done with the recorder, when the green light had reported safe receipt of his neural patterns, he turned to Caliph. "I no longer have legal jurisdiction here. The 'me' speaking to you is not even legally entitled to call itself Adam Fernando. But I hope you won't consider it improper of me to offer some small thanks for your assistance."

"Will someone come back to take over?" Caliph asked.

"Probably. But don't be surprised if they come to shut down Pegasus. I'm sure my legal self will put in a good word for you, though."

"Thank you," the aerial said.

"It's the least I can do."

Fernando stood from the recorder, and—as was his usual habit—took a running jump at the dissolution field. It wasn't the most elegant of ends—the lack of an arm hindered his balance—but it was quick and efficient and the execution not without a certain dignity.

Caliph watched the tiger burn, the stripes seeming to linger in the air before fading away. Then it gathered its spheres into an agitated swarm and wondered what to do next.

Dead Men Walking

PAUL J. McAULEY

Paul J. McAuley (www.omegacom.demon.co.uk) *lives in London, England. He often writes hard SF, and is one of the group of writers responsible for the British version of the hard SF/space opera renaissance of the 1990s. He has published more than a dozen SF novels, of which the most recent is* Mind's Eye *(2005). He has three collections of short fiction,* The King of the Hill and Other Stories, The Invisible Country, *and* Little Machines.

"Dead Men Walking" was published in Asimov's. *It is part of the Quiet War series of stories, the seventh to date, that began with "Second Skin" (1996). Like the killer android Roy Batty in the film Bladerunner, Roy Bruce is in hiding and living out his days, in this case on Ariel, an icy moon of Uranus, until the retrovirus built into special programmed killers, doppelgangers, terminates his life. But there appears to be another android on Ariel, killing actively, and Bruce has to track down his peer or risk discovery as the killings are investigated. All scenarios end in death.*

guess this is the end. I'm in no condition to attempt the climb down, and in any case I'm running out of air. The nearest emergency shelter is only five klicks away, but it might as well be on the far side of this little moon. I'm not expecting any kind of last-minute rescue, either. No one knows I'm here, my phone and the distress beacon are out, my emergency flares went with my utility belt, and I don't think that the drones patrol this high. At least my legs have stopped hurting, although I can feel the throb of what's left of my right hand through the painkiller's haze, like the beat of distant war drums. . . .

If you're the person who found my body, I doubt that you'll have time to listen to my last and only testament. You'll be too busy calling for help, securing the area, and making sure that you or any of your companions don't trample precious clues underfoot. I imagine instead that you're an investigator or civil servant sitting in an office buried deep inside some great bureaucratic hive, listening to this out of duty before consigning it to the memory hole. You'll know that my body was found near the top of the eastern rimwall of the great gash of Elliot Graben on Ariel, Uranus's fourth-largest moon, but I don't suppose you've ever visited the place, so I should give you an idea of what I can see.

I'm sitting with my pressure suit's backpack firmly wedged against a huge block of dirty, rock-hard ice. A little way beyond my broken legs, a cliff drops straight down for about a kilometer to the bottom of the graben's enormous trough. Its floor was resurfaced a couple of billion years ago by a flood of water-ice lava, a level plain patched with enormous fields of semi-vacuum organisms. Orange and red, deep blacks, foxy umbers, bright yellows . . . they stretch away from me in every direction for as far as I can see, like the biggest quilt in the universe. This moon is so small and the graben is so wide that its western rim is below the horizon. Strings of suspensor lamps float high above the fields like a fleet of burning airships. There's enough atmospheric pressure, twenty millibars of nitrogen and methane, to haze the view and give an indication of distance, of just how big this strange garden really is. It's the prison farm, of course, and every square centimeter of it was constructed by the sweat of men and women convicted by the failure of their ideals, but none of that matters to me now. I'm beyond all that up here, higher than the suspensor lamps, tucked under the eaves of the vast roof of transparent halflife polymer that tents the graben. If I twist my head I can glimpse one of the giant struts that anchor the roof. Beyond it, the big, blue-green globe of Uranus floats in the black sky. The gas giant's south pole, capped with a brownish haze of photochemical smog, is aimed at the brilliant point of the sun, which hangs just above the western horizon.

Sunset's three hours off. I won't live long enough to see it. My legs are comfortably numb, but the throbbing in my hand is becoming more urgent, there's a dull ache in my chest, and every breath is an effort. I wonder if I'll live long enough to tell you my story . . .

All right. I've just taken another shot of painkiller. I had to override the suit to do it, it's a lethal dose . . .

Christos, it still hurts. It hurts to laugh . . .

My name is Roy Bruce. It isn't my real name. I have never had a real name. I suppose I had a number when I was decanted, but I don't know what it was. My instructors called me Dave—but they called all of us Dave, a private joke they never bothered to explain. Later, just before the war began, I took the life of the man in whose image I had been made. I took his life, his name, his identity. And after the war was over, after I evaded recall and went on the run, I had several different names, one after the other. But Roy, Roy Bruce, that's the name I've had longest. That's the name you'll find on the roster of guards. That's the name you can bury me under.

My name is Roy Bruce, and I lived in Herschel City, Ariel, for eight and a half years. Lived. Already with the past tense . . .

My name is Roy Bruce. I'm a prison guard. The prison, TPA Facility 898, is a cluster of chambers—we call them blocks—buried in the eastern rim of Elliot Graben. Herschel City is twenty klicks beyond, a giant cylindrical shaft sunk into Ariel's icy surface, its walls covered in a vertical, shaggy green forest that grows from numerous ledges and crevices. Public buildings and little parks jut out of the forest wall like bracket fungi; homes are built in and amongst the trees. Ariel's just over a thousand kilometers in diameter and mostly ice; its gravity barely exists. The citizens of Herschel City are arboreal acrobats, swinging, climbing, sliding, flying up and down and roundabout on cableways and trapezes, nets and ropewalks. It's a good place to live.

I have a one-room treehouse. It's not very big and plainly furnished, but you can sit on the porch of a morning, watch squirrel monkeys chase each other through the pines . . .

I'm a member of Sweat Lodge #23. I breed singing crickets, have won several competitions with them. Mostly they're hacked to sing fragments of Mozart, nothing fancy, but my line has good sustain and excellent timbre and pitch. I hope old Willy Gup keeps it going . . .

I like to hike too, and climb freestyle. I once soloed the Broken Book route in Prospero Chasma on Miranda, twenty kilometers up a vertical face, in fifteen hours. Nowhere near the record, but pretty good for someone with a terminal illness. I've already had various bouts of cancer, but retroviruses dealt with those easily enough. What's killing me—what just lost the race to kill me—is a general systematic failure something like lupus. I couldn't get any treatment for it, of course, because the doctors would find out who I really am. What I really was.

I suppose that I had a year or so left. Maybe two if I was really lucky.

It wasn't much of a life, but it was all my own.

Uranus has some twenty-odd moons, mostly captured chunks of sooty ice a few dozen kilometers in diameter. Before the Quiet War, no more than a couple of hundred people lived out here. Rugged pioneer families, hermits, a few scientists, and some kind of Hindu sect that planted huge tracts of Umbriel's sooty surface with slow-growing lichenous vacuum organisms. After the war, the Three Powers Alliance took over the science station on Ariel, one of the larger moons, renamed it Herschel City, and built its maximum security facility in the big graben close by. The various leaders and lynchpins of the revolution, who had already spent two years being interrogated at Tycho, on Earth's Moon, were moved here to serve the rest of their life sentences of reeducation and moral realignment. At first, the place was run by the Navy, but civilian contractors were brought in after Elliot Graben was tented and the vacuum organism farms were planted. Most were ex-Service people who had settled in the Outer System after the war. I was one of them.

I had learned how to create fake identities with convincing histories during my training; my latest incarnation easily passed the security check. For eight and half years, Roy Bruce, guard third class, cricket breeder, amateur freestyle climber, lived a quiet, anonymous life out on the fringe of the solar system. And then two guards stumbled across the body of Goether Lyle, who had been the leader of the Senate of Athens, Tethys, when, along with a dozen other city states in the Outer System, it had declared independence from Earth.

I'd known Goether slightly: an intense, serious man who'd been writing some kind of philosophical thesis in his spare time. His body was found in the middle of the main highway between the facility and the farms, spreadeagled and naked, spikes hammered through hands and feet. His genitals had been cut off and stuffed in his mouth; his tongue had been pulled through the slit in his throat. He was also frozen solid—the temperature out on the floor of the graben is around minus one hundred and fifty degrees Centigrade, balmy compared to the surface of Ariel, but still a lot colder than the inside of any domestic freezer, so cold that the carbon dioxide given off by certain strains of vacuum organisms precipitates out of the atmosphere like hoar frost. It took six hours to thaw out his body for the autopsy, which determined that the mutilations were postmortem. He'd died of strangulation, and then all the other stuff had been done to him.

I was more than thirty klicks away when Goether Lyle's body was discovered, supervising a work party of ten prisoners, what we call a stick, that was harvesting a field of vacuum organisms. It's important to keep the prisoners occupied, and stoop labor out in the fields or in the processing plants leaves them too tired to plan any serious mischief. Also, export of the high-grade biochemicals that the vacuum organisms cook from the methane in the thin atmosphere helps to defray the enormous cost of running the facility. So I didn't hear about the murder until I'd driven my stick back to its block at the end of the shift, and I didn't learn all the gruesome details until later that evening, at the sweat lodge.

In the vestigial gravity of worldlets like Ariel, where you can drown in a shower and water tends to slosh about uncontrollably, sweat lodges, saunas, or Turkish-style hamams are ideal ways to keep clean. You bake in steam heat, sweat the dirt out of your pores, scrape it off your skin, and exchange gossip with your neighbors and friends. Even in a little company town like Herschel City, there are lodges catering for just about every sexual orientation and religious belief. My lodge, #23, is for unattached, agnostic heterosexual males. That evening, as usual, I was sitting with a dozen or so naked men of various ages and body types in eucalyptus-scented steam around its stone hearth. We scraped at our skin with abrasive mitts or plastered green depilatory mud on ourselves, squirted the baking stones of the hearth with water to make more steam, and talked about the murder of Goether Lyle. Mustafa Sesler, who worked in the hospital, gave us all the grisly details. There was speculation about whether it was caused by a personal beef or a turf war between gangs. Someone made the inevitable joke about it being the most thorough suicide in the history of the prison. Someone else, my friend Willy Gup, asked me if I had any idea about it.

"You had the guy in your stick last year, Roy. He have any enemies you know of?"

I gave a noncommittal answer. The mutilations described by Mustafa Sesler were straight out of my training in assassination, guerrilla tactics, and black propaganda. I was processing the awful possibility that Goether Lyle had been murdered by someone like me.

You must know by now what I am. That I am not really human. That I am a doppelgänger who was designed by gene wizards, grown in a vat, decanted fully grown with a headful of hardwired talents and traits, trained up, and sent out to kill the person whose exact double I was, and replace him. I do not know how many doppelgängers, berserkers, suicide artists, and other cloned subversives were deployed during the Quiet War, but I believe that our contribution was significant. My target was Sharwal Jah Sharja, a minor gene wizard who lived alone in the jungle in one of the tented crevasses of East of Eden, Ganymede, where he orchestrated the unceasing symphony of the city-state's closed loop ecosystem. After I took his place, I began a program of ecotage, significantly reducing the circulation of water vapor and increasing the atmospheric concentration of carbon dioxide and toxic trace gases. By the time the Quiet War kicked off, some four weeks later, the population of East of Eden was wearing breathing masks, the forests and parks were beginning to die, most food animals and crops had died or were badly stricken, forcing the city to use biomass from vacuum organism farms to feed its citizens. A commando force of the Three Powers Alliance annexed East of Eden's farms in the first few hours of the war, and after two weeks its starving citizens agreed to terms of surrender.

I was supposed to turn myself in as soon as the city had been secured, but in the middle of the formal surrender, dead-ender fanatics assassinated half the senate and attacked the occupying force. In the subsequent confusion, the tented crevasse where I had been living was blown open to vacuum, Sharwal Jah Sharja was posted as one of the casualties, and I took the opportunity to slip away. I have successfully hidden my true identity and lived incognito amongst ordinary human beings ever since.

Why did I disobey my orders? How did I slip the bonds of my hardwired drives and instincts? It's quite simple. While I had been pretending to be Sharwal Jah Sharja, I had come to love life. I wanted to learn as much about it as I could in the brief span I'd been allotted by my designers. And so I adopted the identity of another casualty, and after the war was over and the Three Powers Alliance allowed trade and travel to resume, I left East of Eden and went out into the Solar System to see what I could see.

In all my wanderings I have never met any others like me, but I did find a hint that at least one of my brothers and sisters of the vat had survived the war. All of us had been imprinted with a variety of coded messages covering a vast range of possibilities, and a year after going on the run I came across one of them in a little-used passageway between two chambers of the city of Xamba, Rhea.

To anyone else it was a meaningless scrawl; to me, it was like a flash of black lightning that branded an enciphered phone number itself on my brain. The walls of the passageway were thickly scribbled with graffiti, much of it pre-war. The message could have been left there last year or last week; it could have been a trap, left by agents hunting renegades like me. I didn't have the nerve to find out. I went straight to the spaceport and bought a seat on a shuttle to Phoebe, the gateway port to the other moons of Saturn and the rest of the Outer System. Six months later, wearing the new identity of Roy Bruce, I became a guard at TPA Facility 898.

That's why, almost nine years later, I couldn't be certain that any of my brothers and sisters had survived, and I was able to convince myself that Goether Lyle had been the victim of the vicious internal politics of the prison, killed and mutilated by someone who knew about the black propaganda techniques in which we'd been trained. But that comforting fiction was blown apart the very next day, when another mutilated body was found.

The victim was a former senator of Baghdad, Enceladus, and a member of the prison gang that was intermittently at war with the gang to which Goether Lyle had belonged. A message written in blood on the ground next to the senator's body implied that he'd been murdered by Goether Lyle's cronies, but whoever had killed him must have done the deed in his cell some time between the evening count and the end of the night's lockdown, spirited his body out of the facility without being detected, and left it within the field of view of a security camera which had been hacked to show a recorded loop instead of a live feed. Members of the rival gangs lived in different blocks, had chips implanted in their skulls that constantly monitored their movements, and in any case were under lock-down all night. If the killer was a prisoner, he would have had to bribe more than a dozen guards; it was far more likely that the senator had been killed by one of the facility's staff. And when I heard what had been done to the body, I was certain that it was the handiwork of one of my brothers or sisters. The senator had been blinded before he'd been strangled, and his lungs had been pulled through incisions in his back. It was a mutilation called the Blood Eagle that had been invented by the Vikings some two thousand years ago. I remembered the cold, patient voice of the instructor who had demonstrated it to us on a corpse.

Someone in the warden's office reached the same conclusion. Posted at the top of our daily orders was an announcement that a specialist team was on its way to Ariel, and emergency security measures were put in place at the spaceport. That evening Willy Gup told the sweat lodge that the warden reckoned that it was possible that the two murders were the work of the kind of vat-grown assassin used in the Quiet War.

"So if you come across anything suspicious, don't be tempted to do anything stupidly heroic, my brothers. Those things are smart and deadly and completely without any kind of human feeling. Be like me. Stay frosty, but hang back."

I felt a loathsome chill crawl through me. I knew that if Willy and the others realized that one of "those things" was sitting with them in the steamy heat of the lodge, they would fall on me at once and tear me limb from limb. And I knew that I couldn't hang back, couldn't let things run their course. No one would be able to leave Ariel for the duration of the emergency security measures, and the specialist team would search every square centimeter of the facility and Herschel City, check the records and DNA profile of every prisoner, member of staff, citizen and visitor, and release a myriad tiny halflife drones designed to home in on anyone breathing out the combination of metabolic byproducts unique to our kind. The team would almost certainly uncover the assassin, but they would also unmask me.

Oh, I suppose that I could have hiked out to some remote location on the surface and hunkered down for the duration, but I had no idea how long the search would last. The only way I could be sure of evading it would be to force my pressure suit to put me in deep hibernation for a month or two, and how would I explain my absence when I returned? And besides, I knew that I was dying. I was already taking dangerously large daily doses of steroids to relieve the swelling of my joints and inflammation of my connective tissue caused by my pseudo-lupus. Suspended animation would slow but not stop the progress of my disease. Suppose I never woke up?

I spent a long, bleak night considering my options. By the time the city had begun to increase its ambient light level and the members of the local troop of spider monkeys were beginning to hoot softly to each other in the trees outside my little cabin, I knew what I would have to do. I knew that I would have to find the assassin before the team arrived.

My resolve hardened when I started my shift a couple of hours later and learned that there had been two more murders, and a minor riot in the prison library.

I found it laughably easy to hack into the facility's files: I had been trained well all those years ago, and the data system was of a similar vintage to my own. To begin with, I checked the dossiers of recently recruited staff, but I found nothing suspicious, and didn't have any better luck when I examined the dossiers of friends and family of prisoners, their advocates, and traders and businesspeople currently staying in Herschel City. It was possible that I had missed something— no doubt the assassin's cover story was every bit as good as the one that had served me so well for so long. But having more or less eliminated the obvious suspects, I had to consider the possibility that, just like me, the assassin had been hiding on Ariel ever since the war had ended. I had so much in common with my brothers and sisters that it would not be a wild coincidence if one of them had come to the same decision as I had, and had joined the staff of the prison. Perhaps he had finally gone insane, or perhaps the hardwired imperatives of his old mission had kicked in. Or perhaps, like me, he had discovered that he was coming to the end of his short life span, and had decided to have some fun. . . .

In the short time before the specialist team arrived, it would be impossible to check thoroughly the records of over three thousand staff members. I had reached a dead end. I decided that I needed some advice.

Everyone in Herschel City and the prison was talking about the murders. During a casual conversation with Willy Gup, I found it easy enough to ask my old friend if he had any thoughts on how someone might go about uncovering the identity of the assassin.

"Anyone with any sense would keep well clear," Willy said. "They'd keep their nose clean, they'd keep their stick in line, and they'd wait for the specialists."

"Who won't be here for a week. A full-scale war could have broken out by then."

Willy admitted that I had a point. One of the original intake of guards, a veteran who'd served in one of the Navy supply ships during the Quiet War, he had led the team that put down the trouble in the library. Three prisoners had died and eighteen had been badly injured—one had gouged out the eyes of another with her thumbs—and the incident had left him subdued and thoughtful. After studying me for a few moments, he said, "If it was me, I wouldn't touch the files. I hear the warden is compiling a list of people who are poking around, looking for clues and so forth. He tolerates their nonsense because he desperately wants to put an end to the trouble as soon as he can, and he'll be pretty damn happy if some hack does happen to uncover the assassin. But it isn't likely, and when this thing is over you can bet he's going to come down hard on all those amateur sleuths. And it's possible the assassin is keeping tabs on the files too. Anyone who comes close to finding him could be in for a bad surprise. No, my brother, screwing around in the files is only going to get you into trouble."

I knew then that Willy had a shrewd idea of what I was about. I also knew that the warden was the least of my worries. I said, as lightly as I could, "So what would you do?"

Willy didn't answer straight away, but instead refilled his bulb from the jar of iced tea. We were sitting on the porch of his little shack, at the edge of a setback near the top of the city's shaft. Banana plants and tree ferns screened it from its neighbors; the vertical forest dropped away on either side. One of Willy's crickets, a splendid white and gold specimen in a cage of plaited bamboo, was trilling one of Bach's Goldberg Variations. Willy passed the jar to me and said, "We're speaking purely hypothetically."

"Of course."

"You've always had a wild streak," Willy said, "I wouldn't put it past you to do something recklessly brave and dangerously stupid."

"I'm just an ordinary hack," I said.

"Who goes for long solitary hikes across the surface. Who soloed that route in Prospero Chasma and didn't bother to mention it until someone found out a couple of years later. I've known you almost nine years, Roy, and you're still a man of mystery." Willy smiled. "Hey, what's that look for? All I'm saying is you have character, is all."

For a moment, my hardwired reflexes had kicked in. For a moment, I had been considering whether or not this man had blown my cover, whether or not I should kill him. I carefully manufactured a smile, and said that I hadn't realized that I seemed so odd.

"Most of us have secrets," Willy said. "That's why we're out here, my brother. We're just as much prisoners as anyone in our sticks. They don't know it, but those dumbasses blundering about in the files are trying to find a way of escaping what they are."

"And there's no way you can escape what you are," I said. The moment had passed. My smile was a real smile now, not a mask I'd put on to hide what I really was.

Willy toasted me with his bulb of tea. "Anyone with any sense learns that eventually."

"You still haven't told me how you would catch the assassin."

"I don't intend to catch him."

"But speaking hypothetically . . ."

"For all we know, it's the warden. He can go anywhere and everywhere, and he has access to all the security systems too."

"The warden? Really?"

Willy grinned. "I'm pulling your chain. But seriously, I've done a little research about these things. They're not only stone killers, but they're also real good at disguising themselves. The assassin could be any one of us. The warden, you, me, anyone.

Unless this thing makes a mistake, we haven't got a hope of catching it. All we can do is what we're already doing— deploy more security drones, keep the prisoners locked down when they aren't working, and pray that that'll keep a lid on any unrest until that team arrives."

"I guess you're right," I said.

"Don't try to be a hero, my brother. Not even hypothetically."

"Absolutely not," I said.

But one of Willy's remarks had given me an idea about how to reach out to the assassin, and my mind was already racing, grappling with what I had to do.

I decided that if the assassin really was keeping an eye on the people who were hacking into the files, then he (or at least, his demon), must be lurking in the root directory of the data system. That was where I left an encrypted message explaining what I was and why I wanted to talk, attached to a demon that would attempt to trace anyone who looked at it. The demon phoned me six hours later, in the middle of the night. Someone had spotted my sign and wanted to talk.

The demon had failed to identify the person who wanted to talk, and it was infected with something, too: a simple communication program. I checked it out, excised a few lines of code that would have revealed my location, and fired it up. It connected me to a blank, two-dimensional space in which words began to appear, emerging letter by letter, traveling from right to left and fading away.

>>you got rid of the trace function. pretty good for an old guy—if that's what you really are.

>they trained us well, I typed.

>>you think you know what i am. you think that i am like you.

Whoever was at the other end of the program wanted to get straight down to business. That suited me, but I knew that I couldn't let him take the lead.

>we are both children of the vat, I typed. that's why I reached out to you. that's why i want to help you.

There was a pause as my correspondent thought this over.

>>you could be a trap.

>the message got your attention because it is hardwired into your visual cortex, just as it is hardwired into mine.

>>that kind of thing is no longer the secret it once was, but let's say that i believe you . . .

A black disc spun in the blank space for less than a second, its strobing black light flashing a string of letters and numbers, gone.

>>do you know where that is?

I realized that the letters and numbers burnt into my brain were a grid reference.

>i can find it.

>>meet me in four hours. i have a little business to take care of first.

It was the middle of the night; the time when the assassin did his work.

>please don't kill anyone else until we have talked.

My words faded. There was no reply.

The grid reference was at the precise center of a small eroded crater sixty klicks south of the facility, an unreconstructed area in the shadow of the graben's eastern rimwall. Before I headed out, I equipped myself from the armory and downloaded a hack into the security system so that I could move freely and unremarked. I was oddly happy, foolishly confident. It felt good to be in action again. My head was filled with a fat, contented hum as I drove a tricycle cart along an old construction road. The rendezvous point was about an hour away: I would have plenty of time to familiarize myself with the terrain and make my preparations before the assassin, if that was who I had been talking to, turned up.

I want to make it clear that my actions were in no way altruistic. The only life I wanted to save was my own. Yes, I knew that I was dying, but no one loves life more than those who have only a little of it left; no one else experiences each and every moment with such vivid immediacy. I didn't intend to throw away my life in a grand gesture. I wanted to unmask the assassin and escape the special team's inquisition.

The road ran across a flat terrain blanketed in vacuum-cemented grey-brown dust and littered with big blocks that over the eons had been eroded into soft shapes by impact cratering. The rimwall reared up to my left, its intricate folds and bulges like a frozen curtain. Steep cones and rounded hills of mass-wasted talus fringed its base. To my right, the land sloped away toward a glittering ribbon of fences and dykes more than a kilometer away, the boundary of the huge patchwork of fields. It was two in the morning by the clock, but the suspensor lamps were burning as brightly as they always did, and above the western horizon the sun's dim spark was almost lost in their hazy glow.

I was a couple of klicks from the rendezvous, and the road was cutting through a steep ridge that buttressed a great bulge in the rimwall, when the assassin struck. I glimpsed a hitch of movement high in a corner of my vision, but before I could react, a taser dart struck my cart and shorted its motor. A second later, a net slammed into me, slithering over my torso as muscular threads of myoelectric plastic tightened in constricting folds around my arms and chest. I struggled to free myself as the cart piddled to a halt, but my arms were pinned to my sides by the net and I couldn't even unfasten the safety harness. I could only sit and watch as a figure in a black pressure suit descended the steep side of the ridge in two huge bounds, reached me in two more. It ripped out my phone, stripped away my utility belt, the gun in the pocket on the right thigh of my pressure suit and the knife in the pocket on the left thigh, then uncoupled my main air supply, punched the release of my harness and dragged me out of the low-slung seat and hauled me off the road. I was dumped on my back near a cart parked in the shadow of a house-sized block and the assassin stepped back, aiming a rail-gun at me.

The neutron camera I'd fitted inside my helmet revealed scant details of the face behind the gold-filmed mirror of my captor's visor; its demon made an extrapolation, searched the database I'd loaded, found a match. Debra Thorn, employed as a paramedic in the facility's infirmary for the past two years, twenty-two, unmarried, no children. . . . I realized then that I'd made a serious mistake. The assassin was a doppelgänger, all right, but because she was the double of someone who hadn't been an adult when the war had ended she must have been manufactured and decanted much more recently than me. She wasn't insane, and she hadn't spent years under cover. She was killing people because that was what she'd been sent here to do. Because it was her mission.

A light was winking on my head-up display—the emergency short-range, line-of-sight walkie-talkie. When I responded, an electronically distorted voice said, "Are you alone?"

"Absolutely."

"Who are you?"

I'd stripped all identifying tags from my suit before setting off, but the doppelgänger who had killed Debra Thorn and taken her place was pointing a gun at my head and it seemed advisable to tell her my name. She was silent for a moment, no doubt taking a look at my file. I said, "I'm not the doppelgänger of Roy Bruce, if that's what you're thinking. The person I killed and replaced was a gene wizard by the name of Sharwal Jah Sharja."

I briefly told the assassin the story I have already told you. When I was finished, she said, "You've really been working here for eight years?"

"Eight and a half." I had made a very bad mistake about my captor's motives, but I must have piqued her curiosity, for otherwise I would already be dead. And even if I couldn't talk my way out of this and persuade her to spare me, I still had a couple of weapons she hadn't found . . . I risked a lie, said that her net had compromised my suit's thermal integrity. I told her that I was losing heat to the frozen ground, that I would freeze to death if I didn't get up.

She told me I could sit up, and to do it slowly.

As I got my feet under me, squatting on my haunches in front of her, I glanced up at the top of the ridge and made a crucial triangulation.

She said, "My instructors told me that I would live no more than a year."

"Perhaps they told you that you would burn briefly but very brightly—that's what they told me. But they lied. I expect they lied about a lot of things, but I promise to tell you only the truth. We can leave here, and go anywhere we want to."

"I have a job to finish."

"People to kill, riots to start."

The assassin took a long step sideways to the cart, took something the size of a basketball from the net behind its seat, bowled it toward me. It bounced slowly over the dusty ground and ended up between my legs: the severed head of an old woman, skin burnt black with cold, eyes capped by frost.

"The former leader of the parliament of Sparta, Tethys,"

the assassin said. "I left the body pinned to the ground in one of the fields where her friends work, with an amusing little message."

"You are trying to start a war amongst the prisoners. Perhaps the people who sent you here are hoping that the scandal will close the facility. Perhaps they think it is the only chance they'll have of freeing their comrades. Who are you working for, by the way?"

"I'll ask the questions," the assassin said.

I asked her how she would escape when she was finished. "There's a special team on the way. If you're still here when they arrive, they'll hunt you down and kill you."

"So that's why you came after me. You were frightened that this team would find you while they were hunting me."

She may have been young, but she was smart and quick.

I said, "I came because I wanted to talk to you. Because you're like me."

"Because after all these years of living amongst humans, you miss your own kind, is that it?"

Despite the electronic distortion, I could hear the sneer in the assassin's voice. I said carefully, "The people who sent you here—the people who made you—have no plans to extract you when you are finished here. They do not care if you survive your mission. They only care that it is successful. Why give your loyalty to people who consider you expendable? To people who lied to you? You have many years of life ahead of you, and it isn't as hard to disobey your orders as you might think. You've already disobeyed them, in fact, when you reached out to me. All you have to do is take one more step, and let me help you. If we work together, we'll survive this. We'll find a way to escape."

"You think you're human. You're not. You're exactly like me. A walking dead man. That's what our instructors called us, by the way: the dead. Not 'Dave.' Not anything cute. When we were being moved from one place to another, they'd shout out a warning: 'Dead men walking.'"

It is supposed to be the traditional cry when a condemned person is let out of their cell. Fortunately, I've never worked in Block H, where prisoners who have murdered or tried to murder fellow inmates or guards await execution, so I've never heard it or had to use it.

The assassin said, "They're right, aren't they? We're made things, so how can we be properly alive?"

"I've lived a more or less ordinary life for ten years. If you give this up and come with me, I'll show you how."

"You stole a life, just as I did. Underneath your disguise, you're a dead man, just like me."

"The life I live now is my own, not anyone else's," I said. "Give up what you are doing, and I'll show you what I mean."

"You're a dead man in any case," the assassin said. "You're breathing the last of your air. You have less than an hour left. I'll leave you to die here, finish my work, and escape in the confusion. After that, I'm supposed to be picked up, but now I think I'll pass on that. There must be plenty of people out there who need my skills. I'll work for anyone who wants some killing done, and earn plenty of money."

"It's a nice dream," I said, "but it will never come true."

"Why shouldn't I profit from what I was made to do?"

"I've lived amongst people for more than a decade. Perhaps I don't know them as well as I should, but I do know that they are very afraid of us. Not because we're different, but because we're so very much like a part of them they don't want to acknowledge. Because we're the dark side of their nature. I've survived this long only because I have been very careful to hide what I really am. I can teach you how to do that, if you'll let me."

"It doesn't sound like much of a life to me," the assassin said.

"Don't you like being Debra Thorn?" I said.

And at the same moment, I kicked off the ground, hoping that by revealing that I knew who she was I'd distracted and confused her, and won a moment's grace.

In Ariel's microgravity, my standing jump took me high above the assassin's head, up and over the edge of the ridge. As I flew up, I discharged the taser dart I'd sewn into the palm of one of my pressure suit's gloves, and the electrical charge stored in its super-conducting loop shorted out every thread of myoelectric plastic that bound my arms. I shrugged off the net as I came down and kicked off again, bounding along the ridge in headlong flight toward the bulging face of the cliff wall and a narrow chimney pinched between two folds of black, rock-hard ice.

I was halfway there when a kinetic round struck my left leg with tremendous force, and broke my thigh. I tumbled over hummocked ice and caught hold a low pinnacle just before I went over the edge of the ridge. The assassin's triumphant shout was a blare of electronic noise in my ears; because she was using the line-of-sight walkie-talkie I knew that she was almost on me. I pushed up at once and scuttled toward the chimney like a crippled ape. I had almost reached my goal when a second kinetic round shattered my right knee. My suit was ruptured at the point of impact, and I felt a freezing pain as the smart fabric constricted as tightly as a tourniquet, but I was not finished. The impact of the kinetic round had knocked me head over heels into a field of fallen ice-blocks, within striking distance of the chimney. As I half-crawled, half-swam toward it, a third round took off the top of a pitted block that might have fallen from the cliffs a billion years ago, and then I was inside the chimney, and started to climb.

The assassin had no experience of freestyle climbing. Despite my injuries I soon outdistanced her. The chimney gave out after half a kilometer, and I had no choice but to continue to climb the naked iceface. Less than a minute later, the assassin reached the end of the chimney and fired a kinetic round that smashed into the cliff a little way above me. I flattened against the iceface as a huge chunk dropped past me with dreamy slowness, then powered straight through the expanding cloud of debris, pebbles and icegrains briefly rattling on my helmet, and flopped over the edge of a narrow setback.

My left leg bent in the middle of my thigh and hurt horribly; my right leg was numb below the knee and a thick crust of blood had frozen solid at the joint. But I had no time to tend my wounds. I sat up and ripped out the hose of the water recycling system as the assassin shot above the edge of the cliff in a graceful arc, taser in one hand, rail gun in the other. I twisted the valve, hit her with a high-pressure spray of water that struck her visor and instantly froze. I pushed off the ground with both hands (a kinetic round slammed into the dusty ice where I'd just been), collided with her in midair, clamped my glove over the diagnostic port of her backpack, and discharged my second taser dart.

The dart shorted out the electronics in the assassin's suit, and enough current passed through the port to briefly stun her. I pushed her away as we dropped toward the setback, but she managed to fire a last shot as she spun into the void beyond the edge of the setback. She was either phenomenally lucky or incredibly skillful: it took off my thumb and three fingers of my right hand.

She fell more than a kilometer. Even in the low gravity, it was more than enough to kill her, but just to make sure I dropped several blocks of ice onto her. The third smashed her visor. You'll find her body, if you haven't already, more or less directly below the spot where you found mine.

The assassin had vented most of my air supply and taken my phone and emergency beacon; the taser I'd used on her had crippled what was left of my pressure suit's life support system. The suit's insulation is pretty good, but I'm beginning to feel the bite of the cold now, my hand is growing pretty tired from using the squeeze pump to push air through the rebreather, and I'm getting a bad headache as the carbon dioxide concentration in my air supply inexorably rises. I killed the ecosystem of East of Eden by sabotaging the balance of its atmospheric gases, and now the same imbalance is killing me.

Just about the only thing still working is the stupid little chip I stuck in my helmet to record my conversation with the assassin. By now, you probably know more about her than I do. Perhaps you even know who sent her here.

I don't have much time left. Perhaps it's because the increasing carbon dioxide level is making me comfortably stupid, but I find that I don't mind dying. I told you that I confronted the assassin to save myself. I think now that I may have been wrong about that. I may have gone on the run after the Quiet War, but in my own way I have served you right up until the end of my life.

I'm going to sign off now. I want to spend my last moments remembering my freestyle climb up those twenty kilometers of sheer ice in Prospero Chasma. I want to remember how at the end I stood tired and alone at the top of a world-cleaving fault left over from a shattering collision four billion years ago, with Uranus tilted at the horizon, half-full, serene and remote, and the infinite black, starry sky above. I felt so utterly insignificant then, and yet so happy, too, without a single regret for anything at all in my silly little life.

Damascus

DARYL GREGORY

Daryl Gregory (www.darylgregory.com) *lives in State College, Pennsylvania with his wife, a psychologist and university professor, and their two children. He is a full-time writer, although half of what he writes is web code for a software company. He attended Clarion in 1988 and published two stories in the early 1990s, and then two in 2004, and one in 2005 ("Second Person, Present Tense," a real knockout), and a couple of excellent ones in 2006.*

"Damascus" was published in F&SF. *A variant of the disease Kuru is deliberately spread as part of a primitive female-oriented cult religion plausibly establishing a beachhead in the U.S. This is neuropsych hard sf about disease, brain structure, and religion. Maybe we don't have much in the way of free will. Maybe what we believe is the result of biochemistry. A former nurse is infected. Does she want to be cured? This is a really scary story.*

I

When Paula became conscious of her surroundings again, the first thing she sensed was his fingers entwined in hers.

She was strapped to the ambulance backboard—each wrist cuffed in nylon, her chest held down by a wide band—to stop her from flailing and yanking out the IV. Only his presence kept her from screaming. He gazed down at her, dirty-blond hair hanging over blue eyes, pale cheeks shadowed by a few days' stubble. His love for her radiated like cool air from a block of ice.

When they reached the hospital, he walked beside the gurney, his hand on her shoulder, as the paramedics wheeled her into the ER. Paula had never worked in the ER, but she recognized a few of the faces as she passed. She took several deep breaths, her chest tight against the nylon strap, and calmly told the paramedics that she was fine, they could let her go now. They made reassuring noises and left the restraints in place. Untying her was the doctor's call now.

Eventually an RN came to ask her questions. A deeply tanned, heavy-set woman with frosted hair. Paula couldn't remember her name, though they'd worked together for several years, back before the hospital had fired Paula. Now she was back as a patient.

"And what happened tonight, Paula?" the nurse said, her

tone cold. They hadn't gotten along when they worked together; Paula had a temper in those days.

"I guess I got a bit dizzy," she said.

"Seizure," said one of the paramedics. "Red Cross guy said she started shaking on the table, they had to get her onto the floor before she fell off. She'd been seizing for five or six minutes before we got there so we brought her in. We gave her point-one of Lorazepam and she came out of it during the ride."

"She's the second epileptic this shift," the nurse said to them.

Paula blinked in surprise. Had one of the yellow house women been brought in? Or one of the converts? She looked to her side, and her companion gazed back at her, amused, but not giving anything away. Everything was part of the plan, but he wouldn't tell her what the plan was. Not yet.

The nurse saw Paula's shift in attention and her expression hardened. "Let's have you talk to a doctor, Paula."

"I'm feeling a lot better," Paula said. Didn't even grit her teeth.

They released the straps and transferred her to a bed in an exam room. One of the paramedics set her handbag on the bedside table. "Good luck now," he said.

She glanced at the bag and quickly looked away. Best not to draw attention to it. "I'm sorry if I was any trouble," she said.

The nurse handed her a clipboard of forms. "I don't suppose I have to explain these to you," she said. Then: "Is there something wrong with your hand?"

Paula looked down at her balled fist. She concentrated on loosening her fingers, but they refused to unclench. That had been happening more often lately. Always the left hand. "I guess I'm nervous."

The nurse slowly nodded, not buying it. She made sure Paula could hold the clipboard and write, then left her.

But not alone. He slouched in a bedside chair, legs stretched in front of him, the soles of his bare feet almost black. His shy smile was like a promise. I'm here, Paula. I'll always be here for you.

II

Richard's favorite album was Nirvana's In Utero. She destroyed that CD first.

He'd moved out on a Friday, filed for divorce on the following Monday. He wanted custody of their daughter. Claire was ten then, a sullen and secretive child, but Paula would sooner burn the house down around them than let him have her. Instead she torched what he loved most. On the day Paula got the letter about the custody hearing, she pulled his CDs and LPs and DATs from the shelves—hundreds of them, an entire wall of the living room, and more in the basement. She carried them to the backyard by the box. Claire wailed in protest, tried to hide some of the cases, and eventually Paula had to lock the girl in her room.

In the yard Paula emptied a can of lighter fluid over the pile, went into the garage for the gas can, splashed that on as well. She tossed the Nirvana CD on top.

The pile of plastic went up in a satisfying whoosh. After a few minutes the fire started to die down—the CDs wouldn't stay lit—so she went back into the house and brought out his books and music magazines.

The pillar of smoke guided the police to her house. They told her it was illegal to burn garbage in the city. Paula laughed. "Damn right it's garbage." She wasn't going to be pushed around by a couple of cops. Neighbors came out to watch. Fuck them, she thought.

She lived in a neighborhood of Philadelphia that outsiders called "mixed." Blacks and Latinos and whites, a handful of Asians and Arabs. Newly renovated homes with Mexican tile patios side by side with crack houses and empty lots. Paula moved there from the suburbs to be with Richard and never forgave him. Before Claire was born she made him install an alarm system and set bars across the windows. She felt like they were barely holding on against a tide of criminals and crazies.

The yellow house women may have been both. They lived across the street and one lot down, in a cottage that was a near-twin of Paula's. Same fieldstone porch and peaked roofs, same narrow windows. But while Paula's house was painted a tasteful slate blue, theirs blazed lemon yellow, the doors and window frames and gutters turned out in garish oranges and brilliant whites. Five or six women, a mix of races and skin tones, wandered in and out of the house at all hours. Did they have jobs? They weren't old, but half of them had trouble walking, and one of them used a cane. Paula was an RN, twelve years working all kinds of units in two different hospitals, and it looked to her like they shared some kind of neuromuscular problem, maybe early MS. Their yellow house was probably some charity shelter.

On the street the women seemed distracted, sometimes talking to themselves, until they noticed someone and smiled a bit too widely. They always greeted Paula and Richard, but they paid special attention to Claire, speaking to her in the focused way of old people and kindergarten teachers. One of them, a gaunt white woman named Steph who wore the prematurely weathered face of a long-time meth user, started stopping by more often in the months after Richard moved out. She brought homemade food: Tupperware bowls of bean soup, foil-wrapped tamales, rounds of bread. "I've been a single mom," she said. "I know how tough things can be on your own." She started baby-sitting Claire a couple nights a week, staying in Paula's house so Claire could fall asleep in her own bed. Some afternoons she took Claire with her on trips to the grocery or the park. Paula kept waiting for the catch. It finally came in the form of a sermon.

"My life was screwed up," Steph said to Paula one afternoon. Claire had vanished to her bedroom to curl up with her headphones. The two women sat in the kitchen eating cheese bread someone in the yellow house had made. Steph drank wine while Paula worked her way through her afternoon Scotch. Steph talked frankly about her drug use, the shitty boyfriends, the money problems. "I was this close to cutting my wrists. If Jesus hadn't come into my life, I wouldn't be here right now."

Here we go, Paula thought. She drank silently while Steph droned on about how much easier it was to have somebody walk beside her, someone who cared. "Your own personal Jesus," Steph said. "Just like the song."

Paula knew the song—Richard loved that '80s crap. He even had the Johnny Cash remake, until she'd turned his collection to slag. "No thanks," Paula said, "I don't need any more men in my life."

Steph didn't take offense. She kept coming back, kept talking. Paula put up with the woman because with Richard out of the house she needed help with Claire—and because she needed her alone time more than ever. The yellow house women may have been Jesus freaks, but they were harmless. That's what she told herself, anyway, until the night she came home to find Claire gone.

III

Paula knew how to play the hospital game. Say as little as possible, act normal, don't look at things no one else could see. She knew her blood tests would come out normal. They'd shrug and check her out by noon.

Her doctor surprised her, though. They'd assigned her to Louden, a short, trim man with a head shaved down to gray stubble who had a reputation among the nurses for adequacy: not brilliant, but not arrogant either, a competent guy who pushed the patients through on schedule. But something had gotten into him—he was way too interested in her case. He filled her afternoon with expensive MRIs, fMRIs, and PET scans. He brought in specialists.

Four of them, two neurologists and a psychiatrist she recognized, and one woman she didn't know who said she was an epidemiologist. They came in one at a time over the afternoon, asking the same questions. How long had she experienced the seizures? What did they feel like when they struck? Did she know others with these symptoms? They poked her skin to test nerve response, pulled and flexed the fingers of her clenched hand. Several times they asked her, "Do you see people who aren't there?"

She almost laughed. He sat beside her the entire time, his arm cool against her own. Could anyone be more present?

The only questions that unsettled her came from the epidemiologist, the doctor she didn't recognize. "Do you eat meat?" the doctor asked. Paula said sure. And the doctor, a square-faced woman with short brown hair, asked a dozen follow-up questions, writing down exactly what kinds of meat she ate, how often, whether she cooked it herself or ate out.

At the end of the day they moved Paula into a room with a middle-aged white woman named Esther Wynne, a true southern lady who'd put on makeup and sprayed her hair as though at any moment she'd pop those IV tubes from her arms and head out to a nice restaurant.

Doctor Louden stopped by once more before going home that night. He sat heavily beside Paula's bed, ran a hand over his gray scalp. "You haven't been completely open with us," he said. He seemed as tired as she was.

"No, probably not," she said. Behind him, her companion shook his head, laughing silently.

Louden smiled as well, but fleetingly. "You have to realize how serious this is. You're the tenth person we've seen with symptoms like yours, and there are more showing up in hospitals around the city. Some of my colleagues think we may be seeing the start of an epidemic. We need your help to find out if that's the case."

"Am I contagious?"

He scratched his chin, looked down. "We don't think so. You don't have a temperature, any signs of inflammation— no signs that this is a virus or a bacterial infection."

"Then what is it you think I have?"

"We don't have a firm idea yet," he said. He was holding back, treating her like a dumb patient. "We can treat your symptoms though. We'll try to find out more tomorrow, but we think you have a form of temporal lobe epilepsy. There are parts of your brain that—"

"I know what epilepsy is."

"Yes, but TLE is a bit. . . ." He gestured vaguely, then took several stapled pages from his clipboard and handed them to her. "I've brought some literature. The more you understand what's happening, the better we'll work together." He didn't sound like he believed that.

Paula glanced at the pages. Printouts from a web site.

"Read it over and tomorrow you and I can—oh, good." A nurse had entered the room with a plastic cup in her hand; the meds had arrived. Louden seemed relieved to have something else to talk about. "This is Topamax, an epilepsy drug."

"I don't want it," she said. She was done with drugs and alcohol.

"I wouldn't prescribe this if it wasn't necessary," Louden said. His doctor voice. "We want to avoid the spikes in activity that cause seizures like today's. You don't want to fall over and crack your skull open, do you?" This clumsy attempt at manipulation would have made the old Paula furious.

Her companion shrugged. It didn't matter. All part of the plan.

Paula accepted the cup from the nurse, downed the two pills with a sip of water. "When can I go home?" she said.

Louden stood up. "I'll talk to you again in the morning. I hate to tell you this, but there are a few more tests we have to run."

Or maybe they were keeping her here because they did think she was contagious. The start of an epidemic, he'd said.

Paula nodded understandingly and Louden seemed relieved. As he reached the door Paula said, "Why did that one doctor—Gerrhardt?—ask me if I ate meat?"

He turned. "Dr. Gerrholtz. She's not with the hospital."

"Who's she with then?"

"Oh, the CDC," he said casually. As if the Centers for Disease Control dropped by all the time. "Don't worry, it's their job to ask strange questions. We'll have you out of here as soon as we can."

IV

Paula came home from work to find the door unchained and the lights on. It was only 7:15, but in early November that meant it had been dark for more than hour. Paula stormed through the house looking for Claire. The girl knew the rules: come home from school, lock the door, and don't pick up the phone unless caller-ID showed Paula's cell or work number. Richard took her, she thought. Even though he won partial custody, he wanted to take everything from her.

Finally she noticed the note, in a cleared space on the counter between a stack of dishes and an open cereal box. The handwriting was Steph's.

Paula marched to the yellow house and knocked hard. Steph opened the door. "It's all right," Steph said, trying to calm her down. "She's done her homework and now she's watching TV."

Paula pushed past her into a living room full of second-hand furniture and faded rugs. Every light in the house seemed to be on, making every flat surface glow: the oak floors scrubbed to a buttery sheen, the freshly painted daffodil walls, the windows reflecting bright lozenges of white. Something spiced and delicious fried in the kitchen, and Paula was suddenly famished. She hadn't eaten anything solid since breakfast.

Claire sat on a braided oval rug, her purple backpack beside her. A nature show played on the small boxy TV but the girl wasn't really watching. She had her earphones in, listening to the CD player in her lap. Lying on the couch behind her was a thin black woman in her fifties or sixties.

"Claire," Paula said. The girl pretended to not hear. "Claire, take off your headphones when I'm talking to you." Her voice firm but reasonable. The Good Mother. "You know you're not supposed to leave the house."

Claire didn't move.

"The police were at the green house," Steph said. A run-down place two doors down from Paula with motorcycles always in the front yard. Drug dealers, Paula thought. "I went over to check on Claire, and she seemed nervous, so I invited her over. I told her it would be all right."

"You wouldn't answer your phone," Claire said without looking away from the TV. She still hadn't taken off the headphones. Acting up in front of the women, thinking Paula wouldn't discipline her in public.

"Then you keep calling," Paula said. She'd forgotten to turn on her phone when she left the hospital. She'd stopped off for a drink, not more than thirty, forty-five minutes, then came home, no later than she'd come home dozens of times in the past. "You don't leave the house."

Steph touched Paula's elbow, interrupting again. She nodded at the woman on the couch. "This is Merilee."

The couch looked like the woman's permanent home. On the short table next to her head was a half-empty water glass, a Kleenex box, a mound of damp tissue. A plastic bucket sat on the floor. Merilee lay propped up on pillows, her body half covered by a white sheet. Her legs were bent under her in what looked like a painful position, and her left arm curled up almost to her chin, where her hand trembled like a nervous animal. She watched the TV screen with a blissed-out smile, as if this was the best show in the world.

Steph touched the woman's shoulder, and she looked up. "Merilee, this is Paula."

Merilee reached up with her good right arm. Her aim was off; first she held it out to a point too far right, then swung it slowly around. Paula lightly took her hand. Her skin was dry and cool.

The woman smiled and said something in another language. Paula looked to Steph, and then Merilee said, "I eat you."

"I'm sorry?" She couldn't have heard that right.

"It's a Fore greeting," Steph said, pronouncing the word For-ay. "Merilee's people come from the highlands of Papua New Guinea. Merilee, Paula is Claire's mother."

"Yes, yes, you're right," Merilee said. Her mouth moved more than the words required, lips constantly twisting toward a smile, distorting her speech. "What a lovely girl." It wasn't clear if she meant Claire or Paula. Then her hand slipped away like a scarf and floated to her chest. She lay back and returned her gaze to the TV, still smiling.

Paula thought, what the hell's the matter with her?

"We're about to eat," Steph said. "Sit down and join us."

"No, we'd better get going," Paula said. But there was nothing back at her house. And whatever they were cooking smelled wonderful.

"Come on," Steph said. "You always love our food." That was true. She'd eaten their meals for a month.

"I just have a few minutes," Paula said. She followed Steph into the dining room. The long, cloth-covered table almost filled the room. Ten places set, and room for a couple more. "How many of you are there?" she said.

"Seven of us live in the house," Steph said as she went into the adjoining kitchen.

"Looks like you've got room for renters."

Paula picked a chair and sat down, eyeing the tall green bottle in the middle of the table. "Is that wine?" Paula asked. She could use a drink.

"You're way ahead of me," Steph said. She came back into the room with the stems of wine glasses between her fingers, followed by an eighteen- or nineteen-year-old black girl—Tanya? Tonya?—carrying a large blue plate of rolled tortillas. Paula had met her before, pushing her toddler down the sidewalk. Outside she walked with a dragging limp, but inside it was barely discernible.

Steph poured them all wine but then remained standing. She took a breath and held it. Still no one moved. "All right then," Steph finally said, loud enough for Merilee to hear.

Tonya—pretty sure it was Tonya—took a roll and passed the plate. Paula carefully bit into the tortilla. She tasted sour cream, a spicy salsa, chunks of tomato. The small cubes of meat were so heavily marinated that they could have been anything: pork, chicken, tofu.

Tonya and Steph looked at Paula, their expressions neutral, but she sensed they were expecting something. Paula dabbed a bit of sour cream from her lip. "It's very good," she said.

Steph smiled and raised her glass. "Welcome," she said, and Tonya echoed her. Paula returned the salute and drank. The wine tasted more like brandy, thick and too sweet. Tonya nodded at her, said something under her breath. Steph said something to Merilee in that other language. Steph's eyes, Paula noted with alarm, were wet with tears.

"What is it?" Paula said. She put down the cup. Something had happened that she didn't understand. She stared at the pure white tortillas, the glasses of dark wine. This wasn't a snack, it was fucking communion.

"Tell me what's going on," she said coldly.

Steph sighed, her smile bittersweet. "We've been worried about you. Both of you. Claire's been spending so much time alone, and you're obviously still grieving."

Paula stared at her. These sanctimonious bitches. What was this, some kind of religious intervention? "My life is none of your business."

"Claire told me that you've been talking about killing yourself."

Paula scraped her chair back from the table and stood up, her heart racing. Tonya looked at her with concern. So smug. "Claire told you that?" Paula said. "And you believed her?"

"Paula. . . ."

She wheeled away from the table, heading for the living room, Steph close behind. "Claire," Paula said. Not yelling. Not yet. "We're going."

Claire didn't get up. She looked at Steph, as if for permission. This infuriated Paula more than anything that had happened so far.

She grabbed Claire by her arm, yanked her to her feet. The headphones popped from her ears, spilling tinny music. Claire didn't even squeak.

Steph said, "We care about you two, Paula. We had to take steps. You won't understand that right now, but soon. . . ."

Paula spun and slapped the woman hard across the mouth, turning her chin with the blow. Steph's eyes squeezed shut in pain, but she didn't raise her arms, didn't step back.

"Don't you ever come near my daughter again," Paula said. She strode toward the front door, Claire scrambling to stay on her feet next to her. Paula yanked open the door and pushed the girl out first. Her daughter still hadn't made a sound.

Behind her, Steph said, "Wait." She came to the door holding out Claire's backpack and CD player. "Some day you'll understand," Steph said. "Jesus is coming soon."

V

"You're a Christian, aren't you?" Esther Wynne said. "I knew from your face. You've got the love of Jesus in you."

As the two women picked at their breakfast trays, Esther told Paula about her life. "A lot of people with my cancer die quick as a wink," she said. "I've had time to say good-bye to everyone." Her cancer was in remission but now she was here fighting a severe bladder infection. They'd hooked her to an IV full of antibiotics the day before. "How about you?" Esther said. "What's a young thing like you doing here?"

Paula laughed. She was thirty-six. "They think I have a TLA." Esther frowned. "Three-letter acronym."

"Oh, I've got a couple of those myself!"

One of the web pages Dr. Louden gave her last night included a cartoon cross-section of a brain. Arrows pointed out interesting bits of the temporal lobe with tour guide comments like "the amygdala tags events with emotion and significance" and "the hippocampus labels inputs as internal or external." A colored text box listed a wide range of possible TLE symptoms: euphoria, a sense of personal destiny, religiosity . . .

And a sense of presence.

Asymmetrical temporal lobe hyperactivity separates the sense of self into two—one twin in each hemisphere. The dominant (usually left) hemisphere interprets the other part of the self as an "other" lurking outside. The otherness is then colored by which hemisphere is most active.

Paula looked up then, her chest tight. Her companion had been leaning against the wall, watching her read. At her frightened expression he dropped his head and laughed silently, his hair swinging in front of his face.

Of course. There was nothing she could learn that could hurt her, or him.

She tossed aside the pages. If her companion hadn't been with her she might have worried all night about the information, but he helped her think it through. The article had it backward, confusing an effect for the cause. Of course the brain reacted when you sensed the presence of God. Neurons fired like pupils contracting against a bright light.

"Paula?" someone said. "Paula."

She blinked. An LPN stood by the bed with a plastic med cup. Her breakfast tray was gone. How long had she been ruminating? "Sorry, I was lost in thought there."

The nurse handed Paula the Topamax and watched as she took them. After the required ritual—pulse, blood pressure, temperature—she finally left.

Esther said, "So what were you thinking about?"

Paula lay back on the pillows and let her eyes close. Her companion sat beside her on the bed, massaging the muscles of her left arm, loosening her cramped fingers. "I was thinking that when God calls you don't worry about how he got your number," she said. "You just pick up the receiver."

"A-men," Esther said.

Dr. Louden stopped by later that morning accompanied only by Dr. Gerrholtz, the epidemiologist from the CDC. Maybe the other specialists had already grown bored with her case. "We have you scheduled for another PET scan this morning," Louden said. He looked like he hadn't slept at all last night, poor guy. "Is there anyone you'd like to call to be with you? A family member?"

"No thank you," Paula said. "I don't want to bother them."

"I really think you should consider it."

"Don't worry, Dr. Louden." She wanted to pat his arm, but that would probably embarrass him in front of Dr. Gerrholtz. "I'm perfectly fine."

Louden rubbed a hand across his skull. After a long moment he said, "Aren't you curious about why we ordered a PET scan?" Dr. Gerrholtz gave him a hard look.

Paula shrugged. "Okay, why did you?"

Louden shook his head, disappointed again that she wasn't more concerned. Dr. Gerrholtz said, "You're a professional, Paula, so we're going to be straight with you."

"I appreciate that."

"We're looking for amyloid plaques. Do you know what those are?" Paula shook her head and Gerrholtz said, "Some types of proteins weave into amyloid fibers, forming a plaque that kills cells. Alzheimer patients get them, but they're also caused by another family of diseases. We think those plaques are causing your seizures, and other symptoms."

Other symptoms. Her companion leaned against her shoulder, his hand entwined in hers. "Okay," Paula said.

Louden stood up, obviously upset. "We'll talk to you after the test. Dr. Gerrholtz?"

The CDC doctor ignored him. "We've been going through the records, Paula, looking for people who've reported symptoms like yours." She said it like a warning. "In the past three months we've found almost a dozen—and that's just at this hospital. We don't know yet how many we'll find across the city, or the country. If you have any information that will help us track down what's happening, you need to offer it."

"Of course," Paula said.

Gerrholtz's eyes narrowed. She seemed ready to say something else—accuse her, perhaps—but then shook her head and stalked from the room.

Esther watched her go. After a minute of silence, the woman said, "Don't you worry, honey. It's not the doctors who are in charge here."

"Oh I'm not worried," Paula said. And she wasn't. Gerrholtz obviously distrusted her—maybe even suspected the nature of Paula's mission—but what could that matter? Everything was part of the plan, even Dr. Gerrholtz.

By noon they still hadn't come to get her for the scan. Paula drifted in and out of sleep. Twice she awoke with a start, sure that her companion had left the room. But each time he appeared after a few seconds, stepping out from a corner of her vision.

The orderly came by just as the lunch trays arrived, but that was okay, Paula wasn't hungry. She got into the wheelchair and the orderly rolled her down the hall to the elevators. Her companion walked just behind them, his dusty feet scuffing along.

The orderly parked her in the hall outside radiology, next to three other abandoned patients: a gray-faced old man asleep in his chair; a Hispanic teenager with a cast on her leg playing some electronic game; and a round-faced white boy who was maybe twenty or twenty-one.

The boy gazed up at the ceiling tiles, a soft smile on his face. After a few minutes, Paula saw his lips moving.

"Excuse me," Paula said to him. It took several tries to get his attention. "Have you ever visited a yellow house?" The young man looked at her quizzically. "A house that was all yellow, inside and out."

He shook his head. "Sorry."

None of the women still at the yellow house would have tried to save a man, but she had to ask. The boy had to be one of the converts, someone Paula's mission had saved.

"Can I ask you one more question?" Paula said, dropping her voice slightly. The old man slept on, and the girl still seemed engrossed in her game. "Who is it that you're talking to?"

The boy glanced up, laughed quietly. "Oh, nobody," he said.

"You can tell me," Paula said. She leaned closer. "I have a companion of my own."

His eyes widened. "You have a ghost following you too?"

"Ghost? No, it's not a—"

"My mother died giving birth to me," he said. "But now she's here."

Paula touched the boy's arm. "You don't understand what's happened to you, do you?" He hadn't come by way of the yellow house, hadn't met any of the sisters, hadn't received any instruction. Of course he'd tried to make sense of his companion any way he could. "You're not seeing a ghost. You're seeing Jesus himself."

The boy laughed loudly, and the teenage girl looked up from her game. "I think I'd know the difference between Jesus and my own mother," the young man said.

"Maybe that's why he took this form for you," Paula said. "He appears differently for each person. For you, your mother is a figure of unconditional love. A person who sacrificed for you."

"Okay," the young man said. He tilted his head, indicating an empty space to Paula's right. "So what does yours look like?"

VI

God came through the windshield on a shotgun blast of light. Blinded, Paula cried out and jammed on the brakes. The little Nissan SUV bucked and fishtailed, sending the CDs piled on the seat next to her clattering onto the floorboards.

White. She could see nothing but white.

She'd stopped in heavy traffic on a four-lane road, the shopping center just ahead on her right. She'd been heading for the dumpsters behind the Wal-Mart to dispose of those CDs once and for all.

Brakes shrieked behind her. Paula ducked automatically, clenched against the pending impact, eyes screwed shut. (Still: Light. Light.) A thunderclap of metal on metal and the SUV rocked forward. She jerked in her seatbelt.

Paula opened her eyes and light scraped her retinas. Hot tears coursed down her cheeks.

She clawed blindly at her seatbelt buckle, hands shaking, and finally found the button and yanked the straps away. She scrambled over the shifter to the passenger seat, the plastic CD cases snapping and sliding under her knees and palms.

She'd found them deep in Claire's closet. The girl was away at her father's for the mandated fifty percent of the month, and Paula had found the stacked CDs hidden under a pile of blankets and stuffed animals. Many of the cases were cracked and warped by heat and most CDs had no cases at all. The day after the bonfire, Paula had caught the girl poking through the mound of plastic and damp ashes and told her not to touch them. Claire had deliberately disobeyed, sneaking out to rescue them sometime before the garbage men took the pile away. The deception had gone on for months. All the time Paula thought Claire was listening to her own music—crap by bubble-gum pop stars and American Idols—her headphones were full of her father's music: Talking Heads, Depeche Mode, Pearl Jam, Nirvana.

Paula pushed open the passenger door and half fell out the door, into the icy March wind. She got her feet under her, stumbled away from the light, into the light. Her shins struck something—the guard rail?—and she put out a hand to stop from pitching over. Cold metal bit her palms. Far to her right, someone shouted angrily. The blare and roar of traffic surrounded her.

Paula dropped to her knees and slush instantly soaked her jeans. She covered her head with both arms. The light struck her neck and back like a rain of sharpened stones.

The light would destroy her. Exactly as she deserved.

Something touched the top of her head, and she shuddered in fear and shame and a rising ecstasy that had nothing to do with sex. She began to shake, to weep.

I'm sorry, she said, perhaps out loud. I'm sorry.

Someone stood beside her. She turned her head, and he appeared out of the light. No—in the light, of the light. A fire in the shape of a man.

She didn't know him, but she recognized him.

He looked down at her, electric blue eyes through white bangs, his shy smile for her only. He looked like Kurt Cobain.

VII

"I'm not taking the meds anymore," Paula said. She tried to keep her voice steady. Louden stood beside the bed, Gerrholtz behind him holding a portfolio in her hands as big as the Ten Commandments. They'd walked past Esther without saying a word.

Her companion lay on the floor beside her bed, curled into a ball. He seemed to be dissolving at the edges, dissipating into fog. He'd lain there all morning, barely moving, not even looking at her.

"That's not a good idea," Dr. Louden said. He pulled a chair next to the bed, scraping through her companion as if he wasn't there. Paula grimaced, the old rage flaring up. She closed her eyes and concentrated.

"I'm telling you to stop the drugs," she said. "Unless I'm a prisoner here you can't give me medicine that I refuse."

Louden exhaled tiredly. "This isn't like you, Paula," he said.

"Then you don't know me very well."

He leaned forward, resting elbows on knees, and pressed the fingers of one hand into his forehead. More TLE patients were rolling in every day. The nurses murmured about epidemics. Poor Dr. Adequate had been drafted into a war he didn't understand and wasn't prepared for.

"Help me then," he said without looking up. "Tell me what you're experiencing."

Paula stared at the TV hanging from the ceiling. She left it on all the time now, sound off. The images distracted her, kept her from thinking of him on the floor beside her, fading.

Gerrholtz said, "Why don't I take a guess? You're having trouble seeing your imaginary friend."

Paula snapped her head toward the woman. You bitch. She almost said it aloud.

Gerrholtz regarded her coolly. "A woman died two days ago in a hospital not far from here," she said. "Her name was Stephanie Wozniak. I'm told she was a neighbor of yours."

Steph is dead? She couldn't process the thought.

Gerrholtz took the sheets from her portfolio and laid them on Paula's lap. "I want you to look at these."

Paula picked them up automatically. The photographs looked like microscope slides from her old biochem classes, a field of cells tinged brown by some preserving chemical. Spidery black asterisks pock-marked the cells.

"Those clumps of black are bundles of prions," Gerrholtz said. "Regular old proteins, with one difference—they're the wrong shape."

Paula didn't look up. She flipped the printouts one by one, her hand moving on its own. Some of the pictures consisted almost entirely of sprawling nests of black threads. Steph deserved better than this. She'd waited her whole life for a Fore funeral. Instead the doctors cut her up and photographed the remains.

"I need you to concentrate, Paula. One protein bent or looped in the wrong way isn't a problem. But once they're in the brain, you get a conformational cascade—a snowball effect."

Paula's hands continued to move but she'd stopped seeing them. Gerrholtz rattled on and on about nucleation and crystallization. She kept using the word spongiform as if it would frighten her.

Paula already knew all this, and more. She let the doctor talk. Above Gerrholtz's head the TV showed a concerned young woman with a microphone, police cars and ambulances in the background.

"Paula!"

Dr. Gerrholtz's face was rigid with anger. Paula wondered if that was what she used to look like when she fought with Richard or screamed at Claire.

"I noticed you avoided saying 'Mad Cow,'" Paula said. "And Kuru."

"You know about Kuru?" Louden said.

"Of course she does," Gerrholtz said. "She's done her homework." The doctor put her hands on the foot of Paula's bed and leaned forward. "The disease that killed Stephanie doesn't have a name yet, Paula. We think it's a Kuru variant, the same prion with an extra kink. And we know that we can't save the people who already have it. Their prions will keep converting other proteins to use their shape. You understand what this means, don't you Paula?"

Still trying to scare her. As if the promise of her own death would break her faith.

On the screen, the reporter gestured at two uniformed officers sealing the front door with yellow tape that looked specially chosen to match the house. Paula wondered if they'd found Merilee yet.

"It means that God is an idea," Paula said. "An idea that can't be killed."

VIII

The house shimmered in her vision, calling her like a light-house; she understood now why they'd painted it so brightly. Minutes after the accident her vision darkened like smoked glass, and now only the brightest things drew her attention. Her companion guided her down the dark streets, walking a few feet in front of her, surrounded by a nimbus of fire.

Steph opened the door. When she saw the tears in her eyes Steph squealed in delight and pulled her into a hug. "We've been waiting for you," she said. "We've been waiting so long." And then Steph was crying too.

"I'm sorry," Paula said. "I'm so sorry. I didn't know. . . ."

The other women came to her one by one, hugging her, caressing her cheeks, all of them crying. Only Merilee couldn't get up to greet her. The woman lay on the same couch as four months ago, but her limbs had cinched tighter, arms and legs curled to her torso like a dying bug. Paula kneeled next to her couch and gently pressed her cheek to Merilee's. Paula spoke the Fore greeting: I eat you.

That was the day one life ended and another began.

Her vision slowly returned over the next few days, but her companion remained, becoming more solid every day. They told her she didn't have to worry about him leaving her. She called in sick to work and spent most of the next week in the yellow house, one minute laughing, the next crying, sometimes both at the same time. She couldn't stop talking about her experience on the road, or the way her companion could make her recognize her vanity or spite with just a faint smile.

Her old life had become something that belonged to a stranger. Paula thought of the blank weekends of Scotch and Vicodin, the screaming matches with Richard. Had she really burned his record collection?

When she called him, the first thing she said was, "I'm sorry."

"What is it, Paula." His voice flat, wary. The Paula he knew only used "sorry" to bat away his words, deflect any attack.

"Something wonderful's happened," she said. She told

him about Steph and the women of the house, then skipped
the communion to tell him about the accident and the blind-
ing light and the emotions that flooded through her. Richard
kept telling her to slow down, stop stumbling over her words.
Then she told him about her companion.

"Who did you meet?" he said. He thought it was someone
who'd witnessed the accident. Again she tried to explain.

Richard said, "I don't think Claire should come back
there this weekend."

"What? No!" She needed to see Claire. She needed to
apologize to her, promise her she'd do better. She gripped
the receiver. Why couldn't Richard believe her? Why was he
fighting her again?

She felt a touch on the back of her head. She turned, let
her hand fall to the side. His blue eyes gazed into hers.

One eyebrow rose slightly.

She breathed. Breathed again. Richard called her name
from the handset.

"I know this is a lot to adjust to," Paula said. The words
came to her even though her companion didn't make a sound.
"I know you want the best for Claire. You're a good father."
The words hurt because they were true. She'd always thought
of Richard as a weak man, but if that had once been true,
Claire's birth had given him someone weaker to protect. As
their daughter became older he took her side against Paula
more and more often. The fights worsened, but she broke
him every time. She never thought he'd have the guts to walk
out on her and try to take Claire with him. "If you think she'd
be better off with you for a while, we can try that." She'd win
his trust soon enough.

In the weeks after, Claire stayed with Richard, and Paula
did hardly anything but talk with the yellow house women.
At work the head nurse reprimanded her for her absences
but she didn't care. Her life was with the women now, and
her house became almost an annex to theirs. "We have
room for more," Paula said dozens of times. "We have to tell
others. It's not right to keep this to ourselves when so many
people are suffering." The women nodded in agreement—or
perhaps only in sympathy. Each of them had been saved,

most of them from lives much worse than Paula's. They knew what changes were possible.

"You have to be patient," Steph told her one day. "This gift is handed from woman to woman, from Merilee's grandmother down to us. It comes with a responsibility to protect the host. We have to choose carefully—we can't share it with everyone."

"Why not?" Paula said. "Most of us would be dead without it. We're talking about saving the world here."

"Yes. One person at a time."

"But people are dying right now," Paula said. "There has to be a way to take this beyond the house."

"Let me show you something," Steph said. She brought down a box from a high bookshelf and lifted out a huge family bible. Steph opened it to the family tree page, her left hand trembling. "Here are some of your sisters," she said. "The ones I've known anyway."

The page was full of names. The list continued on the next page, and the next. Over a hundred names.

"How long has this been going on?" Paula said in wonder.

"Merilee's mother came here in 1982. Some of the women lived in this house for a while, and then were sent to establish their own houses. We don't know how many of us there are now, spread around the country. None of us knows all of them." She smiled at her. "See? You're not so alone. But we have to move quietly, Paula. We have to meet in small groups, like the early Christians."

"Like terrorists," Paula said bitterly.

Steph glanced to the side, listening to her companion. "Yes," she said, nodding. And then to Paula: "Exactly. There's no terror like the fear of God."

IX

He woke her at three A.M. Paula blinked at him, confused. He hovered beside the bed, only half there, like a reflection in a shop window.

She forced herself awake and as her vision cleared the

edges of him resolved, but he was still more vapor than solid. "What is it?" she said. He teasingly held a finger to his lips and turned toward Esther's bed. He paused, waiting for her.

Paula slipped out of the bed and moved quietly to the cabinet against the wall. The door came open with a loud clack, and she froze, waiting to see if she'd awakened her roommate. Esther's feathery snore came faint and regular.

Paula found her handbag at the bottom shelf and carried it to the window. Feeling past her wallet fat with ID cards, she pulled out the smaller vinyl case and laid it open on the sill like a butterfly.

The metal tip of the syringe reflected the light.

Paula made a fist of her left hand, flexed, tightened again. Working in the faint light, she found the vein in her arm mostly by feel and long familiarity, her fingertips brushing first over the dimpled scars near the crook of her elbow, then down half an inch. She took the syringe in her right hand and pressed into the skin. The plastic tube slowly filled.

Paula picked her way through the dim room until her hand touched the IV bag hanging beside Esther's bed. The woman lay still, her lips slightly apart, snoring lightly. It would be simple to inject the blood through the IV's Y-port.

But what if it was too late for her? The host incubated for three to six months. Only if the cancer stayed in remission that long would the woman have a chance to know God. Not her invisible, unseen God. The real thing.

Paula reached for the tubing and her companion touched her arm. She lowered the syringe, confused. Why not inject her? She searched his face for a reason, but he was so hard to see.

He turned and walked through the wall. Paula opened the door and stepped into the bright hallway, and for a moment she couldn't find him in the light. He gestured for her to follow.

She followed his will-o'-the-wisp down the deserted corridor, carrying the syringe low at her side. He led her down the stairwell, and at the next floor went left, left again. At an intersection a staffer in blue scrubs passed ten feet in front of them without seeing them.

Perhaps she'd become invisible too.

He stopped before a door and looked at her. It was one of the converted rooms where doctors on call could catch some sleep. Here? she asked with her eyes. He gestured toward the door, his arm like a tendril of fog.

She gripped the handle, slowly turned. The door was unlocked. Gently, she pushed it open.

The wedge of light revealed a woman asleep on the twin bed, a thin blanket half covering her. She wore what Paula had seen her in earlier: a cream blouse gleaming in the hall light, a patterned skirt rucked above her knees, her legs dark in black hose. Her shoes waited side-by-side on the floor next to the bed, ready for her to spring back into action and save her world.

Paula looked back at the doorway. Dr. Gerrholtz? she asked him. Did he really want this awful woman to receive the host?

His faint lips pursed, the slightest of frowns, and Paula felt a rush of shame. Who was she to object? Before Steph had found her Paula had been the most miserable woman alive. Everyone deserved salvation. That was the whole point of the mission.

Dr. Gerrholtz stirred, turned her head slightly, and the light fell across her closed eyes. Paula raised the needle, moved her thumb over the plunger. No handy IV already connected. No way to do this without waking the woman up. And she'd wake up screaming.

"Hello?" Dr. Gerrholtz said. Her eyes opened, and she lifted a hand to shade her eyes.

Jesus is coming, Paula said silently, and pressed the needle into her thigh.

X

Paula and Tonya stooped awkwardly at the edge of the pit, clearing the sand. They dug down carefully so that their shovel blades wouldn't cut too deep, then pitched the spark-flecked sand into the dark of the yard. They worked in short sleeves, sweating despite the cold wind. With every inch they uncovered the pit grew hotter and brighter.

It was hard work, and their backs still ached from this morning when they'd dug the pit, hauled over the big stones, and lined the bottom with them. But Paula had volunteered for this job. She wanted to prove that she could work harder than anyone.

Inside the house, women laughed and told stories, their voices carrying through the half-opened windows. Paula tossed aside a shovelful of sand and said, "Tonya, have you ever asked why no men are invited?" She'd thought about her words for a long time. She wanted to test them on Tonya first, because she was young and seemed more open than the other women.

Tonya looked up briefly, then dug down again with her shovel. "That's not the tradition."

"But what about Donel? Wouldn't you want this for him?" Donel was Tonya's son, only two years old. He shared a bedroom with her, but all the women took care of him.

Tonya paused, leaned against her shovel. "I . . . I think about that. But it's just not the way it's done. No men at the feast."

"But what if we could bring the feast to them?" Paula said. "I've been reading about Merilee's people, the disease they carried. There's more than one way to transmit the host. What if we could become missionaries some other way?"

The girl shook her head. "Merilee said that men would twist it all up, just like they did the last time."

"All the disciples were men last time. This time they're all women, but that doesn't make it right. Think about Donel." Think about Richard.

"We better keep going," Tonya said, ending the conversation. She started digging again, and after a moment, Paula joined her. But she kept thinking of Richard. He'd become more guarded over the past few months, more protective of Claire. When her daughter turned fourteen—another of Merilee's rules—Paula would bring her to communion. But if she could also bring it to Richard, if he could experience what she'd found, they could be a family again.

Several minutes later they found the burlap by the feel under their shovels. They scraped back the sand that covered the sack, then bent and heaved it up onto a pallet of plywood and one-by-fours. After they'd caught their breath they called the others from the house.

More than seventy women had come, some of them from as far away as New Zealand. None of them had come alone, of course. The air was charged with a multitude of invisible presences.

Eight of the women were chosen as pall bearers. The procession moved slowly because so many of them walked with difficulty. God's presence burned the body like a candle— Merilee's early death was proof of that—but not one of them would trade Him for anything. A perfect body was for the next life.

Steph began to sing something in Merilee's language, and the others joined in, harmonizing. Some knew the words; others, like Paula, hummed along. Women cried, laughed, lifted their hands. Others walked silently, perhaps in communion with their companions.

There was an awkward moment when they had to tilt the litter to get through the back door, but then they were inside. They carried her through the kitchen—past the stacks of Tupperware, the knives and cutting boards, the coolers of dry ice—then through the dining room and into the living room. The furniture had been pushed back to the walls. They set the litter in the center of the room.

Paula gripped the stiff and salt-caked cloth—they'd soaked the body overnight—while Steph sawed the length of it with a thick-bladed knife. Steam escaped from the bag, filling the room with a heady scent of ginger and a dozen other spices.

The last of the shroud fell away and Merilee grinned up at them. Her lips had pulled away from her teeth, and the skin of her face had turned hard and shiny. As she'd instructed, they'd packed ferns and wild herbs around her in a funeral dress of leaves.

Steph kneeled at the head of the impromptu table and the others gathered around. The oldest and most crippled were helped down to the floor; the rest stood behind them, hands on their shoulders.

Steph opened a wooden box as big as a plumber's toolbox and drew out a small knife. She laid it on a white linen napkin next to Merilee's skull and said, "Like many of you I was at the feast of Merilee's mother, and this is the story Merilee told there.

"It was the tradition of the Fore for the men and women to live apart. When a member of the tribe died, only the women and children were allowed at the feast. The men became jealous. They cursed the women, and they called the curse kuru, which means both 'to tremble' and 'to be afraid.' The white missionaries who visited the tribe called it the laughing sickness, because of the grimaces that twisted their faces."

As she talked she laid out other tools from the box: a filet knife, a wooden-handled fork with long silver tines, a Japanese cleaver.

"Merilee's grandmother, Yobaiotu, was a young woman when the first whites came, the doctors and government men and missionaries. One day the missionaries brought everyone out to the clearing they'd made by the river and gave everyone a piece of bread. They told them to dip it into a cup of wine and eat, and they said the words Jesus had spoken at the last supper: This is my body, this is my blood."

Steph drew out a long-handled knife and looked at it for perhaps thirty seconds, trying to control her emotions. "The moment Yobaiotu swallowed the bread, she fell down shaking, and a light filled her eyes. When she awoke, a young boy stood at her side. He held out his hand to her, and helped her to her feet. 'Lord Jesus!' Yobaiotu said, recognizing him." Steph looked up, smiled. "But of course no one else could see him. They thought she was crazy."

The women quietly laughed and nodded.

"The doctors said that the funeral feasts caused Kuru, and they ordered them to stop. But Yobaiotu knew the curse had been transformed in her, that the body of Christ lived in her. She taught her daughters to keep that covenant. The night Yobaiotu died they feasted in secret, as we do to-night."

Steph removed the center shelf of the box, set it aside, and reached in again. She lifted out a hacksaw with a gleaming blade. A green price tag was still stuck to the saw's blue handle.

"The body of Christ was passed from mother to daughter," Steph said. "Because of them, Christ lives in all of us. And because of Merilee, Christ will live in sisters who've not yet been found."

"Amen," the women said in unison.

Steph lifted the saw, and with her other hand gently touched the top of Merilee's skull. "This we do in remembrance of him," she said. "And Merilee."

XI

The screaming eventually brought Louden to her room. "Don't make me sedate you," he began, and then flinched as she jerked toward him. The cuffs held her to the bed.

"Bring him back!" she screamed, her voice hoarse. "Bring him back now!"

Last night they'd taken her to another room, one without windows, and tied her down. Arms apart, ankles together. Then they attached the IV and upped the dosage: two parts Topamax, one part Loxapine, an anti-psychotic.

Gerrholtz they rushed to specialists in another city.

A hospital security guard took up station outside her door, and was replaced the next morning by a uniformed police officer. Detectives came to interrogate her. Her name hadn't been released to the news, they said, but it would only be a matter of time. The TV people didn't even know about Gerrholtz—they were responding to stories coming out of the yellow house investigation—but already they'd started using the word "bioterrorism." Sometime today they'd move her to a federal facility.

Minute by minute the drugs did their work and she felt him slipping from her. She thought, if I keep watch he can't disappear. By twisting her shoulders she could see a little way over the bed and make out a part of him: a shadow that indicated his blue-jeaned leg, a cluster of dots in the speckled linoleum that described the sole of a dirty foot. When the cramps in her arms and lower back became too much she'd fall back, rest for a while, then throw herself sideways again. Each time she looked over the edge it took her longer to discern his shape. Two hours after the IV went in she couldn't find him at all.

Louden said, "What you experienced was an illusion, Paula, a phantom generated by a short-circuiting lobe of your brain. There's a doctor in Canada who can trigger these presences with a helmet and magnetic fields, for crying out loud. Your . . . God wasn't real. Your certainty was a symptom."

"Take me off these meds," she said, "or so help me I'll wrap this IV tube around your fucking neck."

"This is a disease, Paula. Some of you are seeing Jesus, but we've got other patients seeing demons and angels, talking to ghosts—I've got one Hindu guy who's sharing the bed with Lord Krishna."

She twisted against the cuffs, pain spiking across her shoulders. Her jaw ached from clenching her teeth.

"Paula, I need you to calm down. Your husband and daughter are downstairs. They want to visit you before you leave here."

"What? No. No." They couldn't see her like this. It would confirm everything Richard ever thought about her. And Claire. . . . She was thirteen, a girl unfolding into a woman. The last thing she needed was to have her life distorted by this moment. By another vivid image of her mother as a raving lunatic.

"Tell them to stay away from me. The woman they knew doesn't exist anymore."

This morning the detectives had emptied her bag and splayed the driver's licenses and social security IDs like a deck of cards. How long has this been going on? they demanded. How many people are involved?

They gave her a pencil and yellow legal pad, told her to write down all the names she could remember. She stared at the tip of the pencil. An epidemiology book she'd read tried to explain crystallization by talking about how carbon could become graphite or diamond depending on how the atoms were arranged. The shapes she made on the page could doom a score of her missionaries.

She didn't know what to do. She turned to her companion but he was silent, already disintegrating.

"You're too late," she told the detectives. She snapped the pencil in half and threw it at them, bits of malformed diamond. "Six months too late."

XII

They called themselves missionaries. Paula thought the name fit. They had a mission, and they would become agents of transmission.

The first and last meeting included only eighteen women. Paula had first convinced Tonya and Rosa from the yellow house, and they had widened the circle to a handful of women from houses around Philly, and from there they persuaded a few more women from New York and New Jersey. Paula had met some of them at Merilee's feast, but most were strangers. Some, like Tonya, were mothers of sons, but all of them had become convinced that it was time to take the gospel into the world.

They met at a Denny's restaurant in the western suburbs, where Steph and the other women wouldn't see them.

"The host is not a virus," Paula said. "It's not bacterial. It can't be detected or filtered out the way other diseases are, it can't be killed by antibiotics or detergents, because it's nothing but a shape." A piece of paper can become a sailboat or swan, she told them. A simple protein, folded and copied a million times, could bring you Kuru, or Creutzfeldt-Jakob disease, or salvation.

"The body of Christ is powerful," Paula said. They knew: all of them had taken part in feasts and had been saved through them. "But there's also power in the blood." She dealt out the driver's licenses, two to each woman. Rosa's old contacts had made them for fifty bucks apiece. "One of these is all you need to donate. We're working on getting more. With four IDs you can give blood twice a month."

She told them how to answer the Red Cross surveys, which iron supplements to buy, which foods they should bulk up on to avoid anemia. They talked about secrecy. Most of the other women they lived with were too bound by tradition to see that they were only half doing God's work.

Women like Steph. Paula had argued with her a dozen times over the months, but could not convince her. Paula loved Steph, and owed so much to her, but she couldn't sit idly by any longer.

"We have to donate as often as possible," Paula said. "We have to spread the host so far and so fast that they can't stop us by rounding us up." The incubation time depended directly on the amount consumed, so the more that was in the blood supply the faster the conversions would occur. Paula's conversion had taken months. For others it might be years.

"But once they're exposed to the host the conversion will happen," Paula said. "It can't be stopped. One seed crystal can transform the ocean."

She could feel them with her. They could see the shape of the new world.

The women would never again meet all together like this—too dangerous—but they didn't need to. They'd already become a church within the church.

Paula hugged each of them as they left the restaurant. "Go," she told them. "Multiply."

XIII

The visitor seemed familiar. Paula tilted her head to see through the bars as the woman walked toward the cell. It had become too much of a bother to lift Paula out of the bed and wheel her down to the conference room, so now the visitors came to her. Doctors and lawyers, always and only doctors and lawyers. This woman, though, didn't look like either.

"Hello, Paula," she said. "It's Esther Wynne. Do you remember me?"

"Ah." The memory came back to her, those first days in the hospital. The Christian woman. Of course she'd be Paula's first voluntary visitor. "Hello, Esther." She struggled to enunciate clearly. In the year since they'd seen each other, Paula's condition had worsened. Lips and jaw and arms refused to obey her, shaking and jerking to private commands. Her arm lay curled against her chest like Merilee's. Her spine bent her nearly in half, so that she had to lie on her side. "You look—" She made a sound like a laugh, a hiccupping gasp forced from her chest by an unruly diaphragm. "—good."

The guard positioned a chair in front of the bars and the older woman sat down. Her hair was curled and sprayed. Under the makeup her skin looked healthy.

"I've been worried about you," Esther said. "Are they treating you well?"

Paula almost smiled. "As well as you can treat a mass murderer."

Some facts never escaped her. The missionaries had spread the disease to thousands, perhaps tens of thousands. But more damaging, they'd completely corrupted the blood supply. New prion filters were now on the market, but millions of gallons of blood had to be destroyed. They told her she might be ultimately responsible for the deaths of a million people.

Paula gave them every name she could remember, and the FBI tracked down all of the original eighteen, but by then the mission could go on without them. A day after the meeting in the restaurant they'd begun to recruit others, women and men Paula would never meet, whose names would never be spoken to her. The church would continue. In secret now, hunted by the FBI and the CDC and the world's governments, but growing every day. The host was passed needle by needle in private ceremonies, but increasingly on a mass scale as well. In an Ohio dairy processing plant, a man had been caught mixing his blood into the vats of milk. In Florida, police arrested a woman for injecting blood into the skulls of chickens. The economic damage was already in the trillions. The emotional toll on the public, in panic and paranoia, was incalculable.

Esther looked around at the cell. "You don't have anything in there with you. Can I bring you books? Magazines? They told me they'd allow reading material. I thought maybe—"

"I don't want anything," Paula said. She couldn't hold her head steady enough to read. She watched TV to remind herself every day of what she'd done to the world. Outside the prison, a hundred jubilant protestors had built a tent city. They sang hymns and chanted for her release, and every day a hundred counter-protestors showed up to scream threats, throw rocks, and chant for her death. Police in riot gear made daily arrests.

Esther frowned. "I thought maybe you'd like a Bible."

Now Paula laughed for real. "What are you doing here, Esther? I see that look in your eye, you think I don't recognize it?" Paula twisted, pressed herself higher on one elbow. Esther had never been infected by the host—they wouldn't have let her in here if she didn't pass the screening—but her strain of the disease was just as virulent. "Did your Jesus tell you to come here?"

"I suppose in a way he did." The woman didn't seem flustered. Paula found that annoying.

Esther said, "You don't have to go through this alone. Even here, even after all you've done, God will forgive you. He can be here for you, if you want him."

Paula stared at her. If I want him. She never stopped craving him. He'd carved out a place for himself, dug a warren through the cells in her brain, until he'd erased even himself. She no longer needed pharmaceuticals to suppress him. He'd left behind a jagged Christ-shaped hole, a darkness with teeth.

She wanted him more than drugs, more than alcohol, more than Richard or Claire. She thought she'd known loneliness, but the past months had taught her new depths. Nothing would feel better than to surrender to a new god, let herself be wrapped again in loving arms.

Esther stood and leaned close to the bars so that their faces were only a couple feet apart. "Paula, if you died right now, do you know beyond a shadow of a doubt that you'd go to heaven?" The guard told her to step back but she ignored him. She pushed one arm through the bars. "If you want to accept him, take my hand. Reach out."

"Oh, Esther, the last—" Her upper lip pulled back over her gums. "—last thing I want is to live forever." She fell back against the bed, tucked her working arm to her chest.

A million people.

There were acts beyond forgiveness. There were debts that had to be paid in person.

"Not hiding anymore," Paula said. She shook her head. "No gods, no drugs. The only thing I need to do now—"

She laughed, but it was an involuntary spasm, joyless. She waited a moment until it passed, and breathed deep. "I need to die clean."

Tin Marsh

MICHAEL SWANWICK

Michael Swanwick (www.michaelswanwick.com) *lives in Philadelphia, Pennsylvania. His novels include the Nebula Award winner,* Stations of the Tide *(1991),* The Iron Dragon's Daughter *(1993),* Jack Faust *(1997), and* Bones of the Earth *(2002), and he has been a prolific short-fiction writer in recent years. His short fiction has been collected principally in* Gravity's Angels *(1991),* A Geography of Unknown Lands *(1997),* Moon Dogs *(2000),* Tales of Old Earth *(2000),* Puck Aleshire's Abecedary *(2000),* Cigar-Box Faust and Other Miniatures *(2001), and* The Periodic Table of Science Fiction *(2005). He published several fantasy stories (some of them pieces of his forthcoming fantasy novel) but just a smidgen of SF.*

"Tin Marsh" was published in Asimov's, *where Swanwick is a regular contributor. It is one of a series of planetary romances he has published in recent years, adventure stories set on one or another of the Solar System planets or moons, in the hard-boiled tradition of Leigh Brackett's stories. We suspect the women central characters are a kind of homage to Brackett herself. This story, about prospecting for valuable minerals, is darker than usual for Swanwick, about how people who like one another, when forced too close for too long, come to hate and torture each other. Fortunately, there is a great life-or-death chase, and a happy ending.*

It was hot coming down into the valley. The sun was high in the sky, a harsh white dazzle in the eternal clouds, strong enough to melt the lead out of the hills. They trudged down from the heights, carrying the drilling rig between them. A little trickle of metal, spill from a tanker bringing tin out of the mountains, glinted at the verge of the road.

A traveler coming the other way, ten feet tall and anonymous in a black muscle suit, waved at them as they passed, but, even though it had been weeks since they'd seen another human being, they didn't wave back. The traveler passed them, and disappeared up the road. The heat had seared the ground here black and hard. They could leave the road, if they wanted, and make almost as good time.

Patang and MacArthur had been walking for hours. They expected to walk for hours more. But then the road twisted and down at the bottom of the long decline, in the shadow of a basalt cliff, was an inn. Mostly their work kept them away from roads and inns. For almost a month they'd been living in their suits, sleeping in harness.

They looked warily at each other, mirrored visor to mirrored visor. Heat glimmered from the engines of their muscle suits. Without a word, they agreed to stop.

The inn radioed a fee schedule at their approach. They let their suits' autonomic functions negotiate for them, and carefully set the drilling rig down alongside the building.

"Put out the tarp," MacArthur said. "So it won't warp."

He went inside.

Patang deployed the gold foil tarp, then followed him in.

MacArthur was already out of his suit and seated at a cast-iron table with two cups of water in front of him when Patang cycled through the airlock. For an instant she dared hope everything was going to be all right.

Then he looked up at her.

"Ten dollars a cup." One cup was half empty. He drank the rest down in one long gulp, and closed a hairy paw around the second cup. His beard had grown since she had last seen it, and she could smell him from across the room. Presumably he could smell her too. "The bastards get you coming and going."

Patang climbed down out of her suit. She stretched out her arms as far as they would go, luxuriating in the room's openness. All that space! It was twenty feet across and windowless. There was the one table, and six iron chairs to go with it. Half a dozen cots folded up against the walls. A line of shelves offered Company goods that neither of them could afford. There were also a pay toilet and a pay shower. There was a free medical unit, but if you tried to con it out of something recreational, the Company found out and fined you accordingly.

Patang's skin prickled and itched from a month's accumulation of dried sweat. "I'm going to scratch," she said. "Don't look."

But of course MacArthur did, the pig.

Ignoring him, Patang slowly and sensuously scratched under her blouse and across her back. She took her time, digging in with her nails hard enough almost to make the skin bleed. It felt glorious.

MacArthur stared at her all the while, a starving wolf faced with a plump rabbit.

"You could have done that in your suit," he said when she was done.

"It's not the same."

"You didn't have to do that in front of—"

"Hey! How's about a little conversation?" Patang said loudly. So it cost a few bucks. So what?

With a click, the innkeeper came on. "Wasn't expecting

any more visitors so close to the noon season," it said in a folksy synthetic voice. "What are you two prospecting for?"

"Gold, tin, lead, just about anything that'll gush up a test-hole." Patang closed her eyes, pretending she was back on Lakshmi Planum in a bar in Port Ishtar, talking with a real, live human being. "We figured most people will be working tracts in the morning and late afternoon. This way our data-bases are up-to-date—we won't be stepping on somebody's month-old claim."

"Very wise. The Company pays well for a strike."

"I hate those fucking things." MacArthur turned his back on the speaker and Patang both, noisily scraping his chair against the floor. She knew how badly he'd like to hurt her.

She knew that it wasn't going to happen.

The Company had three rules. The first was No Violence. The second was Protect Company Equipment. The third was Protect Yourself. They all three were enforced by neu-ral implant.

From long experience with its prospectors, the Com-pany had prioritized these rules, so that the first overruled the second, the second overruled the third, and the third could only be obeyed insofar as it didn't conflict with the first two. That was so a prospector couldn't decide—as had happened—that his survival depended on the death of his partner. Or, more subtly, that the other wasn't taking proper care of Company equipment, and should be elimi-nated.

It had taken time and experience, but the Company had finally come up with a foolproof set of algorithms. The out-back was a functioning anarchy. Nobody could hurt any-body else there.

No matter how badly they needed to.

The 'plants had sounded like a good idea when Patang and MacArthur first went under contract. They'd signed up for a full sidereal day—two hundred fifty-five Earth days. Slightly longer than a Venusian year. Now, with fifty-nine days still to go, she was no longer certain that two people

who hated each other as much as they did should be kept
from each other's throats. Sooner or later, one of them would
have to crack.

Every day she prayed that it would be MacArthur who finally yanked the escape cord, calling down upon himself
the charges for a rescue ship to pull them out ahead of contract. MacArthur who went bust while she took her partial
creds and skipped.

Every day he didn't. It was inhuman how much abuse he
could absorb without giving in.

Only hatred could keep a man going like that.

Patang drank her water down slowly, with little slurps and
sighs and lip-smackings. Knowing MacArthur loathed that,
but unable to keep herself from doing it anyway. She was
almost done when he slammed his hands down on the table-
top, to either side of hers, and said, "Patang, there are some
things I want to get straight between us."

"Please. Don't."

"Goddamnit, you know how I feel about that shit."

"I don't like it when you talk like that. Stop."

MacArthur ground his teeth. "No. We are going to have
this out right here and now. I want you to—what was that?"

Patang stared blankly at her partner. Then she felt it—an
uneasy vertiginous queasiness, a sense of imbalance just at
the edge of perception, as if all of Venus were with infini-
tesimal gentleness shifting underfoot.

Then the planet roared and the floor came up to smash her
in the face.

When Patang came to, everything was a jumble. The floor
was canted. The shelves had collapsed, dumping silk shirts,
lemon cookies, and bars of beauty soap everywhere. Their
muscle suits had tumbled together, the metal arm of one
caught between the legs of the other. The life support systems were still operational, thank God. The Company built
them strong.

In the middle of it all, MacArthur stood motionless,

grinning. A trickle of blood ran down his neck. He slowly rubbed the side of his face.

"MacArthur? Are you okay?"

A strange look was in his eyes. "By God," he said softly. "By damn."

"Innkeeper! What happened here?"

The device didn't respond. "I busted it up," MacArthur said. "It was easy."

"What?"

MacArthur walked clumsily across the floor toward her, like a sailor on an uncertain deck. "There was a cliff slump." He had a Ph.D. in extraterrestrial geology. He knew things like that. "A vein of soft basalt weakened and gave way. The inn caught a glancing blow. We're lucky to be alive."

He knelt beside her and made the OK sign with thumb and forefinger. Then he flicked the side of her nose with the forefinger.

"Ouch!" she said. Then, shocked, "Hey, you can't . . . !"

"Like hell I can't." He slapped her in the face. Hard. "Chip don't seem to work anymore."

Rage filled her. "You son of a bitch!" Patang drew back her arm to slug him.

Blankness.

She came to seconds later. But it was like opening a book in the middle or stepping into an interactive an hour after it began. She had no idea what had happened or how it affected her.

MacArthur was strapping her into her muscle suit.

"Is everything okay?" she murmured. "Is something wrong?"

"I was going to kill you, Patang. But killing you isn't enough. You have to suffer first."

"What are you talking about?"

Then she remembered.

MacArthur had hit her. His chip had malfunctioned. There were no controls on him now. And he hated her. Bad enough to kill her? Oh, yes. Easily.

MacArthur snapped something off her helmet. Then he slapped the power button and the suit began to close around her. He chuckled and said, "I'll meet you outside."

Patang cycled out the lock and then didn't know what to do. She fearfully went a distance up the road, and then hovered anxiously. She didn't exactly wait and she didn't exactly go away. She had to know what MacArthur was up to.

The lock opened, and MacArthur went around to the side of the tavern, where the drilling rig lay under its tarp. He bent down to separate the laser drill from the support struts, data boxes, and alignment devices. Then he delicately tugged the gold foil blanket back over the equipment.

He straightened, and turned toward Patang, the drill in his arms. He pointed it at her.

The words LASER HAZARD flashed on her visor.

She looked down and saw the rock at her feet blacken and smoke. "You know what would happen if I punched a hole in your shielding," MacArthur said.

She did. All the air in her suit would explode outward, while the enormous atmospheric pressure simultaneously imploded the metal casing inward. The mechanical cooling systems would fail instantly. She would be suffocated, broiled, and crushed, all in an instant.

"Turn around. Or I'll lase you a new asshole."

She obeyed.

"Here are the rules. You get a half-hour head start. Then I come for you. If you turn north or south, I'll drill you. Head west. Noonward."

"Noonward?" She booted up the geodetics. There was nothing in that direction but a couple more wrinkle ridges and, beyond them, tesserae. The tesserae were marked orange on her maps. Orange for unpromising. Prospectors had passed through them before and found nothing. "Why there?"

"Because I told you to. Because we're going to have a little fun. Because you have no choice. Understand?"

She nodded miserably.

"Go."

* * *

She walked, he followed. It was a nightmare that had somehow found its way into waking life. When Patang looked back, she could see MacArthur striding after her, small in the distance. But never small enough that she had any kind of chance to get away.

He saw her looking and stooped to pick up a boulder. He windmilled his arm and threw.

Even though MacArthur was halfway to the horizon, the boulder smashed to the ground a hundred yards ahead of her and to one side. It didn't come close to striking her, of course. That wasn't his intent.

The rock shattered when it hit. It was terrifying how strong that suit was. It filled her with rage to see MacArthur yielding all that power, and her completely helpless. "You goddamned sadist!"

No answer.

He was nuts. There had to be a clause in the contract covering that. Well, then . . . She set her suit on auto-walk, pulled up the indenture papers, and went looking for it. Options. Hold harmless clauses. Responsibilities of the Subcontractor—there were hundreds of those. Physical care of the Contractor's equipment.

And there it was. There it was! In the event of medical emergency, as ultimately upheld in a court of physicians . . . She scrolled up the submenu of qualifying conditions. The list of mental illnesses was long enough and inclusive enough that she was certain MacArthur belonged on it somewhere.

She'd lose all the equity she'd built up, of course. But, if she interpreted the contract correctly, she'd be entitled to a refund of her initial investment.

That, and her life, were good enough for her.

She slid an arm out of harness and reached up into a difficult-to-reach space behind her head. There was a safety there. She unlatched it. Then she called up a virtual keyboard, and typed out the SOS.

So simple. So easy.

DO YOU REALLY WANT TO SEND THIS MESSAGE?
YES NO

She hit YES.

For an instant, nothing happened.

MESSAGE NOT SENT

"Shit!" She tried it again. MESSAGE NOT SENT A third time. MESSAGE NOT SENT A fourth. MESSAGE NOT SENT She ran a trouble-shooting program, and then sent the message again. MESSAGE NOT SENT

And again. And again. And again.

MESSAGE NOT SENT

MESSAGE NOT SENT

MESSAGE NOT SENT

Until the suspicion was so strong she had to check.

There was an inspection camera on the back of her suit's left hand. She held it up so she could examine the side of her helmet.

MacArthur had broken off the uplink antenna.

"You jerk!" She was really angry now. "You shithead! You cretin! You retard! You're nuts, you know that? Crazy. Totally whack."

No answer.

The bastard was ignoring her. He probably had his suit on auto-follow. He was probably leaning back in his harness, reading a book or watching an old movie on his visor. MacArthur did that a lot. You'd ask him a question and he wouldn't answer because he wasn't there; he was sitting front row center in the theater of his cerebellum. He probably had a tracking algorithm in the navigation system to warn him if she turned to the north or south, or started to get too far ahead of him.

Let's test that hypothesis.

She'd used the tracking algorithm often enough that she knew its specs by heart. One step sidewards in five would register immediately. One in six would not. All right, then . . . Let's see if we can get this rig turned around slowly, subtly, toward the road. She took seven strides forward, and then half-step to the side.

LASER HAZARD

Patang hastily switched on auto-walk. So that settled that. He was watching her every step. A tracking algorithm would have written that off as a stumble. But then why didn't he speak? To make her suffer, obviously. He must be bubbling over with things to say. He must hate her almost as much as she did him.

"You son of a bitch! I'm going to get you, MacArthur! I'm going to turn the goddamned tables on you, and when I do—!"

It wasn't as if she were totally hopeless. She had explosives. Hell, her muscle suit could throw a rock with enough energy to smash a hole right through his suit. She could—

Blankness.

She came to with the suit auto-walking down the far slope of the first wrinkle ridge. There was a buzzing in her ear. Somebody talking. MacArthur, over the short-range radio. "What?" she asked blurrily. "Were you saying something, MacArthur? I didn't quite catch that."

"You had a bad thought, didn't you?" MacArthur said gleefully. "Naughty girl! Papa spank."

LASER HAZARD

LASER HAZARD

Arrows pointed to either side. She'd been walking straight Noonward, and he'd fired on her anyway.

"Damn it, that's not fair!"

"Fair! Was it fair, the things you said to me? Talking. All the time talking."

"I didn't mean anything by it."

"You did! Those things . . . the things you said . . . unforgivable!"

"I was only deviling you, MacArthur," she said placatingly. It was a word from her childhood; it meant teasing, the kind of teasing a sister inflicted on a brother. "I wouldn't do it if we weren't friends."

MacArthur made a noise he might have thought was laughter. "Believe me, Patang, you and I are not friends."

The deviling had been innocent enough at the start. She'd only done it to pass the time. At what point had it passed over the edge? She hadn't always hated MacArthur. Back in

Port Ishtar, he'd seemed like a pleasant companion. She'd even thought he was cute.

It hurt to think about Port Ishtar, but she couldn't help herself. It was like trying not to think about Heaven when you were roasting in Hell.

Okay, so Port Ishtar wasn't perfect. You ate flavored algae and you slept on a shelf. During the day you wore silk, because it was cheap, and you went everywhere barefoot because shoes cost money. But there were fountains that sprayed water into the air. There was live music in the restaurants, string quartets playing to the big winners, prospectors who had made a strike and were leaking wealth on the way out. If you weren't too obvious about it, you could stand nearby and listen. Gravity was light, then, and everybody was young, and the future was going to be full of money.

That was then. She was a million years older now.

LASER HAZARD

"Hey!"

"Keep walking, bitch. Keep walking or die."

This couldn't be happening.

Hours passed, and more hours, until she completely lost track of the time. They walked. Up out of the valley. Over the mountain. Down into the next valley. Because of the heat, and because the rocks were generally weak, the mountains all had gentle slopes. It was like walking up and then down a very long hill.

The land was grey and the clouds above it murky orange. These were Venus' true colors. She could have grass-green rocks and a bright blue sky if she wished—her visor would do that—but the one time she'd tried those settings, she'd quickly switched back. The falseness of it was enough to break your heart.

Better to see the bitter land and grim sky for what they were.

West, they traveled. Noonward. It was like an endless and meaningless dream.

"Hey, Poontang."

"You know how I feel about that kind of language," she said wearily.

"How you feel. That's rich. How do you think I felt, some of the things you said?"

"We can make peace, MacArthur. It doesn't have to be like this."

"Ever been married, Poontang?"

"You know I haven't."

"I have. Married and divorced." She knew that already. There was very little they didn't know about each other by now. "Thing is, when a marriage breaks up, there's always one person comes to grips with it first. Goes through all the heartache and pain, feels the misery, mourns the death of the death of the relationship—and then moves on. The one who's been cheated on, usually. So the day comes when she walks out of the house and the poor schmuck is just standing there, saying, 'Wait. Can't we work this thing out?' He hasn't accepted that it's over."

"So?"

"So that's your problem, Poontang. You just haven't accepted that it's over yet."

"What? Our partnership, you mean?"

"No. Your life."

A day passed, maybe more. She slept. She awoke, still walking, with MacArthur's hateful mutter in her ear. There was no way to turn the radio off. It was Company policy. There were layers upon layers of systems and subsystems built into the walkers, all designed to protect Company investment. Sometimes his snoring would wake her up out of a sound sleep. She knew the ugly little grunting noises he made when he jerked off. There were times she'd been so angry that she'd mimicked those sounds right back at him. She regretted that now.

"I had dreams," MacArthur said. "I had ambitions."

"I know you did. I did too."

"Why the hell did you have to come into my life? Why me and not somebody else?"

"I liked you. I thought you were funny."

"Well, the joke's on you now."

Back in Port Ishtar, MacArthur had been a lanky, clean-cut kind of guy. He was tall, and in motion you were always aware of his knees and elbows, always sure he was going to knock something over, though he never did. He had an odd, geeky kind of grace. When she'd diffidently asked him if he wanted to go partners, he'd picked her up and whirled her around in the air and kissed her right on the lips before setting her down again and saying, "Yes." She'd felt dizzy and happy then, and certain she'd made the right choice.

But MacArthur had been weak. The suit had broken him. All those months simmering in his own emotions, perfectly isolated and yet never alone . . . He didn't even look like the same person anymore. You looked at his face and all you saw were anger and those anguished eyes.

LEAVING HIGHLANDS
ENTERING TESSERAE

Patang remembered how magical the tesserae landscape had seemed in the beginning. "Complex ridged terrain" MacArthur called it, high ridges and deep groves crisscrossing each other in such profusion that the land appeared blocky from orbit, like a jumble of tiles. Crossing such terrain, you had to be constantly alert. Cliffs rose up unexpectedly, butte-high. You turned a twist in a zigzagging valley and the walls fell away and down, down, down. There was nothing remotely like it on Earth. The first time through, she'd shivered in wonder and awe.

Now she thought: Maybe I can use this. These canyons ran in and out of each other. Duck down one and run like hell. Find another and duck down it. Keep on repeating until he'd lost her.

"You honestly think you can lose me, Patang?"

She shrieked involuntarily.

"I can read your mind, Patang. I know you through and through."

It was true, and it was wrong. People weren't meant to know each other like this. It was the forced togetherness, the fact you were never for a moment alone with your own thoughts. After a while you'd heard every story your partner had to tell and shared every confidence there was to share. After a while every little thing got on your nerves.

"How about if I admit I was wrong?" she said pleadingly. "I was wrong. I admit it."

"We were both wrong. So what?"

"I'm willing to cooperate, MacArthur. Look. I've stopped so you can catch up and not have to worry about me getting away from you. Doesn't that convince you we're on the same side?"

LASER HAZARD

"Oh, feel free to run as fast and as far as you want, Patang. I'm confident I'll catch up with you in the end."

All right, then, she thought desperately. If that's the way you want it, asshole. Tag! You're it.

She ducked into the shadows of a canyon and ran.

The canyon twisted and, briefly, she was out of sight. MacArthur couldn't talk to her, couldn't hear her. Couldn't tell which way she went. The silence felt wonderful. It was the first privacy she'd had since she didn't know when. She only wished she could spare the attention to enjoy it more. But she had to think, and think hard. One canyon wall had slumped downward just ahead, creating a slope her walker could easily handle. Or she could keep on ahead, up the canyon.

Which way should she go?

Upslope.

She set the walker on auto-run.

Meanwhile, she studied the maps. The free satellite downloads were very good. They weren't good enough. They showed features down to three meters across, but she needed to know the land yard-by-yard. That crack-like little rille—did it split two kilometers ahead, or was there a second rille that didn't quite meet it? She couldn't tell. She'd've gladly paid for the premium service now, the caviar of info-feed detailed enough to track footprints across a dusty stretch of terrain. But with her uplink disabled, she couldn't.

Patang ducked into a rille so narrow her muscle suit's programming would have let her jump it, if she wished. It forked, and she took the right-hand branch. When the walls started closing in on them, she climbed up and out. Then she ran, looking for another rille.

Hours passed.

After a time, all that kept her going was fear. She drew her legs up into the torso of her suit and set it to auto-run. Up this canyon. Over this ridge. Twisting, turning. Scanning the land ahead, looking for options. Two directions she might go. Flip a mental coin. Choose one. Repeat the process. Keep the radio shut down so MacArthur couldn't use it to track her. Keep moving.

Keep moving.

Keep moving . . .

Was it hours that passed, or days? Patang didn't know. It might have been weeks. In times of crisis, the suit was programmed to keep her alert by artificial stimulation of her brain. It was like an electrical version of amphetamines. But, as with amphetamines, you tended to lose track of things. Things like your sense of time.

So she had no idea how long it took her to realize that it was all no use.

The problem was that the suit was so damned heavy! If she ran fast enough to keep her distance from MacArthur, it left a trace in the regolith obvious enough to be followed at top speed. But if she slowed down enough to place her walker's feet on bare stone when she could, and leave subtle and easy-to-miss footprints when she couldn't, he came right up behind her. And try though she might, she couldn't get far enough ahead of him to dare slow down enough to leave a trace he couldn't follow.

There was no way she could escape him.

The feeling of futility that came over her then was drab and familiar, like a shabby old coat grown colorless with age that you don't have the money to replace. Sometime, long ago, she'd crossed that line where hope ceased. She had never actually admitted to herself that she no longer believed they'd ever make that big strike—just one day woken up knowing that she was simply waiting out her contract, stubbornly trying to endure long enough to serve out her term and return to Earth no poorer than she had set out.

Which was when her deviling had turned nasty, wasn't it? It was when she had started touching herself and telling MacArthur exactly what she was doing. When she'd started describing in detail all the things she'd never do to him.

It was a way of getting through one more day. It was a way of faking up enough emotion to care. It was a stupid, stupid thing to do.

And this was her punishment.

But she couldn't give up. She was going to have to . . . She didn't finish that thought. If she was going to do this un-named thing, she had to sort through the ground rules first.

The three rules were: No Violence. Protect Company Equipment. Protect Yourself. They were ranked hierarchically.

Okay, Patang thought. In order to prevent violence, I'm going to have to destroy Company property.

She waited to see if she'd pass out.

Nothing happened.

Good.

She'd come to a long ridge, steep-sided and barren and set her suit to auto-climb. As she climbed, she scanned the slope ahead, empty and rock-strewn under a permanently dazzling cover of sulfuric acid clouds. Halfway up, MacArthur emerged from the zigzagging valley below and waved jauntily.

Patang ignored him. That pile of boulders up ahead was too large. Those to the right were too small. There was a patch of loose regolith that looked promising but . . . no. In the end, she veered leftward, toward a shallow ledge that sheltered rocks that looked loose enough to be dislodged but not massive enough to do any serious damage to MacArthur's suit. All she wanted was to sweep him off his feet. He could survive a slide downslope easily enough. But could he hold onto the laser drill while doing so?

Patang didn't think so.

Okay, then. She took her suit off automatics and climbed clumsily, carefully, toward her destination. She kept her hel-

met up, pointed toward the top of the ridge, to avoid tipping
MacArthur off to her intentions.

Slantwise across the slope, that's right. Now straight up.
She glanced back and saw that she'd pulled MacArthur
into her wake. He was directly beneath her. Good. All systems go.

She was up to the ledge now.

Stop. Turn around. Look down on MacArthur, surprisingly close.

If there was one thing Patang knew, after all these months,
it was how easy it was to start a landslide. Lean back and
brace yourself here, and start kicking. And over the rocks
go and over the rocks go and—

LASER HAZARD

"Ohhhh, Patang, you are so obvious. You climb diagonally
up a slope that any ordinary person would tackle straight on.
You change direction halfway up. What were you planning
to do, start an avalanche? What did you think that would accomplish?"

"I thought I could get the laser away from you."

"And what good would that do? I'd still have the suit. I'd
still have rocks. I'd still have you at my mercy. You hadn't
really thought this one through, had you?"

"No," she admitted.

"You tried to outwit me, but you didn't have the ingenuity.
Isn't that right?"

"Yes."

"You were just hoping. But there isn't any hope, is
there?"

"No."

He flipped one hand dismissively. "Well, keep on going.
We're not done yet."

Weeping, Patang topped the ridge and started downward,
into a valley shaped like a deep bowl. Glassy scarps on all
sides caught whatever infrared bounced off the floor and
threw it back into the valley. The temperature readings on
her visor leaped. It was at least fifty degrees hotter out there

than anyplace she had ever been. Hot enough that pro-
longed exposure would incapacitate her suit? Maybe. But
there was MacArthur behind her, and the only way forward
was a shallow trough leading straight down. She had no
alternative.

Midway down the slope, the trough deepened. Rock walls
rose up to plunge Patang into shadow. Her suit's external
temperature went down, though not as much as she would've
liked. Then the way grew less steep and then it flattened
out. The trough ended as a bright doorway between jagged
rocks.

She stepped out into the open and looked across the
valley.

The ground dazzled.

She walked out into it. She felt weightless. Her feet floated
up beneath her and her hands rose of their own accord into
the air. The muscle suit's arms rose too, like a ballerina's.

A network of cracks crazed the floor of the valley, each
one blazing bright as the sun. Liquid metal was just oozing
up out of the ground. She'd never seen anything like it.

Patang stomped on a puddle of metal, shattering it into
droplets of sunlight and setting off warning alarms in her
suit. For an instant she swayed with sleepiness. But she shook
it off. She snapped a stick-probe from her tool rack and
jabbed it into the stuff. It measured the metal's temperature
and its resistance to pressure, ran a few baby calculations,
and spat out a result.

Tin.

She looked up again. There were intersecting lines of
molten tin everywhere. The pattern reminded her of her
childhood on the Eastern Shore, of standing at the edge of
a marsh, binoculars in hand, hoping for a harrier, with the
silver gleam of sun on water almost painful to the eye. This
looked just like a marsh, only with tin instead of water.

A tin marsh.

For an instant, wonder flickered to life within her. How
could such a thing be? What complex set of geological
conditions was responsible? All she could figure was that
the noontide heat was involved. As it slowly sank into the

rock, the tin below expanded and pushed its way up through the cracks. Or maybe it was the rocks that expanded, squeezing out the liquid tin. In either case the effect would be very small for any given volume. She couldn't imagine how much tin there must be down there for it to be forced to the surface like this. More than she'd ever dreamed they'd find.

"We're rich!" she whooped. She couldn't help it. All those months, all that misery, and here it was. The payoff they'd set out to discover, the one that she'd long ago given up all hope of finding.

LASER HAZARD
LASER HAZARD
LASER HAZARD

"No! Wait! Stop!" she cried. "You don't need to do this anymore. We found it! It's here!"

Turning, she saw McArthur's big suit lumber out of shadow. It was brute strength personified, all body and no head. "What are you talking about?" he said angrily. But Patang dared think he sounded almost sane. She dared hope she could reason with him.

"It's the big one, Mac!" She hadn't called him Mac in ages. "We've got the goddamned motherlode here. All you have to do is radio in the claim. It's all over, Mac! This time tomorrow, you're going to be holding a press conference about it."

For a moment MacArthur stood silent and irresolute. Then he said, "Maybe so. But I have to kill you first."

"You turn up without me, the Company's gonna have questions. They're gonna interrogate their suit. They're gonna run a mind-probe. No, MacArthur, you can't have both. You've got to choose: money or me."

LASER HAZARD

"Run, you bitch!" MacArthur howled. "Run like you've got a chance to live!"

She didn't move. "Think of it, MacArthur. A nice cold bath. They chill down the water with slabs of ice, and for a little extra they'll leave the ice in. You can hear it clink."

"Shut up."

"And ice cream!" she said fervently. "A thousand different flavors of ice cream. They've got it warehoused: sherbet, gelato, water ice . . . Oh, they know what a prospector likes, all right. Beer in big, frosty mugs. Vodka so cold it's almost a slurry."

"Shut the fuck up!"

"You've been straight with me. You gave me a half-hour head start, just like you promised, right? Not everybody would've done that. Now I'm gonna be straight with you. I'm going to lock my suit down." She powered off the arms and legs. It would take a good minute to get them online again. "So you don't have to worry about me getting away. I'm going to just stand here, motionless and helpless, while you think about it, all right?" Then, desperation forcing her all the way into honesty, "I was wrong, MacArthur. I mean it this time. I shouldn't have done those things. Accept my apology. You can rise above it. You're a rich man now."

MacArthur roared with rage.

LASER HAZARD

LASER HAZARD

LASER HAZARD

LASER HAZARD

"Walk, damn you!" he screamed. "Walk!"

LASER HAZARD

LASER HAZARD

LASER HAZARD

He wasn't coming any closer. And though he kept on firing, over and over, the bolts of lased light never hit her. It was baffling. She'd given up, she wasn't running, it wasn't even possible for her to run. So why didn't he just kill her? What was stopping him?

Revelation flooded Patang then, like sudden sunlight after a long winter. So simple! So obvious! She couldn't help laughing. "You can't shoot me!" she cried. "The suit won't let you!"

It was what the tech guys called "fossil software." Before the Company acquired the ability to insert their programs into human beings, they'd programmed their tools so they couldn't be used for sabotage. People, being inventive buggers, had found ways around that programming often enough to render it obsolete. But nobody had ever bothered to dig it out of the deep levels of the machinery's code. What would be the point?

She whooped and screamed. Her suit staggered in a jittery little dance of joy. "You can't kill me, MacArthur! You can't! You can't and you know it! I can just walk right past you, and all the way to the next station, and there's nothing you can do about it."

MacArthur began to cry.

The hopper came roaring down out of the white dazzle of the sky to burn a landing practically at their feet. They clambered wearily forward and let the pilot bolt their muscle suits to the hopper's strutwork. There wasn't cabin space for them and they didn't need it.

The pilot reclaimed his seat. After his first attempts at conversation had fallen flat, he'd said no more. He had hauled out prospectors before. He knew that small talk was useless.

With a crush of acceleration their suits could only partially cushion, the hopper took off. Only three hours to Port Ishtar. The hopper twisted and Patang could see Venus rushing dizzyingly by below her. She blanked out her visor so she didn't have to look at it.

Patang tested her suit. The multiplier motors had been powered down. She was immobile.

"Hey, Patang."

"Yeah?"

"You think I'm going to go to jail? For all the shit I did to you?"

"No, MacArthur. Rich people don't go to jail. They get therapy."

"That's good," he said. "Thank you for telling me that."

"De nada," she said without thinking. The jets rumbled under her back, making the suit vibrate. Two, three hours from now, they'd come down in Port Ishtar, stake their claims, collect their money, and never see each other again.

On impulse, she said, "Hey, MacArthur!"

"What?"

And for an instant she came that close to playing the Game one last time. Deviling him, just to hear his teeth grind. But . . .

"Nothing. Just—enjoy being rich, okay? I hope you have a good life."

"Yeah." MacArthur took a deep breath, and then let it go, as if he were releasing something painful, and said, "Yeah . . . you too."

And they soared.

Taking Good Care
of Myself

IAN R. MacLEOD

Ian R. MacLeod (www.ianrmacleod.com) *lives in England.
He has published more than thirty stories since his first, in
1990, and four novels to date. His next novel,* Song of Time,
*is forthcoming in 2007. He has appeared in one or more
best-of-the-year collections nearly every year since his first
story was selected by three of them. His stories collections
are* Voyages by Starlight *(1997),* Breathmoss and Other Ex-
halations *(2003), and* Past Magic *(2006). He is an impressive
prose stylist, widely admired by other writers.*

"Taking Good Care of Myself" appeared in Nature. *It is a
very complex tale in a very short space, in the SF tradition
of time loop traps. No one knows why people from the future
call upon them to go and take care of their very elderly
selves in that future until they die. This is one man's story.*

The social worker came a day or so before I arrived. He was as briskly pleasant as the occasion, which I'd long been dreading, allowed. He was dressed bizarrely, but people from the future always are.

"We'll need to send a few helpful machines back with you," he murmured as he inspected our spare bedroom and the bathroom and then the kitchen, which no doubt looked ridiculously primitive to him. "But nothing that'll get in your way."

Helen was equally reassuring when she came home that evening. "It's a tremendous challenge," she told me. "You always say you like challenges."

"I mean stuff like climbing, hang-gliding, pushing things to the edge, not looking after some senile version of myself."

"Josh." She gave me one of her looks. "You have no choice."

She was right—and there was plenty of space in our nice house. It was as if we'd always planned on doing precisely this, although I hated the very thought.

I arrived a couple of mornings after, flanked by swish-looking machines, although I was just as pale and dithery as I'd feared. The creature I'd eventually become couldn't walk, could barely see, and certainly didn't comprehend what was happening to him. Exactly how long, I wondered (and secretly hoped), can I possibly last like this?

Scampering around our house like chromium shadows,

the machines performed many of the more obvious and unpleasant duties, but much was still expected of me. I had to
sit and talk, although my elderly self rarely said anything in
response, and none of it was coherent. I also had to help myself eat, and wipe away the spilled drool afterwards. I had to
hold my own withered hand.

"Do you remember this house—I mean, you must have
lived here?"

But I was much too far gone to understand. Not, perhaps,
in a vegetative state yet, but stale meat at very best.

Sometimes, I took me out, pretending to push the clever
chair which was in fact more than capable of doing
everything—except getting rid of this cadaverous ghost—by
itself. My work suffered. So did my relationship with Helen.
I joined a self-help group. I sat in meeting halls filled with
other unfortunates who'd had the care of their future selves
foisted on them. We debated in slow circles why our future
children, or the intelligences that perhaps governed them,
had seen fit to make us do this. Were they punishing us for
the mess we'd made of their world? Or were these addled
creatures, with their lost minds, their failed memories, their
thin grip on this or any other kind of reality, somehow the
means of achieving time travel itself? Predictably, various
means of killing were discussed, from quiet euthanasia to
violent stabbings and clifftop falls. But that was the thing;
complain as we might, not one of us ever seemed capable of
harming ourselves. Not, anyway, the selves we would eventually become.

I declined. The machines, with a will of their own, grew
yet more sophisticated and crouched permanently beside me
as I lay immovably in my spare bedroom cradled in steel
pipes and crystal insertions. They fed me fresh blood, fresh
air. I doubted if this husk I'd become was conscious of any
presence other than its own dim existence now, but still I
found myself sitting beside me, and talking endlessly about
things I couldn't remember afterwards. It was as if I was
trapped in a trance, or that part of me was dying as well. I lay
entirely naked now under clever sheets that cleaned themselves. Occasionally, inevitably, I would lift them up, and

breathe the stale air of my own mortality, and study the thin limbs and puckered flesh of what I would eventually become. The death itself was surprisingly easy. The machines saw to it that there was no pain, and I was there; I made sure I didn't die alone. A faint rattle, a tiny spasm. You're left wondering what all the fuss is about.

After the funeral, which of course I also had to arrange myself, and was far more poorly attended than I might have hoped, and then the scattering of my ashes at the windy lip of one of my favourite climbs, I looked around at my life like a sleeper awakening. Helen had left me, although quietly, without fuss. My house felt empty, but I knew that it was more to do with that old man than with her. I'm back to climbing regularly now. I'm back to freefall and hang-gliding. I find that I enjoy these sports, and many other kinds of dangerous and challenging physical activities, even more. After all, I know they can't kill me, and that the last phase of my life really isn't so very bad. But things have changed, for all that, and I still sometimes find myself sitting alone in my spare bedroom gazing at the taut sheets of that empty bed, although I and all those future machines have long gone. The sad fact is, I miss myself dreadfully, now that I'm no longer here.

The Lowland Expedition

STEPHEN BAXTER

Stephen Baxter (tribute site: www.themanifold.co.uk) *lives in Morpeth, England. He has published more than twenty SF novels to date, starting with* Raft *(1989). Since the mid 1990s he has produced five or ten short stories a year in fantasy, SF, and horror venues, over a hundred in all, and did in 2006 again. He writes, "I've completed my 'Destiny's Children' series with* Resplendent *(2006). 'The Lowland Expedition' is set in the remote future of the same universe. Now I'm working on an alternate-history series called Time's Tapestry."*

"The Lowland Expedition" was published in Analog *and is a story of fantastic technology, adventure, and discovery. In the far future Old Earth is divided into two worlds, called Lowland and The Shelf, separated by some sort of complex time-dilation. Revelations of strangeness keep you reading.*

Enna relished her flights in the spotting balloon.

She loved to see the Expedition train strung out across the Lowland's arid plain, with its spindling-drawn wagons, the chains of servants and bearers, the gleaming coach that transported her father and his precious books, even the small flock of runner-birds. If the weather was fine the Philosophers themselves would walk, marching into the Lowland's mysteries, arguing endlessly. The Lowland Expedition was a grand gesture of the civilization of the Shelf that had spawned it—and it was brave too, for all the explorers knew that they could never go home again, whatever they discovered.

Down there was Tomm, one of the junior cartographers. Whenever Enna flew Tomm always wore a special red cap so she could pick him out, a bright red dot in the dusty line of Philosophers. At twenty-one he was just a year older than Enna herself—and he was her lover, though that was a secret to all but her closest friends, and certainly to her father, or so she hoped. When he saw her, he waved. But his waving was sluggish, like an old man's.

On Old Earth time was layered. When she rode her balloon up into the air, she was ascending into quicker time. If Tomm's ears had been sensitive enough he would have heard her heart fluttering like a bird's, and conversely when she looked down at him he was slowed, trapped in glutinous, redshifted time.

The balloon flights were invaluable aids to navigation, but

Bayle, Enna's father, had strictly ordered that flights should be short, and that his party should take it in turn to man them, so that no one slipped too far out of synchronization with the rest. "This trip is challenging enough for us all," he insisted, "without the wheels of time slipping too." Enna accepted this wisdom. Even now, despite the joy of the flight, she longed to break through the barriers of streamed time that separated her from her love.

But when she spied the city on the horizon she forgot even Tomm.

The light of the Lowland was strange, shifting. Storms of light swept across its surface, silent and flaring white. These founts of brightness were in fact the major source of light on Old Earth, but they made the seeing uncertain. Enna was unsure at first that the bright white line she spied on the horizon was anything but weather: a low cloud, a dust devil, even a minor light storm.

But in a rare instant of clear seeing, it resolved into a cluster of geometrical shapes, unmistakably artificial. It must be a city, stranded in the middle of the Lowland, where nobody had expected to find any signs of humanity but the meanest degradation. And Enna had discovered it.

She turned immediately to the pilot. "Do you see it? There, the city, can you see? Oh, take us down! Take us down!"

The expedition's chief pilot was a bluff good-humored fellow called Momo. A long-time military-service companion of her father, he was one of the few people to whom Bayle would entrust his daughter's life. As he had lost one eye in the wars he "couldn't see a blessed thing," he told her. But he believed her, and began to tug on the ropes that controlled the hot-air balloon's burner.

Enna leaned over the descending gondola, yelling out news of her discovery. As the time differentials melted away, faces turned slowly up towards her.

The Philosophers entered the city in wonder. Enna walked hand in hand with Tomm.

The city was a jumble of cubes and rhomboids, pyramids and tetrahedrons—even one handsome dodecahedron. The walls were gleaming white surfaces, smooth to the touch, neither hot nor cold, and pierced by sharp-edged doorways and windows. The buildings towered over the explorers, immense blocks of a geometric perfection that would have shamed even the grand civic centre of New Foro, Enna thought.

There were no doors, though, and the windows weren't glazed. And there were plenty of other peculiarities. Without inner partitions, each building was like "one big room," as Tomm put it. Between the buildings the ground was just dirt, not paved or cobbled as were the streets of New Foro, back on the Shelf.

"And there's nobody here," Enna whispered. "Not a soul! It's so strange."

"But wonderful," Tomm said. He was tall, strong but sparsely built, with a languid grace that disturbed her dreams. "This must be a terribly ancient place. Look at the finish of these walls—what is this stuff, stone, ceramic, glass? Far beyond anything we are capable of. Perhaps the builders were Weapon-makers."

"Maybe, but don't you think it's all rather eerie? And it's such a jumble—"

"A cartographer's nightmare," Tomm laughed.

"And why are there no windows or doors?"

"We can make windows," he said. "We can hang doors." He took her hands. "Questions, questions, Enna! You're worse than all these grumpy old Philosophers. This is your discovery. Relish the moment!"

There was a deep *harrumph*. Bayle, Enna's father, came walking towards them, trailed by acolytes, lesser men but Philosophers themselves. "But she's right," Bayle said. "There is familiarity, and yet perhaps that blinds us to how much is strange . . ."

Tomm hastily released Enna's hands.

Bayle wore his dress uniform, topped off by his cap of spindling fur and feathers. Though he had devoted the last three decades of his life to science, Bayle had retained an honorary rank in the army of New Foro, and "for the sake of general morale," as he put it, he donned his uniform to mark moments of particular significance during their long journey. But Enna knew that no matter how extravagant his appearance her father's mind was sharper than any around him.

He tapped the walls of the nearest building with his stick. "Certainly the layout follows no obvious rational design, as does the centre of New Foro, say. But there are patterns here." He walked them briskly through the narrow alleys between the buildings. "Can you see how the largest buildings are clustered on the outside, and the smaller huts are trapped in their shade?"

"It almost looks organic," Enna said impulsively. "Like a forest, dominated by its tallest trees."

Bayle eyed her appreciatively. "*I* was going to compare it to a bank of salt crystals." Salt had become something of an obsession of Bayle's during their journey. There was salt everywhere in the Lowlands; there were even plains covered with the stuff, the relics of dried-up lakes. Bayle was gathering evidence for his contention that the Lowland had once been the bed of a mighty body of water. "But I admit, daughter, that your analogy may be more apt. This city is not planned as we think of it. It is almost as if it has *grown* here."

Tomm seemed confused. "But that's just an analogy. I mean, this is a city, built by human hands—though maybe long ago. That much is obvious, isn't it?"

Bayle snapped, "If everything were obvious we would not have needed to come out here to study it." He gave Enna a look that spoke volumes. *A pretty face but a shallow mind*, said that withering expression; *you can do better.*

But Tomm was Enna's choice, and she returned his glare defiantly.

They were interrupted by a raucous hail. "Sir, sir! Look what I've found!" It was Momo. The burly, one-eyed pilot came stumbling around the corner of a building.

And walking with him was a woman. Dressed in some kind of scraped animal skin, she was tall, aged perhaps fifty, in her way elegant despite her ragged costume. She eyed the Philosophers, detached. In that first moment Enna thought she seemed as cold, strange and hard-edged as her city.

Bayle stepped forward, his gloved hand extended. "Madam," he said, "if you can understand me, we have a great deal to discuss." The woman took her father's hand and shook it. The subordinate Philosophers applauded enthusiastically.

In its way this was another remarkable moment in this trek of discovery. This was Bayle's first contact with any of the "lost souls" believed to inhabit the Lowland, stranded here from ages past; to find such people and "rehabilitate" them had been one of his stated goals from the beginning.

But Enna caught a strange whiff about her, an iron stink that at first she couldn't place. It was only later that she realized it was the smell of raw meat—of blood.

As night fell, the explorers and their attendants and servants dispersed gladly into the city's bare buildings. After the dirt of the plain, it was going to be a relief to spend a night within solid walls.

Bayle himself established his base in one of the grander buildings on the edge of the city, bathed in light even at the end of the day. It seemed he planned to spend most of the night in conversation with the woman, as far as anybody could tell the city's sole inhabitant; he said they had much to learn from each other. He kissed his daughter goodnight, trusting her safety to his companions, and to her own common sense.

So it was a betrayal of him, of a sort, when in the darkest night Enna sought out Tomm's warm arms. It wasn't hard for her to put her guilt aside; at twenty she had a healthy awareness of how far her father's opinions should govern her life.

But she dreamed. She dreamed that the building itself gathered her up and lifted her into the sky, just as she was cradled by Tomm's arms. And she thought she smelled an iron tang, the scent of blood. Then the dream became disturbing, a dream of confinement.

Bayle had formulated many objectives for his Expedition.

Always visible from Foro, Puul and the other towns of the Shelf, the Lowland, stretching away below in redshifted

ambiguity, had been a mystery throughout history. Now cartographers would map the Lowland. Historians, anthropolo-
gists and moralists hoped to make contact with the lost people
of the Lowland plains, if any survived. Clerics, mystics, doctors and other Philosophers hoped to learn something about
Effigies, those spectral apparitions which rose from dying
human bodies and fled to the redshifted mysteries of the
Lowland. Perhaps some insight would be gained into the
cause of the Formidable Caresses, the tremendous rattlings
which regularly shook human civilization to pieces. There
were even a few soldiers and armorers, hoping to track down
Weapons, ancient technology gone wild, too wily to have
been captured so far.

There had already been many successes. Take the light
storms, for instance.

On Old Earth day and night, and the seasons of the year,
were governed by the flickering uncertainties of the light that
emanated from the Lowland. Now Bayle's physicists had
discovered that these waves of light pulsed at many frequencies, "like the harmonics of a plucked string," as one mathematician described it. Not only that, because of the redshifting
of the light that struggled up to higher altitudes, the harmonic
peaks that governed the daily cycles here were different from
those to be observed from Foro, up on the Shelf—where,
because of the stratification of time, the length of the "day"
was so much shorter.

Enna had been walked through the logic by her father.
The effects of time stratification, redshifting and light cy-
cling subtly intermeshed so that whether you were up on the
Shelf or down in the Lowland the length of day and night
you perceived was roughly similar. This surely couldn't be
a coincidence. As Bayle said, "It adds up to a remarkable
mathematical argument for the whole world's having been
designed to be habitable by people and their creatures."

That, of course, had provoked a lively debate.

Forons were traditionally Mechanists, adhering to a strand
of natural philosophy that held that there was no governing
mind behind the world, that everything about it had emerged
from the blind working-out of natural laws—like the growth

of a salt crystal, say. However there were hard-line Creationists who argued that *everything* on Old Earth required a purposeful explanation.

After centuries of debate a certain compromise view had emerged, it seemed to Enna, a melding of extreme viewpoints based on the evidence. Even the most ardent Mechanists had had to accept that the world contained overwhelming evidence that it had been manufactured, or at least heavily engineered. But if Old Earth was a machine, it was a very old machine, and in the ages since its formation, natural processes of the kind argued for by the Mechanists had surely operated to modify the world.

At the heart of Bayle's project was a deep ambition to reconcile the two great poles of human thought, the Mechanist versus the Creationist—and to end centuries of theological conflict over which too much blood had been spilled.

In the morning Enna and Tomm were among the first to stir. They emerged from their respective buildings, and greeted each other with a jolly innocence that probably fooled nobody.

Cartographer Tomm had been detailed to take up the balloon for a rapid aerial survey, to provide context for the more painstaking work on the ground. Enna, free of specific chores, decided to ride up with him.

But there was a problem. They couldn't find pilot Momo.

Tomm was unconcerned. "So old One-eye treated himself to a party last night."

"That isn't like Momo." He was a habitual early riser, like Bayle himself—a relic from military days, it seemed.

"He won't be the only one—"

"That isn't like him!" Enna snapped, growing impatient. When Tomm treated her like a foolish child, Enna had some sympathy for her father's view of him. "Look, this is a strange city which we barely explored before splitting up. You can help me find Momo, or use the hot air you're spouting to go blow up the balloon yourself."

He was crestfallen, but she stalked off to search, and Tomm, embarrassed, hurried after her.

She thought she remembered the building Momo had chosen as his shelter. She headed that way now. But something was wrong. As she followed the unpaved alleys, the layout of the buildings didn't quite match her memory of the night before. Of course she had only had a quick glimpse of the city, and the light of morning, playing over these crisp creamy walls, was quite different. But even so, she wouldn't have expected to get so lost as this.

And when she came to the place where she thought Momo's building should have been, there was only a blank space. She walked back and forth over the bare ground, disoriented, dread gathering in her soul.

"You must be mistaken," Tomm insisted.

"I'm good at direction-finding, Tomm. You know that."

Playfully he said, "You found your way to my bed well enough—"

"Oh, shut up. This is serious. This is where Momo's shelter was, I'm sure of it. Something has changed. I can feel it."

Tomm said defensively, "That doesn't sound very scientific."

"Then help me, cartographer. Did any of you make a map last night?"

"Of course not. The light was poor. We knew there would be time enough today."

She glared at him. But she was being unfair; it was a perfectly reasonable assumption that a city like this wouldn't change overnight.

But the fact of the matter was, Momo was still missing.

Growing increasingly disturbed, she went to her father's room. That at least was just where it had been last night. But her father wouldn't see her; a busybody junior Philosopher barred her from even entering the door. Bayle was still deep in discussion with Sila, the ragged city woman, and he had left strict instructions to be disturbed by nobody—not even Enna, who had grown up in her father's shadow.

Tomm, apologetically, said he had to go get on with his work, Momo or no Momo. Distracted, Enna kissed him goodbye, and continued her search.

In the hours that followed, she walked the length and breadth of the city. She didn't find Momo. But she did learn that he wasn't the only missing person; two others had vanished, both servants. Though a few people were troubled, most seemed sure it was just a case of getting lost in a strange city. And as for the uncertain geography, she saw doubt in a few eyes. But the Philosophers, far better educated than she was, had no room in their heads for such strange and confusing notions.

Tomm went sailing over the city in his balloon, a junior pilot at his side, and she dutifully wore the red cap. Time-accelerated, he waved like a jerky puppet. But she didn't find Momo, or dispel her feeling of disquiet.

That evening, to her astonishment, her father let it be known that he was hosting a dinner—and Sila, the ragged city woman, was to be guest of honor. Enna couldn't remember her father showing such crass misjudgment before, and she wondered if he had somehow been seduced by this exotic city of the Lowland, or, worse, by the woman, Sila, of whom Enna still knew nothing at all. But still Bayle's entourage would not let her near him.

She made the best of it. She put on the finest dress in her luggage, and decorated her hair with her best jewelry, including the pretty piece her mother had given her when they bade their tearful goodbyes. But as she brushed her hair by the light of her spindling-fat lamp, the blank walls of the city building seemed to press down over her.

She clambered out to meet Tomm. He was still in his traveling clothes; he had not been invited to the dinner.

"You look wonderful," he said.

She knew he meant it, and her heart softened. "Thanks." She let him kiss her.

"Do you suppose I'm allowed to walk you over?"

"I'd like that. But, Tomm—" She glanced back at the building, the gaping unglazed windows like eye sockets. "Put my luggage back in one of our wagons. I don't care which one. I'm not spending another night in one of these boxes."

"Ah. Not even with me?"

"Not even with you. I'm sorry, Tomm."

"Don't be. As long as you let me share your wagon."

She was stunned by the sight that awaited her in her father's building. Three long trestle-tables had been set up and laid with cloths and the best cutlery and china. Candles glowed on the tables, where finely dressed guests had already taken their seats. At the head table sat Bayle himself, with his closest confidantes—and his guest of honor, Sila, dressed now in a fine flowing black robe. From a smaller building co-opted as a kitchen, a steamy smell of vegetables emanated, while five fat runner-chicks slowly roasted on spits.

Enna had grown up in a world shaped by her father's organizational skills, of which the Expedition was perhaps the crowning glory. But even she was impressed by the speed and skill with which this event had been assembled. After all the party had only reached this mysterious Lowland city a day before.

When he saw Enna, Bayle stood up and waved her forward. Led by Nool, Bayle's sleek manservant, Enna took her place at her father's right hand side. Sila sat on his left.

Enna leaned close to her father. "I've got to talk to you. I've been trying all day."

"I know you have. Priorities, my dear."

That was a word she had heard all her life. But she insisted, "Something isn't right here. People are missing. The geography—"

He looked at her, briefly concerned. "I know you're no fool, my dear, and I will hear you out. But not now. We'll make time at the end of the dinner."

She wasn't going to get any more from him. But as her father sat back, she caught the eye of the city woman, Sila. She imagined there was a calculation in Sila's deep gaze as it met her own. She wondered what Sila truly wanted—and what it would cost them all if she achieved it.

The food was good, of course; her father would have allowed nothing less, and the wine flowed voluminously, though Enna refused to touch a drop. She longed for the meal to be over, so she could talk to Bayle before another

436   STEPHEN BAXTER

night fell. At last the final dish was cleared away, the glasses refilled for the final time.

And, to Enna's intense frustration, Bayle got to his feet and began to make a speech.

He had spent the night and much of the day in conversation with Sila, he said, and a remarkable experience it had been.

Everybody had expected to find people, down here on the Lowland. For generations the judges of Foro had used "time pits" as a punishment measure. The logic was simple. The deeper you fell, the slower time passed for you. So by being hurled into the time pits you were banished to the future. Nobody had ever climbed back up. But as time had gone by rumors wafted up to the Shelf that some, at least, of the criminals of the past had survived, down there in their red-shifted prison.

"The time pits have long been stopped up," Bayle said now, "and we look back on such methods with shame. We long to discover what had become of our exiled citizens, and their offspring—and we long to reach out the hand of rationality and hope to them. Our consciences would permit nothing less.

"And now we have found those lost souls in the person of Sila. She is the daughter of an exile, whose crime was political. Sila grew up almost in isolation with her mother, her only society a drifting transient collection of refugees from many ages. And yet she is educated and articulate, with a sound moral compass; it would take very little grooming indeed for her to pass as a citizen of Foro.

"There may be no society as we know it here, no government, no community. But the inhabitants of the Lowland are not animals, but people, as we are. In her person Sila demonstrates the fundamental goodness of human nature, whatever its environment—and I for one applaud her for that."

This was greeted by murmured appreciation and bangs of the tables. Sila looked out at the Philosophers, a small smile barely dissipating the coldness of her expression.

Now Bayle came to the emotional climax of his speech.

"We all knew when we embarked from Foro that this would not just be an Expedition to the Lowland, but into time. We are all of us lost in the future, and with every day that passes here, the further that awful distance from home grows." He glanced at Enna, and she knew he was thinking of her mother, his wife, who had been too ill to travel with them on this journey—and who, as a consequence, Enna would never see again. "All of you made a sacrifice for knowledge, a sacrifice without precedent in the history of our civilization.

"But," Bayle said, "if this is a journey of no return, it need not be a journey without an end.

"Look around you! We do not yet know who built this city, and why—I have no doubt we will discover all this in the future. But we do know that *it is empty*. The sparse population of the Lowland has never found the collective will to inhabit this place. But we can turn this shell into a city—and with our industry and communal spirit, we will serve as a beacon for those who wander across the Lowland's plains. All this I have discussed at length with Sila.

"Our long journey ends here. This city, bequeathed to us by an unimaginable past, will host our future." He raised his hands; Enna had never seen him look more evangelical. "We have come home!"

He won a storm of applause. Sila surveyed the crowded room, that cold assessment dominating her expression—and again Enna was sure she could smell the cold iron stench of raw meat.

At the end of the dinner, despite her anxiety and determination, Enna still couldn't get to talk to her father. Bayle apologized, but with silent admonishments, warned her off spoiling the mood he had so carefully built; she knew that as Expedition leader he believed that morale, ever fragile, was the most precious resource of all. It will keep until the morning, his expression told her.

Frustrated, deeply uneasy, she left the building, walked out of the city to her wagon, and threw herself into Tomm's arms. He seemed surprised by her passion.

Wait until the morning. But when the morning came the city was in chaos.

They were woken by babbling voices. They hastily pulled on their clothes, and hurried out of the wagon.

Servants and Philosophers milled about, some only half-dressed. Enna found Nool, her father's manservant; disheveled, unshaven, he was nothing like the sleek major-domo of the dinner last night. "I'm not going back in there again," he said. "You can pay me what you like."

Enna grabbed his shoulders. "Nool! Calm down, man. Is it my father? Is something wrong?"

"The sooner we get loaded up and out of here the better, I say . . ."

Enna abandoned him and turned to Tomm. "We'll have to find him."

But Tomm was staring up at the sky. "By all that's created," he said. "Look at that."

At first she thought the shape drifting in the sky was the Expedition's balloon. But this angular, sharp-edged, white-walled object was no balloon. It was a building, a parallelepiped. With no signs of doors or windows, it had come loose of the ground, and drifted away on the wind like a soap bubble.

"I don't believe it," Tomm murmured.

Enna said grimly, "Right now we don't have time. Come on." She grabbed his hand and dragged him into the city.

The unmade streets were crowded today, and people swarmed; it was difficult to find a way through. And again she had that strange, dreamlike feeling that the layout of the city was different. "Tell me you see it too, cartographer," she demanded of Tomm. "It has changed, again."

"Yes, it has changed."

She was relieved to see her father's building was still where it had been. But Philosophers were milling about, helpless, wringing their hands.

The doors and windows, all of them, had sealed up. There was no way into the building, or out.

She shoved her way through the crowd, grabbing Philosophers. "Where is he? Is he in there?" But none of them had an answer. She reached the building itself. She ran her hands over the wall where the door had been last night, but it was seamless, as if the door had never existed. She slammed on the wall. "Father? Bayle! Can you hear me? It's Enna!" But there was no reply.

And then the wall lurched before her. Tomm snatched her back. The whole building was shifting, she saw, as if restless to come loose of the ground.

When it settled she began to batter the wall again.

"He can't hear you." The woman, Sila, stood in the fine robes Bayle had given her. She seemed aloof, untouched.

Enna grabbed Sila by the shoulders and pushed her against the wall of the building. "What have you done?"

"Me? I haven't done anything." Sila was unperturbed by Enna's violence, though she was breathing hard. "But you know that, don't you?" Her voice was deep, exotic—ancient as Lowland dust.

Desperate as Enna was to find her father, the pieces of the puzzle were sliding around in her head. *"This is all about the buildings*, isn't it?"

"You're a clever girl. Your father will be proud—or would have been. He's probably already dead. Don't fret; he won't have suffered, much."

Tomm stood before them, uncertain. "I don't understand any of this. Has this woman harmed Bayle?"

"No," Enna hissed. "You just lured him here—didn't you, you witch? It's the building, Tomm. That's what's important here, not this woman."

"The building?"

"The buildings take meat," Sila said. "Somehow they use it to maintain their fabric. Don't ask me how."

Tomm asked, "Meat?"

"And light," Enna said. "That's why they stack up into this strange reef, isn't it? It isn't a human architecture at all, is it? *The buildings are competing for the light.*"

Sila smiled. "You see, I said you were clever."

"The light?"

"Oh, Tomm, don't just repeat everything we say! He's in there. My father. And we've got to get him out."

Tomm was obviously bewildered. "If you say so. How?"

She thought fast. Buildings that take meat. Buildings that need light . . . "The balloon," she said. "Get some servants."

"It will take an age for the heaters—"

"Just bring the envelope. Hurry, Tomm!"

Tomm rushed off.

Enna went back to the building and continued to slam her hand against the wall. "I'll get you out of there, father. Hold on!" But there was no reply. And again the building shifted ominously, its base scraping over the ground. She glanced into the sky, where that flying building had already become a speck against the blueshifted stars. If they fed, if they had the light they needed, did the buildings simply float away in search of new prey? Was that what had become of poor Momo?

Tomm returned with the balloon envelope, manhandled by a dozen bearers.

"Get it over the building," Enna ordered. "Block out the light. Hurry. Oh, please . . ."

All of them hauled at the balloon envelope, dragging it over the building. The envelope ripped on the sharp corners of the building, but Enna ignored wails of protest from the Philosophers. At last the thick hide envelope covered the building from top to bottom; it was like a wrapped-up present. She stood back, breathing hard, her hands stinking of leather. She had no idea what to do next if this didn't work.

A door dilated open in the side of the building. Fumes billowed out, hot and yellow, and people recoiled, coughing and pressing their eyes. Then Bayle came staggering out of the building, and collapsed to the ground.

"Father!" Enna got to the ground and took his head on her lap.

His clothes were shredded, his hands were folded up like claws, and the skin of his face was crimson. But he was alive. "It was an acid bath in there," he wheezed. "Another few moments and I would have succumbed. It was like being swallowed. Digested."

"I know," she said.

He looked up; his eyes had been spared the acid. "You understand?"

"I think so. Father, we have to let the doctors see to you."

"Yes, yes . . . But first, get everybody out of this cursed place."

Enna glanced up at Tomm, who turned away and began to shout commands.

"And," wheezed Bayle, "where is that woman, Sila?"

There was a waft of acid-laden air, a ripping noise. Philosophers scrambled back out of the way. Cradling her father, Enna saw that the building had shaken off the balloon envelope and was lifting grandly into the air.

Sila sat in an open doorway, looking down impassively, as the building lifted her into the time-accelerated sky.

Bayle was taken to his wagon, where his wounds were treated. He allowed in nobody but his daughter, the doctors, Nool—and Tomm, who he said had acquitted himself well.

Even in this straitened circumstance Bayle held forth, his voice reduced to a whisper, his face swathed in unguent cream. "I blame myself," he said. "I let myself see what I wanted to see about this city—just as I pompously warned you, Tomm, against the self-same flaw. And I refused to listen to you, Enna. I wanted to see a haven for the people I have led out into the wilderness. I saw what did not exist."

"You saw what Sila wanted you to see," Enna said.

"Ah, Sila . . . What an enigma! But the fault is mine, Enna; you won't talk me out of that."

"And the buildings—"

"I should have seen the pattern before you! After all we have a precedent. The Weapons are technology gone wild, made things modified by time—and so are the buildings of this 'city.'"

Once, surely, the buildings had been intended to house people. But they were advanced technology: mobile, self-maintaining. They fuelled themselves with light, and with organic traces—perhaps they had been designed to process their occupants' waste.

Things changed. People abandoned the buildings, and forgot about them. But the buildings, self-maintaining, perhaps even self-aware in some rudimentary sense, sought a new way to live—and that way diverged ever more greatly from the purposes their human inventors had imagined.

"They came together for protection," Bayle whispered. "They huddled together in reefs that look like towns, cities, jostling for light. And then they discovered a new strategy, when the first ragged human beings innocently entered their doorways."

The buildings apparently offered shelter. And when a human was foolish enough to accept that mute offer—

"They feed," said Tomm with horror.

Bayle said, "It is just as the wild Weapons once learned to farm humans for meat. We have seen this before. We share a world with technology that has gone wild and undergone its own evolution. I should have known!"

Enna said, "And Sila?"

"Now she is more interesting," Bayle whispered. "She told me exactly what I wanted to hear—fool as I was to listen! She cooperates with the city, you see; in return for shelter—perhaps even for some grisly form of food—she helps it lure in unwitting travelers, like us. Her presence makes it seem safer than a city empty altogether."

"A symbiosis," Tomm said, wondering. "Of human with wild technology."

Enna shuddered. "We have had a narrow escape."

Bayle covered her hand with his own bandaged fingers. "But others, like poor Momo, have died for my foolishness."

"We must go on," Tomm said. "There is nothing for us here."

"Nothing but a warning. Yes, we will go on. The Expedition continues! But not forever. Someday we will find a home—"

"Or we will build one," Tomm said firmly.

Bayle nodded stiffly. "Yes. But that's for you youngsters, not for the likes of me."

Enna was moved to take Tomm's hand in hers.

Bayle watched them. "He may not have a first-class mind," he said to Enna. "But he has an air of command, and that's worth cultivating."

"Oh, father—"

Outside the wagon there came shouting, and a rushing sound, like great breaths being drawn.

"Go and see," Bayle whispered.

Enna and Bayle rushed out of the wagon.

Displacing air that washed over the people, the sentient buildings of the city were lifting off the ground, massive, mobile. Already the first of them was high in the blueshifted sky, and the others followed in a stream of silent geometry, buildings blowing away like seeds on the breeze . . . ends.

Heisenberg Elementary

WIL McCARTHY

Wil McCarthy (www.wilmccarthy.com) *lives in Lakewood, Colorado. He writes the science column, Lab Notes, for SciFi.com. He writes hard SF, characteristically, and his stories appear regularly in the SF magazines. He has published nine novels to date, the most recent of which is* To Crush the Moon *(2005). He says at his website, "Wil McCarthy is a writer of science fiction and science fact, when he's not launching rockets, designing satellite constellations, or building robots for the aerospace industry. His goal in writing is to find the edge that balances action and depth, entertainment and enlightenment, science and fiction. He is particularly interested in stories which, however outlandish, could actually happen."*

"Heisenberg Elementary" appeared in Asimov's. *It is a wild story of what is happening now and in the future in elementary school, today in the USA a cauldron of kids cooking in a stew of educational theories and standardized testing, but tomorrow, the new weird, virtually and literally. "Real education costs real money," Miss Solarabad says cryptically, "but by measuring the outcome we can change it at the elementary level." Then the Chronarchists show up. Is this a parody of No Child Left Behind? We think so.*

"**N**ine Nine Two!" shouts JimmyTim Exxon in the middle of literacy block. "Five Eight! Four Nine Nine One Seven!" Everyone looks up at the clock but otherwise ignores him. That's his social security number, and everyone knows it by heart already. After hearing it every fifteen minutes all week long, we're not even giggling anymore.

"Let's talk about ticware," Miss Solarbad had said on Monday morning, "and the various ways to avoid infection." Yeah, yeah, don't lick the flag pole don't inload from strangers don't execute neurops no matter what survival traits they seem to offer. Like everyone doesn't know JimmyDim caught the bug at school, from a badly formatted toilet seat. And the week has only gone downhill from there.

Literacy block is a hundred hours long. Fortunately, it takes place in a virtual universe, with minimal leakage. Boy, I feel sorry for that me! Our time, our real time, is spent taking standardized tests, like always.

"Real education costs real money," Miss Solarbad says cryptically. "But by measuring the outcome we can change it at the elementary level. When every chair contains a thousand children, the statistics are universal."

They're just getting ready to blow lunch in through the vents—I catch a whiff of hot dog vapor—when the Chronarchists show up again.

"Again?" says their sergeant recluse. "What do you mean again?"

445

"You've been here five times today and it's barely lunch," answers Miss Solarbad.

"Oh," he says unhappily. "Great. Would you hit me with a chair to break the loop? Please?"

Guardedly: "That depends why you're here."

"Can't say, ma'am. Prime directive."

But I'm tired of this loop, so I hit the sergeant recluse myself.

"Thanks, kid," he says, his hair shifting color from blond to brown. His voice is lower, too. Then it's down to business: he and his three priwates form a circle around Pammy TransAm, line up their funguns and turn her Happy. Ouch. That smile's got to hurt.

"Sorry ma'am," says the sergeant recluse to a frowning Miss Solarbad. "We find it's the best way to neutralize inconvenient people."

"You always say that."

"Actually, ma'am, we never always said that until just now. The changes are retroactive."

"What changes? Who are you?"

"Chronarchists, ma'am. Just liberating the timeline."

Miss Solarbad frowns. "From a happy girl like Pammy TransAm? Why on Earth? Who was she going to be?"

"President of Bitchtopia, ma'am. Very destabilizing. Now she's Union of Unconcerned Citizens."

"Oh," says Miss Solarbad. "Well, uh. Thanks?"

"All in a day's work, ma'am," he says, and ceases to ever have existed. Brother!

Finally we get to breathe lunch, and after that a whiff of playground dust and fresh-cut grass. Then it's back to the CSAPSAT for another four hours.

"Don't bias the statistics," Miss Solarbad reminds us sternly. "Don't think about your answers."

Pretty soon the Chronarchists are back. This time they give Pammy a speech impediment, which her extreme happiness causes her to see as a positive growth experience.

"Tank oo vey much!" she says brightly.

"Unconcerned Citizens my foot," mutters the sergeant recluse before ceasing to ever have existed again.

Finally, finally, the school day is over and I can go play. Unfortunately my parents can't afford point-to-point, so of course I have to tunnel home as a quantum waveform, which is like completely unfair. And of course Mom is waiting for me at the collapse point, looking shrewish. Don't you love that word, shrewish?

"Your waveform shows a peak at the arcade again," says Mom.

"It's on the way," I remind her.

"It's on all possible ways," she says, like that's the end of that.

"Give me a break," I try, putting on a mature voice so she'll maybe listen for once. "It's only a ten percent presence. I didn't even experience it at a Newtonian level."

But I get dish duty anyway, followed by more homework than there are hours to complete it. School doesn't care about the problems of working families; Mom and Dad can't afford a time compactor, so what am I supposed to do? I settle for an optic cram and dump, which utterly makes me ill, then wind down by kicking a virball around the page for half an hour in five parallel muscle groups. I think about inloading a season of TV, but I'm just too tired. I crawl into bed, utterly defeated.

There is of course something wrong with my pillow. All my dreams are in blue, and the audio is laggy. It figures.

In the morning, Mom and Dad and Janey have run the helium chiller dry, so I'm forced to superconduct in liquid nitrogen, like that's going to decohere. If they actually loved me they'd turn the dial down, and never mind the trillion bucks. But noooo. I hate my life.

Outside, the weather is cold and rainy. Yuck. My waveform clusters under trees and awnings, collapsing only reluctantly into homeroom.

The Chronarchists of course are already there, playing some kind of scanner thing over Pammy TransAm.

"Highly effective in the third degree," says the sergeant recluse. "I was afraid of that. No amount of change is going to stop this girl. There's only one thing for it."

The priwates all nod solemnly, pulling a uniform out of nowhere and holding it up against Pammy, who like instantly has always been wearing it.

"We're at your disposal, Kernel," says the sergeant recluse in a fawning kind of way.

"Let's get out of here," she says in the voice of a much older woman. "Far future lookback, full temprum. This line's not going to liberate itself."

I stick my hand up. "Pammy? Can I come, too?"

The Chronarchists turn, noticing me for the first time. The sergeant recluse holds out his scanner, whoob whoob whoob, and lights up with surprise.

"Kernel, this is BennyJam Wheelrut, the lingerie designer!"

"It is? Oh, yeah," says Pammy wistfully. Don't you love that word, wistfully? "I went to Heisenberg with him when we were kids." She turns to me. "Benny, people are like totally wrapped around your work. They love it. They'll edit me right out of the timeline if I so much as speak—"

Oops. I get the feeling there were Chronarchists here or something, but Mom says I've got to stop daydreaming in class.

"Today we'll be taking a standardized test," Miss Solarbad announces.

And then suddenly there are three Chronarchists in the room, looking dark and blurry and scared.

"Ignore us," implores the sergeant recluse. "Go on about your business."

Which is a strange thing to say, because they've been standing right there for as long as I can remember. But then—finally!—the Time Patrol shows up with funguns blazing, and for once school is, like, actually interesting.

Rwanda

ROBERT REED

Robert Reed [info site: www.starbaseandromeda.com/reed.
html*] lives in Lincoln, Nebraska, and constitutes all by himself a Nebraska renaissance in SF. He has been one of the
most prolific short story writers of high quality in the SF
field for the past sixteen years, with more than 140 SF, fantasy, and horror stories published, and seems capable of
any excellence. He has had eleven novels published, starting
with* The Leeshore *(1987) and most recently with* The Well
of Stars *(2004). His story collections,* The Dragons of
Springplace *(1999) and* The Cuckoo's Boys *(2005), skim
only some of the cream from his body of work. He has had
stories appear in at least one of the annual "Year's Best"
anthologies in every year since 1992.*

"Rwanda" was published in Asimov's. *A young boy brings
a cicada to his father to ask him about it, in a near future
where an invading alien virus has wiped the minds of much
of humanity, replacing them with alien consciousnesses, but
only partially destroys civilization. It is a story of character
and of terrible revelation. It is a horror story about being
transformed by disaster, a political allegory, and an interesting comparison to the Michael Flynn story, earlier in this
book.*

Beneath a mangled pine tree, you find the empty shell of a cicada, crystalline and robotic and very lovely. And beside that shell lies something even better—a bug, fat and pale and large enough to halfway fill the palm of your tiny hand. Is the bug alive? Apparently so. It doesn't breathe as you breathe, nor can those dark buggy eyes blink or wink or convey any sense of emotion. But the creature is soft and wet, and its limbs seem to move slowly in response to your little prods. A pair of wings extends from the long back, but they are shriveled and plainly useless, and your first inclination is to guess that the creature you are holding has been poisoned or burned in some horrific, wondrous fashion.

Your father sits on the patio drinking beer. Many elements go into your calculations. What time of day is it? How many cans are stacked near his bare feet? By his posture, can you read his mood, and if so, does it look as if he can endure one of your questions, and after that, maybe twenty more?

The day is still early, not even noon yet, and only three spent cans are set on the concrete slab. After you stare at him for a few moments, he notices, and something that might be a smile surfaces, followed by a clear voice asking, "What is it?"

You go to him, showing him your treasure.

He seems puzzled, but only for a moment. Then he asks, "Did you find its exoskeleton?"

That is an enormous word, but you hear a word inside it that you know. Nodding, you tell him about the cicada shell. Does he want to see that too?

"No need."

You offer the creature to him.

He acts tempted. But then some controlling urge causes him to shake his head, and he surprises you. He doesn't say, "Take it back where you found it." He doesn't say, "You should never have disturbed it." Instead, he smiles again, more warmly this time, and climbing up from the iron chair, he says, "Let's both take this fellow back. Where were you? Under the tree over there?"

The world is vast and jammed full of mysteries and things that aren't mysterious to anyone but you. If there is a smarter man than your father, you have not met him. He has books enough to cover walls and other books that come to him on the computer screen, during those hours when there is power. If he doesn't read much, it is because long ago he consumed and digested the contents of his library. And if he doesn't remember everything that he has read, at least he can go to the proper shelf and open one or two or ten books, finding an answer that will satisfy him, if not quite you.

"Nice," he says, sitting under the tree with you. Then he pops open another beer. You smell it and you can smell him. This is Friday, and there will be hot water tomorrow, at least for a few hours. Then both of you will wash up, the smell of soap defeating the other stinks for a while.

The ground is bare beneath the pine tree, except for the dead needles and some little marks made by your various sticks. In the soft tan earth, you recently drew the outline of a very simple house. Your father examines your drawing for a long moment. He sips his warm beer. He watches the big bug resting on the ground beside the tree trunk, and he stares off at nothing for a long while, finishing the can and nodding at nothing. Then without quite looking at you, he asks, "How old are you?"

He knows your age. Of course he does. But adults like to ask little questions where the answer is common knowledge.

It is not so much a test as it is a means of pointing something out to children.

You recite your age.

And he nods in response, saying what he meant to say at the beginning. "You are old enough."

Old enough for what? You have no clue what he means.

"Look at that house," he tells you.

He doesn't mean the house you drew. He points across the long yard. Only recently you came to realize that this particular tree doesn't stand on your property. Father cuts both of the yards when the grass grows shaggy. But somewhere in the green middle is a line that divides what is yours from what belongs to that other house.

The house is empty. Along your street are several more just as empty, and on the street behind yours are more houses like this one. Everywhere you go in the city, vacant homes sit in shaggy lawns, weeds growing up from the cracks in their sidewalks and driveways.

"Are you looking at it?"

It is very much like your house, except bigger. The shades are down and a thick layer of grime shows on the glass. It has been your impression that no one wants you to look in those windows. But you have done it often enough to have a clear image about what is inside. Dusty furniture and darkness are inside, at least on the ground floor. And silence. And, at least for you, mysteries.

"Think of this exoskeleton," your father tells you.

Surprised, you blink and stare at the delicate empty and exceptionally fragile shell of the cicada.

"The skeleton is something like that house. It used to be a home, but now it has been left behind."

The idea sounds familiar, and then it doesn't. You aren't certain what you are hearing in these words, but more than puzzled, you are worried—your heart quickening and a tightness building in the back of your throat.

"And this pupa," your father says. "Look at it now."

The bug's wings seem to have grown larger in the last minutes. But the body is still soft and colorless, and, by all measures, exceptionally helpless.

"Biology," he says.

That single word sounds ominous and very sad.

"Genetics," he says.

Again, you want to shiver, though you can't decide why.

"What if people were the same as this insect?" he asks. Then before you can make a sound, much less offer a weak answer, he adds, "What if they lived as one thing for a very long time, and then they passed through a sudden transformation, coming out the other side to discover that they weren't people anymore?"

All you can do is nod, your stomach pulling itself into a stubborn knot.

"What we believe happened . . . our best guess derived from hard evidence and quite a lot of informed conjecture . . . is that somebody wanted to colonize the Earth." Your father shakes his head and grins, as if astonished by his own words. "Aliens, I mean. Extraterrestrials. Creatures that must have been similar to humans, both in body and in their ecological niche. They must have sent out robotic probes, probably in the remote past, and sometime after they discovered our world, the aliens mounted a second expedition that brought their colonists here."

You think of the proud rockets in his books and the flashy, muscular starships in the old comics that you read.

But he doesn't let you think about starships for long. "Space is huge," he warns. "The distances are too great to imagine, and even a tiny payload is very difficult to move from sun to sun. And every voyage, even with the best engines, will take centuries, in not many, many thousands of years."

He asks, "How can you colonize a distant world for a cheap, reasonable price?"

Then he shakes his head, answering his own question. "There is no reasonable price, of course. That's the point I'm making here."

You try hard, but you cannot follow his logic.

"No reasonable price," he repeats, "yet there is a relatively cheap method to conquer a new world. Imagine that you can shrink each your brave colonists down to where they are smaller than ants. Shrivel them down to the size of dust mites, say. All the information necessary to replicate each of them is contained inside one of these tiny storage devices, and for the sake of argument, let's say there are millions of them onboard the colony ship. How big would that starship have to be, do you think?"

No guess is correct.

Your father grins, warning you, "You know, your bed has millions of dust mites. They live on it and inside it, on the sheets and blankets and pillow cases."

He says, "Hundreds of millions of colonists could ride inside a vessel no bigger than this."

The empty beer can, he means.

"When you read history, you'll see. You'll see. The successful colonists are those who travel light and make what they need when they arrive." He crushes his can and sets it beside the half-born cicada. "The invaders came with the tools necessary to build new homes for themselves. And by homes, I mean bodies. Familiar, workable bodies holding brains large enough to contain all of their memories and thoughts and desires. That's what their robot probes had found in the first expedition, we think. I think. Not just a living world, but they found a world offering a common species that could be claimed for their own important selves.

"Human beings, I mean.

"Of course."

Your father pauses for a long, long while.

Then softly, sadly, he describes how the tiny starship would strike the Earth and rip apart, scattering its dusty contents across the high dry stratosphere. The colonists could drift undetected, perhaps for many years, riding the cold winds until they were everywhere. Then they would dive into the lower atmosphere, latching rides on raindrops and downdrafts, descending onto the innocent humans who were going about their own little lives.

A mite-sized colonist would enter its host through the lungs or stomach, and in short order, ride the bloodstream up to the brain.

The only symptoms were a mild fever and odd aches, and sometimes, a harmless red rash. And then after a few days, the sick human would drift into a deep sleep that would last until his mind had been rewritten and reborn.

But the new colony had one considerable weakness. When the first expedition examined the Earth, there were barely one hundred million humans. The aliens assumed that the population would grow, but no more than five-fold, which was why only half a billion colonists made the long journey.

"The invaders had no choice but to be less than 10 percent of the population," your father explains. "Instead of dominating their new world, they were a minority, and not a well-received minority, as it happened. . . ."

The cicada's wings are even larger now.

He says, "The natural first conclusion was that some horrible new disease was running wild. The disease would leave its victims confused and possibly brain damaged. Which explained why those poor people spoke nonsense after they woke. And why they were clumsy at first, walking with the same slow, careful shuffle. And that also gave a reason why they didn't seem to recognize friends and family. They had suffered a profound neurological shock. As a precaution, the first couple million victims were quarantined inside hospitals and public buildings, and doctors worked for days to find the virus or bacteria responsible. But there was nothing to find, since of course this was no simple disease. And then teams of specialists, in Atlanta and in Switzerland, noticed that their patients were speaking the same precise gibberish, and the patients seemed to understand what was being said."

He shakes his head for a moment. "More people were falling ill every day," he explains. "Two million victims quickly became twenty million, and there weren't enough hospital beds for everyone. People tried to cope with shuffling, muttering spouses. Or babbling children. And then after a few days of rest and practice, the supposedly sick people would suddenly leave their homes, meeting at predetermined places where they could discuss their circumstances and make plans.

"For a while, nothing made sense.

"For two weeks, the public was terrified but ignorant. The rate of infection continued to rise, and rise. No one was sure how many people would eventually catch the soul-robbing disease. And then suddenly, on the fifteenth day, the truth was learned."

Your father takes a deep breath and holds it, and then he exhales, admitting, "Everybody knew somebody who had died. Everybody had a neighbor or loved one who had been replaced by some kind of creature that was nothing like the dead soul. Linguists had deciphered the new language, and with the help of military interrogators, they held their first and only interviews with the aliens.

"'We just wanted a place to live,' the invaders said. 'Please, give us a chance to make up for this,' they begged. 'We can live with you and be good neighbors. We can offer you technological wonders, for free, and within a few years, your world will be wealthy beyond your most optimistic dreams.'

"That's what they claimed, speaking to the specialists with their new mouths. Residing inside the bodies they had stolen from their rightful owners.

"Which leads to the obvious question: how can you trust a creature that has so willingly and easily killed the mind of a helpless host?"

Again, your father needs a deep breath.

"The decision was inevitable," he says. "And by necessity, the work had to be completed quickly, with whatever tools were on hand."

You say nothing, finding yourself staring off at the empty house.

"The call for action came from everywhere," your father tells you with a hard sorry voice. "It came from the government, and it came from important individuals in the media. And every neighborhood had some loud demanding voice that explained what was necessary now. A cleansing. A purge. And since the disease rate was still accelerating, and since anybody with a mild fever or a slight red rash could be infected, thus dangerous . . . well, it was impossible to be generous or patient, and very quickly, kindness was forgotten entirely."

He lowers his face.

"Suppose," he says. "Suppose somebody in your family was sick, but you couldn't accept her fate. Because people got the flu all the time, and you had to let the disease run its course, if you were going to be sure one way or the other. But then, what if your neighbors heard that she was sick and came to deliver the cure? You told the others to leave or you would fight with them. Because she was your wife and your only true love. You weren't ready to give up hope yet. You promised that you would watch over her for now, and you told them that you had a gun, even when you didn't. But then they broke down the front door and pushed their way upstairs to the bedroom. Your neighbors, they were. Friends for years, in some cases. And you were reduced to screaming insults and promising revenge for what they were doing with their shotguns and garden shovels . . . !"

You aren't looking at the empty house now.

Instead you stare at your own home, and in particular, the upstairs window that always has its shade pulled closed. A room that you have never been inside, not even once.

"Ten percent," says your father.

Then he almost seems to laugh with a bitter, acidic tone. "The world can surrender 10 percent of its population and not miss a beat. Or nearly so. But nothing that swift or large can ever be that simple and clean. I mean, what happens when rumors start? When one authority figure stands before a news camera, mentioning in passing, 'We're worried about aliens hiding, drifting inside unsuspecting hosts.' Not that there was evidence of that happening. There has never been. The mite-sized bodies had drifted to the ground together, and those that hadn't found hosts were soon destroyed by free oxygen and simple erosion. But if you have already invested the last week of your life killing these invaders, then it is natural to be cautious. It is perfectly understandable if you want to take care of those who might be a problem at some later date."

You stare at the maturing cicada.

"And of course, the aliens fought back. Not in an organized fashion or with much effect . . . but they did manage
to kill three or four humans for every ten of them who
perished . . . which means millions more were dead, and
those who weren't felt even angrier and more desperate. . . ."

The cicada kicks its jointed legs, and the swelling wings
begin to tremble, as if eager to fly away.

"And then," your father says. His mouth is open but he
pauses for a moment before asking again, "What if you were
a person for a very long time, and then suddenly you passed
through some enormous event, and on the other side you
discovered that you weren't really human anymore?"

What does he mean by that?

"In history," he says, "this metamorphosis happens with
numbing regularity. The Holocaust. Cambodia. And Rwanda,
to name three."

Three what?

"There are many good reasons to murder," he assures you.

Then he looks toward the empty house, explaining, "She
had a light fever and a bit of a sunburn, and that's all she had.
But they killed her anyway. Hacked her body to pieces and
left the pieces in our bed. And then a couple weeks later,
when the death rate was approaching 50 percent, some de-
spairing soul pried open the back door of that house over
there and knifed two people to death." Then he looks at you,
and with the mildest voice, he says, "Don't believe what you
hear. Revenge really can help heal the deepest hurts."

You say nothing.

With a finger and thumb, your father picks up the almost-
born cicada, and he stands, placing it on the highest branch
that he can reach.

Then he looks down at you. "And even the angriest inhuman soul can be kind," he says. "Even splattered with blood,
he can do something that is right and good. Do you know
what I mean? Two people are dead in their own bed, and
between them lies a baby . . . and for all the evils walking
free in the world, one good impulse can save that child's
very little life. . . ."

Preemption

CHARLIE ROSENKRANTZ

Charlie Rosenkrantz (www.othersideofchristmas.com) *lives in Los Angeles. He says, "I grew up in rural Maryland under dark skies and built my first telescope, a 6 inch F8 reflector (almost as large as myself) when I was 12. We soon moved to the Washington DC suburbs, and my dark skies vanished, though I maintained a strong interest in astronomy and the sciences, as well as science fiction." And "I've owned businesses in several far-flung fields over the years, from art to satellite TV installation to real estate development, and have worked for others in the fields of bank loan servicing and construction estimating. A children's Christmas poem that I wrote, entitled 'The Other Side of Christmas,' was published in a number of newspapers around the country several years ago."*

"Preemption" was published in Analog *and it is his first publication. "I was inspired to start submitting my sf work by the Writers of the Future Contest, and received generous advice from two of the contest judges, Tim Powers and Larry Niven." Here is a story in a very old SF tradition, with all the details wonderfully transformed. Suddenly alien mercenaries invade to make a preemptive strike against the future threat of Earth to the races of the galaxy. The answer is funny enough to convince us to make this story the last in the book this year.*

One brilliant April morning, the red-eye flight of a Boeing 757 was on its final approach to Houston International from Las Vegas when a portion of its underbelly disintegrated. The resultant shock wave and missing hull section caused it to make prepunctual contact with the Earth's unforgiving surface, just short of the runway.

Three miles south-southwest, a local who was barely finished coughing into his cell phone at his boss, feigning the flu, was driving two buddies and his dog, Spartacus, to a Monster Truck Pull Rally when his SUV was vaporized. In the front, only the radiator and items forward of it remained. In the rear, only a foot and a half section of glossy red metal and sparkling chrome survived, along with one third of the gas tank. The remaining gasoline erupted as it was blown backwards, setting fire to a barbershop and incinerating a smiling cardboard cutout of the mayor—an indisputably self-described man of the people, who was locked in a vicious bid for re-election.

Just to the north, a traveling circus—currently not in the act of traveling—lost one of its larger trailers as an eight-foot spherical section of its center magically disappeared. The two ends of the trailer were blown in opposite directions, destroying a couple of valuable midway tents, but in this instance no fires materialized.

In the center of town, a pet psychic was in the process of describing the profound sense of loss and self-loathing associated with a case of overly compulsive scratching (and preparing to collect her fee) when she and her divination vacated the Earthly plane. The eight-foot spherical zone of sublimation—where solids transformed instantly into gas—also made a casualty of the neighbor's chandelier in the apartment below. Though nearby windows were blown out, the majority of the heat and force of the disintegration inexplicably vanished along with the seer.

Panic erupted as hundreds of similar incidents occurred throughout the greater Houston area in rapid succession. But the panic was not limited to Houston, or to the great state of Texas, for that matter. This was also happening in every other state—and in every nation on Earth.

The men on either arm were half carrying Andrew Harrison as they flew through the tunnels. Eventually they made it to the end. Over the sound of the internal pile driver hammering blood past his ears, he heard the steel door thud into place, felt the vibration underfoot.

"You nearly pulled my arm out of its socket," he said with a scowl to the one on his left.

"I'm sorry, Mr. President. I'll be more careful next time."

"Next time? Write yourself a directive: there will never be a next time." He looked around. The bunker was spacious but nonetheless felt cramped, as if he had just been banished to a hovel in someone's back yard next to their garage. Never had accommodations costing so many taxpayers so much felt so subhuman, so second-class. He marched over to another Secret Service man, this one seated at the conference table in front of a computer, pecking at the keyboard with his right hand while talking into his left sleeve.

"What the hell's going on?"

"We don't know, Mr. President. Some type of high tech assault. Explosions or disintegrations or . . . we don't know what they are, but they're happening all across the country."

"What are you talking about, 'all across the country'?"

"Everywhere, sir. Thousands of them. So many we can't even count. Reports coming in from every city in the U.S."

"My God." His knees, like a pair of garden hoses with their water source cut off, were useless. He slumped into a chair. In the last few minutes of chaos he had only been told of unexplained explosions in D.C., including one on the sidewalk in front of the White House.

"Who's doing it?"

"We don't have a clue, sir."

"Get Swick down here immediately. And locate the directors of the CIA and FBI." He switched seats and grabbed a phone. "This is Harrison. Get me McNab. Now."

The Secretary of Defense came on the line. "Andy, are you okay?"

"What's going on?" he demanded, ignoring pleasantries. "Who's attacking us?"

The first reply he received was silence.

The second reply he received was, "We have absolutely no idea."

"What? Is that the best you can do?"

"Andy, look. We've got several thousand people on this. And people from every other agency that might be of any help. So far . . . zip. People and buildings everywhere are being destroyed, and there's not the slightest sign as to how or why."

"Unacceptable. I want answers. Who has the capability to do something like this?"

Again, silence.

"No one. This is far in advance of anything we ever thought possible."

Harrison's hands felt cold even as his neck grew hotter. He felt the impulse growing to insult his long-term friend— to start yelling to relieve the pain choking his thoughts. But he didn't get the chance.

"Wait a minute, Andy. We're getting some data. Hold on."

When Secretary of Defense McNab came back on the line, his voice was shaky. "Mr. President," he began. Formal. That wasn't good. "NASA and Air Defense both confirm the appearance of a number of unidentified objects encircling the Earth."

Realizing the incomprehensible must now somehow be comprehended, Harrison slumped forward, a frozen image of pure helplessness. The facts trickled in: Estimated altitude of enemy vessels, 800 miles; seventeen located so far; out of range for retaliatory action; destruction occurring with spherical areas being vaporized; diameters of kill zones estimated from eight to fifty feet; similar reports from other nations; methodology unknown; attacks already suspected to be in the hundreds of thousands, possibly millions; no pattern or reasoning evident; cities, towns and communities everywhere in chaos.

The phone seemed to increase in mass, becoming a burden to hold. His strength had been sucked away along with his ability to think. His impulse never to give in, never to back down from a fight, was annihilated. Through a numb stupor, he envisioned the end of his own life, the end of his family, and that of humanity. His Defense Secretary, dismayed and helpless, asked if he had any suggestions—again not what he wanted to hear.

He said nothing. All he could do was wonder how to say, "We surrender," in whatever alien tongue the attackers spoke, if indeed they spoke any language at all.

The FBI Director had been injured; she had been hit with flying glass from an attack. The CIA Director, having called in sick, thereby extending his vacation at his second home in Easton, Maryland, across the Chesapeake, had not been heard from since the attacks began. Two CIA analysts, Kimmells and Blix, were poring over reports on their laptops, directing occasional nervous glances toward the President. He eyed them suspiciously. They should be trustworthy: they were career analysts, but he was paranoid at the moment. The people around him weren't giving him answers, and giving him answers was the primary job of the people around him. They should all know this by now.

Additionally, emergency talks with other world leaders had been as helpful as a chat with an IRS telephone information center. The Russians, the Chinese, and various NATO leaders could do little but confirm they were enduring the same fate. They all agreed to stand firm against the aggression, not give an inch. Useless posturing.

He looked to his right. "I've got to get on the air and say

something. Something to calm and reassure them. They expect leadership, deserve it, demand it. If we survive this, if we don't all get fried, they'll just turn around and roast me at the polls next November."

His ashen speechwriter nodded and gazed at an empty note pad. Three TV screens high on the wall gave flickering images—endless reports of major amounts of minor destruction on all continents. On one station, the citizenry was being interviewed. One woman said, "It's like way totally unfair. We didn't do anything to anybody and they're totally bombing us. Are we supposed to like . . . hide or something? I'd be way pissed off if I weren't so totally freaked. What do I do now?"

Others being interviewed were equally confused and unenlightened.

"It just doesn't make any sense, sir," came a voice from across the table. Bernard Swick, National Security Advisor, was visibly shaken. His chin quivered; his jowls wagged. "Their technology is so far advanced we can't even remotely determine how it works and don't have the slightest clue as to what it is. There's no detectable beam or energy transmission. They could easily have wiped us out by now. But the attacks are completely random. Not on our key infrastructure, defense, or high technology. Mostly civilian. Totally chaotic. There's no logic to it at all."

"Unless they want to create terror before eliminating us. Unless they have some other motivation. Unless. Unless. You and the Secretary of Defense need to determine what they're doing and how they're doing it. Immediately. Find any weakness to exploit. Whatever their plan is, I expect you to stop it. Understood?"

"Yes sir." Swick got up to leave, at which point the Secret Service refused to open the blast door until the President turned around and barked at them to let him out.

Harrison grasped at a frenzied dust devil of random thoughts, trying to hold each of them still where he could look at them. At least his wife, Brittany, and the two kids were safe. At least for now. They were in another bunker— an Uncle Sam cave with all the amenities. But what did the supposed illogic behind these attacks mean? What did any of it mean?

He went over and sat across from the CIA analysts. "What patterns are there to the attacks? There's got to be something."

Kimmells pursed his lips, thinking about this, as if there were time for idle pondering. "Well, Mr. President, I can't say there's a pattern to whom they're attacking, but we have been able to deduce a couple things."

"Which may be mostly irrelevant," said Blix.

"Yes, but not entirely irrelevant," said Kimmells.

"That's true," said Blix.

Kimmells looked to his left. "Stop interrupting. You're distracting me."

Blix clamped his mouth shut and stared defiantly at the wall.

"You see, Mr. President, most of the attacks have been on the surface. Houses, cars, parks, apartment buildings. The zone of annihilation is always spherical. And normally eight feet or so in diameter."

"But not always," said Blix.

Kimmells shot him a look. Blix returned to his computer.

"Some of these spherical zones are larger. A few. But below ground they're all larger. All reports of attacks on basements, root cellars, and the like have had kill zones of twenty feet or more. And depth seems to be significant. For example, there was an attack on an office building over on K Street, one level below ground, twenty feet in diameter. A few minutes later, on the other side of that same building, an attack two levels down, twenty-eight feet in diameter. Sad, actually: it was a policeman and his dog, highly decorated, and he was investigating—"

"The policeman, not the dog," Blix interrupted.

"What?" Kimmells spun around.

"The policeman was the decorated party. Just clarifying. The way you structured that sentence, it sounded like—"

"Of course, the policeman! Blix, you're not helping!" Kimmells turned back to Harrison. "My point, Mr. President, should I be permitted to finish it: the farther below ground the room is, the bigger the sphere." He took a deep breath. "It could mean they're testing their weaponry in some fashion."

"But we think that unlikely," said Blix.

"That's right. Unlikely. They could have tested it anywhere. Not here and now when they're in the process of attacking us. Now it could mean their weaponry requires more power to be activated when surrounded in five out of six directions by soil and rock—"

"But we think that unlikely also," said Blix.

Kimmells sighed. "Yes. Unlikely also."

Harrison leaned forward, his temper long since missing in action, his patience on a short leash. "Get to the point. What's the most likely conclusion?"

"Well, it could well mean their detection and/or targeting technology utilizes data gathered multi-directionally—in three dimensions—and therefore is less effective below ground."

"I don't understand. Why would that result in larger explosions?"

Kimmells held up his index fingers and stared at the space between them as if the answer resided in, and could be divined from, that exact location. "Well, if they're having difficulty obtaining a bio-sign reading, or getting an exact lock on the individual's location, they could simply boost their power output and destroy a larger area . . . theoretically."

Difficulty obtaining a bio-sign reading. Growing slightly hopeful, Harrison said, almost whispered, "Any reports of attacks this deep?"

"Oh, no sir. Not even close."

Harrison felt his shoulders relax and experienced a rush of hope. Only then did he become aware of the ignoble fact that most of his tension had been tied into concern for his own survival, not that of his fellow Americans. Partially cognizant that this might be something he would have felt guilty about in years past, he nonetheless managed not to let it derail his feeling of relief.

Blix chuckled. "But statistically speaking, Mr. President, that doesn't mean very much. After all, very few people work at this depth. So, if attacks are random, based on probability it might take quite a while—"

"Yes. I get your point." So much for relief. He looked at Kimmells. "Is there any pattern to the attacks? Anything at all?"

"Well, Mr. President, there's so much chaos, it's hard to tell. And there's so much raw data, it's a gargantuan task for headquarters to sort it all. We're being sent any relevant information as fast as they compile it. The targets have been homes, offices, veterinary clinics, beauty salons, police stations, airplanes, municipal parks, duck blinds, urban, rural . . . you name it."

Harrison looked down but held up his right index finger to indicate he had heard enough for the moment. An image of a duck blind flitted nervously through his mind, frantically searching for a place to settle down and make sense, on a quest for meaning where it could fit properly into a greater whole. It failed.

"Okay. What about the size of the . . . kill zone. You said some were larger."

Kimmells smiled, a slightly goofy and sheepish grin. "Well, the largest one reported so far was, uncharacteristically, above ground and was on what Blix and I are calling the 'busload of blind bigots.'"

"You're joking." Harrison stared at the pair of analysts, wondering who hired them. He also wondered how he had gotten stuck with these two, of all people, in the middle of this crisis. "A busload of blind bigots," he said incredulously.

"Yes sir," said Kimmells. "It seems there was a charter bus full of blind members of the KKK on their way to an annual party in Biloxi, Mississippi. They go there each year for Easter, to gamble away the holiday. The attack took out the driver, the passengers, the entire bus, and a healthy chunk of Interstate 10. We estimate a diameter of 60 feet. And a whole mess of other cars behind them drove right into the crater."

Harrison rubbed his eyes. Despite himself, he wondered how blind people gambled. Then he wondered—if they were both KKK and blind—how they would know they hadn't put their hoods on backwards. Shaking his head, he wondered if present company was possibly getting to him.

He confronted Blix accusatively. "What's taking so long with my order to attempt communication with the aliens?"

"Well, sir, they're working on it, but we're a bit short-handed. Some people went home to their families as soon as the chaos began. And some of our guys overslept. A big Caribbean-theme party last night. I wasn't invited, but . . . Wait." Looking at his computer screen, he grinned. "What do you know? They've just informed me they're ready! Just when you need something, if you try, sometimes, well, you get what you need. I was just telling Kimmells, here—"

"Shut up and prepare to send my message." Harrison forced himself to concentrate on the issue at hand. He thought of all the exhortations of foreign leaders—to stand firm, to talk tough with the aliens, threaten massive retaliation. A big bluff. He thought of all the people dying with every minute that passed and all the additional people that would die while he pretended he could fight them—a nameless them, likely as advanced over us as we are over our cave dwelling ancestors. He wondered what kind of a leader he would be if he didn't at least try to stand up to them. He thought of the cheering crowds at his campaign stops, the friendly, innocent faces.

"Tell them we surrender. Tell them we will cooperate with them in any way they require if they will stop the attacks."

The message was relayed along a circuitous path to conceal the whereabouts of the President, then sent skyward on multiple frequencies. They waited.

Harrison repeatedly walked the length of the conference table, trying to shrug off a suffocating aura of guilt at his impotence and concentrate on a solution. He stopped pacing and turned to face Kimmells.

"Where aren't they attacking?"

"Sir?"

"Where aren't they attacking? You told me what types of places they are attacking. What types of places aren't they attacking?"

"Well, sir . . . I—"

"Movie theaters," said Blix. "Not one report of an attack on any theaters."

"Well, come to think of it, Mr. President," said Kimmells, "we don't know of any attacks on grocery stores yet."

"Or hospitals," said Blix. Except for one. We did get one report just in the last few minutes of an attack on a hospital basement. Three levels down. Forty foot diameter. Took out everyone hiding there. And a chunk of the morgue. But that's the only one so far."

"Are people dying in every attack?"

"Not at all," said Kimmells. "Many houses have been hit when the owners were out."

"Possibly at the theater," said Blix.

Kimmells glared at his associate, looked back at the President, took a deep breath, and said, "Anyway . . . no. One report from a man says an attack took out several of his prize sheep. And his best sheepdog. And we have reports from park rangers in the Angeles National Forest, north of LA, of blasts out in the woods, in completely unpopulated areas. And from forest rangers elsewhere as well. And then, well, there was what could only be described as an odd one—"

"We're receiving an answer!" Blix shouted. "They've sent back a message. It's coming through now."

Harrison quickly slid over the conference table and landed on the floor next to Blix. On the screen was their reply: WE DO NOT REQUEST YOUR SURRENDER. WE DO NOT REQUIRE YOUR COOPERATION.

Harrison stared at the screen with a stiffness that mirrored his catatonic wits. That was their reply?

After a moment, he said, "Send this message. 'Then why, in the name of humanity, are you attacking us?'" He collapsed into the chair.

"This next response should be quicker," said Blix. Weary and frustrated, Harrison raised his head and stared at him. "Well, sir, they had to learn how to respond. Maybe even how to learn our language. And look, they answered intelligibly and with proper grammar."

He then returned to his computer, his enthusiastic countenance withered by the President's glare.

Blix was right. Soon the answer came: WE ARE NOT ATTACKING YOU.

Seething with anger, Harrison said, "What the hell are they trying to pull? Okay. Send this: 'You have attacked us around our entire world. Stop immediately. We will not sit idly by as you exterminate us.'" He gazed at the ceiling. "As if we could stop them," he muttered.

He went to the other end of the conference table and argued with his speechwriter, whose note pad was suspiciously devoid of anything resembling a speech. Kimmells and Blix took the opportunity to bicker with each other, after which they returned to their research, but not before Blix accused Kimmells of possessing neither the insight nor the courage that Mulder would show in a similar situation.

Soon Harrison was called back over. The response had arrived: WE ARE NOT ATTACKING YOU. WE ARE NOT EXTERMINATING YOUR SPECIES.

Blix raised an eyebrow at Kimmells, who bristled at Blix like the more irritable half of a long-married couple. "So?"

Blix then raised both eyebrows. Kimmells's eyes flared. "I don't want to hear it!"

Harrison—whose whirlwind of thoughts had lost its speed but had disrespectfully dumped the clutter of ideas on him in a heap—ignored their bickering. "This is insane! What are they doing? How do we stop it? Okay. Send this: 'If you are not attacking us, what the hell are you doing?' Yes, that's exactly how I want you to say it. 'If you are not attacking us, what the hell are you doing and why?' Send it now."

He looked at Kimmells in despair. "Does it appear they're trying to deceive us with these answers? Or could it be . . . we think so differently that they don't understand us . . . or we don't understand them?"

"Any of those possibilities could exist," said Kimmells.

Blix looked away, clearing his throat.

Kimmells continued. "They seem to be responding only to the direct communications you give them. So we get terse answers. But this time you asked what they were doing and why. Perhaps that will elicit a more detailed response. But it's also possible they misunderstand our communication somehow."

"Or not," said Blix.

Kimmells sighed abruptly, nervously. "Mr. President, there is one theory developing, and Blix thinks it probable. You see, based on some of the attacks and now this reply by the aliens that they are not exterminating our species . . . well, sir . . . there's the . . . the possibility that they're actually attacking our . . . well, sir, there's the possibility they're actually attacking our pets. . . . Sir."

Harrison coughed uncontrollably for a few seconds, silently vowing that if his CIA Director proved to be still alive, he would strangle him at the first opportunity.

"You're joking. Or you're insane."

Blix eagerly turned to face him. "To be more specific, Mr. President, I believe they're attacking our dogs." He looked at Harrison with a wide-eyed innocence that made him appear even more ridiculous. "It was hard to filter this out at first with all the confusion, but it's possible that dogs have been the target of all attacks. Human deaths are likely just collateral damage. Or sheep deaths, for that matter," he said with a chuckle.

Stunned now more than angry, Harrison tried to process the information. Okay, so there was a dog that a man lost along with his sheep. There was that policeman and his dog. Parks are often filled with people walking their dogs. Families trying to hide would go into their basements or public shelters with their . . . Veterinary offices filled with . . . Okay. Okay. But this did not in any way constitute proof. As he was about to say so, the image of the duck blind flapped its way back into his consciousness, exhausted from its migration and still searching for a place to rest. This time it was complete with two hunters and an English Setter. No. How in the name of cross-eyed, crack-smoking Uncle Sam was he supposed to believe something like this?

"What about the airplanes?" he blurted out.

"The airplanes were all destroyed from blasts to the cargo area," said Blix. "Where the dogs are carried. Also, we've recently had two reports of people cut in half by the spherical blast zones while walking their dogs: either poor targeting or the humans weren't the target to begin with. And lots of houses attacked when the owners were out. It was your question about where they weren't attacking that got me going. Movie theaters. When's the last time you saw a dog in a movie theater?"

Far from ready to embrace either the premise or its messenger, Harrison ignored the question. "What about the blasts in the woods?" He found himself compulsively making a fist on the surface of the table.

"Coyotes, I suppose. Or wolves. All the same species, you know."

"They are not," said Kimmells.

"Are too," said Blix, through gritted teeth.

"Well, what about those . . . that KKK bus?"

"Blind, sir. Guide dogs. A whole pack of Klan guide dogs, I presume."

As much as Harrison wanted to believe a scenario that didn't end with the destruction of humanity, he still was not about to take this person's idea seriously. And he tightened his fist a little more. "Have you always been prone to wild and crazy delusions?"

"No, Mr. President. Not at all. . . . Well, actually . . . Oh, look! They've responded!"

As motionless as granite, three Grand Tetons in a bunker, they stared at the screen as the message came in. It said: AT THE REQUEST OF A SPECIES THAT WE HAVE ENTERED INTO A MUTUALLY BENEFICIAL ARRANGEMENT WITH, WE ARE ELIMINATING A THREAT TO THE FUTURE BALANCE OF POWER IN THIS PART OF THE GALAXY. YOUR SPECIES, NOT REPRESENTING A THREAT, IS NOT BEING EXTERMINATED. PREDICTIONS INDICATE THAT YOUR SPECIES WILL NOT EXPAND BEYOND THIS STAR SYSTEM, DUE TO ITS SELF-DESTRUCTIVE AND INDOLENT NATURE. FURTHERMORE, WE ARE BOUND BY INTERSTELLAR CODES THAT FORBID THE TOTAL ELIMINATION OF ANY SPECIES THAT HAS ALREADY ACHIEVED FULL SENTIENCE.

OUR CONTRACTED TASK IS THE COMPLETE ELIMINATION OF YOUR CANINE SPECIES. PREDICTIONS INDICATE THAT, IF UNCHECKED, THEY WILL ACHIEVE FULL SENTIENCE AND INTELLIGENCE IN 178,000 OF YOUR YEARS, SOONER IF ASSISTED BY HUMANS. PREDICTIONS ALSO INDICATE THEY WOULD THEN RAPIDLY SPREAD THROUGHOUT THE GALAXY AND DESTROY THE PLANS OF THOSE WE REPRESENT.

Harrison felt an unannounced and unwelcome creaking in the fuzzier recesses of his harried mind and stared at Blix suspiciously. No. No, not even this loon would jeopardize his job by writing a fake response as some type of perverse joke. It had to be the real thing.

He shook his head. "Contracted assassins. Mercenaries. Sent across interstellar space in a preemptive attack to kill our dogs? Preposterous. I can't address the nation with a story like this and then find out it's wrong. It will be tough enough to do even if I'm certain it's true. How can we be sure they aren't still interested in wiping us out?"

Blix was frowning, staring at his computer screen, and didn't seem to hear the question, but Kimmells answered readily. "Well, sir, one thing that's puzzled us from the start is the lack of damage. It's—"

"Lack of damage?"

"Yes, sir. What I mean is the low amount of damage with each individual incineration, not the total number of attacks. You see, obliterating that much solid matter instantly should cause tremendous heat and an enormous shock wave. But most of the heat and force is being dissipated, somehow. It's as if they're actually trying to protect us. Sir."

"And the planet," said Blix, while still puzzling over the alien message. "Otherwise, 200 million of such energy releases would almost certainly devastate the Earth."

"200 million?" Harrison asked with a shudder.

"Yes. The number of dogs on Earth. But that's a very rough guess. It's likely more. I could—"

Harrison jumped from his chair. The latest bizarre parade

of facts steamrollering its way through his mind had just coalesced into bleak understanding. He ran to his speech-writer. "No time to prepare a speech. Just give me notes. I need to be on the air in two minutes. I need to warn every-one to stay away from their dogs!"

Staring at his president with an expression customarily reserved for a lunatic sporting a weapon, his mouth stayed open, unmoving. There was a tremor in the eyes as he tried to keep them focused on his boss. But after Harrison sat down and explained the situation he relaxed (somewhat) and they quickly started working out what to say.

"I understand some dog owners can be a bit fanatic," Har-rison said. "Do you think they'll all listen to me? Or will some refuse, hugging their dogs into oblivion in some sort of defiant act of devotion and self sacrifice?"

"I really wouldn't know, Mr. President. I'm a cat person."

"Yeah. Me too," Harrison said, contemplating whether it had been a mistake not to get a dog within the last couple years. Suddenly a new worry descended upon him.

He scurried back to Kimmells and Blix. "We need to at least attempt to change their minds. We can't just let them destroy our dogs while we sit and do nothing." No longer worried about the destruction of humanity (or his own sur-vival), he was now fighting back irrepressible and prophetic images of enraged dog ex-owners marching on the White House for the next eighteen months.

Blix jumped up. "I'm so glad you said that, Mr. President! There's no way dogs can achieve sapience in a mere 178,000 years. They're just, well—no disrespect intended—they're just not that smart."

They sent a formal protest: there had to be an error—dogs could not possibly develop such highly evolved intelligence so fast.

This gave Harrison the opportunity, in his speech to the nation, to pronounce that he was personally attempting ev-erything humanly possible to stop the alien assault diplo-matically, as we had no chance of stopping them militarily.

But the bulk of his speech was simply an appeal to get everyone to put immediate distance between themselves and their dogs. Due to the urgency of the situation, he had not even spoken with other world leaders yet. Lives had to be saved, and his first responsibility was to the citizens of the United States.

That was a good touch, he thought. Of course, his subordinates were communicating with every government in the world, but that was a small detail better left out at a time when he would need all the political capital he could get.

He poured empathy into his speech. He knew their pain, but this was the only way. He felt the intense sorrow and depth of their sacrifice, but every dog owner must act immediately to protect their lives and the lives of their children. Like a mighty redwood that has had the core of its trunk hollowed out by cruel forces of nature, yet still lives, we must do our duty, we as a nation must soldier on.

No sooner had he finished his speech than a message came back from the aliens: WE HAVE MADE NO ERROR IN PREDICTION. THE TIME INTERVAL STATED IS ACCURATE.

After deliberating, they sent a new message—one designed to give a response of more than thirteen words: "Our data on evolutionary development, canine brain capacity, and intelligence levels suggest it would take more than ten times as long as you state for dogs to evolve as you claim. How do you account for such rapid development?"

Soon the answer came: YOUR PRIMITIVE EVOLUTIONARY THEORIES AND ASSUMPTIONS ARE INACCURATE. THE MANIFEST CAPACITY OF A SPECIES TO LEARN IS NOT AS IMPORTANT A FACTOR IN LONG-TERM DEVELOPMENT AS A WILLINGNESS TO LEARN. NO OTHER SPECIES ON YOUR PLANET EXHIBITS AS MUCH EAGERNESS TO LEARN AS YOUR CANINE SPECIES DOES. THIS SHOULD BE EVIDENT TO YOU BASED ON THEIR ENTHUSIASM FOR DOING TRICKS, STUNTS, OR OTHER TASKS, NO MATTER HOW CONDESCENDING OR ANNOYING. IT IS THIS CAPACITY, ALONG WITH ALARMINGLY PROLIFIC BREEDING, THAT WOULD HAVE SWIFTLY PROPELLED THEM TO

FULL SENTIENCE AND DOMINATION OF THIS ARM
OF THE GALAXY.

That would have swiftly propelled them. . . . Harrison
contemplated the bleak finality of those words. He wrestled
with what to do, even as he puzzled over how they knew so
much about us. TV, no doubt. TV signals blabbing about us
every day, heading omni-directionally into space. The same
TV he repeatedly told his wife and nanny to keep the kids
from watching. His kids, who were so proficient at avoiding
their schoolwork. His offspring, his progeny, who apparently represented no threat to the cosmos.

Over the next several days, he tried in vain to persuade
them to cease. They refused. He tried to get a delay, time to
negotiate or come up with other options. They again refused;
time was of the essence in their contract with the species
they represented. In short order, all dogs were eliminated
from the surface of the Earth, along with wolves, jackals and
coyotes. Then, as promptly as the aliens came, they left.

The devastation and terror created by the attack caused a
worldwide economic slump. It was sharp and severe, though
not as great as some in decades past. But this one felt deeper.
The emotional loss, many would even say the spiritual loss,
was unmitigated. The planet had been violated.

There was vitriolic anger toward the nameless aliens, who
came to be known as The Butchers. Those who mourned the
loss of their companions could not strike back at them and
were even cheated out of the opportunity to have a physical
image to curse, a face to hate.

Numerous incidents of unprovoked attacks on cat owners
and an increase in wars around the globe seemed to prove
The Butchers' claims about our species. Mankind did indeed know how to be self-destructive.

In the U.S., which had been particularly hard hit, the human population gave its best shot at returning to normal.
They sought out ways to carry on.

After statues, monuments, and other shrines had been lov-
ingly erected in memory of their pets, people turned to other
sources of companionship. They adopted turtles, hamsters,

parrots, and pigs. Many prior dog owners got cats—and were forced to make the necessary adjustments. Others took in raccoons, ferrets, otters, and even skunks . . . after prudent alterations had been made. They even did it despite laws to the contrary. And laws were changed. Rapidly. The times cried out for change (as much as any increment of time could possibly be expected to cry out for anything), and even old politicians can learn new tricks when forced to do so.

By the time the Earth pirouetted its way around the sun again to the spot in its orbit we call Easter, the intense demand for rabbits was overwhelming. But, as fortune would have it, the rabbits complied enthusiastically. Rabbits always do.

Many former dog owners, with ceaseless devotion, endeavored to teach their new cats any number of tricks. The cats proved to be wholly uncooperative, some even disdainful.

Others had better luck. Crows were said to be able to learn a few words, and some would even play fetch with marbles or small rubber balls. One man from Minnesota trained his parrot to sing the Star Spangled Banner. In defense of his bird and its rendition, he said, "Well, he ain't perfect, but he sure is better than some people I've heard sing it."

No one could argue with that.

Otters, it was found, would hang their heads out of moving car windows just like dogs, and—as a bonus—they could learn a wide array of tricks. Being the providential creatures that they were, they became popular overnight.

Pigs could be taught to wake their owners (albeit with a limited degree of finesse) at just the right time of the morning, and altered skunks were discovered to be amazingly affectionate. They also had the side benefit of scaring off burglars and pesky door-to-door salesmen.

But parrots would not fetch the morning paper, and pigs were sadly lost when it came to the finer points of how to retrieve a stick. Cats could not be trained to bark in an attempt to frighten the mailman, and skunks would not bring slippers to their owners. Despite mankind's best efforts, life was not the same.

Very few people blamed President Harrison for the disaster, and he received high marks for many eloquent, consoling speeches. But when November rolled around, they voted him out of office in one of the most crushing landslides in modern American history.

He was trounced by the junior Senator from Missouri, a father of four, who had been the proud owner of a Malamute and two Dachshunds.

On the morning of January 16th, President Harrison descended in the elevator along with four Secret Service agents, whose protests he had overridden by coming here. But for now, he was still President, and they still worked for him.

"It's safe, guys. Relax." Carefree lately, having fully accepted his defeat, he smiled at them as they got off on the bottom floor. But they weren't much for smiling back.

It wasn't in their nature.

Major Parker, head of the local operation, greeted him. "Glad you could make it, Mr. President."

"Oh, I couldn't pass up this opportunity, Dane. It was now or never for me."

They passed through four blast doors, each one closed in their wake. Harrison contemplated the two thousand feet of rock above them. He also contemplated the brave members of the intelligence and military communities who had been lost in this campaign.

"What's the latest count?"

"1287, sir."

"1287? That's up quite a bit, isn't it?"

"It sure is. In fact, six more just this morning," he said proudly.

As they walked into the main hall, Harrison was surprised to find himself overcome with emotion. Nearly seven hundred dogs were neatly assembled in rows and columns in front of him.

"This room's more packed than some of my campaign rallies," he said, feigning a puzzled scratch of the head. "And a more enthusiastic crowd, too."

And they were. Tails were wagging that belonged to Irish

Setters, Dalmatians, German Shepherds, and Pomeranians. From Golden Retrievers to English Sheepdogs, Labradors to Papillons, there were thirty-seven breeds represented, as well as a broad assortment of mutts.

He had been briefed prior to coming, just as he would have been for a press conference. Stay away from the Husky in the front row—you give him a little attention and he'll demand more. And the Cocker Spaniel next to him bites. Yes, exactly like the press.

"These are all local dogs, Mr. President."

"Yes, I know." Only thick lead containers with no air holes had proven safe to transport the dogs in. Other attempts had resulted in dogs and the government officials moving them being destroyed. Limited air supply had necessitated carrying sedated dogs from nearby locations only.

"And a proud lot they are," Harrison said.

"Sir, I understand we may be working out a cross-breeding program with the Russians. Any word?"

"Oh, that's for the next administration to decide. I'm out of that picture. But the Russians do have a sizeable population. And the Brits, too. The Brits have more than we have in Colorado."

"Really. I didn't have details. They keep me in the dark down here."

Harrison laughed. "They probably do. They do that sort of thing. Well, I'll tell you something you don't know, then. When the Egyptians were informed of the alien inability to see through solid rock they successfully barricaded about fifty of them in a tunnel underneath one of the pyramids."

"That's fabulous, sir."

"I tell you, Major. Those Butchers may be right about us. We may not make it. We may end up destroying ourselves . . . perhaps with the same finality with which they destroyed my career. But I'll be damned if we're going to let them cheat Earth out of its rightful place in the galaxy."

A Pembroke Welsh Corgi barked in agreement.

"I have something to show you, sir. Over here." He led the President to the far side of the room, where forty-two dogs were separated into seven rows of six each. One of the trainers held up three fingers. They all stood on their hind legs and raised their right front paws, giving the President a salute.

"Ho! That's wonderful!"

"Well, Mr. President, you are still the Commander In Chief, after all."

"Ah, not for long. Not for long."

"Well, I can guarantee you, sir, every one of them would have voted for you if they could."

"Hah. I could have used their support. But I'm afraid that would have required a Constitutional Amendment."

He knelt in front of a Golden Retriever. "What's your name, soldier? Would you like to be given the right to vote?"

"His name is Buddy, Mr. President," his trainer said.

Buddy indicated his voting preference with his tail.

He looked into Buddy's eyes. And at that moment President Harrison understood, far too late, what a fool he had been for never having owned a dog.

The Corporal grabbed the disk and turned around. "Get the Frisbee, Buddy!" he yelled. He tossed it toward the Golden Retriever.

Buddy came to full alertness as the plastic disk sailed his way. It was headed over him, a fairly long throw. His tail wagged randomly, but his eyes followed the disk's movements exactly.

"Catch it, Buddy!"

Buddy was watching the exact angle and speed of the disk. With an eager burst of enthusiasm he ran after it, not taking his eyes off it even to blink. It was rising up on the right hand edge ever so slightly . . . it would soon change course, curve back, dip to the left. He kept running. He knew full well he would soon have to turn and run back the other way; he wasn't fooled a bit. But he enjoyed chasing it in both directions, then catching it at the earliest possible moment. That was the best way to play the game, the way that made it the most fun.

He reversed course, whipping his head up to stay on track

with the disk. It was losing speed and altitude now, and he could project exactly when and where he would be able to jump and grab it. Another second went by, and he confirmed the projection. Two and three-quarter seconds after that, he jumped. This moment represented the culmination of the game, the point of success or failure.

He had timed it perfectly. His teeth bit down, and it was now his. The plastic of the disk tasted like triumph.

"Great catch, Buddy!"

He trotted proudly toward his owner. He liked this new owner who gave him these games to learn. At first, this person had smelled like a stranger. Soon thereafter he smelled like an acquaintance, maybe even a neighbor. But now he smelled like an owner, and Buddy loved that. It filled him with a sense of belonging and security.

He surrendered his prize and then started to trot back to his position, to practice the game once more. He even was beginning to like this new home—these big, square caves with doors and smooth walls and ceilings. But he missed going to the park: the old place with the soft grass that smelled like nature, the fresh breezes that smelled like exhilaration, and the brilliant sky overhead that shone like freedom.

The man prepared to throw the disk again, and, in less than the brief flicker of a dog's heartbeat, faster than the wag of a joyous tail, Buddy forgot all about the park. Because the game was ready to begin anew. He loved all these amazing games: this flying disk, the balls, the stick, and many more. He even liked the new ones where he held up a paw or spoke when his owner showed him a particular object or held up the same object two times in a row. Those games were harder, but he vowed to keep learning them.

The man threw the disk again, and he studied it to see precisely how it would behave this time. He would keep analyzing this game until he mastered it. Just like the other games, he would learn them all. The disk soared overhead, and once again exhilaration ruled the universe. He bounded after it. It was leaning differently this time . . . this disk was delightfully, deviously tricky. But no matter what, he would keep working at it until he was flawless. At every opportunity, with every breath, he would keep striving, he would keep learning. His reasoning for this was as resolute as it was straightforward.

It's what life is all about.

Story Copyrights